The MYSTERIOUS BENEDICT SOCIETY and the PERILOUS JOURNEY

From The Chicken House

The kids are back! And this time the members of the Mysterious Benedict Society must travel right across Europe on their new mission, because their old adversaries are back too and have kidnapped Mr Benedict.

Once again the kids' talents are stretched to the limit. There are puzzles to solve, twists and turns to negotiate, constant threats from the sinister Ten Men. Can courage, intelligence and the power of friendship win through? Of course they can!

Barry Cunningham
Publisher

The MYSTERIOUS BENEDICT SOCIETY and the PERILOUS JOURNEY

TRENTON LEE STEWART

Illustrated by Diana Sudyka

2 Palmer Street, Frome, Somerset BA11 1DS

First published in the United States of America in 2008
Little, Brown and Company
Hachette Book Group, New York, USA

First published in Great Britain in 2010
The Chicken House
2 Palmer Street
Frome, Somerset BA11 1DS
United Kingdom
www.doublecluck.com

Cover Design by Steve Wells
Typeset by Dorchester Typesetting Group Ltd
Printed and bound by CPI Group (UK) Ltd, Croydon, CR0 4YY

The paper used in this Chicken House book is made from wood grown
in sustainable forests.

9 10 8

British Library Cataloguing in Publication data available.

ISBN 978-1-906427-14-6

For Fletcher
—T.L.S.

Lemon-Juice Letters and Key Disappointments

On a bright September morning, when most children his age were in school fretting over fractions and decimal points, a boy named Reynie Muldoon was walking down a dusty road. He was an average-looking boy – with average brown hair and eyes, legs of average length, nose an average distance from his ears, and so on – and he was entirely alone. Other than a falcon soaring high over the road and a few meadowlarks keeping a low profile in the fields on either side, Reynie was the only living creature around.

To an observer, Reynie might well have appeared lost and far from home, and in fact such an observer would have

1

been half right. At least Reynie found it amusing to think so, for he had just determined that his present situation could be described entirely in terms of halves: he was half a day's drive from the suburbs of Stonetown, where he lived; half a mile from the nearest small town; and, according to the man who had given him directions, he had another half mile to go before he reached his destination. The most important thing, however, was that it had been half a year since he had seen his three closest friends.

Reynie squinted against the sun. Not far ahead, the dirt lane went up a steep hill, just as the man in town had said it would. Beyond the hill he should find the farm. And on that farm he would find Kate Wetherall.

Reynie walked faster, his shoes kicking up dust. To think he would see Kate any minute! And Sticky Washington – Sticky would be here by evening! And tomorrow they all would drive to Stonetown to see . . . well, to see Constance Contraire, but that was all right too. Even the thought of Constance insulting him in rhyming couplets made Reynie happy. She might be an impudent little genius-in-the-rough, but Constance was one of the few people in the world Reynie could count as a true friend. Constance, Kate and Sticky were like family to him. It didn't matter that he'd met them only a year ago. Their friendship had been formed under extraordinary circumstances.

Reynie broke into a run.

A few minutes later he stood at the crest of the hill with his hands on his knees, panting like a puppy, his enthusiasm having got the better of him. He had to laugh at himself. After all, he wasn't Kate, who probably could have run the whole way from town without breaking a sweat. (In fact, she probably could have done it running on her hands.) Reynie's gifts were not of the physical variety – he was average in that respect, too – and he was left mopping his brow and gasping for breath as he surveyed the farm spread out before him.

So this was Kate's home: a modest farmhouse and barn, both freshly painted, with an old truck in the farmyard; a tiny white henhouse; a pen with sheep and goats milling about in it; and beyond the pen, an expanse of rolling pastures. Across the lane from the buildings was an orchard, a few of its trees studded with fat red apples, though most of the fruit was undeveloped and scarcely visible. The farm still needed a lot of work, Kate had said in one of her letters. And that was almost *all* she'd said. Her letters were never what you would call wordy, though they were always cheerful. Rather too cheerful, actually – they sometimes made Reynie feel as if he were the only one who missed his friends.

Just as Reynie started down the hill, a bell sounded among the farm buildings below. He scanned the area hopefully for Kate but saw only the goats and sheep filing out of their pen, which must have been left open so they could graze in the pastures. Reynie drew up short in surprise. He could have sworn the last goat to leave the pen had turned around and nudged the gate closed.

Reynie's brow wrinkled. That conscientious goat was not the first unusual thing he'd seen this morning. He was reminded of something else – something curious to which, in his excitement, he hadn't given much thought until now. Reynie shaded his eyes and searched the sky. There, circling quite low overhead, was the falcon he had noticed earlier.

He could just make out its facial markings, which resembled a black cap and long black sideburns. Reynie didn't presume to know much about birds (though in fact he knew more than most people), but he felt sure that this was a peregrine falcon – and in this region, at this time of year, peregrine falcons were very rare indeed.

Reynie grinned and hurried downhill to the farmyard. Something odd was going on, and he couldn't wait to find out what it was.

The barn lay closer than the house, so Reynie went and poked his head in through the open doors, just in case Kate was there. It took a moment for his eyes to adjust from the brilliant sunlight to the relative gloom inside the barn, but once they did they could not have fallen on a more welcome sight.

There was that familiar blonde ponytail, those broad shoulders, that fire-engine-red bucket. He'd found Kate, no doubt about it. She stood with her back to him, hands on her hips, staring toward the far wall. Reynie considered sneaking up on her, then quickly reconsidered. It was probably a very bad idea to sneak up on Kate. Anyway, he hated to disturb her. She was still staring straight ahead, apparently lost in concentration. Reynie, who could see nothing on the barn wall, suspected she was concentrating on something inward. Perhaps she was contemplating some useful new tool to carry in her bucket.

Suddenly Kate doubled over and began to cough. Then to splutter. And then to make truly horrific gagging sounds. Was she choking? Reynie was just about to rush forward and help her when Kate cried out in frustration and stamped her foot. 'Not again!' she moaned, straightening

4

up. Then she turned and saw Reynie watching from the barn entrance.

'I have no idea what that was all about,' Reynie said, 'but I have a feeling I'll think it's funny.'

'Reynie!'

Kate dashed over to him, her bright blue eyes shining with delight. Reynie threw his arms out wide – and instantly regretted it. Kate's greeting, delivered at full tilt, was more of a football tackle than a hug, and as the two of them fell hard to the ground, Reynie felt his breath knocked clean away.

'Did you just get here?' Kate said excitedly, rising onto her knees. 'Where's Miss Perumal and her mother? And what took you so long? You were supposed to be here *yesterday*. I double-checked the letter just to be sure.'

Reynie, suffering from the panicky feeling that always accompanies having one's wind knocked out, was nonetheless trying to smile – indeed, to make any expression other than that of a stranded fish – but he could only move his lips, unable to utter a sound.

'Why, Reynie, you're speechless!' Kate said with a laugh. She hauled him to his feet and began dusting him off with sharp, painful swats. 'I know, I'm excited, too. And not only about Mr Benedict's big surprise. I'm thrilled just to see you boys again! You can't imagine how disappointed I was when you didn't show up last night.'

Recovering his breath, Reynie stepped out of range of Kate's swatting and said, 'You aren't the only one. Our car broke down, and we had to have it towed into town. We spent the night in the motel.'

'The motel in town?' Kate cried. 'If only we'd known!

5

We could have come for you in the truck.'

'Sorry, I would have called, but since you don't have a telephone . . .'

Kate groaned. 'Milligan and his rules! You know I love him, but honestly, some of the things he insists on . . .'

'Anyway,' Reynie said, laughing, 'I couldn't stand to wait for the car to be fixed, so I got permission from Amma' – *Amma* was what Reynie called Miss Perumal, his former tutor who had recently adopted him – 'and directions from the mechanic, and here I am. Amma and Pati will be along as soon as the car's running.'

Kate caught Reynie's arm, her face creased with worry (an unusual expression for Kate, who was not the worrying type). 'Is the car big enough for all three of us to ride together? I mean along with Miss Perumal and her mother and all the luggage? Sticky's parents are coming too you know, and their car is tiny. I can't imagine one of us spending six hours separated from the other two – not after we've just spent six months apart!'

'We rented an estate car. There'll be plenty of room. Now listen,' Reynie said, holding up his hand to check Kate, who had begun to speak again, 'before we stray too far from the subject, won't you tell me what you were doing just now? The last time I heard a sound like that was when the orphanage cat spat up a hairball.'

'Oh, that?' Kate said with a shrug. 'I'm training myself to regurgitate things, but it's a lot harder than you'd think.' Seeing Reynie's horrified expression, she quickly explained, 'It's an old escape artist's trick. Houdini and all those guys could do it. They'd swallow a lockpick or something, and later they'd use their throat muscles to bring it back up.

You're supposed to train with a string tied to whatever it is you're swallowing, so you can help pull it back out. I did that at first, but then I thought I might manage it without the string. No luck yet though.'

'So I was right,' Reynie said. 'It *is* funny. But isn't it – dangerous?'

Kate pursed her lips, considering. Evidently this had never occurred to her. She wasn't one to worry about danger much. 'I suppose it isn't the safest thing in the world,' she admitted, and with a serious look she said, 'You'd better not try it.'

Reynie laughed (for nothing could possibly induce him to try such a thing himself), then affected an equally serious look and said, 'All right Kate, I promise never to swallow – well, what was it you swallowed, anyway?'

Kate rolled her eyes and waved off the question. 'I don't want to talk about it.'

'And, hey, what happens to it now?' Reynie persisted, looking horrified again. 'I mean, since you couldn't—?'

'I don't,' Kate said firmly, 'want to *talk* about it.'

They had plenty of other things to talk about anyway. Not only did Kate want to show Reynie around the farm, she desperately wanted to know his thoughts about the big surprise Mr Benedict had planned for them. Exactly one year had passed since Mr Benedict had recruited the four of them for an urgent mission – a mission that only the most remarkable children could have accomplished – and now, on the anniversary of their first meeting, he had arranged for a reunion at his home in Stonetown. In one of his letters he had explained, 'Here you will be met with a surprise that

I hope will please all of you – a surprise that, while it inadequately expresses my gratitude, not to mention my great and lasting affection for you, nevertheless strikes me as an appropriate . . .' And he had gone on like this for a while, elaborating upon his appreciation for the children's unique qualities and his eagerness to see them all again. Kate had skimmed the letter happily and put it away. Reynie had read the letter several times and learned it by heart.

'You memorized the whole thing?' Kate said, leading Reynie up a ladder to show him the hayloft. 'You're starting to sound like Sticky.'

'Sticky would only have needed to read it once,' said Reynie, which was perfectly true, but Reynie mentioned Sticky mostly to draw attention away from himself. The fact was that he'd memorized every letter he'd received these past six months – not just from Mr Benedict, but also the breezy notes Kate had sent, the slightly boring but faithfully detailed reports from Sticky, and even the quirky poetry Constance had mailed him along with whatever curious button, dust bunny, or paper scrap had struck her fancy on the way to find a stamp. Reynie felt more than a little sheepish about how tightly he'd clung to every word from the others, none of whom had ever said anything about missing him.

'Speaking of Sticky,' Kate said, hauling Reynie through the trap door into the loft, 'have you heard much from him lately? He says you two write more often than he and I do. Says that *you* actually take the trouble to answer his questions, unlike *some* friends he knows. I don't think he quite understands my situation. This is the loft, by the way.'

Reynie looked around. The hayloft resembled every

other hayloft he'd seen – though admittedly he'd seen them only in pictures and movies – but Kate seemed immensely proud of it, so he nodded approvingly before he said, 'What doesn't Sticky understand? About your situation, I mean.'

'Well, for one thing,' Kate said, swinging open the loft's exterior door, which overlooked the animal pen, 'I've been awfully busy, what with going to school and trying to get the farm up and running again. Milligan's often away on missions, you know, and I have to help out.'

Reynie did know this. Milligan was Kate's father. He was also a secret agent. Neither of these facts had been known until recently, though – not even by Kate. She'd been just a toddler when Milligan was captured on a mission, lost his memory, and failed to return. Since her mother was dead and her father had abandoned her (or so everyone believed), Kate had been sent to an orphanage, which she eventually left for the circus. Milligan, for his part, had escaped his captors and gone to work for Mr Benedict. Not until Mr Benedict brought them together, exactly a year ago this month, had Kate Milligan discovered the truth.

'The farm really fell to pieces over the years,' Kate was saying. 'There's been enough work to keep me busy around the clock. Not that I mind work, of course. What I find most difficult is sitting still long enough to write a good letter. Sticky should know that, shouldn't he?'

'He probably should,' Reynie admitted. He stepped over to the door, where Kate was taking something from her bucket (the bucket had a flip-top now, Reynie noticed) and placing it between her lips. It was some kind of whistle. She reached into her bucket again.

'But the real problem with writing letters,' Kate

continued, speaking around the whistle as she tugged a thick leather glove onto her hand, 'is that the government reads all my post. Daughter of a top agent, you know. They have to be sure I'm not revealing any secrets. It's bad enough that everything about our mission was made hush-hush – by rights we ought to be famous for what we did – but I can't even send private letters to my best friends? It's outrageous!'

As if to demonstrate her outrage, Kate puffed her cheeks and blew mightily on the whistle, which emitted a thin squeal like that of a kettle.

'Is that what I think it is?' Reynie asked.

'Probably,' said Kate, 'since you're usually right about everything. Honestly, though, don't you think it's unfair that Sticky blames me for writing so little?'

Reynie decided to come out with it. 'I have to admit I sort of felt the same way, and not just about your letters, but about everyone's. No one has ever really said much about . . . about . . . Well, I was starting to think I was the only one, you know, who . . .'

Kate looked at him askance. 'Reynard Muldoon! I would never have thought you, of all people . . .' She shook her head. 'Not everyone has your gift for expressing things, Reynie. You have no *idea* how much I've missed all of you. I even miss Constance, for crying out loud!'

Reynie grinned. It was just as he'd hoped. He'd been here only five minutes and already felt a hundred times better.

'Ah, here she is!' Kate said, holding her arm aloft. An instant later the air in front of them burst into a flurry of talons and wings. Reynie leapt back. The falcon had swooped down to perch upon Kate's thick leather glove, which extended well past her wrist, and was now flicking its head from side to side, regarding them. 'Reynie, meet Madge.'

'Madge?'

'Short for Majesty. Actually, her full name is Her Majesty the Queen. Because, you know, she's queen of the birds.'

'I see,' said Reynie. 'Naturally. Queen of the birds.'

'Don't give me that look! It's an excellent name whether you like it or not. Isn't it an excellent name, Madge?' Kate gave the falcon a strip of meat from a sealed pouch inside her bucket. She urged Reynie to stroke the bird's feathers (Reynie nervously obliged) and then sent her off again. 'Milligan gave her to me for my birthday – it only took a dozen hints and a month of begging – and I've been training her. She's very smart.' Kate lowered her voice, as if Madge, already a hundred yards away, might overhear. 'Which, between you and me, is kind of rare for a bird of prey. Of course I'd never tell *her* that.'

Reynie was watching the falcon sail away over the farm. It was just like Kate Wetherall to show you something so dramatic and then act as if you shouldn't be surprised. 'I thought you needed a licence to own a falcon,' he said, 'and to go through years of special training.'

'Oh, you do,' said Kate, slipping the leather glove back into her bucket. 'I did all that when I was in the circus. One of the animal trainers was a falconer, and he let me be his apprentice. I learned all sorts of things from that guy . . . but we can talk about that later,' she said, dismissing the subject with an impatient wave of her hand. 'You were going to tell me about Sticky. Have you heard from him lately?'

Reynie produced a folded sheaf of papers from his

pocket. 'Actually, he sent me this a few days ago. It's an account of our mission – for posterity, he says, assuming the mission's ever declassified. He said I could show it to you. He wants our opinion.'

'You mean he wrote about everything that happened? Like a story?'

'Well . . . something like that.' Reynie unfolded the papers and handed them to Kate, who immediately sat down in the hay to read. There were five pages, covered front and back with tiny, cramped print, and the title alone was almost as long as one of Kate's letters. It read:

The Mysterious Benedict Society's Defeat of the Terrible Brainsweeping Machine Called the Whisperer (along with its inventor, Ledroptha Curtain, who was revealed to be the long-lost identical twin of Mr Nicholas Benedict, for whom the Society is named): A Personal Account

'Holy smoke!' Kate said.
'The title?'
Kate nodded and continued to read:

In the event that you, the reader, are unaware of Mr Curtain's foiled plan to become a powerful world ruler using the mind-altering effects of his Whisperer, this account will inform you of it.

The account commences with the forming of the Mysterious Benedict Society. Through a series of tests it was determined that George 'Sticky' Washington (the author of this account), Reynard Muldoon (whose full name is now Reynard Muldoon Perumal, as he has been adopted),

Kate Wetherall and Constance Contraire were sufficiently skilled to enter Mr Curtain's Learning Institute for the Very Enlightened (the acronym being LIVE) and act as secret agents for Mr Benedict. At the aforementioned Institute these children discovered many disturbing things. Then they disabled the Whisperer, although Mr Curtain and his closest assistants (his Executives, as they were called) unfortunately avoided capture. But I see I have already come to the end. Allow me to back up and make a proper introduction to the course of events . . .

The account went on like this, backtracking and side-tracking and circling around as Sticky laboured to produce an accurate summary of their adventures. An entire paragraph, for instance, was devoted to the origin of the word 'terrified,' another to the curious sense of isolation that can occur on islands (as opposed to peninsulas) and still another to a consideration of cruel punishment in schools. By the time Kate reached the second page, her shoulders were sagging. With a sigh, she flipped to the last page and read the final sentence: *And that is the end of the account.* She looked up at Reynie. 'Is it . . . um, *all* like this?'

'I'm afraid so.'

'But how could he make the most exciting, the most dangerous, the most important event in his life – in anyone's life – so . . . so . . .'

'So dull?' Reynie offered.

Kate flopped back onto the hay and started giggling. 'Oh, I can't wait to see him!'

'Don't give him *too* hard a time. He may be coming out of his shell, but he's still sensitive, you know.'

'I'll be sure to hug him before I tease him,' Kate said.

Reynie cringed. Kate's hug would probably hurt Sticky much worse than her teasing.

'Well, enough lying around,' said Kate, who had been lying around for perhaps three seconds. She sprang to her feet. 'Aren't you going to say anything about my bucket?'

'I was about to,' Reynie said. 'I see you've made some modifications.'

Kate hurried over to show it to him. The bucket's clever new lid opened easily but closed securely, which kept her things from spilling out as they sometimes had done in the past. What was more, inside the bucket Kate had attached several pouches that closed with snaps, straps and zippers, so that everything could be snugged into a designated place. Her rope lay coiled in the bottom as always, tucked neatly beneath the pouches.

'Impressive,' Reynie said, examining the hidden catch that made the lid spring open.

Kate beamed. 'Milligan designed the lid. He pointed out that a utility belt would be less cumbersome than a bucket, but I reminded him that you can't stand on a utility belt to reach things—'

'Or fill it with water and drop it on pursuers,' said Reynie, remembering how Kate had done just that to escape Jackson and Jillson, Mr Curtain's most thuggish Executives, who had menaced the children at the Institute.

'Exactly! And Milligan saw my point, so he offered to help me improve the bucket instead of replacing it. Look,' she said, stepping up onto its closed lid. 'No more emptying it and flipping it over. That saves time, you know.'

It was hard to imagine Kate doing anything more quickly

than she already did, but Reynie acknowledged the improvement. 'And what are you keeping in it these days? I mean other than falcon snacks and whistles.'

Pouch by pouch, Kate showed Reynie the bucket's contents. Luckily, she said, Milligan had recovered some of the things she'd been compelled to leave behind at the Institute – her spyglass (which she disguised as a kaleidoscope), her Swiss Army knife, her horseshoe magnet, and her torch – and she had also replaced some of the items that had been lost or ruined, such as her catapult and marbles, her spool of clear fishing twine, her extra-strength glue, and her penlight. In addition, she'd recently put in a pencil-sized paintbrush and a bottle of lemon juice.

'I had to wait to tell you in person,' Kate said with a mischievous look. 'You know the lemon-juice trick, don't you? From now on I'll brush secret notes onto my letters, and those government snoops won't be able to see them. All you have to do is hold the paper over a candle and the words will appear.'

Reynie chuckled. He was familiar with the lemon-juice trick but had never had an opportunity to use it. 'And what's in the last pouch?' he asked, pointing to one that remained unopened.

'Oh, just these,' Kate said, somewhat drearily, producing a ring of at least two dozen keys of all different sizes and varieties. 'Keys for the house. Keys for the truck. Keys for the barn padlock, the henhouse padlock, all the gates and cupboards and sheds, you name it. Milligan believes in keeping things secure.' She sighed and stuffed the keys back into their pouch.

'What's the matter?' Reynie asked.

'Nothing, really,' Kate said. 'Nothing important, at least – and I think that's the trouble. I love the farm, you know, and I'm glad to be here. It's just that sometimes it feels a little dull. After all the exciting things we went through, the important things we accomplished – well, everything since then has seemed a bit ordinary. We were secret agents, Reynie!' Even as she spoke the words, Kate's eyes lit up in a very familiar way. Then she laughed at herself. 'It's kind of hard to get excited about having the key to the cellar. That's all I mean.'

'Well, you're not alone,' Reynie said. 'Since Miss Perumal adopted me, things have been great, but I still feel restless all the time – like I should be doing something urgent and can't say what.'

'Really?' Kate said, and for a moment the two friends regarded each other in silence. It was a look that communicated everything they shared: the dangers, hardships, and triumphs of their mission, of course, but also the knowledge – as isolating when they were alone as it was thrilling when they were together – that they understood things about the world that no one else did, things they might never speak of except to each other.

'I suppose it's just a normal letdown,' Kate said at last. She walked over to the corner of the hayloft. 'Anyway, it's not *that* bad. And I do what I can to keep things interesting.'

With that, she leapt high into the air and pulled a cord hanging from the rafter above her. A trap door fell open beneath her, and with a playful wave Kate fell through the hole and disappeared. Reynie heard her land with a thud on the earthen floor below. 'Come on!' she called up. 'Let's go and pick some apples.'

Reynie shook his head and went to use the ladder. Kate did keep things interesting, after all, and there was no point pining for bygone adventures. If anything Reynie should be grateful – he *was* grateful – that being with his friends no longer meant being in danger. Who needed danger, anyway? Certainly not Reynie!

But whether Reynie needed it or not – and though he had no way of predicting it – danger most certainly awaited him and his friends.

And it would not be waiting long.

Kate and Reynie spent the rest of the morning doing chores. It was enjoyable work, especially since they were engaged in conversation the whole time. As they picked apples from the few trees giving fruit, Kate told Reynie about her last school year (classes were easy enough, but there was far too much sitting at desks). As they filled the water troughs, she described what a terrible state of disrepair the old farm had been in when she and Milligan had returned to it. And as they oiled the gate to the animal pen, she related how Milligan would sometimes come home from a mission in the middle of the night, wake her up, and talk with her for hours.

'Which is fine by me,' Kate said, working the gate hinge to be sure it was entirely smooth and squeakless. She cast Reynie a sly look. 'He tells me all sorts of top-secret things.'

Reynie raised his eyebrows. 'Like what?'

'I'd better wait and tell you and Sticky at the same time,' Kate said. 'He'll want to hear it, too, you know.' She considered for a moment, then added reluctantly, 'For that matter, I suppose we should wait until Constance is with us, too.'

'Then at least tell me about *that*,' Reynie said, pointing toward two hens he had just seen come around the corner of the barn. The hens were harnessed to a tiny wagon filled with grain and – with chickeny little stutter-steps and a great deal of clucking and flapping – were towing the wagon toward the henhouse.

'Chicken delivery,' Kate said with a nod of satisfaction. 'One of my pet projects.' She glanced at Reynie to see if he caught her joke, but he seemed too preoccupied by the feathery spectacle to have noticed.

'A chicken-drawn wagon,' said Reynie (who was politely pretending not to have heard Kate's joke). 'Now how did you manage that?'

'Oh, training the chickens was easy,' Kate said. 'The hard part was training Madge not to hunt them – I lost two hens before she caught on.' She paused for a moment to honour the memory of the unfortunate hens, then continued brightly, 'I told you I learned a lot from that animal trainer, remember? I've been training the farm animals to do chores. Milligan's often away, so we need a lot of help around here. Might as well use what we have, right?'

'I think it's brilliant,' said Reynie with perfect sincerity.

'The chickens feed themselves, and the livestock open and close their own gate.'

'You saw that?' said Kate, looking pleased. 'Yes, they come and go whenever Moocho sounds the farm bell.' She pointed toward the orchard. 'Speaking of Moocho, there he is now. Hey, Moocho! Here's Reynie!'

Kate had mentioned Moocho Brazos in her letters, so Reynie knew a few things about him. He knew, for instance, that Milligan had wanted someone to help out on the farm, as well as to look after Kate when he was away on missions, and that Kate had persuaded him to hire one of her old circus friends. But now, as the swarthy figure of Moocho Brazos emerged from the apple trees, Reynie realized that Kate had neglected to mention a detail or two. She certainly didn't need to fill him in now, for it was perfectly clear from Moocho's enormous muscles, slicked-down hair, and handlebar moustache that he'd been the circus's Strong Man.

Moocho was carrying a heavy tub full of apples that Reynie and Kate had picked earlier that morning. They'd left it at the far edge of the orchard to be retrieved by Moocho – in the farm truck, Reynie had supposed, not having conceived that anyone could carry it more than a few steps. But Moocho had gone on foot, and in his hands the apple tub looked no more substantial than a bowl of cherries.

'So you're the wonderful Reynie Muldoon,' he said as he came up. 'I've heard so much about you.' Given his daunting appearance, Moocho's soft, melodious voice was every bit as unexpected as his attire – a flowery apron worn over overalls and house slippers. He set the apple tub down and gave Reynie's hand a gentle squeeze. 'Very pleased to meet you.'

'Overslept, have you, Moocho?' Kate said.

Moocho yawned as if on cue. 'We were up so late waiting, you know.'

'Madge and I were up late. *You* went to bed at nine.'

'Which, as you know perfectly well, is long past my bedtime,' Moocho said, 'so no scolding, young lady. Unless, of course, you don't care to eat any of my apple pies tonight.'

Kate immediately repented of her teasing, then told him about the broken-down car. Moocho offered to fetch Miss Perumal and her mother in the farm truck, but Reynie said he expected them to arrive soon. The mechanic had promised the car would be fixed before lunch.

'Well, if they aren't here by then I'll go for them,' Moocho said, scooping up the apple tub and starting for the house. 'We can't let them eat in town – the café is dreadful.'

Reynie watched him go, still marvelling at how effortlessly he carried the tub. 'I see why you asked Milligan to hire him. He must do the work of several people.'

'Oh yes, I suppose he does,' said Kate. She grinned. 'But wait till you try his pies. Then you'll know the real reason.'

Noon found Reynie and Kate perched high atop the farmhouse roof. They had gone up to replace a broken shingle and to right a listing weather vane, and afterwards they had lingered to survey the countryside. The view was excellent from that height, and Kate was pointing out the distant millpond, scene of her earliest memory (that of swimming with Milligan), when a faraway sound caught their attention. They turned to see a plume of dust rising over the lane in the distance.

'That must be Amma and Pati,' Reynie said, but Kate, fixing the dust plume in her spyglass, gave a little gasp and cried, 'They're *all* here, Reynie! I mean Sticky's here, too!'

Reynie took the spyglass – Kate was thrusting it upon him with such zeal he feared she would knock him off the roof – and sure enough, down the dusty lane came Miss Perumal and her mother in the estate car, followed by an old saloon: the Washingtons had arrived earlier than expected.

Kate scrambled nimbly to the edge of the roof, gripped the sides of the ladder, and slid down it like a firefighters' pole, bypassing the rungs altogether. By the time Reynie had descended in a more conventional fashion, the farm-yard was full of cars, the Perumals and Washingtons were chatting with Moocho Brazos (who had hurried out to greet them), and Kate was helping Sticky up from the ground and dusting him off.

To Reynie's surprise, Sticky looked exactly as he'd looked a year ago: a skinny boy with light brown skin, anxious eyes (though perhaps the anxiety came from not yet having recovered his breath) and a completely bald head. The baldness was the surprising part. The last time Reynie had seen Sticky, all his hair had grown back; it had since disap-peared. His spectacles were missing, too, but this was only because Kate was just now picking them up from where her hug had knocked them free.

Clutching his ribs, Sticky gave Reynie a feeble smile. Then the two boys laughed and hugged and clapped each other on the back. All around them, the adults were chattering about faulty carburettors and making good time on the roads and bumping into one other unexpectedly in town. Mr Washington was getting a wheelchair out of the boot for Mrs Washington, whose troubled knees kept her from walking much, but who nonetheless took a few painful steps to embrace Reynie and Kate. A short woman with walnut-coloured skin, narrow shoulders and a rather pouty mouth belied by the kindness in her eyes, Mrs Washington couldn't stop shaking her head as she turned the children's faces left and right in her hands.

'You both look years older already,' she said ruefully, as if she couldn't bear the thought. Mr Washington came up with the wheelchair, and his wife lowered herself into the seat and dabbed at her shining eyes. Mr Washington, who resembled a larger version of Sticky – tall, slender, and bespectacled – was not much of a man for words, but he smiled fondly and greeted the children with reserved pats on their shoulders.

Meanwhile, Miss Perumal (her arms crossed protectively over her ribs) had come over to hug Kate. 'Don't you look wonderful, dear? Oh! And I see you've put a lid on your bucket! How clever!'

Kate beamed – she was always flattered when someone complimented her bucket – and only her desire to steal away and talk privately with the boys prevented her opening the bucket and showing Miss Perumal its entire contents. They were already going to have to wait much too long to be alone, for first the luggage had to be brought in, and lunch eaten, and the dishes cleared away, and the guests settled in their rooms – all of which was perfectly pleasant but took ages to accomplish. By mid-afternoon the three

23

young friends were casting nearly constant, yearning glances at one another, and when Miss Perumal finally asked them to make themselves scarce so the adults could speak in private, they lost no time in bolting for the door.

Still, as they walked out into the orchard, Sticky looked suspiciously back toward the farmhouse. 'Why do they want to speak privately, I wonder?'

'It's Mr Benedict's surprise,' Reynie said. 'They're in on it.'

'They are? So that explains why my parents have been whispering. I thought they were discussing Mum's getting a second job. They know I'm dead set against it. I'd sooner go back to quizzing, you know, but they're dead set against *that*.'

Reynie knew from Sticky's letters that his father was already doing two jobs. Their family's finances were terribly strained due to the unhappy events leading up to the last year. Sticky's prodigious memory and reading abilities had made him an incomparable quiz champion, but he had suffered badly under the pressure to make his family's fortune and ultimately had run away from home. The Washingtons had spent every penny – in fact had gone deep into debt – in order to find Sticky and bring him back to them. They had been distrustful of money's allure ever since, and were stubbornly unwilling to let Sticky be subjected to unusual pressures. ('They can hardly stand even to hear me talk about our time at the Institute,' Sticky had written. 'The very thought of my being in danger makes them tremble.') And so the Washingtons remained quite poor.

'How did you find out they know about the surprise?'

Sticky asked as they settled down in the shade of the apple trees.

'Amma got a letter from Mr Benedict,' Reynie said. 'I saw it on her dresser, but she neglected to mention it to me, and later I overheard bits of a conversation she had with Pati. Pati's hard of hearing, so Amma had to say a few things rather louder than she meant to. None of it was enough to give me any clues, but I could tell they knew something I didn't. Not long after that I got my own letter from Mr Benedict – the one he sent to all of us – and I knew we were in for something good.'

'Of course it will be good! How could it not be good?' said Kate, leaning back on her elbows with a satisfied smile. 'It's *already* good. We're together, aren't we? And tomorrow we'll see Mr Benedict!'

'Not to mention Rhonda and Number Two,' Reynie said, referring to Mr Benedict's brilliant assistants (who also happened to be his adopted daughters, though this wasn't widely known). 'I can't wait to see them, either.'

'Neither can I!' Sticky said. In a somewhat more subdued tone he added, 'And, well . . . Constance, too, of course. And what about Milligan, Kate? At lunch you said he'd meet us at Mr Benedict's house, but wasn't he supposed to be here?'

'That was the plan, but then he got called away on a mission.'

'What kind of mission?' asked Reynie and Sticky at the same time. They were both hungry for details.

Kate shrugged. 'No idea. He never tells me anything beforehand, only afterwards. I always read the paper for clues, of course – I'd love to be able to tell him I figured out what he'd been up to – but I never find anything.'

'So you *have* been keeping up,' Sticky said. 'I asked about that in my last letter, but you never replied.' His tone was slightly resentful, but Kate either ignored it or else was blithely unaware.

'Of course I've been keeping up! But I'm not like you, Sticky. I can't read ten newspapers every morning, and half of them in foreign languages. I only read the *Stonetown Times*. Why? Have you seen anything suspicious?'

Sticky grunted. 'I wish. What about you, Reynie?'

Although this conversation might have seemed strange if overheard (for it is rare to hear children discuss the newspaper, and still more so to hear one ask whether anything 'suspicious' has been found), to Reynie and his friends it felt perfectly natural. All of them had long had the habit of reading the paper – in fact it was a newspaper advertisement that had first led them to Mr Benedict – and ever since their mission they had scanned the daily headlines with particular interest. It was doubtful any activity concerning Mr Curtain would be declassified and printed, but it was always possible that some seemingly innocent story might reveal a connection to something deeper and darker – something the children would recognize even if other readers would not. In this single respect they still felt like secret agents, though reading the daily paper was hardly exciting field work.

This morning's front page of the *Stonetown Times*, for instance, had been devoted to nothing more sinister than finance, freight and forestry: INTEREST RATES SHARPLY ON THE RISE, read one headline; CARGO SHIP *SHORT-CUT* TO MAKE MAIDEN VOYAGE, read another; while still another read, PINE WEEVIL

MAKES MEAL OF SOUTHERN FORESTS. And the news only grew less interesting on page two.

'Suspicious?' Reynie said. 'Not unless you think pine weevils are suspicious. Everything I've read has been dull as doorknobs.'

Kate's eyes twinkled. 'Hey, that reminds me! Sticky, I—'

Reynie cleared his throat and gave her a warning look. It was too late, though. Sticky might be slow to make certain connections, but he was exceptionally quick at recognizing personal insults. 'Go on,' he said, burying his face in his hands. 'It's about my account of the mission, isn't it?'

Now Kate looked regretful. 'Oh . . . no . . . I was, uh, just going to . . .' She looked helplessly at Reynie, unable to think of what to say.

Much to their relief, Sticky lowered his hands and smiled. It was a sheepish smile, but at least he didn't seem wounded. 'Out with it.'

'Well, it's . . . factual,' Kate said.

'And thoughtful,' Reynie added, hurriedly taking the account from his pocket in the hope of finding something to praise.

Kate nodded vigorously as Reynie unfolded the papers. 'Oh, yes, it's *very* thoughtful! And grammatical!'

Sticky winced. 'Is it that bad? Oh well, I knew it was probably rubbish. You should have seen the earlier drafts. This was my sixth attempt.' He took the account from Reynie and looked it over ruefully before stuffing it into his pocket. 'Don't worry, I figured I could never publish it anyway. I just wanted to do something to celebrate the occasion.'

Reynie had a sudden insight. 'That's why your hair's

gone, isn't it? For old times' sake!'

'I thought you might get a kick out of that,' Sticky admitted. 'This time Dad helped me shave it – no more hair-remover concoctions.' He shuddered at the memory.

'Well, I love it!' Kate said, giving Sticky's scalp an affectionate rub, and Reynie grinned and nodded his appreciation.

For a long time the three friends lingered in the orchard, revelling in one another's company and reminiscing about their mission to the Institute. Laughing, groaning, occasionally shivering as they recalled their experiences – all of which remained perfectly vivid in their memories – they let the afternoon slip past them. When Kate noticed how long the shadows had grown in the farmyard, she gave a start and hopped up.

'Good grief! They're going to call us inside soon, and Sticky hasn't even met Madge yet!'

'Who's Madge?' Sticky asked.

'Her Majesty the Queen!' Kate said, as if this explained everything. Impatiently she hauled the boys to their feet and ushered them out into the farmyard, where she blew on her whistle and tugged on the protective glove. Almost instantly the falcon appeared, streaking down from an unseen height to settle upon Kate's wrist.

Sticky's puzzlement faded, replaced by anxiety. Though he readily expressed his admiration for this sharp-taloned creature now regarding him with shining black eyes ('*Falco peregrinus*,' he said, nodding as he backed away, 'impressive bird . . . swiftest of predators . . .'), he was not at all keen to make her special acquaintance. As casually as he could,

28

Sticky took a cloth from his shirt pocket and removed his spectacles.

Reynie smiled to himself. He was quite familiar with Sticky's habit of polishing his spectacles when nervous, and seeing him do so now was unexpectedly satisfying. There was a unique pleasure in knowing a friend so well, Reynie reflected, rather like sharing a secret code. Also, it was nice not to be the only one afraid of Kate's bird.

'Don't worry, Madge,' Kate was saying as she fed the falcon a strip of meat, 'I'll be back before you know it.' And after she'd sent Madge aloft again, she clucked her tongue and said, 'Poor thing, did you see how fidgety she was? She knows I'm going away. I think it makes her nervous.'

'Oh yes,' said Sticky, with a doubtful glance at Reynie. 'Poor thing.'

Reynie patted Kate's back. 'I'm sure your little raptor will be fine.'

Moocho Brazos had prepared a sumptuous meal, and dinner was a boisterous, satisfying, happy affair, with everyone chatting at once and platters constantly being passed this way and that. For dessert Moocho served his much-anticipated apple pies – six of them, in fact, although that number seemed less extravagant once Moocho's own appetite was taken into account.

After the dishes were washed, the pleasant tumult died down and the talk fell away. Everyone was overcome with drowsiness. It had been a long day for all, and another full day awaited them. The children were determined to stay up regardless, but though only a year ago they had been on a secret mission making life-and-death decisions, now they were subject to the dictates of their guardians – which meant bathing, bidding one another goodnight and going to bed.

'Oh well,' Kate said through a yawn. 'We'll be up again soon. The cockerel crows at sunrise, you know.'

And indeed it was the sound of crowing that woke Reynie the next morning. He sat up blearily – he'd slept on a pallet on the floor – to see grey dawn beyond the window and Miss Perumal sitting up in bed, smiling at him.

'Today's your big day,' she said. 'I know you're excited. You didn't sleep until after midnight.'

'You were awake?' Reynie asked. He'd been so involved in his thoughts that he hadn't paid attention to Miss Perumal's breathing. Obviously, though, she'd been paying attention to his.

'I'm excited, too,' Miss Perumal said. 'I know you're going to love your surprise.'

There was something about her expression that made Reynie pause. She was happy for him, he could tell – but there was something else, too. It reminded him of the day she had driven him to take Mr Benedict's tests, when she had felt convinced he would no longer need her as a tutor. Her eyes, now as then, reflected a mixture of pride, expectation and a certain sadness. But they were family now, and Reynie knew nothing could induce Miss Perumal to leave him. So what was she musing about?

Miss Perumal's eyes suddenly changed. With a little laugh of surprise, she turned her face away from him, and when she turned back she'd adopted a scolding look. 'I forget how good you are at reading expressions,' she said. She waggled a finger. 'You mustn't study things too closely,

Reynie, if you don't want to spoil your surprise.'

Together they roused Miss Perumal's mother – whose slumber had been unaffected by the cockerel's crow, but who was always susceptible to foot-tickling – and after she'd woken up laughing and calling them villains, they all set about getting ready.

With a feeling of resignation Reynie put on the shirt Number Two had sent him last month for his birthday. He knew it was a token of her affection, but he still couldn't look at the shirt without wrinkling his nose. Number Two's apparent conviction was that good fashion meant matching one's clothes to one's skin tone (her own wardrobe consisted almost entirely of yellow fabrics that accentuated her yellowish complexion), and so naturally she'd thought this muddled, flesh-coloured shirt would suit Reynie perfectly. It did fit him – sort of – but Reynie couldn't have imagined an uglier shirt, or for that matter a less comfortable one (it was made of canvas, 'for durability,' Number Two had written), and he wore it now only because he expected to see her today.

'You too?' Sticky muttered when Reynie met him in the hall. Sticky was wearing a light brown shirt made of some kind of thickly padded material– his torso appeared to have swollen – and he was perspiring heavily despite the morning's chill air. (Reynie recalled that Sticky's birthday was in January; no doubt the shirt had seemed more suitable then.) 'They made me wear it,' Sticky said, jerking his thumb toward the room he'd shared with his parents. He looked Reynie up and down. 'Do you realize you look like a tote bag?'

'At least I'm not *puffy*,' Reynie said. 'Let's go find Kate.'

They hadn't long to look. Before they could start up the stairs, Kate came sliding down the banister. To their disappointment she was wearing blue jeans and a perfectly normal shirt. She landed beside them with a delighted grin. 'Why, you both look so handsome! Are you going to a party?'

Sticky crossed his thickly padded arms. 'This is unacceptable, Kate. You need to go right back up and put on your birthday present.'

'Absolutely,' Reynie said. 'You're outvoted, Kate. We all suffer together.'

Kate was rubbing his canvas sleeve to see how it felt. She whistled and gave him a pitying look. 'Sorry, but mine was much too small for me, so I cut it up and made my pouches out of it. Did I show them to you?' She eagerly flipped open her bucket's lid. 'It was very sturdy material, so—'

'You showed us already,' Sticky said in a defeated tone. 'What *was* your present, anyway?'

'Mine? Oh, it was a vest. With a fringe.'

Reynie eyed her suspiciously. 'Was it really too small?'

'Well,' said Kate with a sly smile. 'It was *going* to be.'

The day was still quite young when the estate car and the saloon pulled away, their eager occupants half-rested but well fed. Moocho Brazos stood in the farmyard waving goodbye until the cars had disappeared beyond the hill. Then he sighed and stroked his moustache sadly. He was much attached to his exuberant young friend, and with Kate gone the farm seemed dull already. With a melancholy shake of his head, Moocho headed off into the orchard, where a number of trees required tending.

And so it was that the young man who arrived on a scooter a few minutes later was met by an empty farmyard.

The young man dashed first to ring the doorbell – he rang it several times – then to the barn, where he discovered a hen depressing a lever with its beak to fill a tiny wagon with grain. He was startled by this sight, but he quickly overcame his wonder and renewed his search for the addressee of the telegram he carried. As he headed out behind the barn (it would be some time before he tried the orchard), the young man – an employee of the town's general store and wire service – was hoping that *someone*, at least, would be here. His job was to deliver the telegram to 'anyone on the Wetherall farm'. There was no telephone here, he knew, which explained the need for a telegram. The old store owner had told him this was the first telegram they'd been asked to deliver in many years. And a very curious, very urgent one it was. It read:

CHILDREN YOU MUST NOT COME STOP TOO
DANGEROUS STOP CALL ME AT ONCE AND I WILL
TELL YOU THE NEWS STOP OH IT IS BAD NEWS
INDEED STOP REPEAT DO NOT COME BUT CALL AT
ONCE AS I FEAR FOR YOUR SAFETY STOP WITH LOVE
AND REGRET
RHONDA

33

Beyond the Glass,

or Windows for Mirrors

The drive to Mr Benedict's house in Stonetown would take several hours, but they had hardly been on the road twenty minutes before Reynie, in his mind, was already there. He was daydreaming. In the front seat of the estate car, Miss Perumal's mother was humming to herself, unaware that her voice resounded throughout the car. Miss Perumal was suppressing a smile. And beside Reynie in the back seat, Kate and Sticky were catching up on each other's lives. Having arrived earlier than Sticky and being a better correspondent than Kate, Reynie already knew everything the other two were telling each other now. The fact that

Sticky had briefly had a girlfriend, for instance, until she broke up with him for remarking upon her pulchritude. ('She didn't believe me when I told her it meant 'beauty',' Sticky said. Kate shook her head. 'It's always best to stick to small words. If you'd said that to me, I'd have punched you.') Or the fact that – unlike Miss Perumal, who considered Reynie unusually mature for his age and was contemplating his enrolment in college – the Washingtons had forbidden any such possibility for Sticky, to whose emotional well-being they were especially attentive now. ('I've told them again and again that I can handle it,' said Sticky. 'But they aren't budging.')

As his friends talked, Reynie let his thoughts wander ahead of the estate car to the house in Stonetown – with its familiar ivy-covered courtyard and grey stone walls – and, of course, to Mr Benedict himself. Reynie could see him now: the perpetually mussed white hair; the bright green eyes framed by spectacles; the large, lumpy nose; and, of course, the green plaid suit he wore every day. To those who didn't know him, Mr Benedict might well look like a joker. The thought made Reynie indignant, for the man was not only a genius, he was exceptionally good – and in Reynie's opinion, good people were decidedly rare.

Mr Benedict himself had disagreed with Reynie about this. Reynie remembered the conversation perfectly. It had occurred some months after the children returned from their mission to the Institute, when Reynie had still lived in Stonetown. Despite Mr Benedict's countless pressing duties, he had arranged to meet Reynie, and did so every week. (Kate, by this time, had gone to live on the farm, and Sticky had returned to live with his parents in a city several hours away. Of the four children, only Constance – whom Mr Benedict was in the process of adopting – would remain in Stonetown, for Miss Perumal was moving their family to a larger apartment in the suburbs, where Reynie could have his own room and, equally important, a library within walking distance.) After Reynie moved away, these weekly conversations with Mr Benedict had become impracticable, and he recalled them now with fondness – even reverence.

On this particular occasion, Reynie had found Mr Benedict alone in his book-crowded study. As usual, Mr Benedict had greeted him with great warmth, and the two of them had sat down together on the floor. (Mr Benedict had a condition called narcolepsy and was subject to bouts of unexpected sleep, often triggered by strong emotions. In those rare instances when he was not fretfully shadowed by Number Two or Rhonda Kazembe, he protected himself from painful falls by keeping low to the ground.) As had happened so many times before, Mr Benedict had discerned immediately that Reynie had something on his mind.

'Though as I've previously remarked,' Mr Benedict said, smiling, 'this is not such a feat of deduction as it might seem, since you, my friend, *always* have something on your mind. Now tell me what it is.'

Reynie considered how to begin. It was all so complicated, and he could find no good starting point. Then he remembered that Mr Benedict always seemed to intuit what he meant, whether or not Reynie had managed to express it properly. And so he said simply, 'I see things differently now, and it's . . . it's bothering me, I suppose.'

Mr Benedict gazed at Reynie, stroking a bristly patch on his chin that he'd missed with his razor. He exhaled through

36

his lumpy nose. 'Since your mission, you mean.'

Reynie nodded.

'You mean to say,' said Mr Benedict after reflecting a moment, 'that you're disturbed by the wickedness of which so many people seem capable. My brother, for example, but also his Executives, his henchmen, the other students at the Institute—'

'Everybody,' Reynie said.

'Everybody?'

'Or . . . or almost everybody. I certainly don't think that about you – or about any of us who've come together because of you. And there's Miss Perumal and her mother, of course, and a few other people. In general, though . . .' Reynie shrugged. 'I thought with the Whisperer out of commission – with Mr Curtain's hidden messages no longer affecting people's minds – well, I thought things would start to seem different. Better. But that hasn't happened.'

'You aren't doubting what you accomplished, I hope.'

Reynie shook his head. 'No, I know we stopped terrible things from happening. It's just that I hadn't expected to start seeing things – to see people – this way.'

Mr Benedict made as if to rise, then thought better of it. 'An old habit,' he said. 'I occasionally feel an urge to pace, which, as you know, is ill-advised. If I dropped off and brained myself against the bookcase, Number Two would never let me hear the end of it.'

Reynie chuckled. He was well aware of Number Two's fearsome protectiveness.

Mr Benedict settled back against his desk. 'It's natural that you feel as you do, Reynie. There is much more to the world than most children – indeed, most adults – ever see

37

or know. And where most people see mirrors, you, my friend, see windows. By which I mean there is always something beyond the glass. You have seen it and will always see it now, though others may not. I would have spared you that vision at such a young age. But it's been given you, and it will be up to you to decide whether it's a blessing or a curse.'

'Excuse me, Mr Benedict, but how can it possibly be a blessing to know that people are untrustworthy?'

Mr Benedict looked at Reynie askance. 'Rather than answer that, allow me to call attention to the assumption you're making – the assumption that most people are untrustworthy. Have you considered the possibility, Reynie, that wickedness is simply more noticeable than goodness? That wickedness *stands out*, as it were?'

When Reynie looked doubtful, Mr Benedict nodded and said, 'I wouldn't expect you to change your mind so quickly. You're used to being right about people – we all know you have marvellous intuition – and it's difficult for you to question the conclusions you've drawn. But as I do with my pacing, Reynie, you must guard against old habits leading you astray.' Mr Benedict crossed his arms and regarded Reynie shrewdly. 'Let me ask you: have you ever had a dream in which, having spied a deadly snake at your feet, you suddenly begin to see snakes everywhere – suddenly realize, in fact, that you're surrounded by them?'

Reynie was surprised. 'I *have* had that dream. It's a nightmare.'

'Indeed. And it strikes me as being rather like when a person first realizes the extent of wickedness in the world. That vision can become all-consuming – and in a way, it, too, is a nightmare, by which I mean that it is not quite a proper assessment of the state of things. For someone as observant as you, Reynie, deadly serpents always catch the eye. But if you find that serpents are *all* you see, you may not be looking hard enough.'

Reynie had mulled this over – was still mulling it over, in fact, and not a little doubtfully – but had let the subject drop as he and Mr Benedict played a game of chess. Reynie had never beaten Mr Benedict; in the relatively few games they'd played, however, he had learned a great deal from him – and not always about chess. As often as not, their games were interrupted by long discussions of other matters, and this time was no different. Mr Benedict gave no indication of surprise when, half an hour later, Reynie responded to an announcement of check by asking, 'So you've had the snake nightmare, too?'

'Oh, certainly,' said Mr Benedict, gently setting aside the rook he'd just taken. (He was always respectful of Reynie's pieces, as if he considered their capture an unfortunate necessity.) 'It's a common nightmare, and I've had it many times, as well as a great many others that are more rare. Part of my condition, I'm afraid.'

'What do you mean?' Reynie had always known that Mr Benedict's narcolepsy made him prone to unpredictable episodes of sleep; beyond this, he realized now, he knew almost nothing.

For a moment Mr Benedict didn't speak, only gazed contemplatively at his fingers as if considering them for the first time. It seemed to Reynie that for some reason he was reluctant to answer, but that he didn't wish to dismiss Reynie's question, either. The latter impulse won out, apparently, for at length Mr Benedict looked up and said,

'For someone like me, Reynie, night time can be just as trying as day time. It's always a relief to give over to sleep, of course – to stop fighting against it, as I must do during the day – but I am often beset by nightmares, strange fits of waking paralysis and even hallucinations, which can be quite terrifying.'

'That's awful!' Reynie said. 'I had no idea.'

'Well,' Mr Benedict said, 'I am long since used to it. I've even made friends with the Old Hag.'

'The Old Hag?'

'An ancient name for one of the more common hallucinations. I sometimes awake to the vision of a hunched figure at the end of my bed. Sadly, this hallucination is usually accompanied by paralysis.'

Reynie was aghast. 'You mean to say there's a strange person lurking by your bed – in the darkness – and you're not able to move?'

'Nor even to cry out,' said Mr Benedict. 'It's rather inconvenient.'

Reynie shuddered, imagining it. 'I'd be scared out of my mind!'

'That *is* the most common reaction,' Mr Benedict said with a smile. 'And I admit I'm only joking when I say I've befriended her. Let's just say I recover more quickly from our encounters than I used to. At any rate, the hallucinations and the paralysis rarely last more than a minute.'

That minute must seem like an eternity, Reynie thought. Then something occurred to him. 'What about Mr Curtain? Do you think that happens to him, too? Do you think it might be why he's so obsessed with controlling things?'

Mr Benedict tapped his nose. 'Very astute, Reynie. I've often wondered that myself. It wouldn't surprise me to learn that my brother's nightly torments and daily struggles have contributed to his obsession. Though I've long since come to terms with my *own* spells of helplessness, it did take years before I stopped feeling ashamed of them. Evidently my brother has taken a different tack and has achieved no such resolution.'

This was an understatement, to say the least. Reynie recalled with frightening clarity Mr Curtain's eerie silver glasses and his high-powered, customized wheelchair – props he used to conceal his condition. The man might look exactly like Mr Benedict, and he might possess a similar degree of genius, but his approach to the world couldn't have been more different.

For a minute Reynie was lost in the uncomfortable memory of his encounters with Mr Curtain. (The memory was uncomfortable not just because of the danger he'd been in, but also because Reynie himself, in a terrible moment, had once doubted which of the two brothers he was more like.) Thankfully, however, he was soon snapped out of his reflections by the sound of soft snoring. Mr Benedict's head had dropped forward, his hands twitched at his side, and he appeared on the verge of slumping over onto the chess-board. Reynie's impulse was to slip out and let him sleep, but Mr Benedict had repeatedly instructed Reynie to wake him whenever such episodes occurred. Or *try* to wake him, at least – it wasn't always possible.

'Mr Benedict!' Reynie said. 'Mr Benedict, sir!'

Mr Benedict came to with a start. Then, yawning, he ran his hands through his rumpled hair and regarded Reynie apologetically. 'I hope you haven't been waiting long.'

'Not even a minute,' Reynie said.

Mr Benedict sighed. 'My brother has influence, I'm afraid, even in his absence. Thinking of him so often upsets me. . .'

Reynie thought he understood this – his own thoughts of Mr Curtain were nothing if not upsetting. And yet, seeing Mr Benedict's expression, Reynie realized it was not anger or fear or even outrage that troubled him so. It was sadness.

'Well, now,' Mr Benedict said, with a quick gesture toward the chessboard, 'I don't wish to rush you, but I believe it's mate in six. Do you agree?'

Reynie turned his attention to the board, but his concern clouded his thoughts. Clearly Mr Benedict wanted to be alone. And so climbing to his feet he said, 'Next time I'll give you a better run for your money.'

'I look forward to it,' Mr Benedict said, also rising. He gave Reynie's shoulder an affectionate squeeze as they moved for the door. 'Until then, my friend, may you have pleasant dreams.'

Reynie *was* having pleasant dreams when Kate nudged him awake. He blinked and looked around to discover that his dreams were, in fact, reality. He was with his friends, and through the car window he saw the tall buildings of Stonetown ahead, which meant they would soon be reunited with Mr Benedict and the others. He gave Kate a sleepy grin. 'I guess I dozed off.'

'Zonked out is more like it,' Kate said. 'And you weren't the only one. Sticky dropped off in the middle of a speech about orchid varieties. I think he bored himself to sleep.'

Sitting on the other side of her, Sticky only smiled. He

was awake now and happily polishing his spectacles, in much too good a mood to be snappish. Reynie could see bits of fuzz stuck to his scalp where he'd slumped against Kate's shoulder.

Into Stonetown they rode, passing several landmarks familiar to Reynie. There was the orphanage where Reynie had lived until a year ago; there was the park where he and Miss Perumal used to take their walks; and now, as they passed into the busy downtown district near the harbour, Reynie could see the Monk Building. It was there he'd met Sticky and Kate, who like Reynie had come to take Mr Benedict's tests.

'Strange to think,' Kate said, almost to herself. She was gazing at the Monk Building with a look of wonder. When she'd met Milligan there, she had thought it was for the first time; neither of them had known the truth about their kinship.

'Can you believe it?' Sticky said as Miss Perumal turned onto the street that led to Mr Benedict's house. 'A year ago we hadn't even met Mr Benedict. We had no idea what we were in for! Can you imagine—'

Reynie interrupted him. 'What's the matter, Amma?'

Miss Perumal was staring at something, her brow furrowed with concern. The children strained against their seat belts, trying to see ahead. Miss Perumal pulled the estate car to the kerb, and then they saw what she had seen: three police officers stood under the elm tree in the courtyard of Mr Benedict's house. They were talking to a cluster of government officials (the children recognized the officials, who had questioned them after their mission), and their expressions were very serious.

'Something's happened,' Miss Perumal said. 'You children wait—'

But the children were already leaping from the car. With Kate in the lead, they dashed to the iron gate that led into the courtyard. They were met by a stern, unfamiliar man who held out his hand to stop them. He was a small man – hardly taller than Kate – but his unpleasant expression and his raspy, sharp voice gave him a distinct air of threat.

'Where do you think you're going?' he demanded. 'Who are you?'

'We're friends of Mr Benedict,' Kate said.

The man narrowed his eyes. 'Friends, you say.'

'Oh dear!' a voice cried from the house. The children looked past the man to see, standing in the front doorway, a lovely young woman with coal-black skin and braided hair. It was Rhonda Kazembe, of course, and as she hurried down the steps she seemed greatly dismayed to see them. 'You came? You didn't get my telegram?'

Kate tried to press past the man, but he took her roughly by the shoulder and held her back. 'Who are these children?' he asked Rhonda.

'It's all right, Mr Bane, they're friends. In fact, the girl you've grabbed so rudely is Milligan's daughter.'

With a start, the man released Kate (who at any rate had been about to release herself), and Rhonda gestured toward the government officials. 'Everyone here but you knows these children,' she said. 'Feel free to check with your superiors.'

As Mr Bane stalked off to do just that, Rhonda opened the gate and embraced them all at once. 'Oh dear,' she said again, squeezing them tightly. 'You shouldn't have come, but now that you have, at least I can stop worrying about you.'

'What's happened, Rhonda?' asked Reynie.

Before Rhonda could answer, Miss Perumal and her mother came up, followed by the Washingtons. Rhonda greeted them with apparent relief. 'Come inside,' she said soberly. 'Come inside and I'll tell you everything.'

'Tell us everything about what?' Kate insisted.

'Mr Benedict and Number Two,' Rhonda replied, and her eyes suddenly brimmed with tears. 'They've been taken.'

The children stared at her in shock. Taken?

'But . . . but who . . . ?' Sticky began.

Rhonda angrily wiped her eyes. 'Who do you think?'

They all knew the answer at once. Reynie said it aloud. 'It's Mr Curtain, isn't it?'

'I'll explain everything when we're in the house. I don't know if you're safe out here. Someone had to deliver it, after all. They may yet be close by, and who knows what they intend?'

'Deliver what?' Reynie asked, but Rhonda wouldn't say more until she had ushered them inside.

Gone were Reynie's visions of a happy reunion inside Mr Benedict's old house. The rambling, three-storey stone building was perfectly familiar, yet the knowledge that Mr Benedict and Number Two were missing gave the place an alien feel. As Mr Washington helped his wife up the front steps and Rhonda carried up her wheelchair, Reynie and his friends kept casting anxious looks all around.

Through the front door they entered Mr Benedict's maze, which Rhonda and the children knew by heart. The maze had been the last of Mr Benedict's tests, as well as a line of defence against intruders. Together they moved quickly through its many identical rooms, up the staircase at the far side and at last into a sitting room, where their entrance surprised another group of officials, all of whom turned toward the doorway with apprehensive expressions.

'Oh, it's just you,' a silver-haired woman said to Rhonda. 'Sorry, we're a bit on edge.' She glanced inquiringly at the children. 'I take it these are—?'

'Yes, Ms Argent,' Rhonda said. 'And I would like them to see it.'

Exchanging uncertain looks, Ms Argent and the other officials nevertheless stepped aside to let the children approach. On a table in the centre of the room sat a brown box.

Rhonda gestured toward the box. 'What happens to Mr Benedict and Number Two depends on that,' she said grimly. She sounded as if she still couldn't believe it, and indeed, as if speaking to herself, she repeated in a whisper, 'Everything depends on that.'

The children moved closer. It was an ordinary-looking box, about the size of a fruit crate, with several holes punched into it. Together they peered through the holes into the box's dark interior, anxious to see just what it might be – what the box might possibly contain that would deter-mine the fate of those they held so dear.

It was a pigeon. Only that. A pigeon.

THE SOCIETY

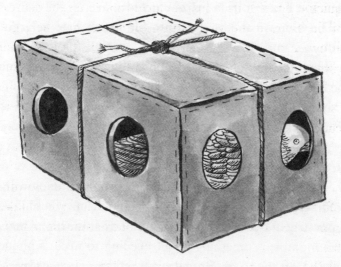

RECONVENES

'**W**hat can this bird have to do with the kidnapping?' Kate asked.

The government officials seemed reluctant to speak until Rhonda pointed out that the children might be directly affected by this situation. Finally a blond man with prominent cheekbones stepped forward to address them. 'It's a carrier pigeon,' he said, 'sent by Mr Curtain. It had a message strapped to its leg. We're expected to send a reply by the same method.'

'Actually,' Sticky interjected, 'it's a homing pigeon.'

Everyone in the room looked at him. The Washingtons,

who were standing with Miss Perumal and her mother inside the doorway, shifted uncomfortably, unsure whether their son had just been helpful or rude.

The blond man coughed into his fist. 'I hate to argue with you, son—'

'Then please don't,' said Rhonda impatiently. 'I assume the difference is important, Sticky?'

'It could be,' Sticky said. 'Homing pigeons can fly great distances – sometimes thousands of miles. Carrier pigeons aren't really suited for long flights.'

Ms Argent, the silver-haired woman, said, 'So we can't necessarily expect it to fly somewhere around Stonetown?'

Sticky shook his head. 'Its roost could be anywhere.'

Ms Argent cast a dark, meaningful look at the blond man, who mumbled something about needing to make a phone call and left the room. Rhonda watched him go, her expression grave.

'Tell me you haven't started a search,' she said.

'Don't worry,' Ms Argent replied. 'We're taking appropriate measures.'

'That's what I'm afraid of,' Rhonda said, turning on her heel. Beckoning her friends to follow, she left the sitting room without another word. She led them down the hallway to the dining room, where she asked them to sit at the long table. 'It's exactly what they should not be doing,' she muttered, closing the door behind her. 'Not until they know more. I'm going to have to be aggressive, I see.'

'Rhonda,' said Miss Perumal, 'what did the message say?'

I would show it to you,' Rhonda said, 'but they've already confiscated it as evidence. In essence, it said—'

'Can you quote it exactly, Rhonda?' asked Reynie, who

knew Rhonda had a prodigious memory almost as good as Sticky's. 'There might be something important in the phrasing, you know.'

'You're absolutely right,' Rhonda said. 'Ready, then?'

And she quoted the message, which was as follows:

Dear Miss Kazembe,

I write to report that your friends are in grave danger, and – lest there be any doubt – that it is I who endangers them.

Let me explain. Despite his efforts to keep silent on the matter, my prisoner, Nicholas Benedict, has been compelled to reveal a secret regarding a certain rare plant. According to his reluctant confession, 'only one person can secure the information' I seek – namely, the exact location and description of the plant – and this person is neither Benedict nor his yellowish assistant but someone, regardless, who is 'extremely close' to Benedict. I know for a fact that he is telling the truth. I must assume that if you are not this person yourself, you will at least know of whom he speaks. For Benedict's sake, I certainly hope so.

You have exactly four days to release this pigeon with the information I require. Be assured that if you attach any tracking devices to the bird, or make any sort of attempt to follow it to its destination, I will know. Such treachery will not bode well for your friends. If you hope to see either of them again, you will give me exactly what I wish, and without delay.

Oh, do not delay, Miss Kazembe. We shall all be most unhappy if you delay.

Cordially,

L. Curtain

When Rhonda had finished reciting the letter, there was a disturbed silence as everyone felt its meaning sink in. At length the silence was broken by Mrs Washington stifling a sob with her handkerchief, and then everyone started to speak at once. Rhonda held up a hand. 'Nobody say anything yet.' She went to make sure nobody was listening at the door, then returned to the table and spoke to the children in a low voice. 'Do any of you know what this is about?'

None of them did.

'Good, then at least you won't be subjected to more than the usual unpleasant questioning.' Rhonda jerked a thumb over her shoulder to indicate the officials down the hall. 'They're very concerned about what Mr Curtain is trying to get. They're worried it's connected to the Whisperer.'

Everyone at the table knew that Mr Curtain's infamous machine was now situated here in Mr Benedict's house, powered by a huge bank of computers that had been moved into the basement. Several months ago, Mr Benedict had finished altering the Whisperer's sophisticated functions, and since then he'd been using it to help people whose memories had been suppressed by the Whisperer under Mr Curtain's guidance. In fact, in Mr Benedict's last letter he had happily reported that he'd restored the memories of almost everyone ever affected by the Whisperer, and that after a year of constant labour he might even allow himself a short vacation.

'What would a plant have to do with the Whisperer?' Sticky asked.

'I don't know,' Rhonda said. 'Mr Benedict's never mentioned anything about a plant to me. All I know is that he was away doing some personal research. Of course he had to take Number Two with him – she'd never let him go alone, and I had to stay to prepare for your visit – but if she knew where they were going, she didn't let on. I doubt she knew. Mr Benedict loves his surprises.'

'Hold on,' Kate said. 'Mr Benedict went away on purpose? He wasn't going to meet us here?'

'He and Number Two left last week,' said Rhonda. 'It was supposed to be part of your surprise.' She was about to say more, but a look of crushing sadness came over her face, and she fell silent.

Miss Perumal spoke up, addressing the children. 'We adults all knew about it, of course. Mr Benedict asked our permission before he made the arrangements. You were to go on a mysterious adventure.'

Sticky looked at his parents in surprise. After this last year of being so carefully sheltered, he found it hard to believe they had granted permission for him to go on an adventure of any kind – mysterious or otherwise.

Mrs Washington lowered her handkerchief. 'We'd been fretting about your education, you see. You're such extra-ordinary children, and none of us thought you were being suitably challenged. Yet we were reluctant to send you off to college so young. We must have had a dozen telephone conversations on the subject, wouldn't you say, Miss Perumal?'

'We did,' said Miss Perumal. 'And we were still deliberating when we heard from Mr Benedict, who happened to be planning an anniversary reunion for you. When we mentioned our concerns to him, he suggested that a field trip – a very special field trip – might be just the thing to supplement your educations. He'd always regretted you were exposed to such dangers on your mission, he said, but it was undeniable that you had thrived under the challenge. None of us could disagree. It was obvious how much you'd grown as a result of that mission – to say nothing of how much you missed one another now.'

'So Mr Benedict proposed an adventure,' Mrs Washington said. 'A completely safe one this time, but an adventure nonetheless. The timing was perfect, he said, because he intended to take a research trip anyway and would be happy to expand its purpose. He and Number Two would leave sometime before you, and then you four would follow in their footsteps, with Rhonda and Milligan accompanying you. That was to be your big surprise.'

Miss Perumal leant to murmur into Reynie's ear. 'You were going to be away for two weeks. I knew you'd have a wonderful time, but I also knew how much I'd miss you.' She gave him a sad smile, and Reynie nodded, understanding now the bitter-sweet look she'd given him that morning.

'Mr Benedict would cover the expenses,' Mrs Washington went on (with a significant look at Sticky, who'd just been wondering how they could afford such a trip). 'Mr Benedict said you were owed that and a great deal more besides, and with Rhonda and Milligan to accompany you we hadn't the least worry for your safety. But now to think' – here Mrs Washington raised her handkerchief to her face again, though not enough to conceal her look of horror – 'to think if you had actually *gone*. What might have happened to you?'

'Nothing would have happened to us,' said Kate soothingly. 'Milligan was going, too, remember? Nobody could have touched us with him along.'

Mrs Washington, who at any rate wished to banish such frightening thoughts from her mind, nodded tightly and lowered her handkerchief. Mr Washington squeezed her shoulder and said nothing – he'd said scarcely a word since they arrived – but his eyes were deeply troubled.

'What exactly was this field trip to be?' Reynie asked. 'Where were we going?'

'That part was secret,' said Miss Perumal. 'Mr Benedict thought you might be nosy enough to glean the details ahead of time, which would defeat the purpose of the exercise, so he provided very few. We knew that you'd eventually meet up with him and Number Two, and that along the way Rhonda would make sure you called home every day – but more than that he didn't reveal. Perhaps Rhonda can tell us more.'

'I wish I could,' said Rhonda, who was at the door again checking for eavesdroppers, 'but Mr Benedict was mum on almost everything. I think he relished the idea of surprising me, as well. He wouldn't even tell me what his research was about, though I sensed he was eager to pursue it.' With a last look down the hallway, she pulled the door closed again.

'Why are you being so careful, Rhonda?' asked Kate. 'Don't those people want to help Mr Benedict too?'

'Some of them, yes,' said Rhonda. Her face hardened. 'Some of them, perhaps not. There's a lot of resentment of the fact that Mr Benedict is the only person who can operate the Whisperer. It's Mr Benedict who calls the shots, and he's stubbornly resisted certain people's suggestions that the government use it for other purposes. Those people might be very pleased if he went away for good. As for the others . . .' She shook her head. 'I don't trust them not to attempt some kind of rescue operation and bungle it terribly. It would be the worst thing they could do. All of them together aren't half as smart as Curtain.'

'What do you think we should do?' Sticky asked.

'We need to speak privately with Milligan. I haven't been able to get in touch with him, but he should be here soon – he's already late, in fact. It's possible Mr Benedict gave him more details about the trip. He did want to be sure it went well for you. Oh, if you could have seen Mr Benedict's face the morning they left! He was so pleased to be giving you this surprise!'

Just then the door flew open with a bang. Everyone jumped and stared. Oddly, though, there seemed to be no one in the doorway. Reynie's first thought was that an unusually strong draught had blown the door open – it was a draughty old house – but then he thought to lower his gaze, and in doing so was rewarded with the sight of Constance Contraire's scowling face.

'You're meeting without me?' she demanded. 'Why wasn't I told?'

'Come in, Constance,' Rhonda said in a weary voice. 'You asked to be left alone, remember? I was just catching everyone up. They've only been here a few minutes.'

This explanation clearly did not satisfy Constance, but she had no opportunity to express her dissatisfaction, for she was immediately swept into the air by Kate, who hugged her so tightly she was unable to speak.

'It's good to see you, Constance,' Kate said sadly, 'even though it's under such awful circumstances.'

Constance's pale blue eyes glistened, her pudgy cheeks reddened, and her feet dangled helplessly around Kate's knees. (She might be of extraordinary intellect for her age – she was only three – but she was of ordinary size, and Kate quite towered over her.) When at last Kate set her down again, Constance had no chance to recover before Reynie and Sticky embraced her as well, quickly followed by the adults. By the time everyone had greeted her, Constance's wispy blonde hair had come free of its slides and fallen about her face, and she wore a wildly disorientated look, as if she were an oversized rag doll that had been magically brought to life.

'Oh,' Constance said confusedly. 'Okay, then. Hello.'

Ms Argent, meanwhile, had appeared in the dining room doorway and stood waiting for the fuss to die down. 'Ms Kazembe,' she said, 'we'd like to ask you a few more questions, please.'

'Very well, I'll be right there,' Rhonda said.

Ms Argent seemed disinclined to leave, but when she realized that everyone in the room was staring at her impatiently, she turned slightly pink and made a hasty exit.

Rhonda made sure Ms Argent was out of earshot, then stepped to a side table, opened a drawer and took out a sealed envelope. She looked solemnly at the children. 'I was to give you this,' she said. 'It contains Mr Benedict's instructions for beginning your adventure. I haven't seen what's inside it yet – I didn't want Ms Argent's crew to know about it, and there hasn't been the least opportunity to read in private – and now that you're all here it seems proper that the four of you should see it first. Mr Benedict wanted you to, after all. I'd better go and see if I can deduce what these people are planning, but we'll discuss this as soon as I return.

'Now, before I hand it over,' Rhonda said, lifting the envelope away from Constance, who had stepped forward to grab it, 'you must promise that if the instructions offer any hint as to Mr Benedict and Number Two's whereabouts, you'll mention it to no one but Milligan or me. It wouldn't surprise me if Ms Argent or one of the others tried to catch you alone, and we must be very careful.' When the children had promised, Rhonda let Constance take the envelope.

'I'm so sorry, everyone,' she said, looking sorrowfully first at the children and then at the other adults. 'Please make yourself as comfortable as you can. Help yourselves to anything in the kitchen – but remember, don't speak to a soul unless I'm present. I have to do everything I can to manage this situation.' Rhonda was fighting back tears again. 'I have to get them home safely. I *have* to . . .'

Miss Perumal walked her to the door. 'It's what we all want, Rhonda. Now, don't worry about us. We'll be fine.'

'And discreet,' Mrs Washington added.

No sooner had Rhonda left than the children turned with anxious, pleading faces to the adults, who could hardly refuse them.

'Go,' Miss Perumal said, waving them toward the door. 'But stay in the house, and remember what Rhonda told you.'

'And come back soon to eat,' Mrs Washington said. 'It will be a long day, and you'll need your strength.'

'Those poor children,' said Miss Perumal's mother. She meant to say it under her breath, but her voice carried after the children as they hurried from the room. 'Oh, the poor, poor dears!'

The children sat in a circle on the floor of Constance Contraire's bedroom. Around them were the piles of Constance's laundry – some dirty and some clean – that they had shoved aside to make room for themselves. Clothes hung on the back of Constance's miniature desk chair, too, and blankets and towels were draped haphazardly across her unmade bed. Given the state of her room, it would have been no surprise to find her chest of drawers utterly empty; and under different circumstances one of the children would have made a point of checking, just to see. But right now, no one was in the mood to tease Constance about her disorderliness or anything else.

The window shade was drawn; the door was locked. They spoke in hushed tones, and every so often one of them checked the hallway for unwanted listeners. The secrecy of their discussion – and the anxiety and urgency that attended it – lent a strange feeling of familiarity to the scene, for only a year had passed since the Mysterious Benedict Society had held meetings just like this at the Institute. In the middle of their circle lay the sealed envelope. Reynie had put off opening it but hadn't said why.

'He didn't tell you anything more?' Reynie asked Constance, who evidently knew as little about Mr Benedict's trip as the others.

'Don't you think I'd have said so if he had?' Constance snapped. 'I've spent the whole morning crying, Reynie – ever since that stupid bird showed up. If I could think of some important fact, you know I'd tell you.'

'I know,' Reynie said gently. He was used to Constance and had a better way with her than the others did. 'Now

57

please don't be upset, but can you tell me how the pigeon got here?'

Constance sniffled and swiped at her eyes. 'There was a knock at the door, and when one of the guards went to open it, that box was on the doorstep. He didn't see who left it, but one of the upstairs guards was watching through a window. She said it was a man in a suit. He was carrying a briefcase.'

'I knew it,' said Kate, curling her lip, and in a tone that implied considerable loathing she said, 'a Ten Man.'

The others looked at her.

'A what?' Sticky asked.

'This was something I was going to tell you about. Do you remember Mr Curtain's Recruiters?'

Constance stared at Kate. 'Do I *remember* them?' she said, her face darkening. 'Hmm, let me think, Kate. Oh, wait! You mean like the men who tried to kidnap me – the ones who shot wires out of their watches, shocked the wits out of me and stuffed me into a bag?'

'Exactly,' Kate said. 'Those guys. Well, they're still working for Mr Curtain, only they aren't called Recruiters any more. Milligan and the other agents call them Ten Men.'

'Because they're heartless?' asked Reynie, thinking of *The Wizard of Oz*.

'Not Tin Men, Reynie. *Ten* Men. It's true they're heartless, though, and they've got even more dangerous. The agents call them Ten Men because they have ten different ways of hurting you.'

'Not just the shockwatches?' Sticky asked, cringing as if he didn't really want to know.

'Apparently they've expanded their wardrobe,' Kate said.

Reynie was rubbing his chin. 'If a Ten Man delivered the pigeon,' he mused, 'then another Ten Man could be waiting at its roost. Mr Curtain wouldn't have to be there himself. They could just call him when the reply came. That means Mr Curtain could be anywhere in the world – and wherever *he* is, that's where Mr Benedict and Number Two are.'

'I have a feeling you're going somewhere with this,' Kate said.

'Not just me,' Reynie said. 'All of us.'

'We're going somewhere?' Sticky asked, confused.

'Okay, Reynie, why haven't we opened the envelope yet?' Constance said. 'Why have you been stalling?'

'Because I think we need to come to an agreement,' Reynie said, taking the envelope and staring at it intently. 'Whatever Mr Benedict has written in here could put us on his trail.' He looked up. 'And I think we should follow it.'

'You mean actually go on the trip?' Sticky said, his eyes widening.

'By ourselves?' Kate said. She considered for perhaps half a second. 'Okay, I'm in.'

Constance looked faintly hopeful. 'You think we could actually find them?'

'It's worth a shot,' Reynie said.

Sticky was polishing his spectacles now. Beads of sweat had appeared on his bald head. 'It might be dangerous. You realize it might be dangerous, right?'

'Yes,' Reynie said. 'But if we find them – or if we can just get close – we won't do anything foolish. We'll contact Rhonda and Milligan, and they can decide what to do.'

'What if we come across a Ten Man?' Constance asked.

'Don't worry about that,' said Kate, with a dismissive wave of her hand. 'We'll just need to keep an eye out for suits and briefcases – and, you know, be prepared to run for our lives.'

'Thank you,' said Constance with a quaver in her voice. 'That's ever so comforting.'

'A Ten Man probably wouldn't even notice us,' Reynie said. 'Four children don't exactly look like a rescue team, you know.'

'Well, I suppose *that's* true,' Constance said in a somewhat stronger voice, and Reynie smiled encouragingly. He didn't quite believe what he'd just said – he suspected at least some of Mr Curtain's henchmen would have heard about them. But Mr Curtain, of all people, would hate to admit he'd been outsmarted by children, and it was possible he'd avoided mention of them. At any rate, Reynie thought it best to shore up Constance's courage, for he could tell she intended to come along regardless.

Kate cracked her knuckles. 'If we're going to do this we need to get started. Four days, the letter said, and we may need every minute.'

'So what's the plan?' Sticky asked, putting away his polishing cloth and resettling his spectacles.

'If we're in agreement,' Reynie said, 'we'll go wherever these instructions lead us. Secretly, of course. The adults would never let us go now – not even if Rhonda and Milligan came with us.'

'Of course not,' said Kate. 'We'll have to sneak out.'

'Oh boy,' said Sticky, who hadn't thought about this yet. 'If a Ten Man doesn't kill me, my parents surely will.'

Reynie grimaced, imagining how Miss Perumal would

react when she discovered he'd gone. He quickly forced the image out of his mind (just as, moments before, he had forced away the image of a Ten Man seizing him in some far-off place where no one could protect him).

'Are we agreed, then?' Kate asked.

'Agreed,' said Constance and Reynie.

Sticky let out a deep breath. 'Agreed.'

Everyone looked at the envelope then, wondering where in the world – and into what unknown dangers – it was to take them.

THE JOURNEY BEGINS

Reynie opened the envelope, took out two sheets of stationery, and began to read:

Dear friends,

I greet you from afar! By now I trust you're enjoying one another's company again. I'm very pleased to think of it.

Rhonda will have given you a few details concerning your trip. The rest are these: she and Milligan will accompany you, but you should think of them as passengers and yourselves as pilots. It is you who must solve the clues that will bring us together again for our celebration. I know you are more than up to the challenge, and I do look forward to hearing stories from your journey.

That journey begins here, where the four of you are gathered. Your first steps should be in the direction that the riddle on the following page takes you. May your adventures bring you closer together, even as they take you far from home.
Warm regards,
Mr Benedict

For a short time the children sat in silence. Now that they'd been given a moment to reflect upon it, they were deeply moved by Mr Benedict's gesture. He'd gone to a great deal of trouble to offer them something special. Little had he known that his own fate was about to take such a terrible turn, or that his gift would lead the children into danger. He would never want them to put themselves at risk – least of all on his account – which was one reason they cared enough about him to do so.

'Are you ready?' Reynie asked finally. The others murmured their assent, adopting expressions of concentration as Reynie read the riddle aloud:

'Looking for something? Open me.
I'm sure that your something inside of me lies.
Of course you can always find hope in me
(Though despair must come first; and later, surprise),
What's sought, though, depends on the seeker –
One looks for bobbin; another, for beaker;
Others, for nature; still others, for nurture –
The quarry will vary from searcher to searcher.

And yet (I suspect this will strike you as strange),
My contents are set and will not ever change.
If you still cannot guess what I mean, here's a clue:
The answer – what I mean – lies inside of me too.'

'You must be kidding,' Kate said when Reynie had
finished. 'That's the riddle? But it's nonsense! Nothing can
hold all those things!'

Reynie looked at her curiously. 'It isn't nonsense, Kate.'

'It's impossible, that's what it is,' said Constance, rolling
her eyes. 'I wouldn't have thought I could feel angry with
him – not right now – but did he really have to make it so
hard? How are we supposed to help him?'

'It sounds like magic,' Sticky said in an awed tone. 'After
all, he wouldn't give us an impossible riddle. Maybe the
answer just *seems* impossible, but isn't really! Like magic!'

Constance made a point of getting Sticky's attention,
then rolled her eyes again. 'It isn't magic, Sticky.'

Sticky glared at her. 'Well, do you have a better idea?
If it isn't nonsense, and it isn't impossible, and it isn't
magic . . .'

'It's a dictionary,' Reynie said, standing up. 'Now let's go
and find it.'

When Kate had stopped smacking herself on the forehead;
and Sticky had worked through the riddle aloud ('So 'hope'
comes after 'despair' but before 'surprise' because the words
are in alphabetical order! I get it!'); and Constance had
rudely pointed out that the riddle had been solved already
and didn't require Sticky's decoding; and Reynie had
grabbed Sticky's arm to prevent him from giving Constance

a painful finger-thump on the head – when, in short, they were ready, the children developed their plan.

Mr Benedict's house, as they all knew perfectly well, contained more books than boards of wood. Almost every available surface held stacks of books; almost every wall was lined with bookshelves. According to Sticky – who remembered the exact placement of every book in the house – there were seventeen dictionaries (twenty-six if you counted foreign languages), any one of which might contain the next clue. The children decided to start on the third floor, where Constance's bedroom was located, and work their way downstairs if necessary.

The third floor consisted of three long hallways, a dozen rooms, and quite a few nooks and crannies – space enough for thousands of books, and searching for the dictionaries would have taken hopelessly long if not for Sticky. As it was, the children were able to move swiftly from shelf to shelf (and from coffee table to windowsill), examining one dictionary after another as Sticky pointed them out. In minutes they had looked at most of the dictionaries on the third floor – including the Greek, Latin, and Esperanto dictionaries in Mr Benedict's tiny room, which saddened them even to enter – but although they'd found lots of silverfish, a pretty silk bookmark (which Constance pocketed) and the definition of a Greek word Sticky had been meaning to look up, they came upon no clue.

'What about Number Two's bedroom?' asked Kate.

'No dictionaries in there,' Sticky said. 'Number Two told me she prefers to go and find a dictionary when she needs one. Searching the shelves helps her remember where everything is.'

Constance was staring at Sticky as if he'd just said he liked to eat sawdust. 'You two have conversations about dictionaries?'

'We used to,' Sticky said sadly. 'I haven't seen her in months, you know.' Then he realized Constance had been making fun of him. 'It wouldn't hurt *you* to look in a dictionary every now and then, Constance. Some new words might improve your rotten poetry.'

'My poems would sound *good* if your ears weren't of *wood*,' Constance said.

'My ears,' Sticky said through gritted teeth, 'are fine.'

'For whittling, maybe, your ears are well suited. For poetry, though—'

'Please don't finish that, Constance,' interrupted Reynie. 'We don't need a rhyme attack right now. We need to find that dictionary.' To Sticky he made a private gesture that clearly meant, 'stay calm and ignore her'.

'I saw that,' Constance said, giving him a very cross look.

Reynie sighed.

Only one hallway on the third floor remained to be searched. They had put it off until last, for on that hallway lay the chamber that contained the Whisperer. Two guards were always posted at the chamber door, and the children had hoped to avoid speaking to anyone. But Sticky said two dictionaries were to be found there, so they were compelled to go and look. Luckily there were none in the chamber itself, Sticky said, for as they all knew, no one was ever allowed in there without Mr Benedict. (Reynie didn't point out that Mr Benedict wouldn't have left the clue where they couldn't possibly get to it, and he was relieved when it didn't occur to Constance to say so.)

The children had been inside that guarded chamber only once, when Mr Benedict took them in to look around. They had admired the soothing colours and soft lighting he used to calm his visitors (or 'guests', as he called them, to make them feel welcome). It came as no surprise that Mr Benedict's guests might stand in need of calming, for they were the Whisperer's former victims, the extremely unfortunate people whose memories Mr Curtain had hidden from them – memories Mr Benedict now employed the Whisperer to restore. The cosy room was a far cry from the cold, austere atmosphere of Mr Curtain's Whispering Gallery.

'It can be disturbing to have one's memory suddenly return,' Mr Benedict had said, 'to remember all at once the important things that have been missing for so long. I do my best to lessen the shock.' He indicated an overstuffed chair in the corner. 'That is where my guests sit. It is easily within the Whisperer's range, and I should think they find it more comfortable – and far less threatening – than the seat my brother designed.'

Mr Benedict kept the Whisperer hidden behind a decorated screen, but the children didn't need to see it to remember it. All but Kate, in fact, had sat in its hard metal chair, their wrists cuffed, a helmet pressed tightly over their heads. And all four of them remembered the terrifying moment when they'd realized Mr Curtain could use his device to wipe away their memories – brainsweeping, he called it – even when they were standing more than a metre away. Yes, they all remembered the Whisperer perfectly well, and they were quite content to leave it hidden behind the screen in that locked and guarded chamber.

As the children entered the hallway on which the

chamber lay, the two guards at its door offered them faint, polite smiles. They were not supposed to fraternize while on duty, of course, and they knew the children were free to roam the hallways – they might well let them pass without comment. But depending on their security clearance (depending, in other words, on their access to classified information), the guards might also know something of the children's history, and this made Reynie worry they would be suspicious of any unusual activity.

'Are you sure there's a dictionary here?' he said to Sticky, as if they were in the middle of a discussion.

'Yes, there certainly is, Reynie, I am sure of it,' Sticky replied in a tone so stiff that Reynie almost winced. They needed to brush up on their acting.

To her credit, Kate was more convincing than either of the boys had been. Casually retying her ponytail, she winked at the guards and said in a breezy tone, 'Just looking up a word.'

The guards nodded, but one of them – a burly, bulldoggish man – watched the children with an appraising look that verged on suspicion. Reynie turned his back, the better to hide his own nervous expression. Sticky had already located the first dictionary and was rapidly examining it as the others looked on. He closed it with a discouraged sigh. 'No luck.'

The burly guard leant toward them. 'Must be an unusual word, eh? You ought to try the other dictionary. It's really big.'

'How do you know there's another dictionary?' asked Sticky, surprised.

'What else do we have to look at all day but these

bookshelves?' said the guard. He pointed a little way down the shelves. 'It's right over there, a great huge fat one. Wait, now where is it? I remember it perfectly – terrible condition, falling apart at the seams. It was right there, I'm sure of it.'

'I know the one you mean,' Sticky said, pointing to a gap on the shelves. 'It *was* right there.'

The other guard spoke up. 'Oh, Mr Benedict took that one! Couple of weeks ago. You were on a break, Russ,' he said to the burly guard. 'Said he was going to fix it up, but I don't suppose he got around to it before he left. I saw it in his study not two days ago, and it was still in awful shape.'

Reynie's heart leapt. 'His study? I guess we should go down there, then.' He and the others quickly turned to go, only to find their way blocked.

'Listen, you kids, I know what you're doing,' said Russ, the burly guard.

They stared at him in bewildered dismay. How could he know? Was this over before they'd even begun?

Reynie forced himself to speak. 'You know what we're . . . doing?'

'You're trying to distract yourselves,' Russ said. 'I understand. You're worried about Mr Benedict and Number Two, and you're just aching to think about anything else. Am I right?'

'Yes!' cried Sticky from behind Reynie. He sounded much too eager to agree, and Russ might have paused to consider this had Constance not crossed her arms and grumpily remarked, 'If you say so.'

'Let me give you some advice,' said Russ, scratching a dry patch on his left jowl. 'If you really mean to be distracted, don't go down to Mr Benedict's study. Go back to your room and play a nice little game. Okay?'

'Why?' Reynie asked. 'Why not go into his study?'

'It's serious business down there, son. They're going through all his papers right now – every folder, file, and book – looking for clues to his whereabouts. They won't let you in there, anyway. Not until they're finished, at least.'

'Thank you,' said Reynie as calmly as possible. 'It's . . . good advice. Come on, everyone, let's go play a game.'

The children hurriedly said goodbye to the guards, who watched in bemusement as they bumped into one another, sorted themselves out, and walked with strange jerky steps down the long hallway, looking for all the world as if they were trying not to run in panic.

'Poor kids,' said Russ in a low tone. 'They'll do anything to avoid the scary stuff.'

As soon as the children were out of sight of the guards, they ducked into the first available room (it happened to be Number Two's bedroom) to discuss their dilemma.

'If they find that clue,' Kate said, closing the door, 'you know we'll never see it.'

'They may *already* have found it,' Constance said. She dropped despondently onto the yellow rug Number Two had woven for her floor. 'For all we know, they're planning some disastrous rescue mission even as we speak.'

'We have to assume they haven't found it yet,' Reynie said. 'Mr Benedict has an awful lot of books and papers in that study, and they probably won't think to check the dictionary until they've checked everything else.'

'We need a distraction,' said Kate. 'Something to get them out long enough for us to slip in and grab it.'

'Any ideas?' Reynie asked.

Sticky began to look around the room as if seeking inspiration. Everything he saw was familiar to him already: the open wardrobe with its array of yellow clothing; the basket of sewing materials and stacks of science journals by the bed (Number Two scarcely slept – seldom more than an hour or two – and filled her long night hours with quiet activity); the tidy writing desk with its bouquet of pencils in a cup; and of course the well-stocked cupboard full of snacks (for though she required little sleep, Number Two had to eat almost constantly or else grow irritable and faint).

'I wish we hadn't come in here,' Sticky muttered, depressed by so many reminders of their missing friend. He went to the window to give himself something different to look at.

Different, though, hardly described what Sticky saw through the window. Indeed, it was one of the strangest spectacles he'd ever witnessed. In the courtyard below, the three police officers were spinning round and round with their legs flying out behind them, as if they were the spokes of a wheel. They were all trying to hold onto whatever it was that was spinning them; they had all lost their caps; and one had even lost his toupee, which lay on the ground nearby like a stunned ferret. At the same time, on the pavement beyond the fence, the unpleasant Mr Bane appeared to have just attempted an unsuccessful headstand, for he lay on his back staring confusedly at the sky. And as if all this weren't enough to make Sticky suspect he was dreaming, no sooner had his brain registered the bizarre scene than a large bird swooped down into it, snatched the policeman's toupee, and flew up into the eaves of the house.

Sticky rubbed his eyes, stared out again, and suddenly understood. 'I think we have our distraction – Moocho Brazos has just arrived.'

The others rushed to the window (Sticky gave Constance a boost so she could see) and quickly made sense of the commotion below: Moocho had come to see Kate for some reason; Mr Bane had rudely refused to admit him, which had got him tossed over the fence; and the police officers had then felt compelled to restrain the huge man, which they did first by grabbing him, then by clinging desperately as he tried to spin them off on his way to the front door.

A buzzer rang somewhere in the house below, followed by the sound of doors banging open and people rushing down hallways and stairs. The guards were swarming to the exits, and everyone else was hurrying to windows to see what was the matter.

'Sticky's right!' said Reynie. 'Now's our chance!' And whirling around as fast as he could, he discovered the bedroom door wide open and Kate Wetherall already gone.

They found Kate coming up the stairs just as they were starting down. In her arms was a massive old dictionary, and her blue eyes twinkled with excitement. She pointed back the way they'd come. Everyone turned and headed straight to Constance's room, where Kate locked the door and went to the window.

'Good,' she said, peeking out, 'Rhonda's down there trying to clear things up. That buys us time.' She clucked her tongue. 'Poor Moocho. I bet he got her telegram and was worried out of his head.'

'You weren't seen?' Sticky asked.

Kate shrugged. 'Nope.'

Even knowing her as they did, the others stared at Kate, flatly amazed. In a matter of seconds – in the time it took the rest of them just to reach the stairway – she had flown down the stairs into the study, found the dictionary, and come out again without being spotted. It seemed impossible.

Kate noticed their expressions. 'What?' She bent to look at herself in Constance's wall mirror. 'Do I have something on my face?'

'Just show us the stupid dictionary,' said Constance resentfully. (*She* still had trouble tying her *shoes*.)

Kate laid the thick book on the floor, and everyone knelt for a closer look. The dictionary was a tattered old thing with warped covers – evidence of some long-ago water spill – and a hopelessly ruined spine. Gingerly, so as not to damage it further, Reynie opened it and began turning pages. Some were irrevocably stuck together; some fell out at the merest touch. An odour of must and mildew filled the room.

'He should have thrown this away years ago,' Constance said, wrinkling her nose at the mildew smell. 'It isn't even usable.'

Reynie turned a page to reveal a deep, rectangular space cut out of the dictionary pages. Nestled inside the cut-out space was another book. 'Not usable as a dictionary, maybe. But as a hiding place it's perfect.'

The second book had brown leather covers and was rather large itself. Reynie quickly turned to the first page, which was blank except for the following inscription:

73

Travellers should always keep journals, and journals should always keep secrets. This journal is no exception. I have taken the liberty of writing the first entry. Read it quickly and move on. Bon voyage! – Mr Benedict

With the others peering over his shoulder, Reynie flipped through the next few pages. It was difficult to gauge whether the journal was an expensive gift or something Mr Benedict had snatched from a bargain pile – something discarded as a botched product and sold for a few pence. Its pages, although made of fine, heavy paper, had been cut unevenly, so that some were much wider than others. Each page was blank except for a single word written in the outer bottom corner. Reynie flipped to the back of the book. The same. One word per page, but taken in order the words did not form intelligible sentences.

'Let's go through it nice and slowly,' Kate said.

Reynie returned to the front and began turning the pages one at a time, working all the way to the end. The first several pages yielded the following sequence of words:

TAKE DOWN ROSES AND THREE TAKE YOUR CHANCES TAKE TIME TO BELIEVE TAKE UP CINNAMON CANDLES TAKE NOTES TAKE MY RULER TOO TAKE OFF GLOVES TAKE HOME.

About a third of the way through the journal a different sequence began:

THE LUCK OF MY BROTHERS THE NOTION OF CONSEQUENCE THE SCOUNDREL THE FLY IN THE

OINTMENT THE NERVE THE PUZZLE THE DOGFISH
ATE THE CATFISH THE ANSWER.

And in the last third of the journal, the words in the bottom corners ran like this:

SHORTCUT HAIRCUT SHORTCUT BLUE SHORTCUT
CREWCUT SHORTCUT DO SHORTCUT COLDCUT
SHORTCUT YOU SHORTCUT UPPERCUT SHORTCUT
THROUGH.

Sticky scratched his head. 'It's some kind of word puzzle, I take it.'

'It does mention the word 'puzzle',' Kate said. 'Maybe that's a hint?'

They were both looking to Reynie for help, but Constance surprised them all by speaking first. 'Take the shortcut,' she whispered, as if to herself.

'What?' Sticky said.

'That's the answer,' Constance declared, more confidently now. 'Take the shortcut.'

Reynie gave Constance a long, searching look. She stared back as if daring him to argue. Instead he turned to the others and said, 'I agree with Constance.'

Sticky was baffled. 'But . . . but how . . .'

Kate was glancing back and forth between Reynie and Constance. 'What makes you think that?' she asked, though she didn't appear to know which of them to ask.

Reynie held out his hand to Constance, indicating that she should answer.

'It's obvious,' Constance said. 'Those are the only three

words that keep being repeated. The other words are meaningless – they're just there to make things look weird.'

'They may be repeated a lot,' said Sticky, 'but how can you be sure that matters?'

'Take a look at them,' Constance said. 'They're always in the corner of a wide page, never in the corner of a narrow one. Doesn't that seem significant?'

Sticky didn't have to look. He remembered perfectly where the words fell on every page. 'Okay, that's true, too. But why are the wider pages significant? Who's to say we can rule out the narrow pages?'

Constance shrugged. She had no answer for this. 'I know I'm right, though,' she said. 'I can just tell.'

Reynie gazed at her wonderingly. It should have occurred to him, he thought, that Constance would surprise them. Given what she'd been capable of at the age of two, there was no telling what she could do now that she was three. After all, she must have developed considerably in the past six months.

'Reynie?' said Kate. 'Any idea about the wide pages?'

Reynie opened the journal to Mr Benedict's inscription and drew his finger along this phrase: *Read it quickly*. 'Remember that? I figured it was important, since Mr Benedict knows how quickly some of us read already – especially Sticky.'

'What does speed have to do with what the words mean?' Kate asked.

'Speed has to do with what words you *see*,' Reynie said, and with the others looking on, he fanned the pages of the journal from left to right. Sure enough, the only words that appeared in the bottom corners were these: *TAKE THE SHORTCUT.*

'Well, what do you know!' said Kate with a laugh. 'Of course! The other words are on narrow pages, so when you fan through like that—'

'—only the corners of the wider pages show up,' Sticky finished, nodding. 'Yeah, I get it too.'

Kate whistled. 'I wouldn't have figured that out in a million years.'

Constance looked exceedingly pleased.

'Okay, so we're one step closer,' Reynie said. 'We need to take the shortcut. But what shortcut? A shortcut to *where*?'

The group fell silent, and Reynie thrust his chin into his hands, trying to concentrate. Out of the corner of his eye, he saw Constance do the same thing. At first he thought she was mocking him, and he started to tell her to knock it off. Then he saw her close her eyes, obviously trying to think. Reynie felt oddly, deeply touched. He had no time to linger on the feeling, though, for just then someone knocked on the door.

'Are you all in there?' said Rhonda. 'You have a visitor.'

The children exchanged frustrated glances. If they didn't want to raise suspicion, they had no choice. For the moment, this meeting of the Society was adjourned.

Half-Truths and Deceptions

'I left as soon as I received Rhonda's telegram,' Moocho Brazos was saying. 'I hoped to catch up and warn you, but you were too far ahead. I'm afraid I was rather agitated when I got here.'

'Perfectly understandable,' said Miss Perumal, passing him a platter of cold cuts. 'It was good of you to try to warn us.'

Everyone was gathered in the dining room again except Rhonda – who'd returned to the questioning interrupted by Moocho's arrival – and the recent confusion had been sorted out. Moocho and the police officers had apologized to one another (much to the displeasure of Mr Bane, who would not be soothed), and Kate had whistled Madge down from the eaves – for the bird Sticky had seen was indeed Kate's clever falcon.

('What a bird!' Kate had exclaimed. 'She must have seen me get into the estate car and followed it all this way! Oh, you must be exhausted, you foolish, naughty thing!' she scolded, stroking the bird's feathers. She was clearly flattered to discover her falcon was so attached. Nevertheless, she felt obliged to leave Madge outside, for a bird of prey could hardly be trusted in the same house as the precious homing pigeon.)

'Does Milligan know about any of this?' asked Moocho, politely taking only enough cold cuts to feed a normal-sized person.

'Rhonda's been unable to reach him,' said Mrs Washington.

Mr Washington, who had been staring out of the window, spoke up for the first time since they'd arrived. 'What is Milligan doing, anyway? I thought he'd already tracked down everyone Mr Benedict wanted to help.'

'Everyone but the Executives who disappeared with Mr Curtain,' Kate said through a mouthful of turkey cold cut. She swallowed and continued, 'Lately he's been going on other kinds of missions. He's . . . uh . . . I'm actually not supposed to know about them,' she said nervously.

'Don't say anything you shouldn't, dear,' said Mrs Washington.

'If the missions have had anything to do with Mr Curtain,' said Reynie (who was hoping to stall questions about the envelope Mr Benedict had given them), 'it might be important for us to know about them.'

'That's true,' said Mr Washington, coming to sit at the table. 'This concerns all of us. Do you know anything that might be relevant, Kate? You should keep quiet about anything that isn't, of course.'

Kate cast a wary glance at the dining room door. Miss Perumal's mother, seeing this, rose from her seat. 'I'll stand guard,' she said. 'You can fill me in later. I can't hear a word when you're all whispering, anyway, and this is certainly a time for whispering.' She went out. The others looked expectantly at Kate.

'He's been investigating the activities of Mr Curtain's creepy henchmen,' Kate said. 'The Ten Men. They've been up to something these past few months – breaking into offices, stealing things from laboratories – but no one can figure out what it is.'

'Ten Men?' said Miss Perumal. 'What a curious name.'

'They're called that because they have ten different ways of hurting you,' Sticky said knowingly.

Sticky's parents turned to stare at him. 'I see you've already heard about them,' said Mr Washington.

'We don't know any details, though,' Reynie said quickly, as Sticky averted his eyes.

'Ten Men look pretty much like ordinary businessmen,' Kate said, 'which can make them hard for the authorities to spot. But everything they carry is a weapon. You already know about their shockwatches, right? Well, they also use their neckties like whips. And their pocket handkerchiefs are soaked in something – if they hold it to your nose you'll be knocked right out – and their briefcases are chock-full of evil stuff, too: razor-sharp pencils, poisonous chewing gum, even a laser pointer that fires a real laser – not just a red light, I mean, but a beam they can cut your *ears* off with!'

At this, everyone at the table looked uncomfortably at their plates of cold cuts. Sticky's hands went to his ears. 'They really cut them off?'

'Well, I don't know if they really do,' Kate admitted, 'but they could if they wanted to.'

'We get the picture,' said Mrs Washington, pushing her plate away. 'These are bad men.'

'*Nasty* men,' Kate corrected. 'Milligan has been in some awful scrapes, I can tell you. If he weren't Milligan, I'd be worried about him all the time.'

Beside her, Sticky was polishing his spectacles, feeling even more troubled now at the prospect of bumping into a Ten Man. The adults were disturbed as well. All around the table they were shaking their heads, clucking their tongues, and looking very sombre indeed. Only Reynie felt unsurprised by Kate's report, for he retained the feeling – despite Mr Benedict's argument against it – that wickedness was something to be expected.

'That's all I know,' Kate said apologetically. 'It doesn't really shed any light on our situation.'

Reynie noticed Miss Perumal looking thoughtful and prepared himself. He figured he knew what was coming. Sure enough, she turned to him and said, 'I'm assuming the envelope Rhonda gave you doesn't clear anything up. Otherwise you'd have told us right away.'

'It didn't give us the least idea of where they might have gone,' Reynie said, which was true in a sense. 'Maybe Milligan will have some answers. Surely he'll be here soon.'

'In the meantime, may we see the letter?' Mr Washington asked.

'Of course,' said Reynie at once, before his friends betrayed any alarm. 'We left it up in Constance's room. Should I get it now?' He made as if to rise.

'Finish your lunch first,' Miss Perumal said, which was what Reynie had hoped she'd say. 'You can go up afterwards.'

Reynie settled into his seat again. He was so nervous he had no appetite, but he did try to eat something. If he and the others were going to sneak out, they had to do it right after lunch. After that, who knew where his next meal would come from?

Eventually Rhonda Kazembe rejoined them in the dining room, closing the door behind her. With a weary shake of her head, she reported that Ms Argent very much wanted to interview the children but had been put off until later. 'I insisted she allow you time to recover from the shock, and that at any rate you could hardly be expected to know anything. Now tell me,' she said with a keen look, 'what was in the envelope? Did you learn anything?'

Reynie quickly repeated his half-truth, saying that the letter hadn't given them any idea about where their friends had gone. Rhonda, who had no reason not to trust him – indeed she put great stock in his opinions – looked bitterly disappointed. In that case, she said, she would wait to see the letter until she'd dealt with another matter. Reynie nodded, feeling every bit as guilty as he did relieved.

Rhonda moved to sit beside Constance (who squirmed uncomfortably, as if in danger of being shown affection) and placed a small, clumsily wrapped box on the table. 'I couldn't give you this earlier,' she said. 'It was in Mr

Benedict's study, and the inspectors wouldn't let me take anything out until they'd gone over it with a fine-toothed comb. I'm sorry to say they've already examined this, even though it was a personal present to you from Mr Benedict. I did make them rewrap it.'

'They did a terrible job,' Kate observed. 'They put the paper on inside out!'

'I know,' said Rhonda, and in a melancholy tone she added, 'Mr Benedict would have found that amusing, don't you think? No doubt he'd have laughed himself to sleep.'

'What is it?' Constance asked.

'An early birthday present,' Rhonda said.

Everyone immediately understood. After the children's mission last year, Mr Benedict had baked a cake for Constance's birthday even though it was a month early. He'd known too well that they would all be separated soon enough. It was at that unexpected celebration that the other children had learned Constance was only two years old. Until then they'd thought she was just an unusually small, awkward, and stubborn child with poor manners.

'So it's a sort of commemoration,' Sticky said. 'To remind us of last year.'

The first thing Constance pulled from the box was a card that read: *Happy birthday, my dear! Always remember that the world is your oyster. Affectionately, Mr Benedict.*

Constance seemed ready to cry, but she cleared her throat and passed the card roughly to Reynie. She needed several tries to take out her present – it was small and delicate, and Constance had neither patience nor dexterity – but at last she produced a lovely pendant on a slender gold chain. The pendant was a miniature globe, painted in deep

83

greens and blues, with a bright, tiny crystal set into it.

'Oh, it's beautiful, dear!' said Mrs Washington.

'It's all right,' Constance said, but now she really was crying and in no mood to be watched. 'I'm going to my room now.' Clutching the pendant tightly in her pudgy fingers, she hastened from the room.

'We should go and be with her,' Reynie said.

The adults murmured their approval as Sticky and Kate nodded and rose from the table. Before he left the room, Reynie stopped in the doorway to take one last glance at Miss Perumal, who happened to be looking right back at him. Her forehead was wrinkled with concern – she was worried about him, of course – and Reynie did his best to give her a reassuring look before he closed the door, wondering when he would see her again.

He could have used a reassuring look himself.

Constance Contraire sat among the heaps of linens on her bed, wearing her new pendant and a sullen expression. When her friends came in, she muttered something cranky and looked away. Not even Reynie, an excellent judge of people's moods, could tell exactly how upset Constance was, for with Constance crankiness was routine.

It wasn't entirely her fault. Though older, wiser, and slightly bigger than she had been a year ago, Constance knew perfectly well that her obstinacy – her sheer, un-rivalled determination not to do what she was told – had played a key role in the success of their mission. She knew, of course, that her friends also had played important roles, and that her wilfulness was not generally a likable trait – in fact, it sometimes ran counter to her *own* desires. But she'd received a great deal of positive attention for her defiant behaviour, and she was, after all, only three years old. She might be a budding genius, but her emotions were still as complicated and ungovernable as those of any child her age. So while on the one hand Constance wanted to be pleasant, courteous, and helpful, on the other she was inclined to be argumentative and grumpy, and indeed this was the sort of behaviour that came most naturally to her.

Her friends were used to this. To a certain degree they all faced the same difficulty – that conflict between heart and brain that arose from being gifted beyond their years – and in sensitive moments such as this one, they felt keenly what it meant to be children in a world of grown-ups. Without a word, the three of them climbed onto the bed and sat with Constance. It might not have been her style to say so, but Constance loved Mr Benedict more than anyone in the world, and they all knew it.

They sat a while in silence. It wasn't long, however, until Constance made a whining sound and climbed down from her bed. She could never stand to be the object of others' pity unless she had purposely aimed for that effect, and this time she hadn't. Moreover, her irritation crowded out her self-pity, which came as a relief. So it was in a slightly sturdier mood that she uncovered the journal Mr Benedict had left them (she'd hidden it under a pile of clothes) and stared at it intently, as if hoping it would reveal its secret of its own accord.

'Somehow it seems like I should know what that shortcut is,' Constance said. 'I have a nagging feeling about it, like it should be familiar. But I can't place it.'

'I've had the same feeling,' Reynie said.

85

'Hey, so have I!' said Kate. 'What about you, Sticky?'

Sticky shrugged. 'I'm always having nagging feelings. The trouble is knowing which one to pay attention to.'

'Well, one thing's for sure,' Kate said. 'If Mr Benedict had mentioned some kind of shortcut before, you boys would remember the conversation. I think even I would remember it. So why does this mention of a shortcut seem so familiar to all of us?'

'We must all have heard about it somewhere,' Reynie said, 'or else . . . do you suppose it could have been in the newspaper?'

'Hey, that would make sense!' said Kate. 'Mr Benedict knows we all read the newspaper every day.'

Reynie rubbed his chin. 'So the question is what—'

But Sticky, having already consulted his memory, interrupted him excitedly. 'It's that cargo ship – the MV *Shortcut*! Remember? It was in all the papers yesterday.'

'Remind us,' said Constance.

'Here, I'll quote one of the articles I read,' said Sticky, and in a rather self-important tone he recited: 'Tomorrow the speediest cargo ship in history will make its maiden voyage, launching from Stonetown Harbour at four o'clock—'

'Four o'clock!' Kate cried. 'We have to get down there!'

'We still have a few hours,' said Sticky, who felt hurt at having been so quickly interrupted, to say nothing of how nervous he felt at the thought of leaving.

'It will take a while to reach the docks, though,' Reynie said. 'And first we have to sneak out of the house.'

'That part's easy enough,' said Kate, pulling out her rope. 'There's a hidden laundry chute down the hall that empties behind the maze.'

'How do you know that?' Sticky asked. 'I mean, if it's hidden . . .'

'Found it on our last visit. When you were looking at bookshelves, I was exploring. The chute hasn't been sealed off or anything, has it, Constance?'

'How should I know? I didn't even know about it,' said Constance. She gestured at the laundry piles around them. 'Normally this just builds up until Number Two hauls it away in a basket. She says she hates to spoil me, but she can't stand the mess. I call it her laundry quandary.'

'That must annoy her no end,' Sticky said.

'Oh, it does!' said Constance, and she smiled a little, cheered by the memory.

Kate was taken aback. 'You mean you live in this house and don't even . . . ?' She shook her head. 'You amaze me, Constance. Anyway, I can lower you all down the chute with my rope, and then I'll come down after you.'

'The police have gone,' said Reynie, peering out of the window into the courtyard, 'but Mr Bane's still guarding the gate. I'll bet he has orders not to let anyone come or go without permission.'

'Now that's a problem,' said Kate. 'If he tries to stop us it'll draw attention to what we're doing.'

'I'll think of something,' said Reynie. 'Meanwhile, could you sneak down and get different shirts for Sticky and me? Mine's giving me a rash.'

Kate balked at this. 'I doubt any shirts in this house would fit you. Don't you think you should just . . . ?'

'My dad brought in the suitcases,' Sticky said. He gave her a suspicious look. 'Didn't you see them by the stairs?

We walked right past them.'

'Oh, right, the suitcases,' said Kate, sighing on her way out. She'd rather enjoyed seeing the boys look so silly and hated them to change.

By the time she returned with the shirts, Reynie had cleared off Constance's desk and was hurriedly writing a note to explain everything and to apologize for causing the grown-ups any worry. They would be extremely careful, he wrote, and would contact Rhonda and Milligan as soon as they found anything useful. They all signed their names at the bottom (Constance's signature was a wild scrawl) and afterwards gazed sombrely at one another, for signing the note had brought home the seriousness of what they were about to attempt. Then, one by one, they nodded resolutely and headed out.

When Kate came down the chute, she found Constance and Reynie cramped between the washing machine and the door, and Sticky, for lack of room, sitting on the clothes dryer. The laundry area, crowded into a space beneath the stairwell at the back of the maze, was more of a closet than a room.

'What took you so long?' Sticky whispered.

'Rhonda came looking for us,' Kate said. 'I heard her knocking on Constance's door, so I hurried back before she could go inside and find our note. I told her we'd be down in a minute. Which technically is true. I didn't say down *where*.'

'We need to get out of here fast,' Sticky said.

'Lower your voice or we won't get anywhere at all,' said Kate, squeezing through them to peek out the door. 'You too, Reynie. 'Try not to breathe so loudly – you sound like a whale spouting. Okay, coast is clear.'

The children quickly made their way through the maze. The route was second nature to them now, and in no time they arrived at the front door, where everyone looked at Reynie. He took a deep breath, steadied himself, and threw the hidden switch that unlocked the door.

Mr Bane sat on a bench beneath the elm tree, keeping a watchful eye on the gate. His face tightened at the sight of the children. Before he could ask their business, Reynie blurted, 'Mr Bane, you need to escort us to the Washingtons' car. We're supposed to bring in some packages.' He pointed down the block. 'It's just around the corner.'

Mr Bane gave him a dark look. 'For one thing, sonny, I don't like to be told what to do, especially not by the adolescent darlings of Rhonda Kazembe. For another, I'm on duty. Or don't you want the entrance guarded?'

'It'll only take a few minutes!' Reynie said, plainly irritated. He went down the steps with the others just behind him.

Mr Bane rose to head them off. 'Apparently you don't understand what's meant by 'duty'.' I'm *watching* the *gate*!'

The others stared at Reynie. Was this his plan? To outrage Mr Bane? Weren't they trying to *avoid* a confrontation?

'Well . . .' Reynie hesitated as if considering something. 'You will let us back in, though, won't you? We have permission to be here, you know.'

Mr Bane's expression changed. The change was subtle,

but it was exactly what Reynie had hoped to see – a shift from defiance to craftiness. Moving to open the gate, Mr Bane said, 'I suppose you kids think you can do whatever you want. You don't think you even have to say please.' With a mocking bow, he stepped aside, and the children hurried out.

Mr Bane closed the gate behind them with a disagreeable smile.

'We'll need your help taking the packages upstairs,' Reynie called as they walked away down the pavement. 'They're very heavy.'

'I'll be here,' Mr Bane called back, then muttered something the children couldn't hear.

'Well, that was clever, Reynie,' said Kate in a low voice. 'I had no idea what you were up to.'

She knelt and held her hand out to Constance, who climbed onto her back (it was their habit for Constance to ride piggyback when they were in a hurry) saying, 'Did you see the look on his face? He obviously can't *wait* to make us stand there begging to be let back in.'

'And then watch us struggle up the steps with the packages,' said Sticky. 'Well done, Reynie.'

Reynie said nothing. He was relieved the ploy had worked, but it wasn't exactly satisfying to have taken advantage of Mr Bane's unpleasantness. The man was supposed to be on their side, after all. His behaviour didn't improve Reynie's opinion of people very much.

'I hope Madge will be all right,' Kate said, hitching Constance into a more comfortable position on her back. 'I didn't see her in the eaves. She's off hunting pigeons, I suppose.'

'We need to get out of sight,' said Sticky, who was anxious about being caught and felt rather like a hunted pigeon himself. 'Does anyone have enough for a taxi?'

No one did. Even pooling their money together produced only a few dollars and some change. That was enough to get them on a city bus, however, and they set out at a rapid pace for the nearest bus stop. Halfway there, Constance uttered a cry of dismay. She'd forgotten the journal Mr Benedict gave them.

'Great,' Sticky muttered. 'This hardly makes for an auspicious beginning.'

'What does 'auspicious' mean?' asked Constance. She looked ready to be furious.

'Never mind,' said Kate. 'It's probably good you left it. One less thing to carry, you know.'

'But I wanted us to write in it like Mr Benedict said,' Constance whined. 'You know, as we travelled.'

'We'll write about everything when we get back,' said Reynie. 'Right, everyone? We'll all promise to write something about . . . well, about whatever's going to happen.'

Sticky and Kate promised they would. Constance wasn't much comforted, but there was no going back now. The children hurried on to the bus stop and boarded the first bus that came, even though its route didn't pass as close to the harbour as they would have hoped. They couldn't risk waiting for a different one.

They rode for some time in silence, watching the more familiar streets and buildings pass behind them as the bus travelled into a different part of Stonetown. Kate was perhaps the only one who didn't half wish they hadn't got away, but even she was subdued. The children were alone and penniless now in a big city. And if everything went as expected, they would soon find themselves – still alone and penniless – in the even bigger world beyond.

If the city of Stonetown was a busy place, its port – Stonetown Harbour – was positively frantic. The harbour, in fact, seemed like a city unto itself. The concrete and steel docks stretched endlessly along the water's edge, bristling with cranes and towering stacks of cargo, and teeming with stevedores and sailors, all of whom dashed about in a mad hurry. Looming over the docks were the ships themselves, their sides rising up like gleaming, metallic cliffs. Some were being loaded or unloaded; others had weighed anchor and were heaving off into the bay, looking for all the world as if a chunk of the city had broken free and was drifting away. The entire place clamoured with the sounds of bells, horns, machinery, whistles – of clanking and screeching and booming and grinding – a shocking bombardment of noise that all but muted the cries of seagulls dipping and soaring overhead.

The children, standing outside the harbour's main security gate, stared wide-eyed.

'I'm not going in there,' said Constance, backing away.

Reynie was in no hurry to descend into that chaos himself, but hurry they must if they wanted to find the *Shortcut* in time. Before he could think how to prod Constance forward though, a barrel-chested young man in a blue uniform and cap whizzed up to them in a motorized passenger cart.

'Don't see many kids down here!' the young man shouted over the din. He circled the children in his cart, looking them up and down with friendly brown eyes. 'And you do fit the description! Here for the *Shortcut*, right?'

The children nodded, and Kate said, 'Do we, um, need tickets or anything?'

'Tickets? No, you're guests of the captain! He expected six, though . . .' The young man glanced left and right, as if someone might have materialized in the last instant. 'This all of you? No grown-ups?'

'Just us,' Reynie replied, and to prevent any questions he added, 'no time to explain!'

'Right you are!' the young man said, clearly pleased. He slammed on the brakes and gestured for them to get into the cart. 'Glad you made it! If you weren't here in two minutes Captain Noland said I was to go and fetch you.'

The cart lurched forwards and shot toward the gate. The

young man looked back at his passengers. 'Name's Joe Shooter, by the way, but you can call me Cannonball. All my friends do! I'm third officer on the *Short* – oh, hold on!'

Joe Shooter – that is, Cannonball – whipped out a piece of paper and waved it at the gate guards, who obviously knew him and only nodded as the cart passed through. The cart, which had already been moving frighteningly fast, began to accelerate. 'We're headed all the way down to the end of the docks!' Cannonball shouted, now weaving crazily among forklifts and stacked cargo and terrified dock workers. The children gripped the sides of the cart. 'So you all ready for your journey? I see you didn't pack any bags! This whole thing's awfully mysterious, if you ask me! Why are you going to Portugal, anyway? Or are you just coming aboard for the experience?'

The cart jerked sharply to the left, and Constance flew out of her seat with a little squeak. Kate caught her by the shirt and pulled her safely down.

'Don't talk much, do you?' Cannonball shouted. 'That's all right! You'll see I don't bite! Now hang on, it gets a bit dicey up here around Terminal Four!'

All the children except Kate closed their eyes. Reynie had never been on a roller coaster, but he imagined it felt much like this. In fact, he was trying to pretend he *was* on a roller coaster – a very safe, properly maintained roller coaster that stood no chance of crashing – when Kate spoke into his ear. 'Reynie, did you know the ship was headed to Portugal?'

Reynie nodded, keeping his eyes tightly shut. 'Port of Lisbon,' he said, then flinched as he heard something whoosh by overhead, followed by a loud crash and the sound of someone cursing.

'Well, I didn't read that part,' Kate said. 'Don't you think we ought to take a plane instead? We can figure out a way to pay for the tickets – I know *you* can, at least – and we'll get there much faster.'

'We don't know whether Lisbon's even important,' Reynie pointed out. 'Mr Benedict said to take the *Shortcut* – he didn't say anything about Lisbon. For all we know the next clue may be hidden on the ship, or it may be revealed to us only at sea.'

'Gosh, that's true. I suppose—' Just then the cart bounced over a bump, and Kate's head knocked sharply against Reynie's.

'What's that?' Cannonball shouted when he heard them cry out. 'Did you say something?'

Kate and Reynie were grabbing their heads, in too much pain to answer, but Constance called out that she would very much like to know where Portugal was.

The sailor laughed and cupped his hand to his ear. 'Sorry, it sounded like you asked me where Portugal was!'

Now everyone was looking at Constance, who made a face and said, 'Well? Is anyone going to tell me?'

'Over the sea,' said Sticky. He was holding onto the cart with one hand and keeping his spectacles on his nose with the other, and he looked rather unwell.

'I know *that* much,' Constance snapped. 'Fine, don't tell me. Why would I want to know?'

'Here we are!' Cannonball announced. The cart skidded to a stop at the bottom of a gangway. 'Everybody out!'

The children piled out of the cart. Cannonball allowed them a moment to stare up in awe. Like any ship, the *Shortcut* was daunting when seen from below. Nor was its size an illusion, for the ship was longer than two football pitches and taller than Stonetown Town Hall.

'She's a beauty, isn't she?' Cannonball said, gazing up admiringly. 'First of her kind, fastest cargo ship in the world! By far! Special hull design! Special jet propulsion system! Believe it or not, kids, in calm seas she can reach—'

'Upwards of sixty knots,' Sticky said. 'She's expected to cross the Atlantic in just two days, right?'

Cannonball snapped his fingers and pointed them at Sticky. 'Exactly right! *Exactly* right!' He grabbed Sticky and hugged him roughly, then just as quickly set him aside. 'Love a boy who knows his ships! Now let's go, everyone! Let's go!'

And with that, Cannonball set his cap on Sticky's head and charged up the gangway.

'I like this guy,' Kate said.

Reynie wasn't surprised. After all, Cannonball was a lot like Kate.

'We're all loaded up!' Cannonball called over his shoulder. 'Just taking care of last minute details! Oh, speaking of which . . .' He stopped on the gangway and knelt down. When the children caught up, he spoke in such a low voice they strained to hear him. He seemed to have no medium volume.

'Listen here, a lot of bigwig company owners decided they wanted to come aboard at the last minute,' Cannonball whispered. 'Top brass. Head honchos.' He puffed out his chest and made a ridiculous face. 'Bullfrogs, if you ask me. Captain Noland's had to make room to accommodate them, so I imagine he'll be pleased to hear there's only the four of you.' Cannonball stood abruptly. 'Now let's go!'

The ship's main deck was every bit as bustling as the docks had been. Dozens of men and women in uniforms hurried in every direction to complete unknown tasks. Cannonball bade the children stay exactly where they were, then dashed away across the deck. He soon returned with a man in a white uniform. 'Here's the captain!'

'Phil Noland,' the captain said, shaking their hands.

Everything about Captain Noland was trim. He had a trim grey beard and well-trimmed grey hair, a trim physique, even trim movements that were not robotic or stiff, exactly, but gave the impression of great efficiency. 'It's a pleasure to meet you. Nicholas Benedict is an old friend of mine, and I've heard a good deal about you all. Now what's this about Milligan and Rhonda? They really aren't here?'

Captain Noland seemed agitated, but Reynie sensed it was for reasons unrelated to the children. Given what Cannonball had said about the captain's unexpected guests, Reynie suspected he was simply under a lot of pressure.

'There was a change of plans,' Reynie said, 'but we can explain all that later, when you're not so busy.'

'I *am* a bit harried,' said Captain Noland. 'And I must apologize. My intention was that you would dine with me this evening. Unfortunately, I'm called upon,' here his expression shifted to one of barely concealed resentment, 'that is, *compelled* to make other arrangements. I'm embarrassed by this, children, and ask your forgiveness. If you don't mind, we'll take a late refreshment together after I've fulfilled my other obligations.'

The children readily agreed, and Captain Noland

hurried away, leaving Cannonball to show them to their quarters below.

'I'm afraid it's just one cabin,' he said, leading them down a ladder. 'The bullfrogs insisted upon having rooms to themselves, so the four of you are squeezed together. Captain's pretty upset. You were to be his guests of honour. But what the company wants, you know, the company gets.'

In the narrow passage at the bottom of the ladder a crew member pulled Cannonball aside and spoke in his ear. 'Right, right,' said Cannonball as the man disappeared up the ladder. To the children he whispered, 'Reminding me to keep my voice down. Good advice, of course, if you like your job. Which I do. Down this way, now!'

They went along more passages and down another ladder, and at last came to their cabin, a cramped space with a single porthole set too high in the wall for any of the children but Kate to look through – and even Kate had to stand on tiptoe. Their bunks were attached to opposite walls (or bulkheads, as Cannonball called them), with a top and bottom bunk on either side. The cabin reminded Reynie of the laundry closet in Mr Benedict's house; there was hardly room for everyone to stand. To spare one another elbow-knocks and squashed toes they each climbed into a bunk as Cannonball closed the cabin door to finish his speech. Or at least to continue it, for apparently Cannonball never finished talking – he only shifted topics.

'When we're properly underway I can give you a tour of the ship,' he said, 'but we'll have to make it snappy. We're shorthanded now, thanks to the bullfrogs.'

'Why shorthanded?' asked Reynie.

'Excellent question!' said Cannonball, flashing him a

bright smile. 'The chief bullfrog is a big jewellery merchant, and he's transporting a huge lot of diamonds to Europe. No problem with this, of course – the *Shortcut*'s an exceptionally secure ship – but at the last minute this bullfrog insists on extra security guards. The captain points out there's no room for so many bodies, says the crew needs space, too, you know. And what does the bullfrog say? Reduce the crew! Says the captain should be good enough to make the ship run with a smaller crew, anyway! So the captain has no choice, and now the rest of us will be working double duty to make sure the trip goes well.'

'That's hardly fair,' said Kate.

'You don't know the half of it! But now's no time to go on about injustice. I'm off to the security hold to make sure everything's in order. Feel free to go back up on deck if you like. Just keep out of the crew's way. And when you see bullfrogs, be polite! If they want us to toss you overboard, you know, we'll have to do it!'

Cannonball laughed and winked, then snatched his cap back from Sticky's head and dashed from the room.

'It's too bad,' Sticky said, rubbing his scalp. 'That cap was keeping my head warm. I'm still not used to the draughts I get with my hair gone.'

Kate tossed her pillowcase to him. 'Here, you can wrap that around your head.'

'You're joking, right?' Sticky said. 'I'd look ridiculous!'

'No more than you did with that cap on,' said Kate matter-of-factly.

Sticky bit his tongue. He knew Kate was only trying to be helpful. After all, a girl who always carried a bucket was clearly more interested in function than style. 'Thank you anyway,' he said, tossing the pillowcase back. 'Now why don't we go up on deck for the launch?'

Everyone got up except Constance, who had fallen asleep. When they tried to wake her she covered her head with her pillow.

'Just like old times,' Kate said.

'She's had a pretty rough day,' said Reynie.

And so they left Constance to her nap and went topside again, where the afternoon sun cast long shadows before them and the harbour breeze whipped in their ears. Far across the deck they saw a group of well-dressed men and women – the ship company owners, presumably – leaning against the dockside rail, attended by Captain Noland. In his brisk, efficient way, the captain was gesturing and pointing, explaining the activity swirling about them as the crew readied for launch.

The children decided to steer clear of all this. Keeping to the opposite rail, they heard but did not see the brass band playing somewhere on the dock below, then the distant tinkle of a bottle being broken against the side of the ship, followed by a burst of applause. ('It's an old tradition,' Sticky told the other two, who already knew this.) Soon they felt the rumble of engines far below them, and the *Shortcut* moved away from the docks and began to nose out of the harbour.

As the ship slowly turned, the children could see all the way across Stonetown Bay to Nomansan Island, the hilly mass of rock upon which Mr Curtain's Institute had been situated, and memories of their time there – memories both dark and thrilling – flooded to the forefront of their minds. Without speaking, possibly without even realizing it, the three friends edged closer together until they stood with shoulders touching. Together they looked out across the waters of the harbour as if across time itself: there they were a year ago, arriving on the island, anxious about what lay ahead. And now, standing at the ship's rail, their thoughts came full circle to their present mission: to save Mr Benedict. What harm did Mr Curtain have in mind for Mr Benedict and Number Two? And was there any chance in the world that they could stop him?

As if they'd been discussing this aloud, Kate said, 'Well, we've made it this far. That's a start, isn't it?'

The *Shortcut* was well clear of the docks now and was picking up speed. In no time the ship would be out of the harbour and ploughing into Atlantic waters.

'Just imagine,' said Sticky, shaking his head. 'A few hours ago I was worried about what Mum and Dad would do to me for leaving without permission. Now we're crossing the *ocean*. And we have no idea what we're in for.'

Kate gave him a sympathetic look. 'Your parents are the least of your worries now, you know.'

Sticky rolled his eyes. 'That was my point, Kate.'

'Oh!' Kate said. She clapped him on the back. 'Well, then. Good point.'

The *Shortcut* was really moving now. The harbour traffic fell astern, the glittering waters the ocean stretched endlessly ahead, and the ship sped faster and faster – so fast that the salty air howled past the children's ears like the winds of a gale – as if the *Shortcut* meant to flash across the water like an arrow and split the horizon. None of them had ever experienced anything like it. For more than an hour they stood transfixed, staring ahead with watering eyes as the ship pressed on and on, trembling with an urgency they felt to their bones. So engrossed were they that none of them thought to look back again until Stonetown itself had disappeared behind them, lost beyond the curve of the earth.

'There you are!' shouted Cannonball. 'We've been looking for you!'

The children turned to see the barrel-chested sailor grinning at them, clutching his cap to keep the wind from carrying it off. Beside him, gripping Cannonball's leg to keep *herself* from being carried off, was a scowling Constance Contraire. Perhaps she felt she'd been abandoned, or perhaps she simply hadn't napped long enough. Her mouth was moving – no doubt she was elaborating upon her foul mood – but the wind on deck was so loud she could scarcely be heard. The others only nodded and tried to look apologetic, the better to avoid a tantrum.

'Ready for your tour?' Cannonball hollered.

The children followed Cannonball from bow to stern, listening with interest as he shouted about the *Shortcut*'s hull design and engines, and the functions of various deck buildings and equipment. There wasn't much room to walk on deck, for most of it was covered with stacks of huge metal containers. Almost all the cargo was carried in these containers, Cannonball explained, which in other cargo ships must be loaded and unloaded with cranes – a long, laborious process – whereas the *Shortcut*'s specially designed containers could be rolled off and on the ship in no time.

'It's all about speed, you see!' Cannonball shouted. 'She may carry less than other container ships, but she's five times as fast!'

Constance, who could hardly get excited about a bunch of giant metal boxes, pointed toward a squat tower behind whose windows she could see Captain Noland and some crew members working. 'What's that thing for?'

'Why, that's the bridge!' Cannonball cried with a look of surprise. It obviously hadn't occurred to him that anyone could fail to recognize a ship's bridge. 'Can't take you in there, I'm afraid!' He glanced about, then tried to shout in a whisper: 'The bullfrogs wouldn't like seeing children on the bridge.'

The children frowned at this, and with a sympathetic shake of his head Cannonball started to move away.

'Good grief!' exclaimed Kate, whose sharp eyes had just spotted a familiar large bird perched atop the bridge tower. 'It's Madge! She followed me *again*! She must have seen me get on that bus!'

'Madge?' asked Cannonball, his eyes growing round with amazement as Kate pointed out the falcon and explained the situation. They grew rounder still when she produced her spyglass and trained it on the bird, and for a moment the young sailor seemed unable to decide whether to stare at the falcon on the bridge tower or the girl with a bucket full of useful tools – both sights being so unusual on a ship. He recovered quickly, however, and with a fond smile said, 'My great-uncle was a falconer. I always loved visiting him as a boy. Wonderful birds, falcons. Royalty of the bird world, if you ask me.'

Kate beamed at this, of course, and when she had passed around her spyglass – none of the other children cared to look long, as Madge was dining upon an unfortunate seabird and the sight made them squeamish – she took out her whistle and her leather glove, thinking to call Madge down. But Cannonball bent close and asked her to put them away.

'Not right now,' he said, with a significant look at a portly company owner who had just appeared on deck. 'Sorry, but that fellow might be displeased to see something so irregular as a girl with a trained falcon. We'll call her down later, if you don't mind. At any rate, it would be uncivil of us to interrupt her meal, don't you think?'

Kate was disappointed, but she followed obligingly enough when Cannonball led them below decks, where the howl of the wind abruptly ceased and they were able to speak in normal voices. (Or, for Cannonball, what passed as a normal voice.)

'Care to see the security hold?' he asked. 'Cargo containers are awfully dull stuff for a tour, I know. But the security hold's something special!'

The children did, of course, want to see the security hold, so Cannonball took them down into the depths of the ship. They passed several scurrying crew members and a phalanx of security guards before coming to a thick metal door with a round, spoked handle on it like that of a bank vault. At a word from Cannonball, one of the guards rather begrudgingly opened the door to let them enter, then positioned himself in the doorway to watch their every movement. The security hold was surprisingly large, almost the size of a tennis court. Its walls were lined with lockers, chests and safes.

'The great thing about the security hold,' Cannonball told them, 'is that it can be locked from the inside, and it's big enough that we could cram the whole crew in here if necessary.'

'Why would you do that?' asked Reynie.

'In case of attack,' said Cannonball in a matter-of-fact tone. 'It's just an added measure of protection. That's one reason the company owners are so pleased about the *Shortcut*. With a ship this fast and a security hold like this, there's no chance of losing your precious cargo to pirates.'

'Pirates!' Constance exclaimed. 'You must be joking!'

Kate laughed. 'I think you have your centuries mixed up, Cannonball.'

'Wrong you are!' said Cannonball. 'Of course modern pirates don't hoist the skull and crossbones, and it's not as common as it used to be, but there's still a good bit of piracy around the world. Costs companies a pretty penny.'

'In fact,' Sticky interjected, 'last year, piracy cost the global economy over fifteen billion pounds.'

Cannonball's eyes bulged with delight, and once again he grabbed Sticky and hugged him. 'Listen to him talk about piracy and global economy! Now how in the world did you know that?'

'Sticky reads a lot,' Reynie said.

'And it all sticks in his head,' Kate said. 'That's why he has the nickname.'

'You don't say!' said Cannonball, chuckling. 'Why, I've never met—'

The guard in the doorway cleared his throat impatiently. 'How long is this going to take, Cannonball?'

'Hard to say,' Cannonball said, giving the guard a withering look. 'And you can call me Officer Shooter.' He turned away from the man and crossed his eyes at the children, who tried not to laugh. 'At any rate, you don't have to worry about pirates. These shipping lanes never see any attacks. But the bul— that is, the company owners want to know they can ship things overseas with absolute security.'

'Like those diamonds,' Constance said.

Cannonball stole a nervous glance at the guard, who was speaking into his radio and seemed not to have heard. 'Yes, well, ahem. Let's not discuss those in present company, all right? I'm not entirely sure you're supposed to know about them, if you see what I mean.'

'I'll tell them,' the guard muttered into his radio. He put it away and said, 'Tour's over, people. Everyone out.'

'Well, since you ask so nicely,' said Cannonball, and with a wink at the children he led them out.

After the tour, the children returned to their cabin to eat their suppers, which Cannonball went to fetch for them. He'd thought they might join the crew for their meals, he said. But the owners had already expressed irritation at the presence of children on the ship, and Captain Noland, with apologies, had sent word for them to keep to their quarters.

'I can't believe the nerve of those people,' Constance said as they waited. 'They treat the captain like their servant – and us like rats. We're starving down here!'

'That's probably what they're hoping for,' said Reynie.

'As long as we're waiting,' Kate said, going to the door, 'I'm off to the heads.'

Constance looked confused. 'The heads?'

'Ship-talk for 'bathroom',' said Kate as she went out.

'Why not call it what it is?' Constance grumbled. 'Just keep it a toilet, no grand names to spoil it.'

'You think 'the heads' is a grand name?' Reynie asked.

'Poetic licence,' Constance said haughtily, as Sticky smirked and rolled his eyes. 'If you boys can come up with a better rhyme to express my annoyance, feel free.'

The boys were still trying to come up with better rhymes when Cannonball returned from the galley. 'I'm afraid Kate hasn't found her sea legs,' he said, handing out sandwiches and bottles of soda. 'I overheard her in the heads as I passed by. Sick as a dog, poor thing. Retching and gagging for all she's worth.'

'That can't be Kate,' Sticky said. 'She wasn't sick at all when she left.'

Reynie masked a smile. He thought he knew what Kate had been up to. 'I'll check on her, just in case,' he said, going out. He met Kate in the narrow passageway outside the cabin. Sure enough, her face was flushed and sweaty, and she was stomping along in obvious frustration. She saw Reynie and tried to look natural, but it was too late. His amusement was too plain.

'Not a word,' she said, brushing past him.

'Still no luck?' Reynie said.

'I don't know what you're talking about,' Kate said without looking back.

As Cannonball had other duties to attend to, the children ate their supper alone. Afterwards Kate placed her bucket beneath the porthole so that Reynie and Sticky could stand on it and look out. A nearly full moon had risen over the ocean, its reflection shimmering on the water. It was a lovely sight, and Kate offered to lift Constance up to see for herself. But Constance was lying on her bunk, gazing at her pendant, and said she wasn't in the mood.

The truth was that Constance was suffering a great deal. Ever since that morning, when the dreadful message was delivered, she had felt caught up in a whirlwind of emotions, and there was no sign of her coming down any time soon. It was no wonder. For the last year of her life she had relied completely upon Mr Benedict – and a year was a very long time indeed to Constance, who had been around for so few to begin with.

Now Mr Benedict was gone, perhaps never to be seen again, and Constance found herself anguishing over his disappearance as much for what he had *not* been to her as for what he had. What Mr Benedict had been was Constance's affectionate guardian and emotional anchor. What he had not been was her father – not yet, at least, and Constance keenly felt the lack. She could never express why this was so, not even to herself, but she had long believed that becoming Mr Benedict's adopted daughter would transform her world, would make her something other than a lost and wandering oddity of a girl. Now she may well have lost her chance.

As it often did, this line of thinking brought to Constance's mind a particular early morning discussion that had occurred a few months previously. The memory was quite vivid, not least for how it began, with Mr Benedict and Number Two entering the dining room just as Constance was sleepily finishing her cereal. Their appearance made for a striking combination of green, yellow, and red – Mr Benedict wore his green plaid suit as usual; and Number Two's rusty red hair was set off, also as usual, by a yellow outfit – and to Constance's bleary eyes the two of them together looked like a traffic light painted by Picasso.

'I don't even like Picasso,' she muttered by way of greeting.

'Good morning to you, too!' Mr Benedict said, as

Number Two began to lay out a variety of charts and folders.

'Not again,' Constance protested. 'It's too early.' She didn't feel like speaking yet, much less submitting to another of Mr Benedict's curious exercises. He'd given her some kind of odd task almost every day since she'd moved in.

Mr Benedict grinned and slid his hands into the pockets of his suit jacket. 'I'm afraid now is the best time, my dear.'

'I'm eating breakfast.'

'Your cereal bowl is empty,' Number Two pointed out. 'There's only milk left.'

Constance wanted to argue with this, but finding she could not she said, 'Why do I have to keep doing these exercises, anyway? Is there some stupid law that requires it?'

'Forgive me, I thought we'd discussed this,' said Mr Benedict, feigning surprise, for of course they had discussed this before, and more than once. He took a seat at the table, and then – only then – the watchful Number Two sat down. Looking a bit faint, she took a handful of almonds from her pocket and popped them into her mouth.

'As your unofficial guardian,' said Mr Benedict, 'I consider myself responsible for your education. That is the reason for all these tiresome exercises. Legally we're obligated to do nothing. The law does not yet factor in.'

'Because I'm not legally adopted yet?' Constance said.

'That's part of it,' said Mr Benedict. 'It's actually rather complicated.'

Constance looked away. She had never openly expressed any special desire to be adopted by Mr Benedict, and she always felt embarrassed to discuss it. Her impatience was finally winning out over her embarrassment, however. She happened to know that Reynie's adoption by Miss Perumal had been made official two months ago, but for some reason her own situation hadn't changed, and Constance had begun to suspect that Mr Benedict was reconsidering. 'What do you mean by 'complicated', exactly?' she asked, trying to sound casual. 'I mean, why haven't I been adopted yet?'

Running a hand through his rumpled white hair (which as usual looked as though it had been groomed with a toothless comb), Mr Benedict sighed and said, 'Technicalities, Constance. You see, according to official records, you do not exist. Oh, I know you probably think you do – and I, for one, agree – but officially you do not. My challenge, then, is to prove your existence to the proper authorities, who apparently are unconvinced by the actual fact of your living, breathing body. Perhaps this is because there is so little of you to offer as evidence. I can't say for sure.'

Here Mr Benedict paused, searching Constance's expression for signs of mirth. They often enjoyed jokes no one else found funny, and Mr Benedict tended to use humour to defuse Constance's explosive moods. But this time she only frowned, and Mr Benedict cleared his throat and quickly continued. 'At any rate, the authorities wish to see official paperwork – paperwork which, like yourself, appears not to exist. So you see we face certain obstacles. I'm confident, however, that once your existence has been established, the adoption process will go smoothly. In the meantime, you should consider yourself part of this family whether the law does or not.'

But this did not satisfy Constance at all. 'What about the Whisperer?'

Mr Benedict raised an eyebrow. 'The Whisperer?'

'You can use it on me to figure out where I came from! You redesigned it so it can retrieve memories, right? So do that with me! We can find out where I was born, who my parents were . . .'

Mr Benedict shook his head. 'I'm afraid I can't do that right now.'

Constance was growing extremely agitated. 'Why? Because the officials won't let you? What about hypnosis, then? Milligan said you're good at it. So hypnotize me! We could find out . . . we could really find out . . .'

She trailed off, discouraged by Mr Benedict's expression. She could tell he was going to refuse her. She could also tell he hated to do so, but her impatience prevented her from focusing on this, and she crossed her arms and glared at him. Number Two was looking back and forth between them, shifting uneasily in her seat and trying to chew her almonds without making too much noise.

'Constance,' Mr Benedict said gently, 'I have doubts about whether hypnosis – or even the Whisperer – would work in your case. The minds of most two year olds are incapable of creating long-term memories. They simply haven't developed enough yet. Most people remember nothing about their toddler years.'

'I'm three and a *half*,' Constance said indignantly, 'and besides, my mind is hardly typical. Isn't that the point of all these stupid exercises?'

'You were two when you came to me,' Mr Benedict reminded her. 'And yes, it's possible your gifts reflect development that would enable you – with assistance – to recall your past. But I don't believe you're prepared for what you might learn. In fact I cannot allow it. There is every indication, Constance, that whatever circumstances led you to find yourself alone at such a young age will be traumatic for you to remember. When you're older, perhaps. At the moment I feel compelled to protect you from any such trauma. You and your friends have been through quite enough already, and lest you forget, you are still very young indeed.'

'Fine, so you can't adopt me, and you won't do anything to make it happen,' Constance growled. She felt deeply wounded. 'Sorry I brought it up. Let's just get on with your dumb tests.'

'Look at me, Constance,' Mr Benedict said.

Constance averted her eyes.

'My dear,' said Mr Benedict softly, almost in a whisper, 'one of your gifts is abundantly clear to me, if not to yourself, and I am going to help you call upon it now. I wouldn't ask it of you if it weren't important, for I know very well how unnerving you find all this. It *is* important, though. So please, Constance. Look at me.'

Partly out of curiosity, and partly because she loved Mr Benedict even though she was furious with him, Constance looked up. Mr Benedict had removed his spectacles and was looking steadily at her with his bright green eyes. Constance's first reaction was to wonder if he was about to fall asleep; her second was to wonder why she'd wondered that.

'You often pretend not to know certain things,' said Mr Benedict, 'because you don't see how you possibly could know them, and this disturbs you. But you do know things, Constance, and right now I want you to pay attention to that fact. When you looked up at me just now, I saw a question in your eyes. You formed an opinion, did you not, about what I was feeling or thinking?'

'I wondered if you were about to fall asleep,' Constance murmured, 'but I didn't know why I thought that.'

Mr Benedict smiled. 'No doubt you noticed something familiar about my expression – something others wouldn't see. Leaving aside explanations for now, let us focus on one thing only, which is that you *can* know things if only you'll allow yourself. Can you agree to do that? Just for a moment?'

Constance hesitated, then nodded. 'I'm not sure what you mean . . . but fine, I'll try.'

'Thank you,' said Mr Benedict. 'While I have your complete attention, then, I'll speak frankly. I have something I want to say to you, and I want you to keep looking at me as I say it. Are you ready?'

Constance braced herself. Her heart was skipping inside her chest, for she had no idea what was coming. 'I'm ready.'

'Then what I want to say is this: Every person in this family loves you. Rhonda loves you, Number Two loves you, and I love you. We already consider you as much a part of our family as any of us, and we would do anything – no, we *will* do anything—'

Mr Benedict's eyes closed before he could finish his sentence, and he slumped forwards onto the table, upsetting Constance's cereal bowl and spilling milk onto the folders and charts.

'Oh dear,' Number Two said, hastening to soak up the

spill with her shirtsleeve before it ran into Mr Benedict's hair. 'I should have seen that coming.'

Constance was blinking in amazement – because she *had* seen it coming. Just before Mr Benedict fell asleep, the thought 'Here he goes now' had flashed into her mind. Mr Benedict was right. She *could* know certain things . . .

'I hope you realize he meant it,' said Number Two. Despite her brusque tone – or perhaps because of it – Constance could tell she'd been touched by Mr Benedict's words.

'I do,' said Constance, recalling the feeling of certainty she'd had while Mr Benedict was speaking. 'At least . . . I mean, I think I do.'

'Good. You should. And now for heaven's sake, are you going to help me clean this up or do you mean to just sit there and watch?'

Constance slowly broke into a grin – she was feeling very happy all of a sudden – and said exactly what Number Two had expected her to say, which was that she did indeed mean to just sit there and watch.

Lying in her bunk in the *Shortcut*, remembering the events of that morning, Constance felt every bit as sad now as she had felt happy then. She had no idea where she came from and no idea where she might be headed. In what little she could remember of her life, the only constant thing – the thing she depended on above all – had been Mr Benedict's presence. And now she had lost even that. Constance sniffled as quietly as she could.

Reynie knelt beside her bunk. 'They're going to be all right.'

'How do you know?' said Constance, rubbing her stinging eyes. 'How do you know that awful man hasn't already done terrible things to them? How do you know they're not . . . not . . .'

'I just do,' Reynie said, and Constance realized that he was speaking with a conviction he didn't actually feel. But it was something, anyway, to hold on to, and she gazed at him with as much hopefulness as she could muster.

'I just do,' Reynie said again, and both of them hoped with all their hearts that he was right.

The Significance of Weather

The hours crawled by as the children waited for Captain Noland. With the exception of one brief spell during which Cannonball thought it safe to allow them on deck (it was raining and the company owners were all below), they'd spent the entire time confined to their cramped quarters. Nor had their appearance on deck, during which they were compelled to hold a tarpaulin over their heads to keep the rain off, proved to be anything like a pleasant diversion.

At least it hadn't lasted long: there'd been time enough for Constance to compose a rhyming complaint about bullfrogs and tarp hogs (by which she meant the boys, whom she accused of crowding her); time enough for the boys to observe how much more miserable a cold wet night could be made by a poetic companion in a foul mood; and time enough for Kate to summon Madge from the bridge tower and smuggle her down to Cannonball's cabin (a courtesy Cannonball insisted upon, since their own cabin was so crowded) – but all of this took less than five minutes. Afterwards the children had retreated below decks, and since then had done nothing but wait.

Constance had finally given up and dozed off, while in the bunk above her, Sticky sat with his feet dangling over the edge, absently rubbing his scalp (which had begun to feel sandpapery with new stubble) and expounding – rather too loudly and at great length – upon modern ocean vessels. Initially Sticky had limited his speech to what he'd read in the newspapers about the *Shortcut*, but once he'd exhausted that topic he had expanded to include all things nautical.

Reynie lay in the other top bunk, propped on an elbow, thinking less about structural innovations than about his friend's recent tendency to show off. It used to be that Sticky couldn't bear to be looked at or listened to. Now it seemed the opposite was true, and the effect was more than a little tiresome. Even a naturally curious person like Reynie disliked hearing lectures that hadn't been asked for. Reynie yawned and stretched – then glanced down at Kate, wondering how she was bearing up. Kate was as good-natured as could be, but she'd also been cooped up for hours. She was sitting on the floor with her legs elaborately crossed and intertwined (in what for most people would be an excruciating position), making sure her bucket's contents were properly secured. By Reynie's count she'd done this five times already, and he suspected she was tolerating Sticky's speech by ignoring it.

At that very moment, however, the speech drew to a sudden, unexpected close, and Sticky – mumbling something indistinct about having a rest – turned onto his side to face the bulkhead. He was burning with embarrassment, for it had just sunk in how long he'd been talking and how pompous he must have sounded.

Sticky would have found such behaviour distasteful in another person, and indeed it was a far cry from how he used to act. Lately, though, he couldn't seem to help himself. It was hard to resist the pleasure he felt when others were impressed by him – and they did so often seem impressed. (Cannonball's exuberant demonstrations of approval, for instance, had made Sticky feel positively rapturous.) And yet, when his efforts fell flat – when he bored people to death or, worse, when he was proved wrong – he either flew out in anger or withered in humiliation. He envied Reynie's calm, imperturbable manner, to say nothing of Kate's unshakable bravado and good cheer. Even Constance inspired some jealousy, for at least *she* had an excuse for her behaviour. Sticky covered his face with his pillow. Was he really jealous of a three year old? There must be something seriously wrong with him.

There wasn't anything seriously wrong with Sticky, though. The truth, which Sticky didn't quite understand, was that pride was a new feeling for him – something he'd rarely experienced before last year's mission – and it was simply taking some getting used to.

'Look who's awake,' said Reynie, who had noticed Constance blinking her eyes and looking around with a

119

disturbed expression. 'It's okay, Constance. You dozed—'

'Someone's coming!' Constance hissed. Her tone was so unnerving that Reynie and Sticky sat bolt upright, and Kate sprang up into a defensive crouch.

'Easy, Constance,' Reynie said, his heart racing. 'You must have been dreaming. You're safe here with—'

A knock sounded at the door. They all froze.

'Hello?' a man's voice called. It was Captain Noland.

Kate looked wonderingly at Constance. 'How did you . . . ? Never mind, we'll talk about it later.' She opened the door.

Captain Noland stood in the passage holding a small chest. His face was drawn with fatigue, but he gave the children a friendly smile as he came in.

'Well, my friends, I regret the circumstances – I'd hoped to entertain you in my own cabin – but regardless, I'm pleased to join you at last. How are you enjoying the *Shortcut*? She's a mighty fast ship, isn't she?'

As the children responded with polite enthusiasm, the captain knelt to open the chest. It was tidily packed with a miniature folding table, a serving tray, a coffee pot and coffee cups, a bottle of cream and two tins of sweets. Captain Noland set up the table and laid out the treats, and Reynie and Sticky climbed down from their top bunks, taking care not to upset the little table, for there was scarcely room on the floor now to step. Indeed, when all four children were seated on the two lower bunks, their knees pressed against the table's edge, and their feet were awkwardly intermingled below. Keeping his elbows close to his side, Captain Noland smiled apologetically and handed each of them a cup.

'So long as no one moves very much, I believe we'll be fine. Ever had navy coffee?'

'What is it?' asked Kate, eyeing the pitch-black liquid in the pot with suspicion.

'It's brewed with a pinch of salt in the grounds,' Sticky answered. 'The salt's supposed to cut the bitterness.'

'So you're familiar with it!' said Captain Noland with an approving look at Sticky. With careful movements he filled the cups, including one for himself. 'Don't worry, Kate, you can't actually taste the salt. Just good, strong coffee.'

The children took turns stirring cream into their cups, and the captain leant against the cabin door and waited politely. When at last they were ready, he toasted their health – as if they were drinking champagne rather than coffee – then closed his eyes and took a long, slow sip, obviously savouring it.

Reynie drank from his own cup and almost choked. It was hard to say whether the coffee tasted more like petrol or cough syrup. Luckily Captain Noland still had his eyes closed and didn't see Reynie grimace as he forced the foul stuff down. He shot a warning look at the others (it was too late for Kate, who was trying to twist her horrified expression into something that resembled a smile) and in a slightly strangled voice said, 'So you were in the navy, Captain?'

'The navy's where I met Nicholas Benedict, in fact,' said Captain Noland. 'He and I – why, what's the matter?' Captain Noland had opened his eyes to discover the children staring at him uncomfortably. They had agreed they must tell him the truth or risk getting nowhere, but now that the time had come, they were anxious. What if he decided to send them back home on the first plane from

121

Lisbon? Or what if he wanted to help them but couldn't? What if there were no more clues to be had?

'We need to speak with you about Mr Benedict,' Reynie said after a pause. 'He's—'

Just then, the cabin seemed to lurch. The children nearly fell from their seats, and the coffee pot and serving tray slid across the table. Captain Noland leapt forward and caught them. The cabin righted itself just as quickly as it had gone askew.

'We're heading into some rough seas, I'm afraid,' said Captain Noland, as if the children could possibly have failed to notice. 'Don't worry, it's nothing very serious, and it won't last the night. By morning we'll . . . wait, what were you going to tell me about Nicholas?'

It took a few minutes for the children to explain, and by the time they had finished Captain Noland was sitting on the little chest, his chin in his hands, looking quite stricken. 'I can't believe it. He called me from Lisbon only last week. He said he and Number Two were having a fine trip.'

'They're in Lisbon, then?' Reynie asked hopefully.

'They were,' said Captain Noland. 'They were leaving that afternoon. He called to make sure everything was properly arranged. You see, I'd invited Nicholas to be a guest on this maiden voyage months ago, and he asked if I would bring you children as guests instead. I was happy to do so. In fact, I was to play a role in the surprise he planned for you.'

'How so?' Kate asked.

'By presenting you with a sealed envelope he sent me several weeks ago. He said he intended to make certain arrangements, and if he succeeded, I was to give you the envelope when we reached port. When he called from Lisbon, he confirmed I should deliver it, along with some official paperwork to ease your passage between countries.'

'Do you have the envelope with you?' Reynie asked.

'In my cabin,' said Captain Noland. 'When we've finished here I'll get it, and we can open it together. I know you meant to do this alone – and I admire your courage – but for your own safety I can't allow it. I won't send you back, but I *am* going to help you.'

'It isn't that we don't want help,' Reynie said, 'and we certainly wouldn't mind some protection. But Mr Curtain is suspicious and extremely smart. His henchmen – the Ten Men – they'll be on the lookout for any kind of rescue attempt, and . . .'

'I understand you,' Captain Noland said. 'We mustn't involve the authorities, we must operate in secret as much as possible. That's all right, Reynie. I'll do whatever's necessary. You probably don't know this, but I owe Nicholas my life. So tell me again, what exactly—'

He was interrupted by a knock at the door. 'Captain, are you in there?'

'I asked not to be disturbed!' Captain Noland called.

'You said except in case of emergency, sir,' said Cannonball, poking his head in. 'Which it is.'

Captain Noland quickly stood up. 'What's happened, Joe?' The young sailor closed the door, and standing with his back against it (there being no other place to stand) said, 'Well, sir, you know how Mr Pressius was going on to the other . . . um, the other owners about his piles of diamonds? About how the jewels themselves are worth more than the *Shortcut* and all her crew?'

123

'I seem to remember that,' the captain said dryly.

'Well, after you excused yourself, Mr Pressius told Mr Thomas about the . . .' Cannonball hesitated, glancing at the children.

'Speak freely, Joe.'

'Aye, sir. He told Mr Thomas about the fakes.'

'Mr Pressius has brought along a chest of plastic diamonds,' Captain Noland explained to the children, 'which he seems to think may serve as decoys in the event of a robbery. I believe he took the idea from a movie.' The captain kept his face impassive, but the children got the distinct impression that he found Mr Pressius perfectly ridiculous. 'Now, Joe, tell me what happened.'

'Aye, Captain. Well, Mr Pressius said the fakes were so good – the best cheap fakes ever made, he said – that he bet Mr Thomas couldn't tell the difference. Of course Mr Thomas didn't like that, as he figures himself an expert on everything—'

'Where's the emergency in all this?' asked Captain Noland.

'Getting to it, Captain. So what happens is Mr Thomas and Mr Pressius insist I take them down to the security hold to open the chests. I didn't know what to do – you said to keep them happy, and seeing as the diamonds do belong to Mr Pressius . . .'

'You did the right thing.'

'Thank you, sir,' said Cannonball, looking relieved. 'Only, the trouble is that Mr Pressius wins the bet. Without a magnifying glass, it's extremely hard to tell the difference between the real diamonds and the plastic ones.'

'Why is that a problem?' asked Captain Noland.

'Because . . . well, sir, did you happen to notice a kind of a joggle in the ship a few minutes ago? A bit of a lurching? Well, Mr Thomas and Mr Pressius were holding the open chests when that happened – they were carrying them across to where the light was better – and seeing as neither of them has his sea legs yet, why . . . the, uh, the diamonds and the decoys, they . . . ahem. They sort of spilled out.'

'Spilled out?'

'Exactly, sir. And mixed together. All across the floor of the security hold.'

'The idiots!' cried Captain Noland, putting a hand to his forehead. 'Don't tell me. Mr Pressius refuses to do the sorting himself. He wants you to do it.'

'Yes, sir. Under heavy guard, of course. He said I'll need to examine each one with a magnifying glass. He'll inspect the diamonds when I've finished, he said, but he certainly isn't going to do the initial sorting himself. That's grunt work, he said. Said it wouldn't have happened anyway if the ship had been sailing properly.'

'Of course that's what he said. And what did you tell him?'

'I said I had to speak with you first. Said you might prefer someone else do it, as it's likely to take several hours, and I'm needed to—'

'*Everyone* is needed!' Captain Noland snapped. He took a deep breath and let it out slowly. 'I'm sorry. The fact is I can't spare *anyone* for several hours, Joe. We're short-handed as it is. The crew is already working double duty, sacrificing their sleep, and now we have rough seas thrown into the bargain. What's more,' Captain Noland said, with a significant look at the children, 'our friends here have alerted me to an urgent situation that requires my attention.'

Cannonball was wringing his cap in his hands. He stared at the floor. 'Sorry, Captain. I should never have—'

'It isn't your fault, Joe. It's the owners' fault. First they compel me to reduce the crew, and now this.' Captain Noland's face contorted with bitterness; his tone was desolate. 'And yet if the *Shortcut* arrives late . . . if the least little thing goes wrong . . .'

'I know,' said Cannonball with an anxious look. 'I know what it would mean for you, sir. It would be . . . well, if there's anything I can . . . you know that I . . .'

Captain Noland's expression softened. He put a hand on Cannonball's shoulder. 'It's all right, Joe. We'll just have to do what we can and hope for the best. Now, help me think. I'll need you on the bridge soon, so who should I assign? Who can I possibly spare?'

Kate raised her hand. 'Why not let me do it? I have good eyes and quick hands. I could make short work of it.'

'I could help too,' Sticky offered. 'We all could.'

Cannonball brightened. 'Now, there's an idea! What do you think, Captain? Set the young ones to sorting?'

'It's very good of you, children,' said Captain Noland, 'and I thank you, but Mr Pressius would never stand for it. You know he wouldn't, Joe. Now, please, we need to hurry. Who can I send?'

Cannonball's face fell. 'You're right, of course. He wouldn't hear of it. All right, then, what about Jenny Briggs? No, wait, you'll need her on the . . . what about Matthew Tanner?'

The captain shook his head. 'Tanner took on Pratt's

dutics. What about Kavanaugh? Or is he —'

'Excuse me,' Reynie interrupted. 'Captain Noland?'

The captain scratched at his beard, evidently straining to be patient. 'Yes, what is it, Reynie?'

'You said the fake diamonds are plastic, right? If that's true, then you ought to just pour everything into a tub of water – the fake ones and the real ones together. The plastic ones will float to the top.'

Captain Noland and Cannonball blinked. Then looked at each other. Then burst out laughing.

'Reynie Muldoon, you've just earned yourself a spot on my crew!' roared Captain Noland. 'Put them in water and see what floats – now, why didn't I think of that? My whole *life* depends on things that float! Joe, will you . . . ?'

'Already on it, Captain!' said Cannonball, and pausing just long enough to tousle Reynie's hair, he hurried out.

'I can't thank you enough,' said Captain Noland. He started to refill Reynie's coffee cup, then saw it was still nearly full. 'Please, drink up! And help yourself to those treats, all of you. They're entirely deserved. Reynie may well have saved me from a fate I can hardly stand to consider.'

Constance had begun stuffing gumdrops into her pockets to prevent the others from eating them. 'What would that be?'

'Why, dismissal, of course,' said Captain Noland. 'This maiden voyage is an important trip! The owners will make money only if the *Shortcut* proves it can deliver what they promise – a reliable transatlantic shipment in two days. If it fails, they'll want to blame something other than the ship design, and it certainly isn't going to be themselves. No, there's no doubt about it. They'll send me packing.'

'Surely you could find another ship,' said Kate. 'Why do you want to work for these jerks, anyway?'

Captain Noland gave her a weary look. 'It's complicated, Kate. If I were dismissed from my command of the *Shortcut* – if the owners claim that I've surprised them with my incompetence – well, you can see it would be difficult for me to secure another position. Meanwhile, I'd be left high and dry. And that is something I cannot tolerate. No, I need to be at sea.' The captain's sincerity on this point was unmistakable. Even as he'd spoken the words 'high and dry,' his eyes had begun to dart back and forth, and his jaw quivered.

'Enough of that, however,' said Captain Noland, composing himself. 'We have more pressing matters to consider. I should return to the bridge now, but I'll bring you that envelope when I can. Shall I bring more coffee when I come? I'll gladly brew a fresh pot.'

The children begged him not to trouble himself on their account. And so, with a promise to return as soon as possible, Captain Noland took his leave.

As the children rifled through the treat tins, they felt somewhat encouraged. If Mr Benedict had called from Lisbon, they were on the right track, and with the captain's help they might even work out where to go next before they reached port. This was their great hope, for when they arrived in Lisbon they would have only two days left to find their friends.

The room had begun to sway again. The movement was less dramatic than that original lurch, but even so Reynie

128

experienced an unpleasant rolling sensation, as if the ocean waves had found their way into his belly. Abandoning his half-nibbled mint cookie – eating seemed like a terrible idea all of a sudden – Reynie began to put away the tiny folding table, which was threatening to tip. Kate moved the treat tins to the floor, munching happily as she decided what to choose next. She seemed unfazed by the motion of the cabin.

'So are we going to talk about what Constance did?' asked Sticky (who like Reynie had sadly given up on the cookies). 'You know, the way she knew Captain Noland was at the door before he knocked?'

Constance rolled her eyes. 'Reynie was right. I was dreaming. Forget about it.'

'Even if you were dreaming,' said Sticky, 'you predicted someone was coming.'

'I think it must have been a coincidence,' said Kate, getting up to help put the table away. Reynie was having trouble keeping his balance and kept banging his shins against the chest. 'Wouldn't you say so, Reynie?'

Reynie dropped heavily to the floor. He was feeling worse by the second. 'I'm not sure,' he admitted. 'Has anything like that ever happened before, Constance?'

Constance shrugged. 'Maybe. I don't know.'

'What does *that* mean?' Sticky said exasperatedly.

Constance made a face at him. 'It means it's happened before, but how can I possibly know whether it's a coincidence or not? Unlike *some* people, I don't happen to think I know everything.'

Sticky, stung by this comment, took out his polishing cloth and made no reply.

'Why don't you just tell us what you do know?' Reynie asked gently. 'What does Mr Benedict say about . . . about your gifts?'

Constance gazed at her shoes, evidently considering how – or whether – to answer him, and after a few moments Kate seemed ready to prompt her. Reynie, sensing Constance's emotional confusion, warned Kate with a subtle shake of his head. He was pretty sure Constance hadn't noticed, yet no sooner had he done it than she looked at him with a grateful expression. It made Reynie very uneasy, as if she'd read his thoughts. Could that be what happened? More likely she was just developing a sense of intuition, like Mr Benedict (and like Reynie himself, for that matter). But what if . . . ?

'Mr Benedict hasn't said much about it,' Constance said, 'except that I can do patterns and stuff, which might explain everything or . . . or maybe not.'

'What do you mean by 'patterns and stuff'?' asked Sticky, trying not to sound demanding this time.

'It's like . . . like . . .' Constance spluttered. 'One thing I'm *not* good at is explaining things.'

'How did Mr Benedict explain it to you?' said Reynie.

Constance thought about this. 'Okay, he said it was like how when most people look at a familiar word, they don't have to spell it out letter by letter. Even with long words like, um – what's a really long word, Sticky?'

'Epidemiological,' Sticky suggested.

'Okay, it's like when Sticky sees that word on paper. He already knows it, so he doesn't have to figure it out letter by letter. Right, Sticky? You just recognize it by the pattern of its letters. I can do the same thing, only with more complicated stuff.'

'Like what?' asked Kate.

Constance seemed embarrassed. She began to pick at her fingernails, and in a barely audible voice she said, 'Like weather, and, you know, stuff like that.'

Reynie raised his eyebrows. 'Weather?'

Constance mumbled something about not feeling very well. This happened to be the truth (nor was she alone in this, for Sticky and Reynie were both holding their bellies now), but the others would not be put off, and so finally she explained, 'I can predict it, apparently. I hadn't realized I could until Mr Benedict pointed it out. He started asking every morning if it was going to rain that day, and I would make what I thought was a dumb guess – only my guesses always turned out to be right.'

'How can that be?' Sticky asked.

Constance shrugged. 'Mr Benedict says people's minds are noticing things all the time, even when we don't realize it. Sights, smells, temperature changes – all sorts of stuff. We notice it without consciously thinking about it. He says we may not be paying attention, but our brains are recording and processing it all the same, and these . . . these observations, or whatever you want to call them, make up a pattern. So if you're good with patterns, the way Mr Benedict says I am, you can sometimes predict things.'

'Because you recognize the pattern,' Reynie said. 'I get it.'

'But I don't see how this explains what happened,' Sticky said. 'What kind of pattern could predict the captain's knocking on the door?'

'Maybe Constance's mind came to recognize the sound of

footsteps in the passageway,' Reynie suggested, 'while to the rest of us that particular sound was still mixed in with the unfamiliar noises of the ship. A lot of the ship sounds must follow patterns, after all. It could be as simple as that.'

Sticky considered this. 'Highly developed, unconscious pattern recognition,' he murmured. 'Okay, I buy that.'

'But couldn't it also be that she's psychic?' Kate asked. 'Did Mr Benedict ever mention that possibility, Constance?'

Constance, who now felt very ill indeed, said irritably, 'You know it's possible, Kate. Now stop asking stupid questions.'

She crossed her arms and closed her eyes, partly because she was so queasy and partly because she disliked being questioned – especially about this particular subject.

Psychic ability *would* be an awful lot to cope with, Reynie thought, especially for someone as young as Constance. The prospect seemed to trouble her extremely. But Reynie said nothing, for at the moment *he* was troubled extremely by the sensation that his stomach was filled with wobbling gelatine.

Kate was unwilling to let the matter drop, however. 'I'll stop asking questions when you start answering them, Constance. Has Mr Benedict ever said anything about your being psychic, or hasn't he?'

Constance moaned. 'If I tell you, can we please stop talking about it?'

'It's a deal,' said Kate.

The boys said nothing. They were both quite nauseous and were trying to hold very still. Unfortunately, with every minute that passed the cabin seemed to sway with greater energy, as if the room itself were a swinging hammock. The captain's little chest was sliding back and forth, first bumping the door, then the wall opposite. Kate took out her rope and tied the chest to a bunk.

'Mr Benedict said it might seem like I'm psychic even if I'm not,' said Constance, sagging over to lie on her side. 'People's expressions and their tone of voice and, you know, just everything about their behaviour – it's all made up of patterns, and my mind's good at recognizing them. So sometimes I know things you might not expect. Like right now, for instance. I can tell you're about to ask me for an example.'

Kate's eyes widened. 'How did you know that?'

'I have no idea,' said Constance. 'Maybe it's something in your eyes, maybe it's just what you always do when I try to explain things. The point is that people have patterns, too. So there's your stupid example.'

'Hey, that's pretty fun!' said Kate, who hadn't noticed that Constance didn't think it fun in the least. 'Of course, it doesn't exactly rule out the possibility that you can read minds.'

'Yes, it does,' said Constance, turning away. 'And don't argue with me. I'm done talking. I feel sicker than sick.'

So did Reynie and Sticky, both of whom were breathing in shallow gasps and longing for the solidity of land. Kate felt fine, however, and as she mulled over what Constance had told her, she snatched another treat from the tins and began to pace the cabin. This required no small feat of balance, as there was scant room for pacing and the floor was disinclined to hold on a level. She was chattering about something the whole while, but the boys had lost

133

their ability to concentrate.

Reynie was trying not to watch her. He would have closed his eyes, but doing so made him feel even sicker. 'Kate, will you please stop moving around? It's only making things worse.'

Kate stopped in her tracks. 'Making what worse? Oh, you don't look so well, Reynie! In fact, neither do you, Sticky! Are *all* of you sick?'

'You should be a doctor,' Sticky groaned.

Before long all three of the invalids were groaning so much that the cabin sounded like a frog pond, and Kate, seeing that her friends' conditions were only worsening, set out to learn the quickest routes to all the ship's bathrooms. (It was also a good excuse to flee the whimpering and moans.) As it happened, the routes Kate learned proved very useful to her friends. But they were all too sick to thank her.

Directions, Recollections, and Outstanding Debts

Reynie's first waking thought was that he was hungry. He hadn't eaten since the evening before, and it was now – well, what time *was* it, anyway? He had no idea how long he'd slept. At least the sickness had passed; Reynie would choose hunger pangs over seasickness any day. Reynie would choose almost anything over seasickness.

He, Sticky and Constance had spent their first night aboard the *Shortcut* feeling sicker than they'd ever felt. (Kate, having shown them to their various bathrooms, slept peacefully in the quiet cabin.) When their illnesses finally subsided early that morning, they had all collapsed into their bunks and passed out. Reynie had a vague memory – or was it a dream? – of Captain Noland speaking in hushed tones to Kate at the cabin door, but otherwise he'd been in complete oblivion until now.

Reynie's mind moved swiftly to Mr Benedict and Number Two. *Only three days left*, he thought, and the urgency he'd felt since yesterday morning gripped him with new intensity. He opened his eyes and sat up. The cabin was dark. Perhaps Kate had taped something over the porthole to help them sleep? No, a glance at the porthole revealed nothing of the sort. He scratched his head and yawned, only to snap his mouth shut – painfully biting his tongue – when Kate sprang up out of the darkness onto his bunk. She shone her penlight into his face.

'What's the matter?' Kate asked. 'Did I scare you?'

'Never mind,' said Reynie grumpily. 'What's going on? How long have I been out?'

'Too long. It's evening now. The captain will be here soon.'

'Evening?'

'Yes, and I've been going nuts waiting for you to wake up,' Kate said. 'Cannonball let me visit Madge a few minutes at lunchtime, but otherwise I've been cooped up in here all day with no one to talk to. She's doing fine, by the way. Cannonball gives her prime bits of meat from the galley – he calls it 'frog food' – and I think she may be falling in love with him.'

'Did the captain come?' Reynie asked. 'Or did I dream that?'

'No, he came by this morning. Do you not remember? You sat up and said something like 'eggness', then fell back to sleep.' Kate thrust a piece of paper at him. 'He brought this. He wasn't sure what it meant, but he said he'd think about it today.'

Reynie looked at the paper, but it was too dark to read. 'The captain read this? He didn't wait for us to see it first?'

'Well, no,' Kate said. 'He'd already looked at it. I'm sure he just wanted to help.'

'I suppose so,' said Reynie uneasily. Rhonda had let *them* open the first envelope, and somehow he'd expected Captain Noland to do the same. But the circumstances had been different at Mr Benedict's house, Reynie reminded himself. Anyway, shouldn't he be glad the captain cared?

'I've been staring at it all day,' Kate was saying. 'It isn't really a riddle at all – more like directions – but I still haven't got very far with it.'

'Let me borrow your penlight,' Reynie said, and shining the light onto the paper he read:

Well done, my friends, and may your ocean crossing be great fun! Please go down for your hint, then up to where the clues lead you – that's where you'll find the next envelope! – Mr Benedict

The middle of the page was blank except for a wide scorch mark. ('No lemon-juice messages,' Kate muttered.) Reynie scanned down to the bottom, where Mr Benedict had written the following lines:

Castle of Sticky's namesake
Against westernmost wall
Not visible

137

Need tool
Olive trees nearby
No cork or pine for two metres

'I figure the castle must be on a hill,' said Kate, 'which is why he made such a point of saying to go *up* to where the clues lead. But I've never heard of a castle named Sticky or George or Washington or anything like it, have you?'

Reynie shook his head. 'I'll bet Sticky has, though.'

'I'll get him up,' said Kate, rolling off the bunk.

A moment later Sticky cried out in the darkness, and Reynie heard Kate ask, 'Did I scare you?'

Sticky was still grumbling at her when Captain Noland arrived with their supper. He'd brought a tray laden with peanut butter sandwiches, fruit, biscuits and milk. Much to his embarrassment, however, there was no coffee.

'I'm afraid I left my coffee pot here last night,' Captain Noland said, once they had roused Constance and turned on the light. 'And Mr Pressius demanded his own pot in his cabin, which left me with no extras.'

The children, assuring the captain that this was perfectly all right, set hungrily upon the food. (Constance, naturally, reached for the cookies first.)

'I'm glad to see you're feeling better,' said Captain Noland, who himself seemed in a poor state of health. His uniform was crisp and trim as ever, but he obviously hadn't slept in some time. His shoulders sagged, his eyes were bloodshot and puffy, and he was stifling a yawn as he asked, 'Any luck with the letter? I'm afraid I haven't had a chance to give it much thought.'

'Actually, neither have we,' Reynie said. 'I've only

glanced at it, and Constance and Sticky haven't even seen it yet.'

He tried to hand the letter to Constance, but she was still very groggy (so groggy she'd forgotten to snatch more than her share of cookies), and she refused to take it. 'I'll look at it later,' she mumbled.

So Reynie passed the letter to Sticky, who hardly glanced at it before he exclaimed, 'Hey, this is easy! That castle's in Lisbon!'

No sooner had the words left Sticky's mouth than Kate was clapping him on the back (so hard he almost choked on his sandwich), and Reynie was saying over and over again, 'I *knew* you'd have the answer,' his face flushed with excitement. Even Constance showed her appreciation by not filching Sticky's cookie while he was distracted. They had been in sore need of hope, and Sticky had just delivered it.

After they'd quieted down, Captain Noland said, 'Is Jorge your given name, Sticky?'

'It's George,' Sticky replied.

'Oh, of course!' said Captain Noland, looking quite impressed. (Sticky, already beaming, now positively shone.)

'Would one of you mind explaining to the rest of us?' Constance said.

'St George's Castle,' said Captain Noland. 'In Portuguese it's called the Castelo de São Jorge, and since it's *in* Portugal, that's how I always think of it. Where did you learn to speak Portuguese, Sticky? Or should I call you Jorge?'

Sticky laughed – a bit nervously, it seemed to Reynie – and said, 'I know lots of languages. It's no big deal, really.' (Reynie noticed that this was not exactly the answer to

Captain Noland's question, but the captain either didn't notice or didn't care.)

'I can imagine why Nicholas chose to send you up there,' Captain Noland said. 'He loves the view from the castle grounds. Probably wanted to share it with you.'

'So the castle *is* on a hill,' Kate said. 'I thought so.'

'The highest hill in Lisbon, in fact.' Captain Noland's tired eyes suddenly looked thoughtful and melancholy, as if he were gazing with them upon a different time. 'Nicholas and I went up there together once, many years ago. He was so moved by the view that he fell asleep and nearly plunged over the castle wall. Oh, I would never have forgiven myself if he had! I'd been watching a ferry down on the river and wasn't keeping an eye on him. I should have been paying better attention.'

'What happened?' asked Constance, a little short of breath, as if at that very moment Mr Benedict were about to topple from the precipice.

'He fell backwards instead of forwards. As simple as that. He got a rather nasty bump on his head, but when I think of the alternative . . .' Captain Noland shuddered. 'Just like that,' he said, snapping his fingers, 'and I would have lost my friend forever – to say nothing of all the lives he saved that year. And it would have been entirely my fault.'

'Was it the westernmost wall he nearly fell from?' asked Reynie. He had a good many questions he wanted to ask – for instance, what was this about Mr Benedict saving lives? Whose lives did the captain mean? But more pressing at the moment was understanding this clue and what they were to do about it.

'It was indeed,' said Captain Noland. He yawned and

pointed toward the chest, still tied to a lower bunk. 'I don't suppose there's any coffee left in the pot, is there? Did you finish it off last night?'

'We, uh – we couldn't,' Reynie said. 'We got seasick right after you left.'

Captain Noland squeezed past him and opened the chest. 'Why, there's still a good half pot left! I'm in luck!' He wiped out his cup from the night before and filled it with the treacly black liquid. Perhaps being cold and stale improved the coffee's taste, Reynie thought; certainly it couldn't make it any worse. Regardless, the captain had forgotten to offer them any, and for this all the children were grateful.

Captain Noland downed half the cup in one gulp, refilled it, then closed the chest and sat on it. 'Much better,' he said. 'I'm of no use to you if I'm asleep. Now then, as for Nicholas's directions, they all make sense to me now. Things should be pretty straightforward when we get up to the castle.'

'How so?' asked Reynie.

'Well, as you might imagine, there aren't any olive trees in the castle itself,' said the captain, 'so Nicholas has to be referring to the outer wall of the castle grounds, which are rather like a big park. I remember quite a stretch of wall on the western side, but I'm sure these other clues – the description of which trees are nearby and which aren't – will narrow the location down exactly. No doubt we'll see right away where he's buried the envelope. We'll look for a spot where the earth has been freshly turned.'

'You think it's buried?' Sticky asked.

'Surely that's what Nicholas meant by 'not visible' and

'need tool'.' He meant for us to dig. I'll have Joe fetch a shovel as soon as we dock.'

The children looked at one another with expressions of relief and surprise.

'Well, *that* was easy,' said Kate, putting the letter away inside her bucket. 'Now all we have to do is get there!'

'You can leave that to me,' said Captain Noland. 'I'll radio ahead to have a taxi waiting at the docks. We'll waste no time that way. Joe and I will change into civilian clothes – the better to avoid notice – and accompany you to the castle.'

'What do you mean by civilian clothes?' asked Constance. 'Aren't you a civilian?'

'Ha!' cried Captain Noland, scratching his beard. 'An old habit, Constance. I was in the navy for so long, I tend to forget things have changed. I only meant to say we won't wear our uniforms.'

'That reminds me,' said Kate. 'Did you say that you and Mr Benedict met in the navy?'

'It's a fact,' said Captain Noland. 'We were in naval intelligence together. Of course, this was very long ago . . . has Nicholas never told you?' Seeing their blank faces, the captain chuckled and shook his head. 'It doesn't surprise me. He couldn't have told you much without seeming to brag – and Nicholas is anything but a braggart. I'm perfectly happy to brag about him, though. I used to joke that he saved a hundred lives every morning before breakfast, and the truth wasn't far from that. We were engaged in a terrible war, you see – a long-forgotten war that no one likes to talk about now – and Nicholas was our best code breaker. Whenever an enemy transmission was intercepted, we brought it straight to him. He usually cracked the code within minutes, if not sooner. Our soldiers avoided any number of surprise attacks thanks to Nicholas.'

The children grinned, pleased to hear good things said about Mr Benedict. In his absence they found themselves especially eager for details about him – as if by gathering details they might, in some small way, bring him back.

'Didn't you say he saved *your* life once, too?' asked Reynie.

Captain Noland had just slugged the rest of his coffee and stood to open the chest. He took out the coffee pot and refilled his cup. 'Actually, Nicholas saved my life more than once. The first time, we'd been sent on a secret assignment. It was an unusually important assignment, too – otherwise they wouldn't have sent Nicholas, who never did field work. His narcolepsy might put him at risk, you see. Well, we managed to complete the assignment, but in the process we were captured by the enemy. I should say that *I* was captured. Nicholas was not. But in order to rescue me he turned himself over to my captors.'

Captain Noland settled onto the chest again. 'I'm sure you're thinking what I was thinking. How on earth did he hope to save me by sacrificing himself? Well, that was when I discovered that Nicholas is the most persuasive man in the world. Mysteriously so. Over the next two days, he spoke with every officer in the enemy headquarters. If he couldn't convince one officer of what he was saying, he would switch tactics, arguing that a different officer ought to be sent in to speak with him. One way or another, he always succeeded, and by the end of the second day he'd found just the right things to say to just the right people, and had convinced our enemy that we should be let go. To this day, I can't quite believe it.'

'That's amazing!' Kate cried. 'How did he possibly manage it?'

'I can't say for sure, but I think part of the answer is that people sense something in Nicholas that makes them trust him. And of course that's with good reason. Compared to Nicholas, even the best of men are untrustworthy.'

Reynie felt a sudden, unexpected twinge of suspicion. This last statement of the captain's sounded rather like a justification, as if one could be untrustworthy and still be considered among 'the best of men'. What was more, the captain's expression had shifted subtly in a way that Reynie couldn't quite interpret. Perhaps he simply felt jealous of Mr Benedict's trustworthy character – or of other people's perception of it. That could be a natural feeling for a good man who wished he were more trustworthy. Still, the thought made Reynie uneasy.

Sticky, meanwhile, was asking Captain Noland how else Mr Benedict had saved his life, and Reynie tried to set aside his suspicions and listen. He did like Captain Noland, after all. And if Mr Benedict trusted him, shouldn't Reynie?

'He saved me once again by saying the right thing to the right person,' Captain Noland said. 'This time the person was me. The war had just ended, and Nicholas was leaving the navy to return to his research. I was thinking of leaving the navy myself, for I was extremely miserable half the time. I'd grown up on ships – my father was a merchant sailor – but by the end of this war I felt I'd missed my calling. How else was I to explain my feeling depressed so much of the time? When I told him this, Nicholas laughed so much he fell asleep. I was fairly annoyed, I can tell you. But then he always did like to laugh, and when he woke up he apologized sincerely and said, 'Phil, it isn't being on ships that makes you miserable. It's getting *off* them. You're always sad when you head for port, and you're sad the entire time you're on land – except for the day you set sail again. The worst thing you could do would be to stay ashore.'

'Well, this was so obvious a child should have seen it, and I hate to say, I almost resented Nicholas for making me look so dumb. But there it was: he knew me better than I knew myself. As long as I'm at sea, I'm happy – which is why this maiden voyage is so important. I can't afford to lose my reputation as a sea captain. Sending me to shore would be like sending me to my doom.'

'Why did you ever leave the navy, then?' asked Constance.

'I felt I had no choice. They had long wanted to promote me, which seems nice enough until you realize that a promotion would have sent me to a comfortable, highly respected post – on land. Torture! I'd always found a way out of it, but finally they insisted. That was when I left the navy and applied for my current position, which seemed perfect. The *Shortcut* will be at sea almost constantly – it loads and unloads faster than other ships, so it spends less time in port – and as I told the owners . . .'

Captain Noland trailed off, looking sheepish. 'I've gone on far too long about your poor old captain. It was Nicholas you wanted to hear about, and rightly so. A better man I've never known – and this despite all manner of ill fortunes, as you children know. To lose his parents so young, and then to struggle so mightily with his narcolepsy . . . I don't mean just the tendency to fall asleep at odd times, but, oh, the nightmares!'

Captain Noland rubbed his bloodshot eyes. He looked as though he had endured a night of bad dreams himself. 'Nicholas and I shared a ship cabin more than once,' he said, 'and the cries of terror he uttered in his sleep were enough to keep me wide-eyed and shivering for hours. He suffered these visitations from phantom creatures almost every night – the Old Hag, I remember, was the worst, such a dreadful hallucination I hated even to hear about her – yet during the day you'd never guess what he'd been through. Always cheerful, always brave. That's Nicholas. Still, he did hope that one day – wait!'

Captain Noland stiffened so suddenly he spilled coffee on himself. 'To think!' he cried. 'Oh, where has my mind gone? To think I almost forgot!' And looking at the children he said, 'Forgive me. I hadn't realized it until this moment, but we have another clue!'

THE OLD HAG, THE SUSPICIOUS GIFT, AND THE QUANDARY AT THE CASTLE

A little over a year before, Captain Noland said, Mr Benedict had received word from a Dutch science museum about the discovery of certain papers – a journal and a packet of documents – in a secret location. The papers had belonged to his parents. Mr Benedict, an orphan since infancy, had wanted to see the papers right away, but at the time he was busy investigating the hidden messages that would eventually lead him to Mr Curtain and the Whisperer. Not until recently had he addressed those more urgent duties enough to take some time for himself – to go on this personal trip.

'So when he called you from Lisbon,' Reynie said, 'he was on his way to Holland?'

'Or else he'd just come from there,' said Captain Noland. 'I don't know. I was pressed for time, and we spoke only briefly. I'm sorry to say I don't know the name of that museum, or even in what city it's located. But I know he intended to go there on this trip.'

'I know his parents were Dutch scientists,' Sticky said, 'but why does the museum have their papers? Shouldn't they have gone to Mr Benedict?'

There was a bit of a legal question pertaining to the case, Captain Noland explained. Mr Benedict's parents had bequeathed all their papers to this museum, but it was unlikely – at least from Mr Benedict's point of view – that these newly discovered documents were meant to be included among those original papers.

'Still, Nicholas was excited,' the captain told them. 'Before now, you see, he'd had only a glimpse into his parents' lives. A few of their early papers had been published in scientific journals, and Nicholas had tracked these down and read them. They were quite sophisticated studies of narcolepsy, he said, which led him to believe his own condition was inherited from one of his parents. Beyond this, though, he's never known anything about them.'

'I've often wondered about that,' said Reynie. 'If anyone could track down information about them, you'd think it would be Mr Benedict.'

'Oh, Nicholas would have loved to find out more if he could,' Captain Noland said. 'But as a young man he was much too poor to travel, and then came that awful war. It

148

was years before he had any money to speak of. By then he'd already got sidetracked with his investigations into Curtain's doings, and of course it's a good thing for everyone that he did. But what a nasty bit of luck it was to learn he had a twin. Separated at birth, apparently, and sent to different relatives – the sort of story that might have made for a joyful reunion. Instead he was devastated to see what a wicked man his brother had become. And who could blame him? After all those years with no family, and then, in effect, to gain a brother and lose him in the same moment!'

At this, the children felt an uncomfortable prickling of guilt. It made sense that Mr Benedict had been wounded by that discovery. But he had hidden his distress from them, and preoccupied as they were with their own problems, none of them had given the situation much thought. Reynie felt particularly guilty, for Mr Benedict *had* mentioned his sadness to him once but had quickly changed the subject – and Reynie had soon forgotten about it.

Captain Noland put a hand to his brow. He looked uneasy. 'I shouldn't have told you that,' he said. 'I'm sorry. Nicholas would never have wanted to trouble you. Now here you are, going about dangerous business for his sake, and I've only added to your concern.'

'It's all right,' Kate said. 'If something's important to Mr Benedict, we all want to know about it – even if he thinks he should protect us.'

This was true enough, yet Reynie couldn't help but wonder again about Captain Noland's trustworthiness. There was no denying that Mr Benedict had kept his feelings from the children, and now Captain Noland had revealed them. He may not have intended any harm, but still . . .

'Well,' said Captain Noland, 'speaking of things important to Nicholas, there was something else about these new papers that excited him. He thought they might contain useful information regarding his narcolepsy. He even joked about shaking hands with the Old Hag and sending her packing.'

'What are you talking about, anyway?' Constance asked. 'This is the second time you've mentioned her.'

'The Old Hag is a notorious hallucination,' Sticky said in an automatic tone, as if reading from a textbook, 'occasionally suffered by people with certain sleep disorders. She appears as a figure crouching near the person's bed, or even sitting on the person's chest. The experience is supposed to be terrifying.'

Captain Noland raised his eyebrows. 'You know a good many things, don't you, Sticky? You're exactly right. It *is* a terrifying hallucination, and Nicholas has experienced it countless times.'

Kate whistled sympathetically. 'No wonder he'd like to get rid of her. He must dread going to sleep at night.'

As if on cue, Captain Noland yawned and looked at his watch. 'Speaking of sleep, my friends, I should attempt a few hours of it. We have a very big day ahead of us tomorrow. And let's be optimistic, all right? Your plan is a good one. We're going to find Nicholas and Number Two – I'm sure of it – and then we'll contact Rhonda and Milligan. Rhonda will have the best ideas for how to proceed, and if anyone in the world can rescue our friends, it's Milligan. So chins up, everyone.'

Reynie, Sticky, and Constance dutifully attempted upbeat expressions, and Kate, already beaming at the captain's praise for her father, winked and gave him a thumbs up.

'That's the spirit,' said Captain Noland. 'Now then, Reynie, will you help me carry these things back to my cabin? I think your help with my little diamond crisis earns you a chance to stretch your legs. I really am sorry to keep you all so confined. Just grab that empty tray and milk bottle, will you? I'll carry the chest.'

The others watched with jealous eyes as Reynie followed the captain out.

'Pay close attention to the route,' Captain Noland instructed as they walked along the narrow passages. 'We'll take a bit of a roundabout path to avoid running into – well, to avoid any unpleasant encounters.'

Reynie disliked having to sneak around to avoid bumping into disapproving bullfrogs – for this was obviously what the captain had meant – but he didn't mind taking the long way. It *was* good to stretch his legs. And yet, Reynie thought, frowning to himself, it was awfully unfair that his friends had no such opportunity. They'd been stuck in that tiny cabin as long as he had. Would it really have been too much to let them come along?

The injustice being done to his friends seemed even worse when Reynie saw Captain Noland's cabin – a large, comfortable, well-furnished room that made the children's all the more closet-like in comparison. Still, the cabin's appeal was greatly diminished by its alarming state of disarray. Reynie had rarely seen a messier room. Dirty plates, platters, silverware and glasses were everywhere, and the floor was strewn with wadded napkins and odd fragments of food. The cabin looked as if someone had emptied a kitchen into it – drawers, cupboards, rubbish bins and all.

Captain Noland made a disgusted noise as he set down his own neatly packed chest. 'I was obliged to host a party for the owners,' he explained, 'and I'm so short of staff I had no one to clean up afterwards. It'll have to wait until we're in port, I suppose. The most important thing now is sleep.'

'I could help you clean up, if you like,' Reynie said. He made the offer reluctantly – the place was truly in a revolting condition – but as he had had plenty of sleep himself it seemed the decent thing to do.

Much to Reynie's relief, Captain Noland said, 'No, no, you've already done more than enough. In fact, young man, I wanted to give you something as a reward for your help with that diamond business. No, don't even think of refusing. I'm convinced that your idea saved me my job – and my job, as you know, means everything to me. So hold out your hand. I'm serious now.'

Reynie's relief faded, replaced by a weird sense of dread. Uncertainly he held out his hand.

Captain Noland closed the cabin door – first looking up and down the passageway to be sure no one was coming – and reached into his pocket. He placed something hard and shiny into Reynie's palm and closed his fingers over it. 'Let's keep this between us, all right, son?'

'All right.' Reynie's heart was beating fast. 'Um . . . thank you, sir.'

'You're more than welcome,' said the captain, opening the door and once again looking both ways along the passage. He nodded and stepped aside. 'Good night, Reynie.'

Reynie wished the captain good night and went out. He hadn't yet opened his hand, which he now shoved deep into his pocket. He didn't want to look at what Captain Noland had given him, nor did he think he should show it to the others. He had caught a glimpse of it, of course, and there was no mistaking the feel of it in his hand. But Reynie didn't want to examine it closely. He didn't want to have his worst suspicions confirmed.

Two days left. Only two days, and the children had no idea how much farther this journey would take them – no idea whether two days would be enough.

These were Reynie's first troubled thoughts the next morning, and he was just moving on to *more* troubled thoughts (he seemed to have a growing supply) when Cannonball appeared and informed them that Captain Noland would not be coming ashore.

'Don't look so dismayed,' Cannonball said, bending to set a platter of toast and jam on the floor. 'I'm still going to accompany you myself. The captain's told me everything about your situation, and I'm sorry about your friends – really and truly sorry. But just you wait. We'll get them back safe and—'

'Captain Noland said both of you were coming,' Reynie interrupted. 'Why has he changed his mind?'

If Cannonball noticed the hint of accusation in Reynie's tone, he gave no indication. 'It's that bullfrog Pressius again. We were *supposed* to have a few days of festivities and celebrations in Lisbon. The captain intended to skip these and go with you. But now Pressius has informed the captain that he wants the *Shortcut* to return to sea at once – just to sail around for a couple days.'

'Why on earth would he want that?' Kate asked, moving the toast before Constance, who was rolling sleepily out of her bunk, could step on it.

'Those ridiculous diamonds,' said Cannonball with a roll of his eyes. 'Pressius is convinced that someone means to rob him. Once we're in the harbour, he's going to make a big show of opening the chest of decoys in front of all the reporters and crew members. He'll announce that the chest is being delivered to a private vault in England. In fact he's taking the *real* diamonds with him on the train to wherever he's going. That's why he insisted on all the extra security – this way he can send some guards along with the decoys to make his story seem authentic. Evidently it's been his plan all along. He just didn't see fit to tell the captain.'

'And of course Captain Noland can't refuse him,' Reynie said. What he really wanted to say was that the captain *wouldn't* refuse Mr Pressius. For a man who believed he owed Mr Benedict his life, Captain Noland certainly seemed unwilling to take many risks on his behalf.

'So what's next?' Sticky asked.

'We'll slip away while the ship's being unloaded, before the ceremonies begin,' Cannonball said. 'I'll have a radio with me. The captain wants us to stay in close touch. He still intends to help – he'll just have to do it from the ship.'

Reynie bit his tongue and looked away.

'What about Madge?' Kate asked. 'Can someone keep her for me? It wouldn't be for long, you know, only a couple of days . . .' She trailed off, suddenly solemn, for a couple of days *wasn't* long, and it was all they had to save their friends.

'I've already made the arrangements,' said Cannonball

154

kindly. 'Don't you worry. Madge will keep my cabin, and she'll be treated like a queen.'

The *Shortcut* was not due in port until late in the afternoon, which allowed the children plenty of time to bathe – an activity that had never seemed quite the luxury it did now. They'd gone a long time without changing clothes or even brushing their teeth, and their general dirtiness had begun to depress them, to say nothing of offending one another's noses. Cannonball had no fresh clothes to offer, but he could provide towels and soap, and he gave them his own half-flattened tube of toothpaste. So the children were able to get rid of the grime, at least, and they brushed their teeth with their fingers.

Afterwards they took turns looking out of the cabin's porthole. For most of the trip they had seen nothing but endless water and sky. But now, with the Portuguese mainland in the distance, they were able once again to appreciate the great speed of the *Shortcut*. The land seemed to transform from a hazy, indeterminate blur on the horizon to a fully-fledged coastline in a matter of seconds.

'It won't be long now,' Sticky said, stepping down from Kate's bucket. 'The port is just a few miles inland on the Tagus River. There's sufficient depth there for—' He stopped himself with a frown – he'd been about to launch into a long and technical speech – and simply said again, 'It won't be long now.'

When at last Cannonball came for them, he was carrying a shovel and was dressed in 'civilian' clothes, or at least he seemed to think so. He wore Bermuda shorts, sandals, and a loud floral-print shirt, and he had smeared his well-tanned face with sunscreen in an effort to make himself look like a tourist. Unfortunately the shirt, which he had borrowed from a shipmate, was no match for his barrel chest. No sooner had he entered the room than a button popped loose and skittered under Constance's bunk.

'I'll get it for you,' said Constance, with a readiness that took the other children by surprise. But then, her voice had quavered when she spoke, and when she emerged from beneath the bunk her expression was unmistakably anxious. She was trying to occupy herself however she could, for now that they'd arrived at this next stage of their journey, she found herself growing frightened.

Cannonball knelt beside her. 'You know what I like about buttons?' he said, taking the button from Constance and gazing at it admiringly. 'They're very small things that hold bigger things together. Awfully important, buttons – little but strong.' He winked and stood up again, leaving Constance with a calmer expression on her face, and having strengthened the good opinion the other children already had of him.

'Now here's the official stuff,' said Cannonball, unfolding a typed document stamped with all sorts of government seals. Reproduced on the back of it was a photograph of the children taken the year before. 'Mr Benedict sent this to the captain to give to you. It's like a passport, apparently, only better. You'll want to keep it secure.'

Kate took the document without thinking and slipped it into her bucket. Her friends didn't argue, for not only did Kate's bucket seem the safest place, the photograph was positively horrible of all of them, and no one cared to see it any longer than necessary.

'Only a minute now,' Cannonball said, holding his head

in an attitude of careful attention. He was listening to the ship's engines and looking out of the porthole at the docks below. The children could hear a brass band playing just beyond the bulkhead. 'There,' he said. 'Now we'll just scoot along.'

Cannonball and the children made their way up into brilliant sunlight, a warm breeze, and a shocking confusion of sound. The ship's deck and the docks below were in utter turmoil – throngs of people were cheering, music was playing, and streamers and confetti drifted everywhere on the breeze. All of Lisbon, it seemed, had come down to greet the record-setting cargo ship. The place looked like a carnival set upon the bank of the river.

By the energetic application of his elbows Cannonball got the children to their taxi, and shutting their doors against the clamour, they were all whisked away toward St. George's Castle. The cobbled streets wound sharply back and forth, maze-like, as the taxi passed through an old fishery district and rose higher and higher up the steep hill upon which the castle sat. With every other turn of the road the castle came into view again, larger each time, until at last they drew near the gated entrance to the grounds. Beyond the stone wall encircling the grounds the castle loomed impressively – but it was the wall that mattered to the children.

The taxi driver stopped the car and spoke to his passengers in accented English. 'Listen, I warn to you,' he said, turning in his seat. 'I do not know your plans, but they will not let you to dig here. I see the bucket and the shovel. But the castle is public grounds. The guards will – how do you say? – they will *throw you up.*'

'Throw us out?' Reynie suggested.

'Yes!' said the taxi driver, smiling. 'That is it! Throw you out!'

'Thanks for the warning,' said Cannonball. He paid the driver and asked him to wait.

For no good reason, Reynie had been imagining an abandoned ruin of a castle with no one around, but St. George's Castle was the exact opposite – a popular tourist site, with people streaming in and out. When he and the others had crossed the street and passed through the open gate, they found quite a lot of visitors milling about the castle grounds, which did resemble a lovely park, as Captain Noland had said. Tourists strolled through little thickets of shrubs, sat on benches, and paged through guidebooks, chattering and pointing at architectural features on the castle. A street musician played guitar and sang near a grove of olive trees. And surrounding everything was the stone wall, in some places low enough to sit on, in others high enough to cast long shadows over those walking below.

'We need to find the westernmost part, right?' Constance said. 'So which way is west?'

'That way,' Reynie said, pointing toward the late afternoon sun.

'Constance!' Sticky said in a reproving tone. 'Don't you know that the sun—'

Luckily Sticky's comment, which surely would have provoked a squabble, was interrupted by a garbled voice blaring from Cannonball's radio. Signalling the children to wait, the young sailor walked off to a quieter spot and spoke into his radio. When he came back he was clearly distressed.

'That was Captain Noland,' Cannonball said. 'The crowds have caused big problems with unloading the containers, and he needs my help sorting things out. Now please don't worry. It's a very quick business once it gets going, and I'm only needed at the start. I should be back within an hour – two at the most.'

'But what if you aren't?' Kate asked. 'We have to hurry, Cannonball! Our friends need us!'

'I know that,' Cannonball said gravely. 'I'm truly sorry, and so is Captain Noland. He said he begs your forgiveness.' He handed Kate his radio and the shovel. 'Start without me, all right? With luck I'll be back before you've even finished digging. Just radio the captain if you run into trouble, and I'll be back as quick as I can!'

With that Cannonball dashed away, but not before Reynie saw the expression on his face. He obviously felt horrible to abandon them and would never have done so had he not been following orders. Reynie shook his head and turned away. Kate put the radio inside her bucket, and with Constance riding piggyback the children set out for the westernmost part of the wall, which lay on the other side of the castle.

Weaving among scattered clusters of sightseers and picnickers, they hurried up a series of steps, crossed a narrow stone plaza, and followed a winding path through a shrub thicket, where their footsteps flushed several peafowl out from under the shrubs. The startled birds darted here and there among the children's feet, clucking and flapping with great agitation before fleeing back to the very shrubs from which they'd emerged.

'Silly, clumsy lot of birds,' muttered Kate, who had nearly

159

tripped over two of them. 'Madge would have a field day here.'

Beyond the thicket the path led the children to the corner of the castle, and just as they turned the corner they all drew up short, blinking in dismay. The westernmost wall lay a short distance from where they stood – but that was the only short thing about it. Indeed, it seemed to stretch on and on forever. Worse, there were people everywhere: people sitting on the wall gazing out over the city and the river below; people admiring the old black cannons set into the wall at regular intervals; people wandering about taking pictures on the grassy lawn between the wall and the castle. And not only were there people everywhere, there seemed to be olive trees everywhere, too. All of a sudden, Mr Benedict's directions seemed hopelessly difficult. Kate took out the paper to read them again:

Castle of Sticky's namesake
Against westernmost wall
Not visible
Need tool
Olive trees nearby
No cork or pine for two metres

'Well, *that's* not very helpful,' Kate said. 'There are olive trees 'nearby' the whole wall, and hardly a pine tree in sight. Which ones are the cork trees, Sticky? I haven't the faintest.'

Sticky pointed. 'There, that's a cork tree. And there and there. Only those few that I can see.'

'That makes for an odd clue, then,' said Reynie. 'Why

160

mention 'olive trees nearby' and 'no cork or pine for two metres' when that can be said of almost the entire wall? It doesn't narrow down the location a bit. Let me see that, will you, Kate?'

As Reynie studied the letter with furrowed brow, Kate shrugged and said, 'Maybe we should just start walking along the wall and see what we find. If Captain Noland's right, it'll be easy to spot where something's just been buried.' She looked around again at all the people. 'The hard part will be digging without getting noticed. If we had time to wait we could sneak back in at night. Maybe that's what Mr Benedict thought we'd do. Otherwise I can't see how he expected us to pull this off without getting in trouble.'

'Neither can I,' said Reynie, still studying the letter. 'Which is why I'm wondering—'

'Get back, everyone!' Constance said. She grabbed Kate's ponytail and jerked on it as if pulling on the reins of a runaway horse. 'Back! Back around the corner! It's Jackson! He's here!'

'What are you talking about?' Kate snapped, trying to pry Constance's fingers from her hair. 'That *hurts*, Con—'

'Do what she says, Kate!' said Reynie, grabbing her arm. 'Step back!'

Puzzled and irritated, Kate stepped back around the corner of the castle. She set Constance on the ground – none too gently – and said, 'This had better be good.'

Constance ignored her, instead looking up at Reynie with searching eyes. 'Why do you think he's here, Reynie? Do you think he knew we were coming? What should we do?'

Reynie put his hands on her shoulders. 'Just stay calm

and tell me what happened. Did you *see* Jackson? Or did you, you know . . .'

'I just suddenly knew. I could just tell.'

'Are you two talking about Jackson the *Executive*?' Sticky asked.

'The one and only,' said Reynie. He peered around the corner of the castle, studying all the people on the wall, near the cannons, on the grassy lawn . . . and then there he was, a swaggering young man stepping out of the shade of an olive tree. Jackson. Their old tormentor, one of Mr Curtain's trusted Executives. He'd seemed unfamiliar at first – he wasn't wearing the tunic and sash he'd always worn at the Institute – but it was him all right. That sharp, knife-like nose, the strutting walk, the stocky build and bright red hair.

Reynie could feel his heartbeat picking up speed. 'She's right. I see him.'

'You've got to be kidding,' Sticky said in a miserable tone. 'Here?'

Constance seemed shaken up. 'I probably just saw him and didn't realize it, right?'

'I'm sure that's what happened, Constance,' said Reynie, trying to sound calm. 'And lucky for us it did. He would have spotted us for sure. He's patrolling the wall.'

'Patrolling it?' Kate said.

'That's what it looks like,' said Reynie, peeking around the corner again. 'He's just pacing back and forth, like he's waiting for something.'

'Or some*one*,' Constance said.

'I knew it was too good to be true,' Sticky said, taking out his polishing cloth. 'And here I'd thought this part, at

162

least, was going to be easy.'

Kate's face darkened. 'Reynie, if Jackson's here . . .'

'Then Jillson's probably here, too. I know.'

If Jackson was dangerous alone, he was doubly dangerous with Jillson, his constant companion. The children had never determined if the two Executives were brother and sister, boyfriend and girlfriend, or simply partners in crime. They didn't even know them by any names other than Jackson and Jillson – which could have been first names, last names, or nicknames. But none of this mattered. What mattered was that Jackson stood between them and their mission, and that Jillson, no doubt, was lurking nearby.

'Constance,' Reynie said, 'do you have a feeling about Jillson?'

'Oh, yes, I hate her,' Constance said. 'Don't you?'

'I meant a feeling about whether or not she's *here*.'

'Oh. No. No, I would have told you if I had, wouldn't I? But that doesn't mean she isn't here. Maybe she's just on the other side of the castle.'

'Or maybe something terrible happened to her,' Kate suggested hopefully. 'She always tied her ponytail with wire, remember? Maybe she got struck by lightning!'

'I'll never understand how you can joke at times like these,' said Sticky, anxiously looking around.

'Who said I was joking?' said Kate. 'Anyway, if she shows up, we can deal with it, can't we? I'm sure I can handle her by myself – Jillson *or* Jackson, either one. With the three of you,' she glanced at Constance, 'well, the two and a half of you to handle the other one, we can probably win if it comes to a fight. At the very least we'll give them a run for their money.'

'It can't come to that, Kate,' said Reynie. 'I don't know why Jackson's here, but if he sees us he'll report it to Mr Curtain, and that will wreck everything. We can't afford for him even to *suspect* that we're here – not without putting Mr Benedict and Number Two in greater danger.'

'So what do we do?' asked Constance. 'How are we supposed to dig? How do we even find *where* to dig?'

Reynie quickly returned to the letter. He felt sure that Mr Benedict had provided an answer if only he knew how to find it. A lot of the directions seemed unimportant or unhelpful, so perhaps they were meant as distractions – like the extra words in the bottom corners of the journal pages. And what was this business about going *down* for their hint, then *up* to where the clues led them? Mr Benedict had written the clues at the bottom of the page, and they did lead uphill to the castle, but why say it like that? For that matter, why did he say 'hint' first – as if there were only one – and then 'clues', which implied *more* than one? Did Mr Benedict mean to suggest a difference between 'hint' and 'clues'? Why would he do that?

Sticky was growing more anxious by the second. It was all well and good for Kate to conjecture about 'handling' Jackson and Jillson – she was so quick she probably wouldn't get handled in return. But he wasn't Kate. He would almost certainly get handled, and just thinking about it was enough to make him sweat. 'Reynie?' he prompted. 'We need to hurry!'

'I know,' Reynie said, still poring over the letter. 'That's what's troubling me. I don't think Mr Benedict meant for us to spend hours searching for our next clue. He expected us to be able to go straight to it – and to recover it quickly, without getting caught. The secret has to be in the letter. It has to be!'

'So find it,' snapped Constance. 'Come on, Reynie, do your thing. Where do we dig?'

Reynie stared at the letter, desperately willing the answer to come to him – and suddenly it did. He started and looked up. 'I don't think we do.'

Constance scowled. 'We don't dig? But Captain Noland said—'

'I don't care what Captain Noland said,' Reynie interrupted, with a sharpness that surprised all of them. 'I'll bet we just have to scrape off some putty and paint. That's why we need a tool. Kate can use her Army knife for that.'

The others stared at him.

'You left out a part,' said Kate. 'What are we scraping putty and paint *from*?'

Reynie handed her the letter. 'Mr Benedict says to go down for the clue. He doesn't mean go down to the bottom of the page – he only wrote the hints down there as a distraction. He wanted to make it seem like he was just being playful: Go *down* for this, go *up* for that. But take a closer look. Go down the hints – read the first letter of each line.'

Kate did as Reynie said. Her eyes widened. Constance and Sticky crowded against her to see what she had seen. And there was the answer, plain as day.

AWKWARD EXCHANGES AND CLEVER DISGUISES

'I can't believe you didn't see that sooner,' said Constance with an incredulous snort. 'It's perfectly obvious!'

'Next time you might trouble to look at it yourself,' said Reynie, trying hard not to snap.

Kate glanced around the corner of the castle wall. 'It's the nearest one. The other cannons all have cork or pine trees within two metres.' (She could speak with perfect certainty given her talent for gauging distances.) Pulling out her spyglass, Kate popped off the kaleidoscope lens and took a closer look at the cannon.

'See anything unusual?' Reynie asked.

'Not yet.'

'Maybe it's down inside the barrel,' said Sticky.

'No, I think I see something now. Yes, that's it! There's a slightly darker area near the base of the cannon . . .' Kate lowered the spyglass and grinned. 'It's rectangular.'

'Like an envelope,' Reynie said.

Kate nodded. 'I think you were right. A little putty and paint and he was able to hide the envelope in plain sight.' She put away the spyglass and took out her Army knife. 'I can get it and be back here in fifteen seconds.'

'Shouldn't we do something to distract Jackson?' Sticky asked.

'Too risky,' said Kate. She slipped her bucket from her belt and set it down, then began untying her ponytail. 'Too many people around, too little time. Jillson could show up any second. I'll just need to go when he's facing the other direction.'

'I agree with Kate,' said Reynie. 'But listen, if he *does* look your way—'

'I'm one step ahead of you, pal.' Kate shook her head vigorously, then ran her fingers through her hair, teasing it up and forwards, until it stuck out on all sides and almost completely obscured her face. 'Sticky, can I borrow your glasses?'

Sticky cringed, but of course he couldn't refuse. 'Be careful with them, will you?'

'When am I ever not careful?' Kate said. She balanced the spectacles low on her nose so she could see over the rims. 'How do I look?'

Sticky squinted. 'Blurry.'

'Weird,' said Constance.

'Perfect,' said Reynie with an approving nod.

Kate untied one of her shoes and peeked around the corner again. 'He's still pacing. Same number of steps in both directions. Looks left, looks right, looks left again. I do like *that* about Jackson. He's predictable. Okay, I'm off!'

Reynie took Kate's place at the corner and watched her go. She walked quickly, but not so quickly as to draw attention to herself, and she even managed to appear slightly bowlegged. For a spur-of-the-moment disguise, it was pretty good. A wild-haired, bow-legged girl with an untied shoe, wire-rimmed spectacles – and no red bucket. If Reynie hadn't known better he might not have recognized her himself. He glanced toward Jackson, who was still walking in the other direction. So far, so good.

Kate swerved around a family that was approaching the cannon to take pictures, pretended to notice her untied shoelace, and knelt by the cannon's base to tie it – which she did with one hand. In the other hand Reynie saw her knife glint. There was no time to marvel at Kate's dexterity, though, for she was every bit as quick as she was dexterous. Already she had scraped the envelope free, tied her shoe, and was rising again, shoving the envelope and knife into her pocket with a triumphant smile. Then she hesitated. The mother in the family was speaking to her, holding out a camera, stepping in front of her. She wanted Kate to take the family's picture together.

'Oh no,' Reynie said.

'What's happening?' Constance hissed.

'Get ready to run,' Reynie said. He heard the other two suck in their breath.

Kate was shaking her head, feigning incomprehension. The mother had grabbed her arm, trying to make herself understood. Finally, with an apologetic smile and an artful twist of her arm, Kate got away. But it was a costly delay. Reynie knew it, and from the expression on Kate's face, she knew it too. She was walking purposefully, but she couldn't risk running. Reynie looked to see if Jackson had noticed her.

Jackson hadn't. But Jillson had.

There was no mistaking Jillson. Six feet tall, greasy brown ponytail, arms like jackhammers. She had just come around the far corner of the castle, and as she approached Jackson, she was pointing in Kate's direction. Her expression was not one of outright recognition, but it was clearly suspicious. Jackson turned to look just before Kate rounded the corner. Whether or not he recognized her Reynie couldn't say – he had to withdraw quickly to avoid being spotted himself.

'Did he notice me?' asked Kate.

'Jillson did,' Reynie said. 'We need to go.'

'Jillson?' Sticky cried.

Kate snatched the shovel from Reynie. 'Move it, then! Give Constance a ride. I'll meet you outside the gate.'

There was no time to argue or ask questions, nor even for Sticky to retrieve his spectacles. With Constance riding on Reynie's back and Sticky, squinting, following close behind, the three of them hurried down the winding path through the thicket, once again startling peafowl from under the shrubs. Across the plaza, down the steps, and toward the gate they ran, and as they ran Reynie looked back to see that Kate had herded several of the peafowl together and was shooing them around the corner of the castle. Even from this distance he could hear a young woman's angry cry of surprise – that would be Jillson – followed by a great clucking, cooing commotion.

Kate, meanwhile, was tossing the shovel like a spear into the middle of the thicket. Reynie glanced ahead at the gate – almost there – and when he glanced back, Kate was disappearing around the castle's farthest corner. Jackson and Jillson came around the other corner just as Reynie darted out through the gate.

'I don't think they saw us,' said Constance, who also had been looking back, 'but what if they ask around? A lot of people saw us running to the gate.' Indeed, some people were looking at them even now. A few were glancing about as if they were wondering where the children's parents were.

'I can't imagine either of them speaks Portuguese,' said Sticky. 'We'll have to hope they don't find someone who speaks English. Maybe they won't even think to ask. They aren't very clever, you know.'

As if to prove Sticky's point, a thwacking sound came from the direction of the thicket, followed by a loud oath. Jackson had stumbled upon the shovel Kate had put there for that very purpose. It sounded as if he'd stepped on the blade, causing the handle to fly up and strike him. The thought would have been amusing were Jackson's angry grumbling not growing louder and more distinct by the moment.

'Clever or not, they're coming this way,' said Reynie, staring anxiously at the gate. 'We need to get out of here. But Kate—'

'What about me?'

Everyone jumped and turned to see Kate grinning at them.

'Where did you come from?' Constance asked.

'I went over the far wall,' said Kate. She handed Sticky his spectacles. 'Listen, I heard them talking. They weren't sure who I was, but they're coming out to look around. Here, Reynie, you'd better let me carry Constance.'

The children took off, hurrying away from the castle. Down, down along the twisting cobbled street, weaving through pedestrians, crossing tiled plazas, down and down to where the street grew still more narrow and began to branch off into other streets and alleyways. They had come into the fishery district. The children stopped to catch their breath and get their bearings. Around them the odour of fish mingled with the more delicate scent of flowering bougainvillea, which draped the old stone walls. Locals and tourists brushed shoulders passing up and down the narrow street, and crowded in the doorways of little shops.

Reynie and Sticky were panting and clutching their sides. Sticky had dropped to one knee and was mopping his brow with his shirt.

'You guys are in awful shape,' observed Constance from her perch on Kate's back.

Kate was looking back up the way they'd come. The spyglass was of no use; the streets were too winding to allow her to see very far in any direction. But at least Jackson and Jillson weren't right behind them, which they had all half-feared.

'We don't even know where we're going yet,' Reynie gasped. 'We need to read the clue.'

They moved into an alley, huddling together behind a

171

stall in which rows of huge fish were stacked like logs. They would not be easily seen from the street. The fish vendor – a burly man wielding a cleaver – glanced at them, saw that they were only children, and returned to his task of lopping off fish heads.

Kate slit the envelope open with her Army knife. Inside was a note and a key. She glanced at the note. 'I can't make head or tail of this,' she said, handing the note to Sticky and directing her attention to the key. It was an ordinary metal key, smallish, with the number 37 engraved upon it. Kate took out her farm keys to compare with it, thinking she might deduce what sort of thing it unlocked. She suspected a cabinet, or no, a locker – this key was much like the one for the grain locker in the barn, and lockers, after all, were usually numbered.

Sticky, meanwhile, was reading the note aloud: '*This station word will train you to send the puzzle.*'

'What's a station word, anyway?' asked Kate.

'I've never heard of any such thing,' said Sticky. 'Maybe it's a—'

'The train station,' said Constance. 'Right, Reynie? *This word puzzle will send you to the train station.* That's the only possible answer!'

Startled, Sticky looked back and forth between Constance and the note in his hand. This new Constance – the one who could detect patterns and sense things others couldn't – took some getting used to.

'Looks right to me,' Reynie said.

'I'll bet this key opens a rental locker there!' said Kate. 'Quick, Sticky! Ask this man how to get to the train station!' She tapped the shoulder of the fish vendor.

Sticky blinked, opened his mouth, closed it again. The vendor looked at Kate, then at Sticky. He waved his cleaver impatiently and said something in Portuguese.

'I . . . I don't speak Portuguese,' Sticky said, and Kate cocked her head in surprise.

Constance looked positively disgusted. 'But on the ship,' she said, 'when Captain Noland asked you—'

'I can *write* it, though!' Sticky said, digging in his pocket for a pen. As the vendor watched – and the others exchanged troubled glances – Sticky turned Mr Benedict's note over and began to write. The vendor said something else in Portuguese. He made a writing motion with his hand, then shrugged and shook his head.

'He can't read,' Reynie said.

'Let me get this straight,' Kate said. 'Sticky can write Portuguese but can't speak it, and this fellow can speak it but can't read it.' She seemed uncertain whether to be frustrated or amused.

Sticky, meanwhile, seemed ready to cry.

Reynie stepped forward. 'Do you speak English?'

The man shrugged apologetically and turned away.

'*Español?*' asked Reynie. He had studied Spanish for a couple of years at the orphanage academy. Portugal bordered Spain, so just maybe . . .

'*Sí,*' the man said, turning back to him. '*Un poquito.*'

'What's he saying?' Kate asked.

'He speaks a little Spanish,' said Reynie, and he quickly asked the man where the train station was located. After a brief, difficult exchange (they both spoke rather clumsy Spanish), Reynie deduced that the station was only a short walk away. The man even agreed to draw them a map, and

173

with a few proficient strokes of the pen he rendered quite an excellent one on the back of Mr Benedict's note. He couldn't write the street names, but these he spoke aloud to Reynie, who thanked him heartily and turned back to the others.

The girls were already set to go, with Constance riding piggyback and Kate looking up and down the busy street to be sure Jackson and Jillson weren't around. Sticky was avoiding Reynie's gaze, but if he expected a complaint, he certainly wouldn't get it from Reynie. Now was hardly the time.

The train station was a bustling, crowded place, with several loading platforms all swarming with people. There was a constant babble of conversation and a barrage of rattling and clacking and hissing as trains pulled in and out of the station, and on top of all that were loudspeaker announcements that echoed everywhere. It was very difficult to hear anything clearly.

'Try again,' said Constance.

Kate again tried to contact Captain Noland on Cannonball's radio. But the squawk that came through its speaker was unintelligible, and for all she knew her own voice on the other end had sounded every bit as squawkish. Even if not, the noisy station might have made her words impossible to comprehend. There was no way to tell if the captain had understood her – or even if it was the captain who had responded. Kate turned the radio off to preserve its battery. They would have to try again later.

Constance scowled. 'You should have radioed from the castle, Kate.'

'If you remember,' Kate said lightly, 'I was a little busy helping us escape.'

Reynie said nothing. He had observed Kate's efforts to contact the captain with a strange mixture of hope and misgiving, and he thought it best to keep quiet until he worked out how he really felt.

Sticky came hurrying over from the ticket counter. 'I got directions,' he said, waving a piece of paper. 'The rental lockers are that way.'

The others followed Sticky through a door and down a short corridor. If the key didn't open a locker, the children had no idea how they were to decide where to go next, so it was with considerable anxiety that they watched Kate insert the key into Locker 37. She turned the key. The lock sprang open.

Inside the locker was an envelope and a stack of paper money. The bills were very colourful, nothing at all like the money the children were used to, and Constance regarded them sceptically. 'Fake money? Why would he give us fake money?'

'Those are euro banknotes,' Sticky said. 'They're common currency in Europe.'

'Okay, so it's real money,' said Constance. 'What are we supposed to buy with it?'

'Train tickets, I imagine,' said Reynie, opening the letter and reading it aloud:

You've used your gifts to come this far
(And done so most terrifically),
The next step also calls for gifts –
Constance's specifically.

* * *

'Me?' Constance said. 'What am I supposed to do? Predict the stupid weather?'

The others looked at one another, stymied.

'Maybe you should look around,' Reynie suggested. 'Maybe the answer will come to you.'

'Give me a break!' said Constance, feeling very much on the spot. She glanced up and down the corridor. 'I see lockers. That's it.'

'No patterns?' Sticky asked.

'Hmm. The lockers do seem to be arranged in numerical order,' Constance said sarcastically. 'I wonder if that's important.'

Kate had begun transferring the money from the locker to her bucket. 'You're joking,' she said, 'but maybe the numbers *are* significant.' She tapped the number on the locker door. 'Maybe '37' means something.'

'It probably means the first thirty-six lockers were taken when Mr Benedict rented this one,' said Constance.

'It isn't a bad idea,' said Reynie. 'Let's think about it.'

But no matter how hard they all thought about it, they couldn't find any significance in the number. Constance, meanwhile, began to pace back and forth. For Constance this was unusual behaviour (it was more like Reynie), and Reynie watched her closely, trying to imagine how Mr Benedict expected them to figure out this clue. If anyone was sensitive to Constance's volatile moods, Mr Benedict was. It seemed unlike him to put such pressure on her. True, he hadn't predicted so much would be riding on this clue, but even so, he probably hadn't intended for Constance to figure it out all by herself.

Constance had stopped pacing now, and Reynie suddenly realized she was staring hard at him.

'What's the matter?' he said.

'You're working this out,' Constance said. 'I can tell.'

'I am?' Reynie said. 'You can?'

Sticky and Kate exchanged glances. They could tell something important was happening.

'Maybe it's a look in your eye,' Constance said, 'or maybe it's your expression, or the way you breathe, or . . . I don't know. I can tell, though. You're about to come up with the answer.' She continued to stare at Reynie, her eyes searching now, half hopeful and half afraid.

Reynie tried to keep his composure. He knew Constance needed him to remain calm, but in fact his heart was racing. It was very strange indeed to have his thoughts revealed like that. For his thoughts on the matter *had* just shifted a little, had they not? He'd begun to broaden his perspective on the clue, to consider how he might look at it in a different way . . .

'There!' said Constance, just as Reynie's eyes widened and he opened his mouth to speak. 'You worked it out!'

Reynie's mouth snapped shut. He took a deep breath. 'Okay, that's pretty unsettling, Constance.'

'Tell me about it,' said Constance. 'Think how it is for *me*.'

Kate couldn't keep quiet any longer. 'What is it, then? What's the answer? Tell us, for crying out loud!'

'It's the pendant,' said Reynie, pointing to Constance's new necklace. 'Mr Benedict didn't mean 'gift' as in 'talent', he meant 'gift' as in 'present'!'

Kate laughed. 'Well, what do you know? Your present

was a clue in disguise! Come on, Constance, let's have a look!'

Constance unclasped the necklace and held the pendant in front of her, turning the miniature globe over and over in her fingers. She gazed at it sadly, admiring anew its rich greens and blues and its brilliant little crystal. 'The world is your oyster,' Mr Benedict had written in her birthday card, and now they all understood that he'd had more in mind than it first appeared. He'd been planning this exciting trip around the world, unaware of the danger into which he was about to fall – and into which Constance and the others would follow him.

Constance thrust the pendant toward Kate. 'Here,' she said in a choked voice. 'Look at it all you want.' She turned and walked a few paces down the corridor, visibly upset.

The others looked after her with concern, but there was little they could do to comfort Constance right now. They still had to work out where to go next, and it wasn't proving as easy as any of them hoped. The continents and oceans on the globe pendant were clearly depicted, but there were no markings anywhere to indicate a destination, and the crystal was set in the middle of the Pacific – no apparent help.

'Any thoughts?' Kate asked.

Reynie was scratching his head. 'Mr Benedict wrote that the world was her oyster, right? I think *this* oyster must have a pearl inside. The question is how we get to it. Maybe there's some kind of internal mechanism. Try pressing on the crystal.'

Kate pressed the crystal. Nothing happened. She tried moving it up and down like a switch, then twisting it like a dial. The crystal was firmly set, however, and wouldn't budge. She turned the globe, inspecting it carefully. There were no discernible seams, no secret hinges. Kate glanced down the corridor at Constance and whispered, 'Do you think we have to crack it open?'

Sticky grimaced. 'I hope not. She's upset enough as it is.'

'Mr Benedict wouldn't do that to Constance,' said Reynie. 'There must be some other way.'

'I could prise the crystal off with my knife,' Kate said. 'Maybe there's a hidden catch or something beneath it. We can have the crystal reset later.' She shrugged. 'Assuming, you know, that we survive long enough.'

Sticky covered his face. 'I hate it when you say things like that.'

'Can you do it without breaking the pendant or scratching it up?' Reynie asked.

'I think so,' Kate said. She peered closely at the edges of the crystal to see exactly how it had been set. 'Wait a minute, there seems to be something . . .' She held the crystal right up to one eye and closed the other. 'Whoa!'

Constance hurried back to them. 'What? What is it?'

Grinning, Kate handed her the pendant. 'That crystal's not exactly what it seems. Don't just look *at* it. Try looking *through* it.'

Constance covered one eye and held the pendant very close to the other. She started. 'Whoa!' She jerked the pendant away, looked at it as if she'd never seen it before, then brought it close to peer into the crystal again.

The crystal, as the boys soon discovered for themselves, was a magnifying glass. Looking through it revealed a map of Holland hidden inside the pendant. The map was smaller than a postage stamp but perfectly legible when seen through the crystal. A bright red X marked a city called Thernbaakagen, and at the bottom of the map was the name of a hotel and a street address.

'I saw that city on the schedule board!' Sticky said. 'There's a train leaving for there in ten minutes!'

'Then it's time to catch a train,' Reynie said.

As the members of the Mysterious Benedict Society hurried to catch their train, Jackson and Jillson – less hurried but every bit as purposeful – entered the station. With frowning faces they scanned the crowd. Neither was especially methodical by nature, and their search, at first, was haphazard. After a few minutes of fruitless looking, however, Jackson had the idea of starting at one platform and walking slowly along all the platforms until they reached the other side of the station. He told Jillson that this was what they would do.

'I don't like being told what to do,' said Jillson.

'Maybe not,' said Jackson. 'But you don't like making decisions, either.'

'That's true,' Jillson said, and she started walking, shoving aside a young businessman who dropped his newspaper and almost fell. 'So you tell me what to do, Jackson, but you don't tell me why. For the last time, why are we at the train station?'

Jackson ignored her. They had just come to the first platform. 'You look that way, into the station,' he said, pleased with himself for having devised a system, 'and I'll look this way, toward the platforms.'

Jillson grunted and did as Jackson said, but after passing

the first two platforms she still hadn't sighted the wild-haired bespectacled girl they'd seen at the castle, the one who'd behaved so curiously and looked so familiar. Then she remembered that Jackson had never answered her question. 'Hey,' she said, 'tell me why we're here or I'm going to club you.'

This time Jackson deigned to answer. 'Because Benedict came here, Jillson. Don't you remember? He and that nervous-looking woman came here on the same morning they went to the castle.'

'Of course I remember. But so what?'

'So they came and left without catching a train. And they never *did* catch a train. They left on a plane. Which means they were up to something at this station, Jillson, something other than catching a train.'

Jillson stared blankly at him. 'That's it?'

'*Yes*, that's it,' Jackson said irritably. 'Besides the castle, this is the only place in the city that we know is connected to Benedict. If we saw someone suspicious hurrying away from the *first* place, and we didn't find her on the street, don't you think we ought to look around the—'

As Jackson was talking they came to the next platform, where a train was about to pull away. The platform was empty now – all the passengers had boarded – except for one girl who leapt aboard the last car just as the train began to move.

A blonde girl with a bucket. Jackson stopped in his tracks. 'I just saw Kate Wetherall get onto that train!'

'So did I,' said Jillson, who'd forgotten that her job was to look away from the trains and into the crowded station. And because she wasn't looking in that direction, she failed

181

to see a businessman emerge from the crowd and come to stand behind her and Jackson.

This businessman was not the young fellow Jillson had shoved aside earlier. This businessman carried a briefcase, and he wore an expensive suit, expensive cologne, and two expensive watches – one on each wrist. Had Jillson seen *this* man earlier, it would never have occurred to her to shove him.

'Kate Wetherall,' Jillson was saying. 'Well, well, well. It did look like her. But can we be sure? I don't want to report it if we're not sure. He hates it when we make mistakes, you know.'

'Can we be sure?' Jackson mimicked with a sneer. 'What other girl in the world carries a bucket wherever she goes, Jillson? It was Kate Wetherall, without a doubt. Let's find out where that train is headed, and then . . .'

Jackson stopped talking. He stiffened. He had caught the scent of expensive cologne. Jillson, noticing Jackson's odd demeanour, likewise stiffened. Together they turned and discovered the businessman standing behind them. The man looked serious, but his eyes displayed an obvious satisfaction, even pleasure. Setting down his briefcase, he placed one hand on Jackson's shoulder, the other on Jillson's.

'Good work,' he said. 'Now come with me.'

PROMISES and REPRIEVES

Because the train journey would take all night, the children had reserved a sleeping compartment, and the first thing Constance did upon entering it was fling herself upon a lower bunk to rest. This was not the irritating behaviour it used to be when the others hadn't known Constance's age. For a three year old, even riding piggyback all afternoon could prove exhausting, to say nothing of being constantly worried and in constant distress. In truth, all of them were worn out – even Kate. But Kate was not one to let fatigue slow her down much.

The moment she closed the door behind her, she popped

open her bucket and took out Cannonball's radio. 'It's quieter in here,' she said. 'With luck we'll still be in range.'

Reynie stood at the compartment window, his hands in his pockets. The train was still in the city, and he could see the setting sun reflected in the windows of passing buildings. It would soon be dark. The children would soon have left far behind them the city, the port, and the ship that had carried them here. In his pocket Reynie could feel the present Captain Noland had given him. He'd never looked closely at it, but with every passing minute he felt more convinced of its significance.

'May I see that radio, Kate?' he asked.

Kate gave him a quizzical look. Something in Reynie's tone had struck her oddly. It wasn't a tone he had ever used with her, and she couldn't guess what it meant. She handed him the radio. 'What's going on? You sound funny.'

Reynie opened the window and tossed the radio out.

'What in the world?' Kate cried. 'Why'd you do that?'

Constance sat up to stare at him, and Sticky ran to the window to look out, as if the radio might have fallen somewhere he could reach. It hadn't, of course, and he stared after it, shaking his head in disbelief.

'I don't want him to know where we are,' said Reynie. 'The captain. I don't trust him.'

Sticky was still gazing forlornly out of the window. That radio – their one connection to adults who might protect them – had been a source of comfort. 'I wish you'd discussed it with us first, Reynie.'

'I'm sorry. I was afraid you would argue.'

'You were being crafty!' Kate said. '*That's* what your tone meant. No wonder I didn't get it. I've heard you be that way

184

with other people, but never with us. I have to say, I don't like it.'

'Sorry,' Reynie said again. His tone was weary. He sat down on the bunk opposite Constance's. His body felt leaden, as if he'd gained a hundred pounds.

'Reynie,' said Constance quietly.

With a feeling of great reluctance, Reynie looked up. 'Yes?'

Constance's pale blue eyes were shining with tears, and in them Reynie detected something like alarm. 'The way you're feeling about Captain Noland right now? I don't ever want to feel that way about you.'

Reynie felt tears spring to his own eyes. He looked away.

'Don't ever do that again,' Constance said. 'Promise me.'

Reynie swallowed hard. He forced himself to meet her eyes again. Then he looked at Kate and Sticky, who were gazing at him wonderingly and with not a little hurt of their own. It would be awful for them to feel they couldn't trust him, Reynie knew. For Constance it would be even worse. But it would be worst of all for him.

'I promise,' Reynie said.

And from the way Constance smiled, he knew that she knew that he meant it.

Reynie awoke early the next morning with a prickling of uneasiness. He had neglected to consider something, but his mind hadn't settled on whatever it was. Opening his eyes he discovered Sticky awake and likewise looking troubled. He stood at the compartment window, staring out at the grey sky with a furrowed brow.

'Our last full day,' Sticky murmured when he saw Reynie

was awake. 'Tomorrow's the deadline.'

Reynie nodded gravely. 'Where are we?'

'Holland. I just saw a sign.'

They had slept through most of Portugal and all of Spain, France, and Belgium. This came as no surprise to Reynie, for extreme weariness had sent all of them crashing into sleep the evening before – they hadn't even made it to dinner. The others had already been yawning when they tried to question Reynie about Captain Noland, only to be interrupted by the arrival of the conductor asking for their tickets. Surprised to find the children travelling alone, the conductor had required some made-up explanations, and by the time of his exit they were all completely done in. They scarcely managed to mutter goodnight before collapsing into their bunks.

At the sound of the boys' voices the girls came awake, Constance looking grumpy with one eyelid half-matted shut, Kate looking quite refreshed as she stretched and tied her ponytail. They rose and joined Sticky at the window, gazing out at the flat, unfamiliar landscape. None of them had ever been to Holland before. There truly were windmills here, and canals, and as the train entered a city they saw lovely old buildings that seemed impossibly narrow, as if they'd been squeezed from the sides. Sticky said the staircases in the buildings were often so narrow and twisty that upstairs furniture had to be hoisted by ropes and brought in through windows. Constance said she was too hungry to care about furniture – that it could be assembled by elves, for all she cared – and that if Sticky wanted to offer *useful* information, perhaps he could tell her where to find the dining car.

'Good morning, Constance,' said Reynie.

They were all hungry – famished, in fact – and in the dining car they ordered so much food that their waiter raised his eyebrows and asked to see their money first. They had more than enough to stuff themselves silly, however, and so they did. Afterwards Sticky said he had something to do and would join them later.

'He's looking for someone to show off to,' said Constance as they returned to their compartment.

'Go easy on him,' said Kate. 'He can't always help himself, you know. I imagine if you know as much as Sticky does, it's hard not to let some of it slip on occasion. Don't you think, Reynie?'

Reynie was at the window, deep in thought. 'Hmm? Oh, yes, probably so.'

'Okay, what's on your mind?' Constance asked him. 'You look funny. I mean more than usual.'

'I've been feeling uneasy about something,' Reynie said, 'and I just realized what it is. If Captain Noland heard you on the radio, Kate – which we can't be sure about – then it wouldn't take much detective work for him to figure out where we're headed. You said we were at the train station. If Captain Noland described us to the ticket agents, they could tell him we bought tickets for Thernbaakagen.'

Kate shrugged. 'So? I know you don't trust him, Reynie – and maybe he isn't the most reliable person we know – but he's Mr Benedict's friend. He has no reason to try to stop us.'

'Maybe not,' said Reynie, who couldn't shake the worry that the captain's loyalty might be swayed – for the right price. 'But even if he wants to help us, can we trust him to make the right decision? What if he decided to tell the police? He might think we need protection. For all we know, the police are waiting at Thernbaakagen to take us into custody. If that happens, we'll never be able to help Mr Benedict and Number Two.'

'You have a point,' Kate admitted. 'What are you suggesting?'

'We should get off the train,' Reynie said. 'Just to be safe. We get off at the next-to-last stop, before we reach the main station.'

Kate and Constance thought this a sensible plan. It certainly wouldn't hurt to be cautious. But they still wanted to know why Reynie was so doubtful about Captain Noland.

'It doesn't matter now, does it?' said Reynie, who felt sad, and not a little guilty, for mistrusting Mr Benedict's friend. Maybe he couldn't help how he felt about the captain, but he could at least avoid speaking ill of him.

'I suppose it doesn't matter,' said Kate in a stern, unforgiving tone, 'seeing as how you chose to cut off all contact with him.'

Reynie looked at the floor. 'I really am sorry for behaving that way. I know it was inexcusable, and—'

Kate snickered and slapped his arm. 'Good grief, Reynie, I was just giving you a hard time! As if anyone could hold a grudge against you!'

'I could,' said Constance, glowering at him. Then she, too, slapped his arm, apparently for the fun of it.

Reynie hurried out to find a train schedule, and consulting it together the three of them determined to get off at a town called Naansemegen, which lay just at the outskirts of Thernbaakagen. From there they would take a bus or taxi to their hotel. They still had enough money for that, Reynie said, and he was about to suggest they buy a street map of the area when to their great surprise Sticky arrived carrying just such a map.

Apparently – or so Sticky reported when they pressed him – he'd written out a request in every language common to western Europe (despite his slight misrepresentation to the captain, he truly did know how to read most languages, if not how to speak them) and shown it to passenger after passenger until someone finally gave him the map. 'I promised to return it before the next stop,' he said. 'Meanwhile I thought we could all take a look.'

Reynie noticed that Sticky did not say what he might have said, which was that he could easily memorize all the streets and intersections on the map by himself. No doubt he intended to do just that – or had already done so – but was trying to be careful about how he presented himself.

'I also learned something else,' said Sticky. 'There's a science museum in Thernbaakagen. I can show you where it is on the map.'

'Outstanding!' Reynie cried, eagerly spreading the map on the floor. 'You've been busy, haven't you?'

'I did have to ask a lot of people,' Sticky said.

'You think it's the same museum Mr Benedict was going to?' asked Kate, peering over his shoulder at the map.

'It seems pretty likely,' Reynie said. 'Why else would he lead us to this particular city?'

After Sticky had shown them where the museum was located – it lay near the outskirts of the city – he traced his finger along a main thoroughfare, then tapped it at an

189

intersection near the middle of the map. 'Our hotel is here. Downtown.'

Reynie nodded. 'So we should go to the museum first.'

'What's all this stupid talk about the museum?' Constance snapped. 'What about the next clue?'

'For all we know,' Reynie replied, trying hard to be patient, 'Mr Benedict never had a chance to leave the next clue. Maybe there's something for us at that hotel and maybe there isn't. We have no idea when or where he was captured. The museum is a lead, Constance. We need to go there, and because it's closer we should go there first, to save time.'

Constance blinked a few times as Reynie's words settled on her. 'I see,' she said. 'That hadn't occurred to me.' And with a quivering lip she shuffled to her bunk and lay down with her eyes closed, her fingers wrapped around her pendant.

The others looked at one another in confusion. What was so upsetting about having a lead? Wasn't that good news?

'Constance, what's the matter?' Kate asked. 'We'll be there soon, you know.'

'I know,' Constance murmured.

'So what's the problem?'

'The problem is what if there *isn't* anything at the hotel?' Constance cried. 'And what if we can't find out anything at the museum? Then it's all over! We'll be at the end of the road, and we won't have saved them!'

Reynie felt like kicking himself. He should have been more careful choosing his words. Constance had been worried enough as it was.

'Listen to me, Constance,' said Kate in a commanding

tone. Constance fell silent at once and listened with grave attention – as did the two boys. It wasn't like Kate to speak so seriously.

'Look at Reynie,' said Kate.

Constance looked at Reynie, who wasn't sure why he was being looked at but did his best to appear confident and resolute.

'Look at Sticky,' said Kate.

Constance did, and under her searching gaze Sticky felt a tremendous urge to polish his spectacles. He resisted, instead giving her a small, sober nod.

'Now look at me,' said Kate.

Constance did – and was almost startled by what she saw. Kate seemed to have doubled in size. She had drawn back her broad shoulders and set her jaw, and something in her stance called to mind the contained ferocity of a lioness. But it was the fierceness in Kate's bright blue eyes that had the most striking effect. The sort of look that made you thankful she wasn't your enemy.

'It's not going to be over,' Kate said firmly, 'until we *say* so.'

When the train pulled into the station, a well-dressed man carrying a briefcase stood in the shadows, waiting. He watched the passengers disembark, keeping an eye out for a blonde girl with a bucket. No such girl appeared. The man's face darkened, and he stepped out of the shadows and boarded the train. Passing methodically through the cars, he checked every seat, every compartment, until he reached the last one.

The train was empty. Turning on his well-polished heel,

the man strode quickly back to the front, where he found the conductor telling jokes to one of the porters. The conductor saw the look in the man's eye and stopped talking, his smile frozen upon his face. A minute later the man exited the train with the information he needed.

The children had got off in Naansemegen.

At that very moment, the children in question were sailing down the streets of Naansemegen on bicycles. They had been looking for the bus stop outside the station when Sticky noticed a sign advertising bicycles for hire. There had been no need for debate, nor even any hesitation. The sun was shining; they had enough money; they hired the bicycles.

Constance rode in a metal basket on the front of Sticky's bike, her legs dangling over the basket edge. The metal pinched her and she felt considerably squashed, but she wasn't complaining. She'd never ridden on a bicycle before and was experiencing, for the very first time, that rare and wonderful sensation of soaring that can occur – especially on a cool, sunny day, and especially when no pedalling is required. For Constance the ride was like coasting down one long, gentle hill, with the breeze fluttering in her ears. She even rather liked her helmet, a sparkly red dome that made her look like a lollipop.

It was impossible not to smile.

Reynie, Sticky, and Kate were smiling, too. They couldn't help themselves. As their bicycles picked up speed, the worries and fears that had burdened them for days seemed to lift away, rising like vapour into the blue sky. However brief their ride might prove to be, it was a reprieve, an escape from their serious concerns, and it was perfectly glorious.

There was a great deal of bicycle traffic in Naansemegen – more so even than car traffic – and so whenever possible the children cut through parks, alleys and side streets. Kate, naturally, was in the lead, and from time to time she would whip her bike around to face the others, beaming at them as she rode backwards, then whip it forwards again and speed ahead.

'That's why I'm riding with *you*,' Constance said to Sticky, who had already guessed as much. If he were Constance, he wouldn't have wanted to ride with Kate, either. But it wasn't lost on Sticky that Constance had insisted on riding with him specifically. He'd taken her demand as a gesture of friendship, a sort of peace offering, and so despite the extra effort it required of him, he had agreed without complaint.

Riding behind them, Reynie could hear Sticky and Constance talking, and he felt encouraged. The last thing those two needed was friction between them – more friction than usual, at any rate. Not when the hardest part of their journey still lay ahead. For Reynie had a strong suspicion that things were about to get extremely difficult indeed, not to mention more dangerous. Jackson and Jillson obviously had been posted at the castle to look out for something, which suggested still more sentries would be posted along the trail of clues.

Reynie frowned. Just like that, the old dread had settled back down upon him. Not ten seconds ago he'd been enjoying the bike ride and feeling pleased to see Sticky and Constance getting along. Now he was thinking about the

193

Ten Men again. The reprieve had been very brief indeed.

'Left!' called Sticky.

Ahead of them, Kate turned left. They had used the borrowed map to determine their route and were relying on Sticky's memory to account for detours. And now that path led them over a canal bridge, out of Naansemegen and into Thernbaakagen. There was no obvious distinction between the two places – Naansemegen being little more than an extension of the larger town – but as the children passed down yet another street of tall, narrow houses, they found that their moods had changed even if the landscape had not.

In Naansemegen they had been *going* somewhere that might prove dangerous. In Thernbaakagen, they had arrived.

The science museum in Thernbaakagen was an old, narrow, elegant brick building, four storeys high, and set off the street by a little stone courtyard. On a bench in the court-yard a bald man sat smoking a pipe and reading a newspaper. A white bandage covered the crown of the man's head – it looked as if he were wearing a doll's cap – and a badge on the breast of his tweed jacket indicated he was a museum employee. When the children pushed their bicycles through the gate, he looked over his paper at them, raised his eyebrows sceptically – no doubt he thought they should be in school – and returned to his reading.

In the museum lobby, the children passed an anxious-looking security guard on their way to the information desk, which was staffed by a dour woman with a recently stitched cut on her cheek and a cast on her left arm. (Reynie wondered if she and the man outside had been in an accident together.) The woman gave the children a brochure and asked them a question in Dutch. Sticky had prepared for this; he handed the woman a note that said they were American exchange students on a field trip. With a grunt, the woman took the first brochure back and gave them one written in English. The museum was free and open to the public, the brochure said. Its exhibits occupied the first three floors, and its library was on the top floor. The children followed a sign to the lift.

Reynie's heart gave a lurch when he entered the library. He loved it instantly, as he did all libraries, but more than this the room – with its dark wooden tables and creaking floorboards – reminded him of the old public library back home, where he and Miss Perumal had spent many an hour walking the aisles. Until now Reynie had tried hard not to think about Miss Perumal. She must be so worried about him . . .

Reynie felt Constance squeeze his hand. It was very quick – she let go almost at once – but it was a kind gesture, and one that reminded him that Constance noticed a great deal more than might be supposed. *Especially with me*, Reynie thought. He must remember to be careful what he said, and even what he allowed himself to think. Constance relied on him. He knew that now.

The museum library's collection was entirely for reference – nothing could be checked out – and except for a few dictionaries and encyclopaedias, all the books and other materials were stored in back rooms, to be retrieved by librarians upon request. The children approached the librarian's desk and Sticky handed a note to the librarian, who had been watching them with interest. They were the only people in the library, and no doubt she rarely saw children here, especially on a school day and without a chaperone. A cheerful-looking young woman with lustrous blonde hair and hazel eyes, the librarian read Sticky's note with an expression of growing wonder.

'Did you write this yourself?' she asked Sticky in English. She looked extraordinarily impressed. 'Your Dutch is excellent. But you do not speak it well? You would prefer to speak English?'

'Yes, please,' Sticky said.

'Good, then,' said the librarian with a friendly smile. 'Most Dutch people speak English, you know.'

Sticky hastened to say that he certainly did know this and that he had written the note merely as a precaution – after all, recent surveys indicated that around fifteen percent of Dutch citizens did *not* speak English, and . . .

Constance rolled her eyes. 'Recent surveys,' she muttered, loud enough for Sticky to hear.

Sticky fell abruptly silent. He shot Constance an angry look.

The librarian, however, smiled at him again. 'My, but you are studious! This must explain why you are here in the library on such a beautiful afternoon. My name is Sophie, children. Now let me see,' she said, returning to the note. 'You are requesting some papers, yes? Special holdings?'

'I explained more on the other side,' Sticky said.

Sophie flipped the paper over. Her eyebrows drew together into a frown. She looked up at the children, then at the door behind them, then back at the note. Her frown deepened. 'I find this very troubling, children. I would like to know what is happening.'

196

Sticky looked nervously at Reynie, who said, 'What do you mean? What would you like to know?'

Sophie regarded him with anxious eyes. 'Why is there all this interest in these papers?'

'All this interest?'

Sophie studied him. 'Could it be a coincidence?' She shook her head. 'And yet you seem like nice children.'

'We *are* nice,' Kate insisted. 'We don't know what you're talking about. What's the big deal about the papers?'

'People are being hurt,' Sophie said gravely, 'because of these papers you wish to see.'

The Duskwort Papers

Often the best way to avoid answering questions is to ask them yourself, and Reynie was quick to do just that. 'We were hoping you could tell us more,' he said to Sophie. 'What exactly has been happening?'

'But I thought you said you knew nothing,' said Sophie, looking confused.

'We heard there was trouble. We wanted to know what *kind* of trouble.'

'I am not sure that I wish to discuss it,' said Sophie, more guarded now. 'It is very unpleasant for me.'

'Please,' said Kate. 'Please help us.'

Sophie gave her a searching look. 'Help you? I do not see how . . .' She sighed and ran her fingers distractedly through her hair. 'Very well. It is nothing you cannot read in the newspaper. Many people wanted to see these materials last week. Some of them . . . men in suits, with little hard bags . . . what do you call them in English? Shortcases?'

'Briefcases,' Sticky suggested grimly.

'Yes. Briefcases. These men did something to the security guard. He is in the hospital now. Some of the museum staff tried to help him. They also are in the hospital now. Everyone is in the hospital except for three of us, who were hurt not as much. We are all afraid now, though. There is a new security guard, but he is afraid too.'

'Did the men steal the papers?' Reynie asked, fearing her response.

'No, because they are fools,' Sophie said bitterly. 'They demanded to see the papers, and when I did not answer fast enough – they were very frightening, you see – they hurt me so that I was not awake. What is the word? Unconscious? They made me unconscious, and when I opened my eyes they were still trying to find the papers. They did not understand how we organize the library, you see. They were angry and creating a bad mess. But there were sirens in the street. The police were coming, and the men decided they must leave. I shouted at them as they left: 'It is a free and public library! All you had to do was ask!"

Sophie shuddered. 'The men, they . . . they shocked me' – she made motions with her hands, as if to show something flying out of her wrists – 'with little wires.' She quickly covered her eyes. It was evident she was trying not to cry.

Constance stepped close to the desk and said quietly, 'I know how that feels, Sophie.' The others looked at her in surprise. They had agreed not to divulge any information about themselves. Reynie in particular had insisted they trust no one and give nothing away. Now Constance had admitted outright that they'd encountered Ten Men before, and therefore must be involved in this unpleasant business. It would be a miracle if they weren't in police custody within the hour.

Sophie had lowered her hand to look wonderingly at Constance, who said, 'The watches and the wires. I know how it feels. They shocked me, too.'

Sophie gazed at Constance without speaking. Then she reached across the desk – she had to stretch a good deal – and placed a hand gently against the tiny girl's cheek. Constance, who usually bristled at so much as a pat on the hand, did not withdraw or even flinch. She returned Sophie's sympathetic gaze with an expression of gratitude and mutual understanding.

'I am sorry,' Sophie said. 'Please, children, go and sit at a table. I do not understand your true reasons, but I will bring you these papers.'

They chose a table at the opposite end of the room, away from the librarian's desk, so that they might speak in low voices and not be overheard. Sophie emerged from a back room carrying a journal and a thin stack of papers in a protective envelope. She placed the journal on the table and carefully removed the papers from the envelope. The top page was covered in handwriting, and not surprisingly it was written in Dutch.

'We can speak again afterwards, if you wish,' Sophie said. 'As for these . . .' She laid a finger on the papers. 'I must ask you to be careful and to keep everything in sight on the table, where I can see it from my desk. It is the policy now, for the protection of the materials. I hope you understand. It is not that I do not trust you.'

The children assured Sophie they understood. She returned to her desk, where they could see her taking slow breaths to calm herself, even as she kept a dutiful, watchful eye on them across the room.

The journal, an old, warped, cheaply constructed book, was held together by a binding, which, given its deteriorated state, was rather more of an idea of a binding than an actual one. The other papers were equally decrepit, all quite yellow with age, and some of them as fragile as onion skin. Not without trepidation, Sticky slid the pile closer to him. The others watched with keen attention. Sticky gave his spectacles a once-over with his polishing cloth, and then – carefully, anxiously – he opened the journal.

It was a strange business watching Sticky read. His eyes hardly seemed to move, for they absorbed great blocks of writing all at once. He would stare at a page for the space of a breath or two, then turn it. Stare, breathe, turn again. At this rate he would finish the journal in minutes, the other papers in just a few minutes more. But Sticky recorded information at a considerably faster pace than he understood it, and once he did understand he sometimes had difficulty summarizing it. He would probably need some time to order his thoughts.

They needed to be patient, Reynie reminded himself, despite the feeling that a Ten Man might burst through the door any moment. They mustn't put too much pressure on Sticky. When he was flustered, Sticky was capable of becoming very agitated and confused. He was less susceptible to such states these days, but the possibility still existed. It had long been a source of embarrassment for him.

Even as he was contemplating this, though, Reynie noticed a subtle shift in Sticky's demeanour. At first it was difficult to place. Sticky, marking a spot in the journal with his finger, had begun to examine the other papers. 'Letters,' he said, glancing up at the others. He studied the topmost letter with great seriousness, then set it aside and returned to the journal, first adjusting his spectacles with a casual, scholarly, almost absent gesture. Almost absent, but not entirely. And now Reynie understood: Sticky was feeling his importance.

It was clear to Reynie that Sticky had been struggling with his ego ever since they met up again at Kate's farm, and Reynie was inclined to forgive his fits of vanity. The boys had been through a great deal together, and Reynie thought he knew Sticky's heart as well as anyone's – knew, in fact, that it was nobler and braver than most. Sticky was a skittish and fearful child, yet he always ended up doing the right thing, no matter how frightening it was. In Reynie's opinion, this made Sticky one of the bravest people he'd ever met. If he occasionally acted like a peacock, it was not such a grave offence, and at any rate Sticky could generally count on Kate and Constance to pluck his feathers.

Sticky soon finished his reading. He pursed his lips and removed his spectacles, evidently deep in thought. Staring into an unseen distance, he polished the spectacles, put them on again, and with a deep, thoughtful breath began rubbing his chin in exactly the same way Reynie often did. Reynie felt suddenly seized with irritation – so much for forgiveness – but he held his tongue, determined not to rattle Sticky out of thinking clearly.

Constance, however, climbed down out of her chair (her arms were too short to reach Sticky from where she sat), stepped over to him, and swatted his hand with all her might. She struck the hand Sticky was using to rub his chin, and the sting of her blow as well as his surprise caused Sticky to jerk the hand up and away, knocking loose his spectacles. Kate reached out, quick as a wink, and caught them – and with the other hand she caught Constance, who was rearing back for another swat.

'Get over yourself!' Constance hissed as Sticky blinked at her in blurry-eyed alarm. 'Stop looking for glory and give us the story!'

Sticky's face turned sullen. 'I was trying to think of how to explain it in English,' he said, taking his spectacles from Kate. You can't just hit people when you're dissatisfied, Constance.'

'Watch me!' Constance said, trying to writhe free of Kate's grip.

'Constance,' Reynie said sharply. He jerked his head toward the librarian's desk, where Sophie had risen from her chair and was staring at the children with concern. He waved at Sophie. 'It's okay. Sorry. We're fine.' And when Sophie, doubtful, sat down again, he murmured, 'You two can fight all you want later. Right now let's just get through this, okay?'

Sticky and Constance glared at each other, but eventually they nodded, and Constance climbed back up into her chair. After Sticky had taken a moment to regain his composure (but only a moment this time, and without any puffery), he told them what he'd learned: the journal had belonged to Mr Benedict's mother, Anki Benedict, while the letters were from her sister in America – Mr Benedict's aunt – and from a fellow scientist, a close friend of Mr Benedict's parents named Han de Reizeger.

'What I've read explains a lot,' Sticky said. 'For one thing, the Benedicts weren't expecting twins. Anki makes several references to the 'baby' coming – one baby, not two – and that if it was a boy they would name him Nicolaas.' Sticky pointed out the name in the journal. 'Obviously the aunt changed the spelling later.'

'Obviously,' said Constance in a mocking tone.

Sticky twitched but made no response to this. 'There are no entries after the birth,' he said, 'which explains why the museum didn't know about a twin. Only Mr Benedict was contacted about these papers, though obviously Mr Curtain has found out about them.' (He stiffened, anticipating another mocking remark, but this time Constance refrained.) 'Those Ten Men may not have got their hands on the journal, but somehow Mr Curtain knows what Mr Benedict discovered in it, which is that their parents may have found a cure for narcolepsy—'

'Really?' cried Reynie and Kate together.

'It's possible,' Sticky said, 'but not certain. There's a rare plant—'

'A rare plant!' Kate exclaimed.

'You mean like the 'rare plant' Mr Curtain mentioned in

his letter?' asked Constance.

Sticky pressed his lips together tightly. It is difficult to explain anything when one is constantly interrupted, and yet Sticky felt he couldn't say so without being accused of haughtiness.

Reynie came to his rescue. 'Sorry, we need to let you finish, don't we? Go ahead, Sticky.' The girls, following Reynie's lead, assumed attentive expressions.

'Okay,' Sticky said. 'Let me go back a little. Apparently Mr Benedict's parents had narcolepsy. Not just one of them. Both of them.' Sticky turned to a passage in the journal. 'Anki writes here that despite having grown up feeling cursed, she and her husband now feel blessed, because it was their shared condition – and their scientific interest in it – that led them to meet.

'She goes on quite a bit about how well they work together, with each of them always on the alert for the other, since they rarely fall asleep at the same moment. And I have to say, they were both pretty amazingly brilliant. They were planning several impressive research projects – all they lacked was the money to get started – and they'd already published a few papers on narcolepsy. But those papers had nothing to do with this rare plant. The plant doesn't enter the picture until near the end of the journal – near the end of their lives, I suppose – when they received this letter.'

Handling them with care, Sticky set aside three sheets of paper from the bundle (the last of which, Reynie had already noticed, had a rectangular space cut out of its middle). 'This letter is from their scientist friend, Han de Reizeger. He wrote to tell them that he'd found living

205

specimens of *translucidus somniferum* – otherwise known as duskwort – previously believed extinct.'

Sticky hesitated. 'I . . . I can tell you a little bit about that plant, if you're interested. I mean I've read about it before.'

'Of course we're interested, you lunkhead!' Kate said, laughing. 'Are you kidding? That plant's the key to this whole business!'

'Well, it's just that sometimes . . .' Sticky shrugged. 'All right. Ahem. Duskwort appears in a few ancient texts, but only a few. It was supposed to be extremely powerful – the slightest taste of it could put people to sleep – and was often considered the stuff of legend. There's an old Norse tale about a party of Vikings storming into a village on a foggy afternoon, only to discover every single inhabitant asleep. Not in their beds, either, but on the ground, against walls, slumped over worktables – everywhere.

'The Vikings were so unnerved that they didn't touch anything. They just walked through the village, staring at all the sleepers. On the far side of the village they found a boy lying next to a smouldering cooking fire clutching a tiny fragment of duskwort. Evidently he'd thrown some into the coals, and the smoke it produced had put everyone in the village to sleep, even though it must have been only the faintest wisp of smoke. Can you imagine?'

'Holy smokes!' Kate said, glancing around to see if the others caught her little joke. They didn't, though, and she had to admit it wasn't worth repeating, so she only added, 'That's some powerful plant.'

'Powerful but fragile,' Sticky said. 'Duskwort only grows in certain unique conditions, and if it's removed from its native environment, it disintegrates. I know this from the journal. The Benedicts had found some specimens the year before – Anki doesn't say where – and taken one back to their lab to study. It quickly turned to dust, but not before they felt pretty confident it could cure narcolepsy, or at least eliminate the worst symptoms. The duskwort would just need to be mixed with certain other chemicals – common chemicals any scientist could easily obtain.'

'And they knew where to find more of it,' Reynie said. 'But they never created the cure. So what went wrong?'

'Unfortunately they were in for a disappointing shock,' said Sticky. 'They went back and retrieved another specimen, only to discover that this second plant wasn't duskwort at all – it was just a clever mimic. It looked exactly like duskwort and lived in exactly the same conditions, but its most important chemical properties were different. In other words, it was useless. Worse than useless, actually, because it was much hardier and more aggressive, which explained why duskwort was so rare – if it even existed any more, now that they'd accidentally destroyed the only known specimen. They believed this mimic plant – Anki calls it 'thwart-wort' in the journal – took over the duskwort's habitat, killing off all the duskwort in the process. The Benedicts went back and scoured the place where they'd found the duskwort, but no luck. Nothing but thwart-wort.'

'So how could they be sure their friend – this Han guy – had found *real* duskwort?' asked Constance.

'The Benedicts had shown him their research,' Sticky said. 'So Han knew what to look for. He used a microscope to study the plants right where he found them. He expected it all to be thwart-wort, and some of it was, but mostly it was duskwort. Lots and lots of duskwort, in fact.'

Reynie wrinkled his brow. Something had been bothering him during Sticky's account, but he hadn't been able to lay his finger on it until just now. If the Benedicts had truly found duskwort, wouldn't it have been the scientific discovery of the century? Why, then, hadn't they published papers about it?

Why hadn't they even announced it to the press?

'So what does duskwort look like, anyway?' Kate asked.

'I don't know,' Sticky said.

Constance gave an incredulous laugh. 'You don't know? But I thought you knew everything! I find that awfully hard to believe, George Washington!'

'I don't care what you *believe*,' Sticky growled. 'I really don't know.'

'Calm down, everyone,' said Reynie with another anxious wave at Sophie. 'Constance, he's telling the truth. I know you're upset, but if you calm down and look at him, you'll know it.'

(Constance was already looking at Sticky, but she was glowering, and glowering tends to obscure one's vision of deeper things. She did her best to relax, and sure enough, she saw the truth in Sticky's defiant, angry expression. He really *didn't* know.)

'It finally makes sense to me,' Reynie said. 'The fact that Anki doesn't specifically mention where they found the first specimen. The fact that the Benedicts didn't announce what they'd found, even though it was an amazing discovery. The fact that these papers were hidden away. It all adds up. They were keeping it a secret.'

'Not just the Benedicts,' Sticky said, with a sullen look at

208

Constance. 'Botanical historians have always considered duskwort one of the great mysteries. In the few ancient texts that refer to it, someone has always removed any description of what the plant looks like or where it's found.'

'Just as the Benedicts did with Han's letter,' Reynie said, pointing to the space cut out of one page. 'I assume it's his description of the duskwort that's missing, am I right?'

Sticky nodded.

'But why keep it a secret?' Kate asked. 'If it's so important . . .'

'Think about it,' Reynie said, looking grave. 'Only a smidgen of this plant put an entire village to sleep. So what do you think would happen if it fell into the wrong hands? Like you said, Kate, this is one powerful plant. Nobody has ever wanted the wrong person to find it.'

'The Benedicts knew, though,' said Sticky. And they only shared the information with their most trusted friend. Han sent them maps, by the way, but the maps aren't here. I assume the Benedicts destroyed them, too.'

'Maps of what?' Kate asked.

'Of the island where Han found the duskwort. He sent one map that showed where the island was located and another of the island itself – including the exact location of the duskwort. He describes the island a bit in the letter, but he doesn't name it or say anything that would pinpoint the place. Otherwise I'm sure the Benedicts would have cut that part out, too. The island could be anywhere in the world.'

'And Mr Curtain wants to find out where it is,' Constance said. 'And he thinks Mr Benedict knows. Or at least that someone 'extremely close' to Mr Benedict knows. Isn't that what his letter said?'

'More or less,' Reynie said. 'And you know what? Now that I think about it, Mr Benedict really *might* know where it is. If he does, then the question is whether he made it to the island or not. We'll have to see—'

'Reynie,' Kate interrupted, 'how could Mr Benedict possibly know where the island is? The maps are gone!'

Reynie was about to explain when the library door opened and the bald, bandaged man they'd seen in the courtyard entered the room. The man glanced at them without interest and went to the librarian's desk, where he engaged in a murmured conversation with Sophie. Suddenly he whipped his head around to stare at them with bulbous eyes. He hastened to their table, followed by an anxious Sophie.

'I am Mr Schuyler,' the man said in curt English. 'And who, may I ask, are you?'

'Students,' Sophie said, coming up. 'They are exchange students, Mr Schuyler.'

Mr Schuyler gestured with his pipe toward the journal and the letters. 'Why are you looking at these?'

'They heard about the trouble,' Sophie interjected. 'They were simply curious. They are *children*, Mr Schuyler.'

Mr Schuyler seemed to consider this declaration with suspicion. At length, however, he grunted, gnawed on the stem of his pipe, and said, 'I suppose I can tell you a few things, then. It *is* a rather interesting story.' He pulled out a chair, forcing Sophie to step back to avoid having her knees knocked, and sat heavily in it. 'Where shall I begin?'

'How about the beginning?' Reynie said.

'Ah. The beginning is very troubling,' said Mr Schuyler. 'You see, these papers legally belong to our library, but an

American man – the son of the papers' original owners – argues that he has claim to them. I had told him he is free to pursue the matter in court, and if the court decides in his favour, he shall have the papers. In fact, I have no doubt the court *will* decide in his favour. But until that decision has been made, the papers must remain in the library! That is simply the way of it.

'This man, however, comes to the desk one morning and asks to see these papers. It is a free and public library, so of course he is given the permission to do so. Afterwards he tells me who he is and asks if I have ever seen him before. I tell him I have not, which is true. Sometimes he uses a wheelchair, he says. Has nobody in the library noticed him before? I assure him that I have not, and Sophie assures him that she has not, either. Do you agree this is what happened, Sophie?'

Sophie opened her mouth to speak.

Mr Schuyler went on, 'Yes, that is what happened. And when we finally convince him that he is not so famous as he believes, he and his companion – a sort of yellow-coloured woman with red hair who reminded me of a pencil – do you not think that is a clever comparison, Sophie? That she looked like a pencil? I believe I said so at the time – what was I saying? Oh yes. He and his companion left. But five minutes later I receive a phone call from him, and he tells me that he only took what was rightfully his. That is all he says, and he hangs up.

'Perhaps you do not know what he meant, children, but I did,' said Mr Schuyler. 'I went straight to the journal and the papers, and I immediately discovered that he has taken two documents that were among the letters, and he has cut

211

out a piece of one page! He has stolen and damaged library property!'

Reynie absorbed these details with keen attention, for Mr Schuyler had just confirmed what Reynie had suspected. Mr Benedict *did* know where the island was. It was he – and not his parents – who had removed the two maps. He also had cut out the part missing from Han's letter. Mr Benedict's parents had hidden these documents in a secret location, after all. They probably hadn't thought it necessary to destroy the sensitive information contained in them.

'The man has committed criminal acts,' Mr Schuyler was saying, 'and I can prove it. He was not so clever as he thinks!' He pointed to a security camera high on the wall behind the librarian's desk. 'You see? I have the evidence. And will you believe, children? He returned to the library the very same day! Well! What do you think happened?'

'You called the police,' Reynie said, privately admiring Mr Benedict's ingenuity, for it was plain to him what Mr Benedict had done. First he'd determined whether Mr Curtain had ever seen these papers (that was why he'd asked if the librarians recognized him). Then he'd tried to make sure that if his twin ever *did* come to the library, he would be arrested.

'Indeed,' said Mr Schuyler. 'I called the police. Nor was it the first time I had called them that day, for earlier the men with the briefcases had come. You have heard about these men?'

'The Ten Men?' asked Constance, and the other children tried not to show their alarm. Constance instantly realized she had spoken imprudently, but it was too late.

Luckily Mr Schuyler was too interested in hearing

himself speak to pay close attention to what a tiny girl said. 'Ten men?' he repeated absently. 'No, you have heard wrong. There were only two. Although they were as dangerous as ten, perhaps even more. They arrived soon after the American man and the pencil woman had left. I was in the courtyard – my position requires much coming and going from the museum, you see,' (the children understood this to mean Mr Schuyler often went into the courtyard to smoke his pipe and read the paper) 'and I saw them enter the gate, but I thought nothing of them until I heard the screams.'

At this Mr Schuyler turned to give Sophie's hand a comforting pat, but Sophie quickly withdrew her hand, so Mr Schuyler patted the arm of his chair, as if this were a perfectly normal thing and just what he'd intended to do.

'The men demanded to see any materials connected to the name Benedict,' Sophie interjected, 'as well as anything that had been requested by previous visitors to the library that day. I knew what they must be seeking, but as I told you, I was at first too frightened to speak. And then—'

'Yes, the screams were terrible,' Mr Schuyler continued, as if Sophie hadn't spoken at all, 'but they did alert me to the situation, and when these men came out again, I charged at them from behind the bench,' (from this the children gathered that Mr Schuyler had peeked over the top of the bench, behind which he was no doubt cowering in terror) 'but one of them pointed a deadly device at me. My reflexes are excellent, and I ducked my head, though not quickly enough to avoid injury.' Gingerly he touched the white bandage on the crown of his head. 'I suffered a great loss of blood, and of course, all of my hair.'

The children raised their eyebrows, and Kate stifled a snigger. Judging from the size and placement of the bandage, there couldn't have been more than a half-dozen hairs on Mr Schuyler's head to begin with. But it did appear he had sustained injury.

'They said I should be glad I was not taller,' Mr Schuyler reflected. 'Then they laughed and went away, and I called the police.'

'Actually, it was Eda who called the police, Mr Schuyler,' said Sophie quietly. 'You called the ambulance. Because of your injury.'

Mr Schuyler made an irritated gesture with his pipe. 'The details are unimportant. And it was most certainly I who called the police the *next* time, children, when the American man returned. He was using a wheelchair now, just as he'd told me he sometimes does, and he was accompanied by an awkward young man with large feet, as well as a teenaged girl with long, shining black hair and a very rude temperament. Very rude indeed! I do not care to repeat what she called me when she left.'

Reynie and the others exchanged furtive glances. They hadn't the least doubt that Mr Schuyler was describing SQ Pedalian and Martina Crowe – the other Executives who had fled the Institute with Mr Curtain. And of course the man in the wheelchair had been Mr Curtain himself.

'The American man,' Mr Schuyler went on, 'asked to see all the materials he had examined that morning. He said he understood there had been an unfortunate incident at the library and wished to verify that the materials were still here. As if he had not committed a crime himself! As if he had never called me on the telephone admitting to it!

214

The nerve of this man!'

Mr Curtain certainly didn't lack for nerve, Reynie thought, but this was an instance of cunning rather than bravado. Clearly he'd wanted to find out why Mr Benedict had visited the museum library, and when his Ten Men failed to secure the answer, he had resorted to duplicity.

'Well, as you might suppose, I was clever,' said Mr Schuyler. 'I gave no sign of distress, the better to lay my trap. He seemed in a hurry this time, and he wanted to photocopy everything – every single page of the journal and letters – to take with him. I told him that with such delicate materials we must use a special machine, and a librarian must make the copies. This is actually true, but that does not make my plan less clever. Not when you consider that as Sophie made the copies, I secretly called the police and told them to come at once, *but not to use their sirens.* Do you see what I was up to, children? This way there was no warning! When the copies were finished, and the man and his companions took the lift to the lobby, they were met by the police. It was all very clever, I assure you.'

'So what went wrong?' asked Reynie, for they all knew perfectly well that Mr Curtain had escaped.

Mr Schuyler spluttered his lips in disgust. 'Despite all I had done, the police let the man escape. He leapt from his wheelchair – greatly surprising them – and did something . . . well, it isn't known exactly what he did. He appeared simply to touch the police officers, and they dropped to the floor and lay helpless for several minutes. The villain fled with his companions, not to be seen again.' He shook his head and looked over his pipe at the children.

'That's a remarkable account, Mr Schuyler,' said Reynie,

when it became clear Mr Schuyler expected such a comment. 'These are very curious and frightening incidents. May I ask one more question about them?'

Mr Schuyler pretended to check his watch, then sighed indulgently, as if he did not care to keep talking and talking but would do so for the children's sake. 'Very well, young man. What is it?'

'The documents that were stolen. What were they?'

'The documents? Oh, they were maps of some kind.'

'Maps?' Reynie repeated, though of course he already knew that. He was hoping Mr Schuyler might have some clue about where the island was located. 'Maps of what, exactly?'

Mr Schuyler seemed to dislike this question. Frowning, he tapped his pipe impatiently against the tabletop. 'We do not know. The materials had been filed and recorded more than a year ago, and no one had reviewed them since.'

'Who filed and recorded them?' Reynie persisted, glancing between Mr Schuyler and Sophie. 'May we speak with that person?'

Sophie looked at Mr Schuyler, and Reynie understood. Obviously Mr Schuyler was that person. And obviously he had not examined the maps.

'I cannot be expected to commit to memory everything I see!' said Mr Schuyler in an exasperated tone. 'I am quite busy with my duties here, children.' He rose abruptly from his chair. 'In fact, I have duties to attend to at this very moment. Good day, all of you. I hope you will cooperate with the police. Please behave with the proper respect.'

'The police?' they all cried.

Mr Schuyler smiled. 'Oh, yes, you must wait here for them, of course. The police wish to question anyone in connection with the attack. You have asked to see these papers, so you must be questioned. Sophie, you *have* called the police, I assume.'

Sophie started. 'Not yet,' she said with an apologetic look at the children.

'Not yet!' Mr Schuyler exclaimed indignantly. 'Very well, if *you* cannot be troubled to call—'

'I will do it right away,' said Sophie, hurrying to her desk.

Reynie leapt to his feet. 'Please, Mr Schuyler. Will you consider—'

But Mr Schuyler wouldn't let him finish. 'No,' he said firmly. 'I will not.' He turned and stalked past the librarian's desk into one of the back rooms.

With the telephone in her hand, Sophie watched him go. She listened for a moment, then turned to the children. 'There is something wrong with this telephone,' she said quietly. 'It is not working. I will try again in one or two minutes. Do you children wish to use the bathroom? It is downstairs.'

'The bathroom?' Sticky said.

Kate grabbed him and whispered, 'She's letting us go, Sticky. Move it.'

They went quickly to the door, pausing just long enough to cast grateful looks toward the young librarian.

'Thank you, Sophie,' Reynie whispered.

'Good luck, children,' Sophie whispered in reply. She watched them leave with an expression of great concern, no doubt wondering whether she'd done the right thing in letting them go. They were children, after all. Whatever they were doing, wherever they were going now – would they be safe?

It was a question shared by the children themselves.

And the answer was no.

The Phone Call, the Money, and the Fateful Envelope

Reynie was confident now that Mr Benedict and Number Two had gone to the island, wherever it was, and that Mr Curtain had followed them there. Whether the children could follow them there, too, remained to be seen, but one thing was certain: if they failed, it would not be from a lack of hurrying.

'I'm sorry! I have to rest!' Reynie gasped, steering his bicycle off the road and into a patch of grass, where he shakily dismounted and flopped onto his back. His legs burned from calf to thigh, his lungs were heaving, and he could barely see for all the sweat stinging his eyes. They had been pedalling madly ever since they left the museum.

Hearing a strange, raspy sound nearby, Reynie wiped his eyes and turned his head to look. Sticky lay wheezing in the grass a few yards away, one leg under his bicycle, like a cavalry soldier whose horse had fallen on him in battle. Too winded to speak and too exhausted to dismount, he'd followed Reynie into the grass and simply let himself crash.

Kate came back to see what was the matter. She sat on her bicycle – by some miracle of balance she kept it upright without pedalling – and Constance sat in the basket. Both girls seemed disappointed.

'We need to hurry, you know,' said Constance, who otherwise wouldn't have agreed to ride with Kate.

'I think . . . I'm done for,' Reynie panted. 'You go on . . . without me.'

'Are you joking?' Kate asked, astonished.

Reynie nodded and hauled himself into a sitting position. He found he couldn't breathe as well this way, however, and so he fell onto his back again. Constance frowned disapprovingly. Meanwhile, an old woman walking a miniature poodle had stopped to let the dog sniff at Sticky. Sticky could only blink at it and gasp. The old woman clucked, said something to the children in Dutch, and moved on.

The route from the museum to the hotel was a long, straight shot along a major thoroughfare, but to avoid attention (since the police might be looking for them) the children had kept to side streets. They were in a quiet neighbourhood now. The patch of grass the boys had collapsed upon was actually a tiny park – a dreary one, unfortunately, scarcely larger than a parking space, with a single rotting bench and a single blighted elm tree.

'I've been thinking,' Kate said as the boys recovered. 'What if Mr Benedict meant for Thernbaakagen to be our last stop? What if he and Number Two took a quick trip to that island with the idea of returning before we got to the hotel? After all, he didn't know about the island until he got here. It wouldn't have been part of his original plans.'

Reynie had considered this but had kept the question to himself. He hadn't wanted to discourage Constance. Sure enough, now that Kate had mentioned it, Constance's troubled expression grew darker still.

'He may very well have tacked the island onto our trip,' Reynie said quickly. 'In which case he'll have left a clue at the hotel. And even if he hasn't, we might be able to track down Han de Reizeger – the Benedicts' friend. He'd be very old by now, but . . .'

'Oh,' Sticky said, looking uncomfortable. 'Um, sorry. Han was already very old. He died a long time ago. Mr Benedict's aunt mentioned that in her letter.'

'She did?' Constance said, turning on him. 'Why didn't you say so earlier?'

Sticky clenched his teeth. 'Because Mr Schuyler came in before we *got* to it, Constance.'

'Can you tell us what it said?' Reynie asked.

'It was in English, actually,' Sticky said. 'Shall I quote it? Or would you rather I . . .?'

'Absolutely,' said Kate. 'Quote away.'

And so Sticky recited the letter:

My dear Anki,

I write in English this time, not only to show you how proficient I've become – I am a regular American now – but to encourage you and Dr Benedict to practise it yourselves, as it has always struck me as ridiculous that you speak ten languages between you yet render your English so clumsily.

But forgive me. I meant first to offer condolences for the loss of your friend Han de Reizeger. It must be a comfort to you that he was so very old. And had he not lived a full and adventurous life? And did he not die travelling the world as he had always hoped he would? If only everyone could be so lucky!

I do regret the financial troubles mentioned in your last letter, Anki, but I cannot help you. I realize you've not gone so far as to ask openly for my help, but I thought the request implicit in your letter, and I am sorry to refuse it. As you should know, my own precarious situation prevents me. I scarcely have enough to pay rent, nor have I ever since Thiedric died these many years ago. But what is this trip you wish to make, anyway? If it is so urgent, must you keep it a secret from your own sister? It only seems proper that a request for travelling funds be accompanied by an explanation. Regardless, I beg you not to attempt the experiment you mention. Sure, the government will pay you handsomely if you achieve success, but are you not concerned about the possibility of an accident? Is this not why others have refused? You may say that most lack your qualifications, but surely in all of Holland there are other scientists who might attempt such a thing.

Personally I believe it is in the nature of explosives to be explosive, and I do not see how you can make it otherwise. No matter how 'noble the purpose,' as you say in your letter, no matter how many lives might be saved, I assure you no one could induce me to attempt such a thing! That, I suppose, is why I did not become a scientist myself. (That, and the fact that science is such a dull business – so much Latin and so many symbols.)

I am relieved, at least, that you intend to wait until the baby has come. But what is the hurry? The baby, the experiment, the mysterious journey – you write as if all must come so quickly! Take your time, Anki! It has never failed to annoy me, I must confess, the way you always write with both hands going at once, as if there were never a moment to be lost. Such haste is hardly proper in a woman to exhibit, however scientific she might think herself to be.

The children were appalled. It was a very disagreeable letter, and as Sticky finished quoting it – the rest was devoted to outrageous prices and noisy neighbours – Reynie wondered what Mr Benedict must have thought of it. Knowing him, he'd probably found his aunt's superior tone amusing; Mr Benedict was not the sort of person to waste a good chuckle on indignation. But then again, Reynie reflected, he must have been disappointed to find yet another example of such unpleasantness in his family.

'I suppose,' said Kate when Sticky had finished, 'they hid her letter because it mentions Han and the secret trip they were planning. They were being awfully careful.'

'Why not just destroy it?' Constance said. 'A nasty letter like that! Why on earth would Anki keep it?'

Kate snorted with laughter. Of the few letters Constance had ever sent her, not one could be considered pleasant, exactly. 'Probably for the same reason I keep *your* letters, Connie girl.'

223

Constance screwed up her face, uncertain if Kate's comment was an insult or an admission of fondness. In fact, she rather thought it might be both.

Strictly speaking, Thernbaakagen lay not on the coast but beyond it. Like so many towns in Holland, it occupied land that the clever Dutch had reclaimed from the ocean. Bordered by the North Sea and crisscrossed by innumerable canals, the town seemed more water than land, and a great deal of its commerce depended on that fact. Fishing, shipping, and water transport had made Thernbaakagen, if not a large city, then at least a thriving, busy one, and the Hotel Regaal sat in the very centre.

Reynie, Sticky and Constance could see the hotel sign from their busy corner two streets away – but they weren't looking at the sign. As they waited for Kate to return from a scouting run, they stood a short distance away from a snack van, staring with watering mouths at all the food. The smell of fried potatoes, especially, made Reynie almost giddy with longing. But they had spent the last of their money on the bicycles.

One of those bicycles came barrelling out of traffic now, ridden by a bespectacled girl with wild hair who hopped the kerb and narrowly missed striking the snack van. The owner of the cart leapt away, fearing for his toes, and said something in terse, disapproving Dutch.

'That's what the old woman with the poodle said,' Constance muttered to herself, and Reynie, hearing her, realized she was right.

'I saw lots of well-dressed people with briefcases,' Kate reported, handing Sticky his spectacles and taking back her bucket, 'but no Martina or SQ. I think we'll just have to chance it, don't you?'

'I suppose we have no choice,' Reynie said, and catching the attention of the snack van owner he asked if the man would keep an eye on their bicycles.

Upon hearing Reynie speak English, the man's disapproving expression faded – as if for some reason he disliked Dutch children but found American ones tolerable – and he said gruffly that he would do so but that they must hurry; he could not spend his afternoon minding bicycles for children. Reynie thanked him, and with another curt nod the man handed Reynie a cone-shaped packet of hot, sliced potatoes – they resembled thick French fries – covered with a mayonnaise-like sauce. 'I saw you looking,' he said. 'Now go and hurry back.'

The children walked slowly toward the hotel, hungrily sharing the potatoes and keeping a wary eye on the people that passed them. The pavement was swarming with pedestrians, many of them in elegant, professional attire, and every time a businessman in a suit looked at the children their hearts skipped. Never had walking down a street been so nerve-racking. They were all relieved when they reached the hotel.

The Hotel Regaal had seen better days – its lobby furniture was rickety, its floors were scuffed and a musty odour hung in the air – but despite having been upstaged by more modern hotels, it was doing its best to retain a semblance of past splendour. The rickety furniture was polished to a shine, the scuffed floors were immaculately swept, and the front desk receptionists were well groomed and professional. One of them, an older man with slicked grey hair, said something in Dutch when the children came in. The other receptionist, a frail, pallid, severe-looking woman with dark circles under her eyes, nodded her agreement.

'There it is again,' said Constance, frowning.

This time Reynie had noticed it, too – the phrase uttered first by the poodle woman and then the snack van owner. The coincidence seemed too significant to let pass. With the others behind him, Reynie approached the receptionists and asked if they spoke English. Instantly a look of understanding appeared on both faces.

'Of course we speak English,' said the grey-haired man, not unkindly. He had bright red cheeks and a goatee so thin and small it looked like a thumbprint on his chin. 'And how may we help you children?'

'May I ask what you just said about us?' Reynie asked. 'We've heard others say it, too, and we're curious.'

'You are attentive children, then!' said the man, sounding both amused and impressed. 'I said that you should be at school! These others you mention must have thought, as I did, that you were Dutch children, and that you were truant. But you are American, yes? On a school trip of some kind?'

'Something like that,' said Kate.

Reynie felt foolish and not a little uneasy. Travelling across town the four of them must have been much more conspicuous than they'd hoped. There was no help for that now, but it was all the more reason to find the clue and leave as quickly as possible. 'Is there a message here for us?' he asked. 'A message from someone named Nicholas Benedict?'

The man broke into a delighted grin. 'Benedict, you say? Here you are at last! Did you hear about this mysterious arrangement, Daatje?' he asked his partner, who only looked away, as if she preferred to bc lcft alonc. 'I suppose not,' the man said and turned back to the children. His enthusiasm was undiminished, not least because of the relief so evident on the children's faces. 'My name is Hubrecht, children, and I am very pleased to meet you! I do have something from Benedict. Yes, indeed I do!'

The children waited, but Hubrecht only looked at them with an encouraging smile. He appeared to be waiting for something himself.

'May we, um, *see* it?' Kate asked. 'Please?'

Hubrecht glanced left and right, and then in a comically conspiratorial manner he leant forward and whispered, 'First you must show me . . . *the item*.' He wiggled his eyebrows dramatically.

'The item?' said Sticky.

'Oh, yes! Your Mr Benedict has booked a room, and I am to make it available to anyone who mentions his name – provided I am shown a certain item. Do you have it? He said you will not have come here without it. I cannot say more.'

'Not another riddle,' Sticky said wearily.

Reynie scratched his head. 'All right, what is it Mr Benedict knew we'd bring?'

'My bucket?' Kate asked. 'I do always have it with me.'

Hubrecht smiled and shook his head. He glanced at Constance as if expecting her to guess, but Constance had noticed a wad of gum stuck under the edge of the desk and was making unpleasant gagging sounds, so Hubrecht looked politely away.

227

'If Mr Benedict's sure we'll have brought it,' said Reynie, 'it's probably something we'd *have* to have with us to get here.'

'Maybe it's clothes,' Sticky ventured.

The others stared at him.

'Oh yes, it must be *clothes*, Sticky,' Constance said, as Kate suppressed a snort of laughter. 'Show him your *clothes* and see if that gets us into the room.'

'It's not such a dumb idea,' Sticky said defensively. 'Without clothes we'd have been arrested by now, right? We couldn't have come here then, could we?' But Hubrecht was shaking his head.

Embarrassed, Sticky gave Constance a sharp poke in the ribs for mocking him. Constance cried out and responded with a kick to the shin; then, pleased with the result (Sticky was grimacing and hopping), she quickly tried for another.

'How about a train schedule?' asked Kate, ignoring the scuffle. 'Or a ticket?'

Hubrecht shook his head. Again he glanced at Constance, as if he expected her to have the answer – and this time Reynie understood why. She *did* have the answer, and Hubrecht had spotted it.

'Your present!' he said, pointing to Constance's globe pendant. (Constance stopped trying to bite Sticky's hand and looked down in surprise.) 'We couldn't have come here without it!'

Hubrecht clapped his hands. 'That is it! A small world – just as your Mr Benedict said! Very well, children, you shall have a key.' He reached beneath the desk. 'This is a scavenger hunt of some kind, yes? What fun! I have been wondering when someone else would come.'

Reynie took the room key from Hubrecht. 'When you say 'someone else,' do you mean another person came before us?'

'Oh, yes! It is a contest, correct? The adults against the children, maybe? Never fear! You are the first to be given a key. No one else has entered the room – not even hotel staff. These were Mr Benedict's instructions.'

'Who else has come?' Sticky asked.

'Two very nice gentlemen. It was the same day your friend Mr Benedict booked the room. They asked if he was staying here. He was not – he and his young associate had simply inspected the room and gone away, leaving the key with me – but because the gentlemen had mentioned his name, I abided by his instructions: I offered them a room, compliments of Mr Benedict, if only they would present a certain item. I thought perhaps it would be in one of their briefcases. They had no item, however, so they thanked me and went away. Polite men, elegantly dressed, the sort who used to frequent this hotel in its finer days. I was left to wonder who else might come. Then, as the days passed, I began to think no one would! Did you think so, too?' he asked his partner, the woman he'd called Daatje, who now seemed to be paying attention.

Daatje started. 'I knew nothing about this, Hubrecht.'

Reynie thought she seemed upset. She was staring at them, not with malice, exactly, but her expression was decidedly unpleasant. Did she feel left out? Obviously Hubrecht found Mr Benedict's arrangement charming and enjoyed being involved. But it wasn't Hubrecht she was staring at. Perhaps she disliked children.

Reynie wanted to believe this but found that he couldn't.

He felt pretty sure Mr Benedict would have left money in the room for them – at least enough to buy a meal or two – and he had a sneaking suspicion that Daatje had stolen some of it, perhaps even all of it. She might easily have done so, knowing the room was unoccupied. Perhaps she'd meant to blame poor Hubrecht or some other member of the hotel staff. That *was* the look she wore, Reynie decided. A guilty look. It made him very uneasy.

You're getting ahead of yourself, he thought. *Let it go for now. You'll find out soon enough.*

But then he noticed Constance.

She was staring at Daatje, staring with a most intense, penetrating look. And the longer Constance stared, the darker her expression grew, until she was positively glowering. Daatje had noticed and was squirming in her seat, avoiding eye contact, as Hubrecht told the children where to find their room. As Kate and Sticky thanked him and headed over to the lift, Reynie had to take Constance by the arm and lead her away from the desk.

'What's the matter?' he said in an undertone. 'What did she do?'

'I don't know,' Constance growled, looking back over her shoulder. 'But it's not good.'

'That's all? Not good?'

'By which I mean extremely bad,' said Constance.

'That's what I was afraid of.'

'What are you two talking about?' Sticky asked.

'Tell you when we're alone,' Reynie said. 'But keep your eyes open. Something's not right.'

'Oh, I hate that you just said that,' said Sticky, reaching for his spectacles.

Kate's eyes narrowed. 'You can tell us in the lift,' she murmured, for the doors had opened now and the lift was unoccupied. The children got on and stood close together, closer than space required, and Kate opened her bucket lid, ready to grab for anything she might need in a hurry. The doors slid closed.

Across the lobby, Daatje watched the children go. She looked upset, so much so that Hubrecht asked if she felt all right.

'Actually, I have a terrible headache,' she said. 'Do you have any medicine?'

'No, but we keep some in the supply cabinet, you know. I'll bring you some.' Hubrecht cast about for the key to the supply cabinet. 'The key must be in the office,' he said, looking puzzled. 'Don't worry, I'll find it.'

When he had gone, Daatje took the supply cabinet key from her pocket and dropped it onto the floor, where it would appear to have fallen by accident. She unfolded a scrap of paper upon which was written a telephone number – a number she dialled with trembling fingers. 'Hello? Yes, this is Daatje – from the hotel . . . yes. Someone has finally come. Just now. It is only a group of children. You may send the money you promised to my address, if you please. I . . . what? No, I cannot possibly tell you which room. Did you hear me say they are only children? No, I never agreed to that. It is against policy, and anyway . . . no, absolutely not! I'm afraid . . . I . . . I'm afraid . . .'

With frightened eyes Daatje glanced over her shoulder. She was still alone. 'Surely you would not do that,' she whispered into the receiver. 'Surely you . . . you . . . I see.'

She swallowed with some difficulty. 'But I insist . . . you must promise no harm . . .'

There was a long pause, during which she chewed her bottom lip in extreme anxiety. And then in one quick breath she gave the room number and slammed down the phone, recoiling from it as if it had given her a most terrible, most excruciating shock.

'I'll go in first,' said Kate, despite feeling very nervous. (And Kate got nervous only when most children would feel terrified.) She and the boys were creeping down the carpeted hallway to the hotel room. Constance had remained at the lift to hold its doors open. They were on the fifth floor. If someone disagreeable confronted them in this hotel room, they needed a means of quick escape.

Kate listened at the door, unlocked it, and peeked into the room. With an uneasy glance at the boys she slipped inside. Reynie and Sticky waited on pins and needles. Kate's confidence always helped them keep their own fears at bay; they disliked it when she seemed uneasy. When after a long, tense minute Kate called out that all was clear, the boys exchanged looks of relief. Her voice had regained its natural breeziness. The boys signalled for Constance to follow, then entered the room.

The door opened into a cramped entryway made all the more awkward by the ill-advised placement of a table in the door's path, so that the door swung only halfway open. On the table, waist-high to the boys, stood a vase of silk flowers, a bowl of sweets, and a note that said *Welcome!* in Number Two's distinct, crabbed handwriting. Reynie's stomach twinged at the thought of what Number Two must be going through at this moment.

Beyond the table a doorway opened onto the large main room, which was furnished with a few chairs, a bed, a sleeper sofa, and two cots folded against one wall. (Enough accommodation for the four of them, Reynie realized, plus Milligan and Rhonda, who were supposed to have come along.) Kate was checking behind the window curtains for any sign of a clue and making noisy, smacking sounds. She was chewing a particularly sticky sweet she'd taken from the bowl.

Reynie couldn't help but marvel. Walking alone into an empty room – a room in which she might face untold dangers – Kate had stopped to help herself to a sweet.

'I don't thee anything unuthual,' she said. 'Bathroom'th clear, too.'

'Maybe this is it, then,' said Sticky, looking around apprehensively. 'Maybe he booked this room for us and planned to come back. Maybe there aren't any more clues.'

'Let's not give up just yet,' said Reynie, hoping Constance hadn't heard what Sticky said. He knelt down to inspect four indentations in the carpet by the wall.

Kate had opened her Swiss Army knife and used its toothpick to scrape loose a bit of candy. 'I noticed those flat spots, too. A chair or something used to be there.'

Reynie stood up quickly. 'The table by the door! It was moved for a reason. I'll bet we have to climb on it or . . .'

Constance walked into the main room, a bunch of sweets in one hand and an envelope in the other. Her pale blue eyes flashed with excitement. 'Didn't any of you see this? It was hanging beneath the table.'

'We didn't,' Reynie said. 'But Mr Benedict knew you'd

233

see it right away. Anyone else would be too tall. He must have wanted you to be the one to find it.'

Constance smiled at this. It pleased her to think Mr Benedict had arranged things that way. But her smile quickly faded as she considered what the letter might say. What if it told them to stay put and wait? What if this was the end of the road? She thrust the envelope toward Reynie. 'You read it. I can't bear to.'

Reynie opened the envelope and read the letter aloud:

My dear friends,

I wanted you to have a comfortable place to rest before the next leg of your journey, which shall take you to . . . well, I leave the destination for you to work out, but there is no great hurry. If you don't know where to look for the answer, you can sleep on it.
Sincerely,
Mr Benedict

'The bed!' they all cried at once, then burst out laughing. It was rare for them to agree on something so quickly. Together they raced to the bed, and in a flurry of flying blankets, sheets and pillows, they stripped it to the mattress in seconds. No envelope. They slid the mattress from the frame. Nothing.

'Let's try the sleeper sofa,' Reynie said, feeling worried now. They cleared the cushions from the sofa, and Kate, grabbing the cloth handle, tugged up and out on the hideaway mattress. It unfolded to reveal a large manila envelope, upon which Mr Benedict had written *To be used in case of hunger, curiosity, or both.*

234

Kate slit the envelope open with her knife and dumped its contents onto the mattress. 'Lunch money,' she said with satisfaction. She set aside the bundle of banknotes and picked up a sheet of paper. 'And an address! 'Risker Water Transport.' It's right here in Thernbaakagen!'

Sticky read the address. 'That street runs along the wharf. I saw it on the map. We're not far from there. All we—'

'What's the matter, Reynie?' Constance said.

Reynie was staring at the money. 'The envelope was sealed. And the money's still there. So what did she do?'

'What did who do?' Kate asked.

'Daatje, the woman downstairs. I thought maybe she'd stolen money that Mr Benedict had left us.' Reynie started to pace, only to find his path blocked by the mattress, cushions, and pillows they'd thrown onto the floor. 'But she *didn't* steal anything. And now that I think of it, those Ten Men that came to the hotel just thanked Hubrecht and left. They didn't make him show them the room. Doesn't that strike you as odd?'

'Probably they didn't realize anything was in here,' Kate said. 'They just thought Mr Benedict booked a room for someone to stay in. Someone who hadn't come yet.'

'Yes, but they would want to know who he rented it for,' Reynie said. 'And the best way for them to learn that would be—' His eyes widened. 'We need to get out of here *now*.'

'You think Daatje told them?' Sticky said, not wanting to believe it. 'You think she called the Ten Men and told them we're here?'

'*Now*, Sticky!' Kate said, grabbing his arm to haul him after her.

But Constance stood in their way, and she wasn't moving. She was staring toward the far wall, staring as if she could see right through it into the hallway beyond.

'It's too late,' she whispered. 'They're already here.'

CAUGHT UP

AT LAST

The children heard the outer door bump against the table in the entryway, and a smell of cologne suddenly permeated the room. A floorboard creaked. And then a tall man with a briefcase leant in through the doorway to look at them. The Ten Man was dressed in a fine blue suit, had very pale white skin, jet-black hair, and thin, almost colour-less lips, which gave the impression that either he'd lost a great deal of blood or else had been recently unfrozen. His dark shining eyes swept the room, taking in the mattress, pillows, and bed linen on the floor.

He gave the children a smile that revealed bright, perfect

teeth. 'Dear, dear, chickies, you've made an awful mess, haven't you? Were you looking for something?'

The children stared at him, not daring to move or speak.

'It's no use pretending you don't speak English,' the Ten Man said with a wink. 'I've heard about you four. Now, then, Constance, be a sugar and bring me the paper in your hand. I want to see it. And you, Kate – bring me whatever it is you're hiding behind your back.' He held out his free hand, the one without the briefcase. It seemed to extend halfway across the room, so exceptionally long was his arm, and his pale, thin fingers, twitching open and shut in a beckoning manner, resembled a dying spider.

Constance made a whimpering sound. She had looked directly into the Ten Man's eyes, and what she'd seen had terrified her. She gripped the letter from Mr Benedict ever tighter, her hand trembling. Beside her, Kate stood half-crouched, poised to respond to any sudden movement.

The Ten Man made no sudden movement, however. On the contrary, his motions were relaxed, even leisurely. With a disapproving cluck, he withdrew his hand and set down his briefcase. His arms were so long he had only to bend a bit at the waist. 'Well, well. I see from your eyes, my little fox, that I risk being bitten if I approach you. You've had your jabs, I hope?'

'Try us,' Kate said through clenched teeth.

'She didn't mean that,' Sticky said.

The Ten Man chuckled. 'Oh, I've no doubt she did. Your reputation precedes you, Katie love. Now, do you suppose if I make an example of you, the other children will behave?' He shook his arms, exposing two large silver watches beneath his shirt cuffs. An electric whine filled the room.

238

'You don't have to do that!' Reynie cried. 'Don't hurt her! We'll give you the papers!'

'Oh dear, I *know* you'll give me the papers,' said the Ten Man with an expression of mock pity. He extended both spidery hands toward Kate. 'But once I've started something, you see, I like to f—'

Kate sprang.

A direct attack was not what the Ten Man had expected, and he flinched in surprise as Kate lunged forward, leaping over the pile of linen and scooping up a pillow as she charged. A split second later there came a muffled *thump-thump* as two wires struck the pillow Kate had lifted – just in time – to use as a shield.

Reynie saw the wires flickering like snakes' tongues as they recoiled into the Ten Man's watches. At the same time he saw Kate bring her other hand around – the one she'd had behind her back – and swing it up toward the man's face. Reynie had thought she was hiding the paper with the address on it. Now he saw it was a small bottle, the contents of which she splashed into the Ten Man's eyes.

'I hope you like lemon juice!' Kate said, as the man howled and covered his face. Already she had dropped the bottle, grabbed the briefcase, and flung it across the room at Reynie, who saw it flying toward him with alarm. He was not the most athletic of children, and he felt lucky indeed when he managed to catch the briefcase before it knocked his teeth out. It was quite heavy, and Kate had thrown it with a great deal of force.

'Reynie!' Kate cried. 'Throw it out of the wind – OW!'

The Ten Man, though temporarily blinded, had used Kate's voice as a guide, snatching her ponytail and yanking her back toward him. He thought better of this when she began to kick at his shins, however, and after a brief tussle he tossed her high into the air away from him. Kate flipped around like a cat, but even so she landed hard on her bucket, and had it not been for the mattress cushioning her fall, she would almost certainly have broken a rib. Wincing with pain, she looked up to see Reynie turning from the window, still clutching the briefcase. 'Reynie! Why . . . ?'

'The pavement's too crowded,' Reynie said. 'I couldn't throw it out. It might kill someone.' He sounded half apologetic and half scared out of his wits. He had wanted nothing more than to get rid of that box of horrors, yet now he stood holding it against his chest. A humming sound came from inside the briefcase, like that of a hive full of angry hornets.

Kate grimaced. Of course Reynie couldn't risk it; she should have thought of that. She'd hoped the briefcase was so precious that the Ten Man would run to retrieve it, giving them a chance to escape. Instead she ought to have snatched it and fled. The Ten Man would have chased her, and the others might have got away. Now they were trapped – and Kate had run out of tricks.

The Ten Man had recovered from the lemon juice and was watching them from across the room. His eyes were puffy and red, and he was no longer smiling. 'I was right about you, ducky. You do bite. But that won't happen again.' His fingers moved up his necktie like a pale and hairless tarantula. With one smooth, practised motion he slid the tie loose from his collar, revealing a thin, metallic fringe at the end like that of a bullwhip.

'I've already said we'll give you the papers,' Reynie said,

speaking with some difficulty. His mouth was dry as dust. 'And I'll give the briefcase back, too. Just please let us go.'

'Oh, tsk tsk,' the Ten Man said. 'Weren't you supposed to be the clever one? And you really think I would let you go? After such rough treatment? Oh, no, Reynard. Naughty children must be punished.' He flicked the necktie, which made a terrible snapping sound as it streaked across the room and knocked a piece of plaster from the wall near Sticky's head.

The children flinched – especially Sticky, who almost fainted – and the Ten Man's lip curled into a sneer. 'That was just to show you what you're in for.'

Reynie's mind was racing. The Ten Man stood between them and the exit, and even if they managed to get past him – which was very unlikely – Reynie now saw another man in a suit, lurking in the entryway just beyond the door. The Ten Man had a partner. This observation did nothing to worsen Reynie's terror (he was already as terrified as he could be), but it did help him understand, fully and completely, that there was no way out, and that he needed to brace himself for what was coming.

Kate, climbing to her feet, had realized the same thing. 'Fine,' she said bitterly. 'Do your worst. You *will* get bitten again, though. Both of you will. That much I promise.'

'Both of us?' the Ten Man said with a frown. He glanced sharply toward the entryway. 'Why aren't you guarding the li . . .' His eyes widened. 'You aren't Mortis!'

'I should hope not,' said the other man.

'What have you done with Mortis?' the Ten Man snarled, spinning toward the doorway and raising his necktie-whip.

'I'll show you,' the other man said, and in the same

241

moment there came a strange whistling sound – *swit*! – and the feathery end of a dart appeared in the Ten Man's shoulder.

Angrily the Ten Man snatched the dart out. But he didn't have time to get a proper look at it before he hit the floor.

The other man entered the room, stepped over the unconscious Ten Man's body, and knelt down with his arms out. Kate threw herself upon him.

'Oh, Milligan!' she cried. 'Oh, Milligan, you're *here*!'

Milligan *was* there, although he was rather difficult to see beneath the pile of jubilant children mobbing him in their excitement. And even when he had freed himself with a lot of hugging and head-patting and handshakes and smiles, Milligan resembled himself but slightly. His normally yellow hair was black, his blue eyes were brown, and his ears, strangely enough, seemed to have shrunk. His ruddy complexion was the same, and he possessed the same tall, lanky build, but at a glance he was hardly recognizable even to those who knew him.

'I thought you were another Ten Man!' Kate said. 'I can't believe I didn't recognize you!'

'You were concentrating on the more immediate threat,' Milligan said. His eyes twinkled. 'You sounded awfully fierce, by the way. Now listen, all of you, the police are coming and we can't spare the time to deal with them. We need to make our exit. Quick now!' He took the Ten Man's briefcase from Reynie, who handed it over with relief.

'The police are coming?' Sticky said.

'Quick now,' Milligan repeated, stepping over the Ten Man's body.

'You're just going to leave him lying here?' Constance said. 'You aren't going to tie him up or anything?'

Milligan turned to see Constance staring at the Ten Man on the floor, afraid even to walk past him. 'Forgive me,' he said, coming back and picking her up. 'Quick now, all of you. And please don't make me say it again.' He carried Constance from the room.

At the end of the hallway the children could see a man's feet sticking out through the lift doors, which kept sliding shut, only to bump the feet and slide open again with a *ding*. Presumably the feet, shod in expensive black shoes, belonged to the Ten Man's tranquilized partner.

'Couldn't you have moved his feet out of the way?' Constance asked. 'That ding is *annoying*.'

'True, but this way the police have to use the stairs,' Milligan said, leading the children in the other direction. They hurried down another hallway and at last to an open window, beyond which a fire escape descended into a side alley. Sticky took one glance out the window and reached for his spectacles. Milligan put a hand on his shoulder. 'Don't look at the ground. Just watch your feet and keep moving. You'll be fine. Kate, you go first and we'll follow you.'

Just then they heard a door bang open, followed by the sound of officers (heavily winded from their climb up the stairs) storming into the other hallway. Kate vaulted the windowsill and led the way down the fire-escape steps, down and down, flight after flight, until she leapt the last few steps and landed beside a parked car. Only then did she realize it was a police car.

'Get in, Kate,' Milligan called from above. 'That's our car.'

'A *police* car?'

'I borrowed it,' said Milligan. 'Quick now, boys.'

Reynie and Sticky scrambled down the final steps of the fire escape and jumped into the back seat with Kate. Milligan put Constance in front with him. 'Keep your heads down,' he said, reversing out of the alley. As he drove past the front of the hotel he murmured, 'Three police cars. Good. And that woman in the lobby must be who called. She looks distraught. Small wonder there.'

'What woman?' Sticky asked, dutifully keeping his head down.

'One of the receptionists. She called the police and told them she'd been bribed and threatened, and that some bad men were on the way to the hotel. She was afraid they were going to do something to a group of children there.'

'How do you know all that?' Constance asked.

Milligan glanced at her. She was sitting up straight in the passenger seat – unlike the others she hadn't needed to duck – and Milligan frowned as something occurred to him. 'You should be in a child's car seat. It's dangerous without one.'

Constance looked at him incredulously. 'Are you joking?'

'A bit. Still, let's do buckle up, everyone.' Keeping his eyes on the road, Milligan reached across and pulled down Constance's seat belt strap, which because of her height (or lack thereof) ran diagonally across her face. She glared at him with her one visible eye.

'Feel free to adjust that,' Milligan said, giving her a lopsided grin. 'Now, to answer your question, I knew what I did by listening to a police radio scanner. My Dutch isn't perfect, but I know enough to do the trick. And luckily I was already in the neighbourhood. The police had mentioned you on the scanner earlier today, too. They said you'd just left the science museum and should be brought into the station for questioning. You four have been busy.'

'I'm glad you found us,' said Reynie. 'Things were about to get awfully unpleasant.'

'I'm so sorry I didn't catch up with you sooner,' Milligan said, the regret plain on his face. 'Five minutes earlier and I could have spared you that encounter – and spared myself the worry. I was detained, unfortunately, or I would have met you the moment you came ashore in Lisbon. It didn't help matters that you're all so horribly clever. I can't tell you how troubled I was to discover you weren't on the train in Thernbaakagen.'

By now the children were all sitting up. Milligan was driving through a gritty warehouse district near the harbour. All but Constance, who was too short, could see the shimmer of the North Sea in the near distance.

'But how did you know we were on that train?' Reynie asked. 'How did you even know we were in Lisbon?'

'It's my job to know things,' Milligan said with a mysterious air. Then he shrugged. 'Also, you left the travel journal Mr Benedict gave you.'

'Oh!' said Kate. 'Then we're lucky we forgot it! I *told* you it was a good thing, Constance!'

'It was indeed,' said Milligan. 'When I arrived at Mr Benedict's house, Rhonda had already discovered your note, and we found the journal soon after. It took us some time to figure out the clues, though, and by the time we did the *Shortcut* had launched. Still, I knew you were in good hands with Captain Noland, and that by catching a plane I would arrive in Lisbon before you, so I didn't really worry until

Joe Shooter – Cannonball, I mean – informed me you were all alone at the castle. I was ready to race up there when you radioed, Kate. I couldn't make out a single word, but it was clear enough from the background noises that you were at the train station.'

Milligan shook his head. 'I barely missed you. I even saw your train pulling away. But at that point I had to take Jackson and Jillson in hand. Yes, they're in custody,' he said in response to the children's exclamations. 'And we had a nice talk. They're stubborn, those two, but luckily they're also quite stupid. They told me more than they realized, and I quickly gathered you were in no danger on that train. So once again I didn't worry; once again I caught a plane – the ticket agent had told me you were headed for Thernbaakagen – and once again I arrived before you. But I didn't take into account your own wariness. I should have guessed you'd get off at a different station . . . ah, this is perfect.'

Milligan pulled the police car off the road and into a warehouse, which somehow he had deduced was empty despite its wide-open bay doors. Shutting off the engine, he turned to make eye contact with all of them – first Kate, then the others, then Kate again. 'You were brave to do what you did,' he said slowly. 'And I know you did it out of love for our friends. But if you ever do something like this again, I can promise you that Ten Men and Executives are going to be the least of your worries – do you understand?' His expression was very severe, his jaw was set, and his words were clipped and terse as if spoken with much suppressed anger.

Kate burst out laughing. Milligan's eyebrows shot up, and Kate, seeing this, laughed even louder. 'Milligan,' she said,

246

'I'll bet you scare the wits out of bad guys, but as a dad you don't scare anyone very much.'

'She's right,' Constance said. 'I can tell you aren't really angry.'

Milligan frowned and looked at Reynie, but Reynie averted his eyes to avoid disappointing him – for he, too, had been unfazed by Milligan's stern admonition. Only Sticky, furiously polishing his spectacles in the back seat, showed the effect Milligan had hoped for. But Sticky was easily unnerved and could hardly be used as a measure.

'Well,' Milligan said, his face relaxing. 'At least I tried.' He jumped from the car and let them all out. Then he went to the boot, out of which he took a large duffel bag and into which he put the Ten Man's briefcase. Shadowing him, the children saw three other briefcases already inside. Milligan slammed the boot closed.

'If this place is abandoned, why are the doors open?' Sticky asked.

'Broken,' Milligan said, reaching inside his suit jacket. He took out a small tool rather like an Army knife, and in seconds he had done something to the winch mechanism that allowed the bay doors to come rattling down.

It was dusky grey in the warehouse now, the only light being that which filtered in through dirty windows and a broken skylight. And though the day was warm, the warehouse was cold, and Constance began to shiver. Milligan took off his suit jacket and draped it over her shoulders. The jacket hung all around her and down to her feet like a cloak.

'Time for a quick change,' Milligan said, picking up his duffel bag. 'Excuse me a minute.'

Kate followed him into what once had been the warehouse office. She was so happy to see Milligan she didn't want to be separated from him even for a minute. In fact, during the car ride she'd kept having the urge to hug him again – and now she did just that, throwing her arms around him and squeezing with all her might. Milligan winced, but as his expression was the same as that of everyone Kate hugged, she thought nothing of it until a minute later, when Milligan was changing shirts and she saw his torso covered with a shocking display of cuts and bruises.

'What happened to you?' she cried, staring. 'Hm?'

Milligan looked down. 'Oh. These. I told you, Katie-Cat. I was detained. That's why I missed you in Lisbon.'

Kate was aghast. 'I thought you got caught up in *traffic*! Or, I don't know, had an urgent, top-secret meeting or something!'

'It was a sort of meeting,' Milligan said, pulling on a different shirt. 'I've had lots of meetings lately. Not all go as smoothly as the one at the hotel.'

Kate suddenly felt worried about Milligan, which had almost never happened, and it was a very disagreeable feeling indeed. She felt guilty, too, for it occurred to her that if she was this worried about Milligan, Milligan must have felt at least as worried about her. Probably more so. She was his daughter, after all.

'Milligan,' Kate said, 'I really am sorry to have worried you.'

'Well, you couldn't have had better intentions,' Milligan said, winking at her. 'I appreciate the apology, though.

When I heard you'd gone – well, I know you're very capable, Kate, but I don't suppose I've slept two hours in as many days. I admit it's taken its toll. I'm not Number Two, after all.'

At this, their faces grew sombre, and Milligan laid his hand on Kate's shoulder. 'We're going to get them back. Don't you worry.'

Her father's words were an unexpected comfort to Kate – who hadn't realized till now that she really could use some comforting – and the effect was to bring tears to her eyes. Kate had always thought crying an acceptable thing for others to do, but she didn't particularly care to be seen doing it herself, so she leant out of the office door, pretending to check on her friends. (The boys had opened the police car's boot and were peeking in at the briefcases, while Constance was hopping up and down to keep warm.) By the time Kate had blinked her eyes clear and turned back to him, Milligan had almost completed his transformation.

Dressed in his usual weather-beaten boots, jacket and hat, Milligan looked nothing like a secret agent and everything like someone who'd got a bad deal at a second-hand shop. Kate was always impressed by the way his clothes so perfectly concealed his utility belt and tranquilizer gun. She thought he ought to look lumpier, somehow.

Milligan adjusted his hat. 'How do I look? More like myself?'

'Except for the black hair and brown eyes,' Kate said, appraising him. 'And your ears look smaller. They're – I don't know, flatter or something.'

'Ah.' Milligan tugged a piece of transparent tape from each side of his head. His ears sprang out to their normal

249

positions. Then he removed the coloured contact lenses, revealing his natural ocean-blue eyes – eyes the same colour as Kate's – and put the lenses away in a tiny container. 'Better? I'm afraid I'm stuck with the black hair for a while.'

Kate was grinning, partly because he looked more like her father now, and partly because she had a great admiration for disguises. 'Were you trying to look like anyone in particular?'

'Anyone but myself,' Milligan replied. 'I've developed a bit of a bad reputation in certain circles. I have an unpopular habit of collecting briefcases that don't belong to me. Speaking of which, the boys weren't actually *touching* the briefcases in the boot, I hope?'

Wondering how Milligan knew, Kate stuck her head out of the office door and gave Reynie and Sticky a warning look. They nodded and tried to close the boot as quietly as possible. 'They aren't now, anyway.'

'Good,' Milligan said, picking up his duffel bag. 'I'd hate to have to speak sternly to them again. It embarrasses me to be so ineffective.'

'What you tell me fits with what I learned from Jackson and Jillson,' said Milligan, when the children had related everything they'd found out. 'My impression is that Curtain has Executives and Ten Men posted all along Mr Benedict's trail. They haven't any clue what they're looking for, because they don't know what Mr Benedict was up to. But they've been keeping an eye out for anything suspicious.'

'So Mr Curtain was just shooting in the dark,' Sticky said. 'Hoping to turn up something he could use.' 'Which he did,' Milligan said. 'He got lucky with this duskwort business. I don't suppose I need to tell you how serious a matter this is. Every law enforcement agency in the world is already nervous about Curtain – and that's without including duskwort. If he gets his hands on real duskwort, if he can send entire *cities* to sleep . . .'

'It will be a dark day,' said Reynie grimly.

'It will be a dark *night*,' said Kate.

Sticky started to say that it would be a total solar eclipse in conjunction with unseasonably heavy cloud cover, but Constance interrupted him.

'Forget all that,' she said crossly. 'What about Mr Benedict and Number Two? We only have until tomorrow to find them!'

'Try not to worry,' said Milligan. 'I intend to stop Curtain before he can harm them – *and* before he learns where to find that plant. There's time enough, Constance. I promise.'

'How can you be sure?' Constance demanded.

'At the airport earlier I was able to confirm that Mr Benedict and Number Two flew here from Lisbon. There was no record of their flying out again, however, so it would appear they travelled to the island by boat, and the fact that he gave you the address of a water transport business makes it all but certain. The island can't be very far – probably somewhere in the North Sea.'

'But the oceans are connected!' cried Constance (who had deduced this from gazing so often at her globe pendant). 'A boat could have taken them anywhere! For all we know they're on the other side of the world!' Her face had gone bright red – she was getting very upset. It seemed to her that Milligan had overlooked a key fact, and if it turned out that he was wrong, that they *couldn't* get to that island in time . . .

'They haven't been gone long enough for that, Constance,' Reynie said gently. 'Not every boat is as fast as the *Shortcut*.'

Constance stared at him a moment, then turned to Sticky, who probably knew everything there was to know about ocean distances and ship speeds and whatnot.

'It's true,' Sticky said. 'The island can't be very far.'

'Well, why didn't anyone *say* that?' Constance growled at no one in particular, but she looked much relieved.

Kate clapped her hands together. 'So what are we waiting for? Let's head for the wharf.'

'We're practically there,' Milligan said. 'I need to scout it out first, though. I'll take a look from the roof.' He headed for the rear of the warehouse, where a very steep and rickety-looking stairway led up to a high door.

'I'm coming, too!' Kate said, hurrying after him.

'We'll all come,' said Reynie.

Milligan spun around and held up his hand in warning. 'No, you won't. These stairs may be unsound. You stay here, and I'll be back in a minute. I mean it, now. Stay put.' Composing his face into a severe expression to show them he meant business, he went up the stairs and disappeared through the door at the top.

The children waited until the door had closed and Milligan was out of earshot. Then they went up after him.

THE BOATHOUSE PRISONER

The door at the top of the stairs opened onto a utility room. From there a ladder and a second door led to the wide, flat roof. The children found Milligan at the roof's edge, peering through a spyglass he'd balanced atop the low wall there.

'You seem to have misunderstood me,' Milligan said in an even tone, without bothering to look at them.

'The stairs held you, so we figured they were sound,' Reynie said.

Milligan grunted. 'For future reference, I walk lightly. Don't ever let that be your guide.' Reynie was unsure if

253

Milligan was teasing him or not. He wouldn't be entirely surprised to learn that Milligan could walk on water. 'Have you found anything unusual?'

'It's what I expected. Several docks and boathouses, a number of seagulls, and one well-dressed fellow with a briefcase.'

Kate took out her own spyglass and swept it along the wharf. Overhanging the entrance to one of the long docks was a sign that had been lettered in both Dutch and English. The English words read: RISKER WATER TRANSPORT – OCEAN TOURS & BOAT RENTALS. A Ten Man stood beneath the sign, his briefcase at his feet and his eyes roving up and down the wharf. Every so often he turned to glance behind him toward the far end of the dock, where a grimy old yacht was moored beside a boathouse.

'I wonder why he keeps looking behind him,' Reynie said, when Kate had passed him her spyglass and showed him where to point it. 'If he's just keeping an eye out for whoever shows up, why watch the boathouse? For that matter, why is he standing in plain sight, unless . . . ?'

'Unless he's guarding the exit?' said Milligan. 'Yes. He's keeping that man prisoner in the boathouse.'

'What man?' asked Reynie. The boathouse had a window, but from this angle he couldn't see through it.

'He came out a minute ago – just before you all so flagrantly disobeyed me – and picked up a carton that had been left at the door. He was staring toward the Ten Man as if he wanted to throttle him. But when the Ten Man glanced back at him, he scurried inside like a frightened mouse.'

'So what do we do?' asked Sticky.

'I know,' said Kate, nudging Milligan and pointing to another warehouse roof much closer to the wharf. 'From over there you can get the drop on the Ten Man with your tranquilizer gun. He'll be out like a light before he knows what hit him.'

Milligan shook his head. 'It's more complicated than that. See how close he's standing to the edge of the dock? I can't risk it. He might fall into the water and drown.'

Kate looked at him cockeyed. 'Are you kidding? These guys are monsters! If that one fell into the water it would serve him right!'

'You might think you mean that,' said Milligan. 'But you'd feel differently if it were to happen and you were responsible. We're not like them, Kate. That's the entire point of trying to stop them.'

'I know we're not,' Kate said irritably. She wanted to argue but could tell it was a waste of time.

Constance was not so easily convinced, however, and in her most strident tone she said, 'So you just let them get away? Like those guys in the hotel?'

Milligan rubbed his temples and explained, as patiently as he could, that he'd already alerted the authorities to the presence of Ten Men in Thernbaakagen. 'The police at the hotel will be vigilant, I assure you. I don't just 'let them get away.' But neither do I risk killing someone – not even a Ten Man – if I can think of a better option.'

'So what's the better option?' Kate asked.

'I'm still trying to think of it,' Milligan admitted. 'I could lure him away from there – preferably to a place where I could engage him at my advantage – but then the prisoner may take the opportunity to flee, and I can't let that happen. He may have vital information.'

'That's easy, then,' said Reynie. 'You draw the Ten Man away, and we'll run down and talk to the prisoner.'

'That's out of the question,' Milligan said. 'You won't be involved in this operation. End of discussion.'

It was not the end of the discussion, however, for the children set at once to arguing with Milligan, pursuing him across the roof and surrounding him and pestering him like honeybees after a bear. With the Ten Man gone there'd be no danger, Reynie said; the clock was ticking and every minute counted, Kate said; if he didn't let them do it they would die on the spot and it would be Milligan's fault, said Constance (who could think of nothing better to say); they'd post a lookout, Sticky said, and if something went wrong they'd leave at once. The children said all this and a great many other things besides, generally speaking at the same time and raising their voices to be heard over one another.

'Enough!' Milligan said finally, clutching at his head as if someone had bludgeoned him. 'We'll compromise. You can hide nearby and keep an eye on the boathouse. But under no circumstances will you come *out* of hiding unless the prisoner appears and seems ready to run. Then – and only then – you may leave your hiding place to speak with him. Is that understood?'

The children swore they understood. And they did. They understood that if something went wrong with Milligan's plan – if the Ten Man got away from him or radioed for help – they might never get a chance to speak with the man in the boathouse, and the consequences for Mr Benedict and Number Two could be dire. So although they understood it was Milligan's duty to keep them safe, they also understood that their own duty required them to disobey him.

It had begun to rain intermittently, fat drops of water so widely spaced one could almost count them. Though it was only mid-afternoon, the sky had grown quite dark, and pedestrian traffic along the wharf had cleared out, anticipating a heavy downpour that Constance said would not develop. The children were huddled under the awning of a tourist shop that had gone out of business. Milligan was behind the shop, picking the lock to the back door. Farther down the wharf the Ten Man stood as before, heedless of the rain.

Reynie looked out over the water, muddy grey and troubled by raindrops, the perfect mirror to his mood. Waiting is never easy, especially when one faces a dangerous task. Even a few moments can allow time to think and feel too much, and Reynie had quite a bit to think and feel. Not only was he struggling to keep his courage up and his dread at bay, but seeing how happy Kate was with Milligan around had given him a painful case of homesickness. Reynie missed Miss Perumal's wry smile, her teasing tones, the frequent hugs from her and Pati. And he missed the feeling of being safe at home – hardly even noticeable most days, a feeling he'd begun to take for granted. How he hoped he might take it for granted again soon!

At that very moment Sticky happened to be gazing at the water, too. Like Reynie he was every bit as wistful as he was nervous, and for much the same reasons. It was one of those rare occasions when two different people feel exactly the same way at exactly the same moment, and somehow both boys sensed this. When at the sound of the front door unlocking they turned and their eyes met, they smiled (however glumly) and nodded with a feeling of mutual understanding and appreciation. If they had to be anxious and homesick, at least they were anxious and homesick together.

Milligan stepped aside to let them enter. Kate hustled right in, but the others needed a moment to recover from the surprise, for Milligan had considerably altered his appearance. He looked markedly shorter, his face seemed oddly puffy beneath a dilapidated fisherman's hat, and when he grinned at them two of his teeth shone gold. Under less urgent circumstances he would have been peppered with questions about this transformation, but as it was, the children scurried silently into the empty shop. Kate was already at the far window, opening the dusty blinds a few inches and looking out through her spyglass.

'This will work,' she said. 'I can see all the way down the wharf.'

'Good. Now remember,' Milligan said, 'even if the prisoner makes a run for it, you're not to leave this building if the Ten Man and I are still in view. If that happens, I'll handle the situation myself. It isn't my preference, but I can manage it as long as I'm not distracted with worrying about you.'

'We get it, Milligan,' said Kate, who knew too well the discomfort of worrying about someone you love. Now that her father was seconds away from a dangerous encounter, she'd begun to grow very worried herself.

'All right then, I'm off,' said Milligan. Reynie, Sticky, and Constance wished him luck, and Kate hugged him (not as fiercely as before – she was mindful of his cuts and bruises – but with a great deal of conviction) until finally Milligan had to unwrap her arms. He tweaked her chin and went out.

With the others at her heels, Kate ran to the window and poked her spyglass beneath the blinds. Milligan was walking slowly along the wharf. The Ten Man had already seen him coming, stooped to pick up his briefcase, and slipped the other hand inside his suit coat. He kept his hand hidden there as Milligan drew near. Kate couldn't tell if Milligan spoke or gave any kind of private signal, but the Ten Man studied him intently as he walked past – and continued to study him after Milligan's back was to him.

Milligan kept walking. The Ten Man glanced toward the boathouse and frowned. He checked his watch . . . then checked his *other* watch . . . and then, with a movement so quick Kate almost missed it, he took something out of his briefcase and slipped it inside his suit coat.

'What was that?' cried Sticky, startled. He had squeezed in next to Kate at the window and was watching without the benefit of a spyglass.

'I couldn't tell,' said Kate. Her pulse was pounding in her ears.

With a final glance at the boathouse, the Ten Man set off along the wharf. Milligan, at this point, was nearing the far end of the wharf, heading for a group of outbuildings. But the Ten Man's stride was twice his, and by the time Milligan turned behind the outbuildings the Ten Man was barely a dozen paces behind him. The Ten Man stopped abruptly, contemplating the corner of the building around which

Milligan had disappeared. Spinning on his heel, he turned to take a different route, circling behind the buildings from the opposite direction.

Kate almost dropped her spyglass. 'He's sneaking up on Milligan! He's going the other way! I have to warn him!' She whirled to race out, but Reynie was standing right behind her – otherwise he'd never have been able to stop her. He threw his arms around her and held on as tightly as he could.

'Hold on, Kate – you don't know what Milligan has in mind! Maybe he *expected* that guy to do that! You can't risk messing up his plan! You—'

Kate had already freed herself from his grip (Reynie wasn't sure how, but he found himself on the ground with his arms empty) and was almost at the door when she drew up short, his words sinking in. He was right, of course. She had no idea how Milligan did what he did. She might very well endanger him when she meant to help him. Difficult as it was, she would simply have to trust Milligan to take care of himself.

'You're right,' Kate said with a resigned sigh. She hurried over and lifted Reynie to his feet, but when she tried to dust off his clothes he emphatically protested. 'Really? You're fine? Good, then, let's go!'

With Constance on her back, Kate led the way along the wharf and down the long dock to the boathouse. Milligan and the Ten Man were nowhere to be seen. Kate dashed in through the boathouse door, then stopped in her tracks, throwing out an arm to prevent the boys (who were less adept at stopping in their tracks) from falling into the empty rectangle of water that took up most of the room.

The children looked quickly about. There were no boats in the boathouse, only the murky water and a walkway on three sides. At a table against the near wall sat a stunned-looking man who'd been making pyramids out of canned goods.

'Who the devil are you?' he cried in English, leaping from his chair and toppling his pyramid. A slump-shouldered man with a face as round as a clock and covered with dark stubble, the boathouse prisoner was dressed in dirty fisherman's clothes, and his black hair, streaked with grey, hung about his face in long greasy strands. He appeared not to have bathed or groomed in days.

'We're friends,' Reynie said as Sticky closed the door and Kate, with her spyglass, took up her position at the window.

'Friends? Ha! If that shadow let you in here I know you ain't my friends.'

'He didn't,' said Reynie. 'We snuck in.'

The man's bloodshot eyes widened, and shoving Reynie aside – almost, in fact, knocking him into the water – he went to the window and looked out over Kate's shoulder. 'So he's gone, is he?'

'Our friend led him away so we could talk to you,' Reynie said. 'Don't worry, that man won't bother you any more. Our friend will take care of that.'

The man looked askance at Reynie, sizing him up. He snorted derisively and looked out of the window again. 'Your friend, eh? Well, too bad for your friend, whoever he is. I don't suppose he knows what he's got himself into.'

With a shake of his head, the man set to pacing, mumbling to himself. 'If the boy's telling the truth, though, now might be the time . . . but it wouldn't take him long,

261

you know it wouldn't, and if he catches you making a break for it . . .' He ran his fingers through his greasy hair and cursed in frustration. 'No, Risker, old boy, you'd better just wait to be sure. Give it a few minutes. Yes, three minutes, maybe four . . .' He went to look out over Kate's shoulder again.

'Mr Risker,' said Reynie, 'please listen to me. You'll see soon enough that everything's all right. We're friends of Nich—'

'Benedict,' said Risker, waving him quiet. 'Oh, I know who you are now, just took me a minute to get a fix on things. I didn't expect a bunch of kids, that's all. Plus there's only four of you, and he paid passage for six.'

'Mr Benedict paid for our passage?' Constance said. 'Passage to where?'

'To his confounded island, that's where! Same place I took him and his friend!' Risker turned from the window to glare at her. He seemed glad to have someone to glare at. 'Nothing but directions with that weird bird. 'Take them here. Tell them this and that. Tell no one else. I'll make it worth your while.' Blah blah blah.'

'What's your problem?' Constance demanded.

'My problem,' Risker growled, 'is I've had nothing but misery since I got back. I wish I'd never met Benedict, I can tell you. And if *you* meet *that* fellow' – he jerked his thumb in the direction of the dock entrance, where the Ten Man had stood guard – 'you'll be wishing the same thing soon enough.'

Reynie was growing very angry. 'What did Mr Benedict do, offer to pay you more money once we arrived safely?'

'Not enough for this!' Risker snarled. He pointed to the

empty rectangle of water. 'My rental boats sunk in twenty feet of water! And my yacht engine sabotaged! And here I sit with no business whatsoever, trapped in my own boat-house with nothing to eat but soup and beans!' In a fit of fury, Risker swept the canned goods from the table. The cans tumbled noisily over the floorboards and splashed into the water.

Reynie tried to master his anger. This man was obviously in a pitiful state; provoking him would only make things worse. 'We're sorry for your trouble,' he said in a calmer voice. 'But things will be better for you now, and we really need your help. Our friends are in danger, and—'

'Join the club,' Risker said with a sneer. He squinted out of the window, craning his head this way and that for a better view in each direction. 'Two more minutes and I'm gone.'

'But all we want is information!' Reynie said. 'Just tell us where the island is and what Mr Benedict told you. Then we'll leave you alone. Is that so hard?'

'Don't you get snappy with me! You don't know what I've been through, do you? The last time I gave out that infor-mation I got myself electrified and cheated all at once! 'Big reward,' they said, but I never saw any reward, did I? *This* is my reward, boy!' Risker waved his arms about, indicating his boathouse prison. But even as he did, the fury seemed to pass from his face, his shoulders sagged, and he returned to staring out the window and muttering to himself. 'Held out a long time, too. Even with those shockers. I held out.'

Reynie bit his tongue. Risker was clearly ashamed, but he was the sort of person whose shame made him bitter and resentful. Saying the wrong thing would only set him more

263

deeply against them. Reynie tried to find the right words . . .

'So you betrayed them,' Kate said, glancing over her shoulder at the filthy man. 'Why not make up for it now and tell us what we want to know? Then you can stop feeling so bad about being a traitor.'

Risker stared at her, trembling violently, his red eyes bulging from his head. 'I'll tell you nothing!' he shouted, and this time he grew so furious he overturned his table. It toppled into the water and drifted to the other side. Risker looked around at the children, his chest heaving. He shook his head and moved toward the door. 'No . . . no, I'm not even going to bother with you. Now's my chance, and I'm taking it. You can wait and find out what's happened to your friend. I'm leaving, and there's no—'

'Let's try it this way,' Reynie said, taking something from his pocket. 'Risker, do you want this or not?'

Risker froze and fell silent, gaping at Reynie's outstretched palm, upon which rested a rather large and brilliant diamond. Even in the murky boathouse the diamond twinkled like a star.

Sticky gasped and put his hands to his head in disbelief. 'How did you get that, Reynie?'

'Captain Noland gave it to him,' said Constance with a knowing expression.

Kate was opening and closing her mouth in shocked indignation. 'Reynie!' she said at last, in a severe tone. 'You can't give that away! It doesn't belong to you!'

'Maybe I will and maybe I won't,' Reynie said, watching Risker's face. The other children's reactions were not lost on the man, whose eyes glinted hungrily as he stared at the sparkling stone. He stepped forward, but Reynie stepped back, and staring directly into Risker's eyes he held the diamond out over the water.

'Tell us what we want to know,' he said firmly, 'and I'll give this to you. Hesitate five seconds and I'll drop it into the water. Your choice.'

Risker was taken aback. 'No! Surely you wouldn't . . . can it possibly be real?'

'Of course it's real,' Reynie said, and it was clear he meant it. 'And now I'll begin counting. One . . .'

'Hold on!' Risker said. 'Don't be hasty now, boy! I can tell you mean what you say. It's real, and you'll hand it over to me if I tell you everything, is that right? We're in agreement?'

Reynie nodded.

'Good, then! Fine indeed. There's not so much to tell, anyway. Why don't you just step away from the water first? Don't want to risk an accident, right? Don't want to drop—'

'Three,' Reynie said. 'Four.'

'I was to take you to the island and give you a message!' Risker said quickly. 'I can't take you there now, of course, but I can tell you where it is. I can tell you the exact place we were to land – the place I dropped your friends off – and the message is this: 'Follow the wind.' That's all, I swear it. 'Follow the wind.' The rest is just details.'

'I happen to be fond of details,' Reynie said. 'Now draw us a map.'

'I've got nothing to draw it with.'

Kate gave him pen and paper from her bucket, then hurried back to the window. It seemed to her that too much time had passed, and her face was taut with worry.

Risker drew a hasty map. 'I'm putting down the longitude and latitude, and I can sketch the eastern part of the island as I saw it, but I never went beyond the shore. I helped them unload their supplies – they brought enough for the lot of you – and then I left. I don't know anything else about it.'

'That's a good start,' Reynie said. 'Now give us the details, and do it quick. Someone will be here soon – either the man in the suit or our friend. Either way, you'd better talk fast.'

Risker did. Their friends, he said, had come to him some days earlier. After a long conversation (during which he got the impression he was being evaluated), Mr Benedict had asked for passage to the island, and he and Risker had come to terms. Risker would take Mr Benedict and Number Two, then return and wait for Mr Benedict's friends to arrive. He would reserve his yacht for their arrival and speak to no one about the trip or the island. If all went as arranged, Mr Benedict would give him more money later. To Risker this seemed an arrangement easily kept. What he couldn't have known was that the men with briefcases would come knocking.

They had a young woman with them, Risker said (from his description the children knew it was Martina Crowe), and their inquiries about Mr Benedict were so cheerful and polite that he mentioned the island before he realized they weren't Mr Benedict's friends at all. When he did begin to suspect, he clammed up, but it was too late. They knew he knew what they wanted to know.

'Must've had their own boat,' Risker said. 'They could have taken my yacht, easy. Instead they sabotaged it and left it sitting out there so things ain't suspicious to the port authorities. And whenever anyone comes by the dock, that shadow down there sizes them up – I've seen him do it – then sends them on their way. He tells them I'm ill, which ain't far from the truth now, I can tell you that.'

The situation was finally growing clear to Reynie. Mr Benedict had decided he could trust Risker, but he hadn't known he and Number Two were being followed, and so hadn't imagined the man would come into such a terrible predicament.

'I didn't tell them everything, though,' Risker said. 'I didn't give them the message about the wind. They didn't ask about it, so that much, at least, I kept from them,' he said, then called the Ten Men an unpleasant name.

'One last thing,' said Reynie, who like Kate was growing extremely nervous about how long Milligan had been gone. 'Why did Mr Benedict come to you? The wharf is full of boats for hire. Why you in particular? Did he give a reason?'

Risker's eyes narrowed. 'You ain't Benedict's own boy, are you? You seem to have that same kind of something going on.' He tapped his forehead. 'Up here, I mean.' When Reynie didn't answer (he thought it best to remain inscrutable), Risker shrugged and said, 'He chose me because we had something in common, he said. First I thought it was because we were both born here but grew up somewhere else.'

'But that wasn't what he meant,' Reynie prompted.

'No, he said his parents were friends of my grandad, Han de Reizeger. That was my birth name, see – de Reizeger. I changed it to Risker years ago. Your Benedict said he felt he owed something to my grandad and wanted to give me some business by way of showing gratitude. Wouldn't say more than that, and I didn't care. I was happy for the business, is all.'

Sticky and Constance looked back and forth between Reynie and Risker, who had grown expectantly tense, his eyes fixed on the hand Reynie held over the water. Reynie nodded, satisfied, and with one last distasteful glance at the diamond, he tossed it in Risker's direction.

Risker was caught off guard – he hadn't expected Reynie to toss such a valuable thing. His eyes bulged, and with fumbling hands he snatched at the diamond in the air. It glanced off his fingertips and went skittering across the floorboards toward the water. 'No!' he shouted, lunging after it. A moment later he had tumbled into the water. And a moment after that he was drowning.

'Help!' Risker gasped, floundering about. His thrashing arms sent up a terrific splash. 'I can't swim!'

In a smooth blur of movement, Kate took her rope from the bucket and tossed one end out to him. 'Grab it, Risker! Grab the rope!' Wild-eyed, Risker snatched at the rope and clung desperately to it. Kate pulled him over to the edge, and with great effort he dragged himself up onto the floor-boards, panting and cursing.

'I wondered why you didn't just swim out of here,' Kate said as she recoiled her rope. 'I guess this explains it.'

Risker stood up, water puddling at his feet. His chest heaved, his legs were shaky, and he looked terribly confused. He wanted to throttle Reynie for being so reck-less with the diamond, but now he owed Kate his life, and throttling her companion wouldn't exactly do. Still trem-bling, he glanced down at the water that had nearly claimed him. With a frown Risker wiped dripping water from his eyes, blinked a few times, and looked again.

There was the glittering stone, bobbing in the water like a fragment of ice.

'Why, that's no diamond!' Risker shouted. 'Diamonds don't *float*!'

'What do you know?' said Reynie, whose opinion of Captain Noland had just improved somewhat. 'It's a fake!'

'But you said it was real!' Risker growled.

'Real, yes, but I never said it was a real *diamond*. I had no idea if it was a real diamond or not.'

Risker's jaw dropped, and Sticky and Kate stared at Reynie, mystified.

Constance, however, was rolling her eyes. 'I'm not sure which is more ridiculous,' she said. 'That you didn't know whether it was real, or that you were going to give it to him without knowing.'

'Saving Mr Benedict and Number Two isn't ridiculous, is it?' Reynie replied, and with a nervous glance at Risker he said quickly, 'Now let's go. We've already been here too long. I don't know what's keeping Milligan, but . . .'

At this, Kate's face clouded with worry, and she spun back to the window as Reynie moved to join the others near the door. He'd taken a great chance with Risker (who was still gaping at him, dumbstruck), and he needed to get out of that boathouse immediately, before the man could—

Too late. Risker sprang forward and seized him by the arm. 'I don't like being tricked, boy!' he snapped, his face contorted with fury. 'Maybe you'd like to see how it feels to splash around while everyone watches. Maybe you won't think you're so clever then!'

'Before you do anything hasty, you might want to look outside,' said Kate, breaking into a grin. She'd just seen Milligan striding toward the boathouse, briefcase in hand, and as Risker peered out of the window she said, 'He's with us. We *told* you he'd take care of that Ten Man.'

Risker's anger and indignation seemed to drain right out of him. 'Fair trade,' he said under his breath. He let go of Reynie's arm, then turned and leant heavily against the wall. 'At least you've got that shadow off my back.'

'Plus Kate saved you from drowning,' Constance pointed out.

'That, too,' said Risker, and after considering a moment he said, 'We'll still call it even.'

Follow the Wind

If the children had given Milligan a headache before, what he was experiencing now was something like the flu combined with a toothache, with lockjaw and mumps thrown in for good measure. In other words, Milligan was suffering. Not only had the children disobeyed him, they made no bones about continuing to do so as they deemed necessary.

Milligan was at a loss. He hadn't a great deal of experience as a father, much less as a guardian to children not his own, and he found himself sorely lacking now in the pertinent skills. To be fair, not many parents *would* know what to do. Not in this situation. Not with these children.

After they told him what they'd learned from Risker (who had wasted no time heading home for a hot meal and dry clothes), Milligan said he would make arrangements for their safe return to Stonetown. He would go on to the island himself, he said. But then the children had argued. And argued.

And argued.

And the trouble was, he thought they had a point. As a team, they were probably better qualified than Milligan to solve whatever riddles and clues Mr Benedict had left behind – and who knew how many more there might be? – especially since Mr Benedict would have created them with the children particularly in mind.

'If you don't bring us along,' Kate was saying, 'we'll just find a way to follow you there. The best thing from a father's standpoint would be to keep us close, so you can protect us.'

Milligan closed his eyes and began knocking his head against the wall of the boathouse.

'It isn't like we want to encounter another Ten Man,' Reynie hastened to remind him. 'Much less Mr Curtain. I'd be very happy never to see that man again. We just want to make sure you can rescue Mr Benedict and Number Two before it's too late.'

'Which is tomorrow,' Sticky pointed out. '*Tomorrow* is too late.'

'Please, Milligan,' said Constance, who so rarely said 'please' that Milligan felt disorientated to hear it coming from her mouth. 'Please, you *have* to let us come. We're their best chance!'

'But how can I trust you now?' Milligan said, exasperated. 'How do I know you'll do exactly what I say? It's the only way I can keep you safe. And that's my top priority here – keeping you safe. Not just Kate, but all of you.'

'We'll make a solemn promise,' Reynie said. 'If you let us come, we'll promise to obey you completely.' He looked at the others. 'Right? We really will.'

'So long as *you* promise not to exclude us,' Kate said to Milligan. 'If there's no direct danger and we can help you, you have to let us. If you promise to do that, I'll promise to obey you.'

'No matter what?' Milligan said doubtfully.

'No matter what,' the children said together.

Milligan studied their faces. 'What if I tell you to stop whatever you're doing, drop to the ground, and pretend to be pigs?'

'Then we root around for grubs,' Reynie said.

'We grunt and smell bad,' said Constance.

'Do you mean feral pigs or domesticated pigs?' Sticky asked. 'Because, you know, their behaviour patterns are considerably . . .' He trailed off. Milligan was staring hard at him. Sticky cleared his throat. 'Not that I would ask that question *then*. I'd be too busy snuffling and oinking.'

Milligan continued to stare hard, and not just at Sticky. He looked down the line of children, gazing into the eyes of every single one, until he felt certain they really were committed to obeying him. 'Make the promise.'

'We promise,' the children said together.

Milligan took off his hat and rubbed his head. He felt somehow that it was the wrong thing to agree, but he also suspected he'd feel the same way if he *didn't* agree. And just as Kate had said, at least this way he could keep an eye on them.

'Fine. I promise, too,' Milligan said, putting his hat back on. 'So let's waste no more time. I need to make a few calls and find transportation. Sit tight, everyone, and I'll be back soon with our ride.'

Their 'ride' turned out to be a bright silver seaplane. The children, who had expected a boat, stood outside the boathouse and gaped as the plane came puttering across the harbour with Milligan at the controls, the sun glinting off its wings so that they had to shield their eyes. (Constance had been right; the downpour never occurred and the clouds had blown over.) Milligan turned the plane at the last moment so that its tail end swung round, its propeller faced the harbour, and its left pontoon gently nudged the dock. He threw open the door and shouted for them to jump in.

'A plane?' Kate said as she scrambled aboard, her eyes sparkling with delight. 'You got us a *plane*?'

'Did you expect horses?' Milligan said. 'It's an island, you know.'

The others clambered aboard and strapped themselves in. Milligan checked the instrument panel, made sure the children were secure, then steered the seaplane out into the harbour, where a crew of fishermen waved from their boat as the plane roared past. Reynie saw them through the window, but he couldn't wave back; his hands were squeezing the armrests of his seat and he couldn't seem to loosen them. He'd never flown in an airplane before. Nor had Sticky, who was polishing his spectacles with slippery, sweaty fingers, or Constance, whose eyes were tightly shut. Only Kate managed to wave at the fishermen (and she did so with both hands, trying to make up for her rude friends). The plane accelerated until finally, with a stomach-dropping lurch, it lifted off the water and into the air. They were up and away.

Constance didn't open her eyes again, for no sooner were they airborne than the plane's vibration put her to sleep. But the others stayed awake pressing Milligan for details: How in the world had he got a plane so quickly? What were the calls he'd needed to make? Was one of them to Rhonda? Who else? And why did he go off by himself to make those calls, anyway? Shouldn't the children know more about it? And wouldn't . . . ?

Milligan chose not to reply to most of their questions (thereby answering the one about whether they should know more), but he did say that he'd called Rhonda and told her to pass along word that the children were fine. And yes, Milligan could confirm that the Washingtons and Miss Perumal and her mother had been in a state of near-panic since the children had sneaked away. And yes, they would be in big trouble when they got home – *huge* trouble, in fact – but since this paled in comparison to the danger they might face on the island, he suggested they concentrate on surviving the next twenty-four hours.

'Speaking of which,' Milligan said, checking his watch, 'three more should bring us there.'

Reynie knew something of geography and had seen Risker's map, so he knew their destination lay in the North Sea, not far off the coast of Scotland. And Sticky, who knew a great deal more, said the island went unnamed on the

275

maps he'd seen of the region (in fact it rarely appeared on maps at all) and had never been the focus of any territorial disputes. To the rest of the world, apparently, the island was of no consequence, yet to Milligan and the children it was now the most important place on earth.

For a long time they flew in silence, everyone lost in thought. So much had happened in so short a time there'd been little chance to reflect upon any of it. Reynie, for one, was contemplating the events of the day in order, trying to determine if anything had gone overlooked. Eventually, after more than an hour had passed, he did think of something – an obvious question he had neglected to ask.

'Milligan,' Reynie said, 'do you have any idea who the person is Mr Benedict mentioned? I mean the one who supposedly knows about the duskwort? I can't think of anyone closer to Mr Benedict than Rhonda or Number Two, but neither of them knows, and you said *you* don't know – so who could it be? Do you think it's a trick of some kind?'

'I have no idea who it might be,' Milligan replied, 'but I believe the person exists. In his letter Curtain said he was positive Mr Benedict was telling the truth. Well, I know what that's about. A group of Ten Men recently broke into a laboratory and stole a rare chemical compound – a new kind of truth serum. It was only enough for a few doses, but I'm sure Curtain used at least one of those on Mr Benedict.'

'If that's true, then why didn't Mr Benedict give the information outright?' Sticky asked. 'Why this mysterious business about someone 'extremely close' to him?'

'The truth serum is tricky. A single drop will make you answer questions truthfully, but it's only effective for a minute. If a person were clever enough – and we all know Mr Benedict is as clever as they come – he might anticipate the questions and invent responses that are essentially true but too vague to be meaningful. I imagine this is why Mr Curtain is holding Mr Benedict and Number Two for ransom. His serum is in short supply, so he's trying a different tactic.'

'So what if—?' Kate began.

Milligan interrupted her. 'Listen, all of you, I can't answer any more questions right now. If you must talk, talk among yourselves. There appears to be a bit of a mechanical issue with this plane. Nothing serious, but I do need to concentrate.'

'Oh, good grief,' said Kate, heaving a sigh. She turned to the boys. 'All right, I suppose we – hey, what's the matter with you two?'

'An . . . issue,' Sticky mumbled, his lips barely moving. 'He said . . . there's an . . . issue. . .'

Kate rolled her eyes. 'Calm down. He's probably just trying to make us stop asking questions. There's obviously something he doesn't want us to know. So fine, let's think about Mr Benedict's clue. What do you suppose 'follow the wind' means?'

'A mechanical issue,' said Reynie, putting his hands on his head.

'With the plane . . .' said Sticky.

'Snap out of it!' said Kate, and she badgered the boys mercilessly until they did – at least enough to have a conversation, though they kept watching Milligan's face for signs of distress. (He seemed untroubled, but then Milligan was sphinx-like in a crisis. He might appear untroubled even if the wings had fallen off.)

' 'Follow the wind',' Kate repeated when she had their attention. 'What do you think that means? Which wind did he have in mind? And follow it *where*?'

'It might not be an actual wind,' Reynie pointed out. 'It might be a symbol of some kind.'

'At the very least,' Sticky said, 'we know we'll be heading east.'

Kate and Reynie looked at him in surprise. (Milligan, in the pilot's seat, pricked up his ears.)

'I didn't tell you?' Sticky said when he saw their expressions. 'No, I suppose I didn't. Sorry, we've been busy.'

'Tell us what?' asked Kate.

'Han de Reizeger's letter said that on this island a strong wind blows out of the west from sunrise to sunset every day. The villagers told him it had always been that way. It's a curious phenomenon. He speculated it was a combination of tidal forces and thermal activity under the island, though personally I suspect—'

'Did you just say 'villagers'?' interrupted Reynie, remembering why it was often better for Sticky to quote things than to summarize them. With so many details to choose from, Sticky sometimes failed to recognize the significance of a particular one.

This time Sticky hadn't left out much. Yes, there used to be a village on the island, he said, though at the time Han de Reizeger wrote the letter it was rapidly losing its inhabitants. The villagers were forgoing that isolated, wind-blasted place for the conveniences (electricity and plumbing, for instance) of the mainland. Han had predicted that within a few years the island would be home only to mountain goats and cliff swallows.

'Sounds like there are mountains, then,' Reynie observed.

'How do you know that?' Kate asked, then blushed and laughed. 'Oh, right. Mountain goats. Cliff swallows. Well, it sounds perfectly charming.'

Two hours later they saw the island for themselves – a very large, oblong land mass in the middle of a watery nowhere. From a distance it had a notably two-faced appearance, for the late evening sun bathed the western half in soft yellow light, while a small central mountain range blocked the sun from the eastern half, relegating that part to something like dusk. The low mountains – of which there were exactly three – ran from south to north in the middle of the island and were dotted sparsely with trees. Seen from above they gave the island the look of some monstrous, unfathomable beast, its head and tail submerged, its spiny back spotted with moss.

To avoid notice, Milligan had approached at a great height, and as the plane flew over the island he and Kate used their spyglasses to survey the terrain, while the boys craned their necks and squinted to see what they could. A few miles across and perhaps twice as long, the island contained such a variety of landscapes it would have made for an excellent geography lesson. West of the mountains it was divided into three easily distinguished regions: the southwest, which was given to meadow; the northwest, which was all thicket and scrub brush; and between them a belt of woodland that ran almost all the way to the western shore. East of the mountains the island consisted mostly of an exposed plain of black rock, with the exception of a little forest that ranged along the shore of a large southeastern bay.

Unfortunately, even with spyglasses, Kate and Milligan observed nothing more than these geographical features. No movement in the open, no boats anchored in the bay, no sign of an encampment anywhere (they searched in vain for tell-tale wisps of campfire smoke). And although the abandoned village was easy to spot – it lay just west of the mountains at the edge of the woodland – there was nothing in it to suggest recent human activity. Nevertheless, everyone in the plane had the powerful feeling that there *was* something down there on the island – that this was indeed the place where their journey, for better or worse, would come to an end.

'That bay to the southeast must be where Risker took them ashore,' Kate said. 'It looks just like the one he drew on his map.'

'That's exactly where we're headed,' said Milligan, already turning the plane. 'At any rate it's the only good place to bring the plane down. Now hang on, everyone. I'll be making a quick descent to lessen our chances of being spotted.'

'When you say 'quick descent',' Reynie said, 'what exactly—?'

The plane suddenly plummeted downwards so fast and at such a steep angle that the children felt as if they'd gone over a waterfall. Reynie was convinced Milligan had lost control; his heart rose into his throat as he wondered whether the plane would smash to bits on the water's surface or plunge straight to the bottom of the bay. Sticky, wondering the same thing, tried desperately to faint from terror. But it is in the nature of a quick descent to end quickly – one way or another – and only a few moments later the seaplane's pontoons were skimming the water.

Milligan had brought the plane down just at the mouth of the bay, passing between low stony hills on either side and heading toward the bay's interior shore. The shoreline there was lined with trees – the edge of the little forest they'd seen from above – and as the plane drew nearer he scoured the trees with his spyglass. The approach took a couple of minutes, for the wind was against them and the water was choppy, and by the time the plane had glided into the shallows and run partly up onto the shore, Milligan was satisfied no ambush awaited them. Other than a few birds, beetles and rodents, the forest was empty.

'Everyone out,' he ordered. 'Quick now.'

Kate woke Constance, who stared at the rocky shoreline and trees in groggy amazement (to her it seemed as if the harbour in Thernbaakagen had been magically transformed), and the children scrambled from the plane into the chill breeze. Milligan was already out, rigging a cable around a wing strut with quick, sure movements, then hurrying to the nearest tree. He had produced a set of pulleys and winches, and using these he began dragging the seaplane up onto the shore. He had only to draw it a few yards before it lay in the shadow of the trees.

The trees did not lack for shadow. With the sun behind the mountains, this part of the island lay in a sort of semi-dusk, and it was growing darker by the moment. In the forest the air was even gloomier and spookier.

'Do I smell petrol?' said Kate, her nostrils flaring. Now that she'd mentioned it, the other children smelled petrol, too. When Milligan didn't answer, they looked at one another with concern.

'You mean there really *is* something wrong with the plane?' asked Sticky, who'd been hoping Kate was right about Milligan just trying to keep them quiet.

'Doesn't matter,' Milligan said, grunting with effort. He wiped sweat from his eyes and continued working at his winch. 'We won't be leaving by plane. The important thing now is to get it out of sight.' He went back into the plane and emerged carrying a large, camouflage-patterned tarpaulin.

'Did you just say we won't be leaving by plane?' asked Reynie.

'You need to stop asking questions now,' Milligan said, unrolling the tarpaulin.

'But how will we get off the island?' asked Constance.

Milligan frowned. 'I said you need to stop asking questions. Remember your promise.'

'Technically you didn't order us to stop,' Reynie pointed out, then quickly added, 'and before you do, you should consider how anxious you've just made us by telling us what you did. It's going to be hard for us to think about anything else, you know.'

At first Milligan made no reply to this. He climbed up and dragged the tarpaulin over the plane, fastening it securely on all sides so the brisk wind wouldn't carry it off. From a distance it would blend fairly well into the background of trees and rocks. Milligan came to stand before the children again. 'Listen to me, all of you. You needn't worry about getting off the island. I've already made other arrangements. As soon as we've determined where Curtain has our friends, I'm sending you away. Now please don't ask any more questions about it. That's a direct order.'

'Can we ask why we can't ask more questions about it?' asked Constance. 'Because that part seems unclear to me.'

Milligan grimaced, took off his hat, and rubbed his head. He obviously hated what he was about to say and had hoped to avoid saying it. 'Because, Constance, in a worst-case scenario – by which I mean if you are captured – it would be best for you to know as little as possible. Curtain will surely get out of you anything you're trying to keep secret. I prefer, therefore, to limit your secrets.'

'Oh,' said Constance, her eyes very wide. 'I don't intend to let that happen,' Milligan said quickly. 'I'm just being cautious.'

'Milligan,' Reynie said, 'can I ask if these arrangements—?'

'Involve the government?' Milligan finished, correctly guessing what Reynie was worried about. 'No, they do not. I've enlisted the aid of some personal friends. If Curtain has spies in the government – and I thought it best to assume he does – they don't know anything about it. Nothing's foolproof, but I promise I've done everything I can to avoid tipping him off. You can trust me, you know, Reynie.'

'I do trust you,' said Reynie, which was perfectly true. Milligan was one of the few people he *did* trust.

'All right,' Milligan said, clapping his hat down on his head again. 'Then let's see about following this wind. We can't be expected to head east, as Sticky suggested. That would only take us out to sea.'

Sticky looked disappointed. 'Well . . . maybe we're supposed to head upwind instead of downwind.'

Everyone fell silent, pondering the clue. It was the first time since they'd arrived that no one was talking or (in Milligan's case) working, and as they stood there they slowly became aware of the island's sounds: wind flapping the edges of Milligan's tarpaulin and shushing in the boughs of the trees, tree trunks groaning and creaking as they swayed, birds chittering and fluttering as they settled into their roosts for the night, the bay waters lapping against the shore . . .

And from somewhere in the forest, a faint yet unmistakable tinkling sound, like that of a chime.

DUSK BEFORE SUNDOWN

They found the wind chime hanging from a low branch a short distance into the forest. It was made of diamond-shaped pieces of thin, painted metal whose edges, according to Milligan, had been cut with a saw. They could find nothing in the tree it was hung from, no markings on the ground beneath it, no signs of any other clues at all. Reynie thought there must be something hidden in the chime's paintwork – which at first glance appeared to be random, disconnected lines and squiggles – but when Milligan took down the chime pieces and laid them on the ground to examine them, everyone suddenly heard another distant tinkling.

'Another chime?' Sticky said.

'So *that's* it!' Reynie said. 'Now that we've taken down this one, we can hear the next one – the one that's farther away. Mr Benedict left us a trail of sound!'

Kate started forward. 'Let's get moving, then. Who knows how many more there are?'

'Wait a minute,' said Constance, bending to take a closer look at the chime pieces. 'Let's figure this one out first.'

'There's no time,' Reynie said. 'The wind dies at sunset, and I doubt we can find the other chimes without it. It's already hard to see in these trees, and it's only going to get darker.'

Constance scowled at him. 'Who says the wind dies at sunset?'

'Han de Reizeger. You were asleep when Sticky told us.'

'Well, that's stupid! Whoever heard of a wind—?'

Milligan scooped up the chime pieces in one hand and Constance in the other. 'Stupid or not, we need to hurry.'

Constance, confused and annoyed, was looking around at the murky forest. 'But isn't it already after sunset?'

'It only seems that way because of the mountains,' said Milligan, setting off in the direction of the tinkling sound. 'Over on the western side there's still light – though not for long.'

'Dusk before sundown,' Constance muttered. 'That's ridiculous.'

They found the second wind chime fifty metres upwind, and a third one fifty metres beyond that. There they came to the edge of the forest and, apparently, the last of the chimes, for after this they heard no more. As Milligan climbed a tree to get a better view of the open terrain ahead, the children loosened the chime pieces from the wires that held them and laid them out on the ground: thirty diamond-shaped pieces of identical size, each painted with different markings.

'I just realized what these are,' Kate said.

'A jigsaw puzzle,' said Reynie, nodding. 'Made with an actual jigsaw.'

Kate flipped one of the pieces over. 'It's really complicated, though. There's paint on both sides, the edges all look the same, and we have no idea what the picture's supposed to be. This could take hours!'

Constance stepped closer, staring intently at the puzzle pieces. 'Turn that piece over, Kate,' she said, pointing. 'No, not that one, *that* one, near the corner. No, the *different* one, for crying out loud! Here, let me.' She knelt and flipped several of the pieces over. 'There. That has to be the right way, doesn't it? It's the only way you can see the jumbled-up map.'

The other children stared at Constance, then at the array of metal pieces on the ground. Where Constance saw a jumbled-up map, the rest of them saw a confusing mess of lines and colours.

Reynie squatted beside her. 'We can't quite make it out, Constance,' he said, trying to seem relaxed. 'Could you rearrange the pieces for us?'

Constance's eyes grew round. 'You mean I'm the only . . . ?'

'Oh, any of us can figure it out eventually,' Reynie said with a casual wave at the puzzle, 'but it'll go faster if you do it. What do you say?'

Constance saw through Reynie's attempt to keep her from feeling the pressure, but his easy, confident manner

287

had a steadying effect nonetheless. She swallowed hard. 'I . . . yes, okay. I'll sort it out.' Fumblingly she took up a piece and immediately dropped it. The same clumsy fingers that couldn't tie a proper bow in her shoelaces were now being put to a far more important test, and her nervousness had set them trembling.

'Just take it easy,' Reynie said. 'Take your time. However long it takes you will still be faster than we could manage.'

Constance took a breath and started again, her awkward fingers struggling to produce the picture she saw so clearly in her mind's eye.

During this time, Milligan had descended the tree and walked out from the forest's edge to inspect something on the ground. Kate went over to join him. The trees gave way to a plain of black rock – beyond which, almost a mile away, loomed the mountains.

'Most of this ground's too hard to take a track,' Milligan said as Kate knelt beside him. 'Except for here.' He indicated a wide patch of gravel in which some kind of heavy tread had left an imprint.

'What is that, a bulldozer track?' Kate asked, wondering how a bulldozer – or any heavy machinery, for that matter – could have come here.

'An amphibious vehicle,' Milligan said. 'I figured this was why we didn't see any boats. Mr Curtain has a Salamander.'

'A what?'

'Picture an armoured boat with tank treads. Fast on land, even faster on water. Big enough to carry Curtain and a whole crew of Ten Men, with plenty of room to spare for prisoners.'

'That figures,' said Kate, who was hardly surprised to

learn that Mr Curtain had an intimidating machine to carry him and his thugs around. He had terrorized the children at the Institute with his screeching, souped-up wheelchair, and the Salamander sounded rather like an oversized version of that wicked contraption.

'It came from that direction,' Milligan said, pointing northeast. 'I imagine they landed in the bay but had to skirt the forest, which is too thick for the Salamander to pass through. Probably they drove the island perimeter, dropping off scouts along the way. Ten Men are good trackers. Mr Benedict and Number Two would have had no chance of hiding and nowhere to run.' Milligan ground his heel into the Salamander track, angry at the thought of his friends being hunted.

'Where do you think they are?' asked Kate, who was feeling the same way. She imagined herself finding Mr Curtain and pummelling him about the ears, though in reality she knew she was no match for him alone.

'I suspect they're holed up in the mountains,' Milligan said. 'We didn't see the Salamander from the plane, so it's probably hidden inside a gully or a cave.'

Sticky came over to tell them Constance was finishing the puzzle. It had only taken her a few minutes. They went back just as she was placing the last piece. Before them lay a map of the island, which must have been modelled after the one Mr Benedict had taken from Han de Reizeger's letter. Mr Benedict had chosen to depict only certain parts of the island, and had done so simply but artfully, with a swathe of upright arrows indicating the little forest, three swooping curves for the mountains and a dense group of squares representing the village on the other side. A dotted line ran straight through the bottom of the middle mountain, ending at the village. 'What's the dotted line, do you think?' asked Constance.

'Most likely a tunnel, given its placement,' said Milligan. He knelt and tapped his finger on the village. 'This must be where you were to meet them, which makes it my next stop.'

'*Your* next stop?' Reynie said. 'Not ours?'

Milligan stood. 'You'll stay here under cover of the forest. I've searched in all directions and seen no sign of anyone coming – and believe me, if we'd been spotted someone would definitely be coming – so here is where you'll be safest. Just don't use your torch, Kate, and keep quiet, all of you. Keep yourselves out of sight and your eyes and ears open. If I don't return by—'

'Milligan!' Constance interrupted in a scolding tone. 'You haven't even seen the other *side* yet.'

'The other side?' Milligan hadn't heard them discussing this part. 'There's more?'

'Give me a minute,' said Kate, reaching into her bucket. She took out her pencil-sized paintbrush and her bottle of extra-strength glue and quickly brushed the glue over the seams between puzzle pieces. 'It takes about thirty-five seconds to set properly,' she said. No one doubted the number – everyone knew Kate would have counted to be sure – and indeed, when Kate lifted the puzzle thirty-five seconds later, its pieces held firmly together. 'This way we can flip it back and forth if we need to,' she said, 'without it all falling apart.'

Kate laid the map face down onto the ground, revealing on its back a series of dashes and dots that were perfectly familiar to everyone.

'Wouldn't you know it?' Reynie said, smiling.

Mr Benedict had made them learn Morse code for their mission to the Institute, and they could all still read it. But because Sticky was the fastest translator, the others had always relied on him to handle their coded messages, and despite the time that had passed they resorted to their old habit and turned to him now. Sticky grinned – a little shyly and a little proudly – and translated the message:

Glad you are here. In the village find supplies and a clue, for we may be out when you arrive. The clue will lead you to us. Until soon. B.

'Another clue!' Kate cried triumphantly. 'So you have to take us, Milligan. You know you do!'

To their surprise, Milligan looked relieved. 'I'd rather keep you close as long as possible, anyway. Still, we can't just assume the village is safe.' He considered a moment. 'All right, here's what we'll do. We'll cross the plain to the foot of the mountains. You'll wait there until I scout out the tunnel and the village. If all's clear, I'll take you to the village and we can see about that clue. Once we've solved it, though, I'm bringing you back here. I want no arguments about that.'

The children agreed and prepared to set out right away, but Milligan said they would wait for it to get darker. The darker it was when they crossed that exposed plain, the better.

'We should also lose the map,' Milligan said. 'Carrying it will slow us down, and I want to get across as fast as possible.'

'Constance and I will hide it,' said Reynie, noticing the sad look in the tiny girl's eyes. He knew what she was thinking. The wind chime map was another example of the trouble Mr Benedict had taken on their behalf – another testament to his fondness for them – and it might well be his last, for there was no guarantee he'd left the next clue before his capture. Reynie suspected Constance might like another minute with the map, a suspicion confirmed when she didn't grumble at him for volunteering her.

'Do you suppose we should bury it?' Constance asked as they moved a little deeper into the trees.

Reynie shook his head. Burying the map would seem too reminiscent of a funeral, he thought, and Constance might fall apart. 'Let's just cover it with spruce needles and twigs.'

Constance nodded enthusiastically. She seemed both grateful and relieved by the suggestion. She also seemed more like a three year old than Reynie had ever seen her – so vulnerable and hopeful and scared – and now it was his turn to be touched.

Before they had taken twenty paces, Kate caught up with them. 'Milligan wants you to stay in sight,' she said. 'I told him I doubted you intended to wander off and have a tea party, but he didn't want to take any chances.'

'Tell him we're going to the bay for a swim,' Constance said, rolling her eyes.

Kate snorted. 'Funny! I *will* tell him that. Oh, I can already see his jaw twitching.' She turned and ran back to the forest edge.

'Kate really is in a good mood,' Reynie reflected.

'I know,' said Constance, 'and it's very annoying.'

Indeed, Kate was feeling as buoyant and cheerful as she

had in a long time. She found it thrilling to see her father do his job – even when it consisted only of watching the sky, as Milligan was doing now – and to be part of a rescue mission which, in her view, could do nothing but succeed.

'You know,' she said to Sticky as they waited, 'hearing you translate that Morse code reminded me of our time at the Institute. I never could get over how fast you did that.' She chuckled. 'I miss those days, don't you? I mean, except for the terrible parts.'

Sticky grinned and nodded. He was inclined to feel nostalgic for any time other than this one (he much preferred having been frightened *then* to being frightened *now*), and Kate's compliment had lifted his spirits. 'I especially miss the way you'd drop down from the ceiling and scare the wits out of us.'

Kate laughed and gave him an affectionate rub on his bald head – only to jerk her hand back as if she'd pricked it on a thorn. 'Youch! You've got some sharp stubble up there!'

Sticky shrugged, still grinning. 'Sorry. Hair grows, you know.'

'That's what Milligan always says,' Kate muttered. 'And he wonders why I never want to kiss his cheek.'

When Reynie and Constance had returned from their task, Milligan told everyone to get ready. It still wasn't dark enough to satisfy him, but it wasn't going to get any darker – a full moon was rising in the east and there were no clouds. And so, having again impressed upon them the need for both silence and speed, Milligan led the children out onto the plain. To limit their time in the open, they set off at a very brisk pace. For Milligan this amounted to a trot, but for the boys it was a sprint, and Milligan carried first one boy and then the other, trading off whenever the one running got too winded. Kate ran the whole distance with Constance on her back. It was a strenuous business indeed, and even if Milligan hadn't forbidden conversation, Kate could never have managed a word.

For a time the mountains seemed to draw no closer, and when at last they did it seemed by centimetres rather than metres, but eventually, finally, the runners reached the place where the land began to rise skyward. The tunnel entrance lay at the bottom of the middlemost mountain, and they had no difficulty finding it. In the moonlight the round black opening was visible from some distance – it looked like a mouse hole at the base of a gigantic cupboard – and Milligan led them straight for it. When at last they came close (but not too close), he ordered them to stay put while he scouted ahead. The children dropped to the rocky ground – everyone but Constance was gasping for breath – and Milligan vanished into the blackness of the tunnel, his footsteps making scarcely a sound.

'All clear,' he said when he returned. 'The tunnel's narrow, so we'll walk in single file. Here, Constance, I'll carry you, and you can carry my flashlight.'

'But I don't *want* to carry—'

'Never mind. I'll carry it.'

Milligan marched ahead with Constance on his back and the others close behind. The rock walls and floor of the tunnel were damp and uneven, and it was indeed narrow. It appeared to have been carved by the passage of an ancient underground stream, though in places it had obviously been widened with chisels and hammers. Reynie imagined the villagers had used it as the quickest passage to the eastern part of the island. These mountains weren't very big – in fact, for mountains they were rather modest – but it would still take hours to hike over them or go around. The tunnel, on the other hand, passed straight through on more or less level ground, and in twenty minutes Reynie was following Milligan out into open air.

They had emerged near the foot of the mountain, yet high enough on its slope to be afforded a good view of the western half of the island – or what would have been a good view had the moon risen over the mountains yet. Even in the gloom, however, they could make out the woodland just down the slope and to the right, and along its near edge the abandoned village – two rows of dilapidated buildings ranging along either side of a broad path. The village reminded Reynie of the frontier towns he'd seen in old Westerns, or at least the main street of such towns, for it had no side roads or outlying structures but was one long, straight shot that ended as abruptly as it began. Milligan scanned the buildings and the surrounding area with his spyglass. He listened carefully. Then he led the children down the slope into the village.

Milligan didn't need to warn them to stay together. The old, rotting structures of the village would probably have seemed lonely and sad in the daytime, but at night they seemed positively spectral. A great many leant precariously to the east, buffeted as they had been by decades of westerly wind, and three or four had seen their roofs carried off by storms. The roofs all lay to the east of their former homes – creeper-covered piles of disintegrating beams and rotten wood shingles.

Milligan and the children moved down the path, looking left and right but also at their feet, for the path – though it might once have passed for a road – was rutted and overgrown now and offered poor footing. In silence they passed building after building, all with dark windows and dark doorways.

About halfway down the path they came upon the village well. As with some of the buildings, the well's roof had blown free in a storm – it lay in a tangle of weeds, far from the barren posts that used to support it – and the rusty winch that was once suspended over the well's mouth had fallen to one side, still tethered to a forlorn wooden bucket with its bottom long since rotted out.

'What a shame,' Kate murmured, for it clearly used to be an excellent bucket.

At a word from Milligan, the group huddled together near the well to discuss what to do. There were no signs, no indications anywhere that a human had passed this way in years. If Mr Benedict had left supplies as his message had promised, he hadn't left any obvious means of locating them.

'Only half these buildings show any sign of being structurally sound,' Milligan observed. 'The rest are on the verge of collapse. Mr Benedict had to know Rhonda and I would never let you venture inside the dangerous ones, so we can rule those out.'

'That still leaves a lot of buildings,' Reynie said. 'This could take a while.'

'Maybe the stuff isn't in a building at all,' said Kate, leaning over the stone wall of the well. She pointed her torch into the darkness. Around six metres down she saw a somewhat distorted version of herself, shining a torch back up. 'Nope, only water. At least we won't go thirsty if we can't find the supplies. I don't know about you all, but that run across the plain left me a bit dry.'

'Dehydrated,' Sticky said, his voice something of a croak.

Reynie nodded. 'Parched.'

Milligan produced a flask from beneath his jacket and tossed it to Kate. 'Three sips each,' he said. As the children shared the water, they continued discussing the best way to proceed, but no one could think of a more efficient strategy than simply to search every sturdy building until they got lucky. 'I was afraid of that,' said Milligan, capping the flask. 'Let's go back and start at the east end. We'll work our way around.'

The first building Milligan deemed safe to enter was a house, and they moved warily through its dark rooms, searching for clues. Judging from the number of old-fashioned woven rope beds in the loft, the place had once been home to a large family. Now it was home to bats and spiders, and its wooden floors were covered with the dust of decades. With a pang the children saw that Mr Benedict and Number Two had been here – their footprints were in the dust throughout the house – but they appeared only to have been looking around, for the house was clearly empty.

They searched two more empty houses before entering an unusual stone and mortar building near the centre of the village. The building, which appeared to be a kind of storage facility or barn (a much larger barn than the modest one on Milligan's farm), consisted of a single large, window-less room with high rafters. What made it unusual was the surprising number of thick wooden beams that rose up from the floor to the rafters, creating the very strange impression of a forest enclosed by walls. The beams, set at equal distances throughout the room, were studded with large iron eyehooks that must once have been used for hanging things. On the dusty floor, the footprints of Mr Benedict and Number Two roamed among the beams from wall to wall.

Kate shone her torch around. 'I don't get it. Those eyehooks are all set at the same height – half a metre and a metre – but why hang anything so low? You'd have to stoop to take things off a hook.'

'Maybe the villagers were really short,' Sticky said.

Kate snorted. 'A village of elf people?'

'The doors and windows are normal size,' Reynie said. He knelt to inspect a couple of the eyehooks, both of which bore knotted remnants of rope. 'I don't think elves lived here.'

'I never said anything about elves,' Sticky said irritably.

'Whatever,' said Kate, 'it's still a weird place.'

'It's remarkably sturdy,' Milligan said, shining his torch up into the rafters, then onto the heavy wooden door with its iron bolts and hinges. 'Sturdiest building in the village by far. The roof would hold up even if the walls fell.'

Reynie stood. 'I think this was a storm shelter. That's why there are no windows. That's why it's so solid. There are enough beams and eyehooks to string up dozens of hammocks. If a bad storm blew in – and obviously there've been some bad storms around here – everyone in the village could come and sleep it out.'

'A community shelter. That makes sense,' said Sticky, trying to sound agreeable, though in truth he was frustrated

298

he hadn't worked this out himself.

Curious though it was, the shelter was empty, and the group moved on. The next building they searched was another house, which also lacked any sign of their friends except footprints in the dust. The house after that lacked even those, and Sticky took one look at the floor and said, 'Let's not waste time here. They didn't come into this one.' He turned to go out.

Reynie caught his arm. 'Actually, Sticky, I'm pretty sure this is the place.' He pointed to the clean wooden floor. 'They did come in here. And they swept.'

Kate discovered the supplies in an upstairs cupboard, along with the makeshift broom that Mr Benedict and Number Two had fashioned from a stick and a bundle of twigs. The house evidently had belonged to the most prosperous villager, or else to the most ardent and skilful carpenter, for it had two well-built floors, each with several rooms whose doors and shutters still hung squarely in their frames. Mr Benedict and Number Two must have thought it the perfect place to serve as the group's temporary home and head-quarters.

The upstairs cupboard lay at the end of a short hallway, and Kate stood at its partly opened door, shining her torch over its shelves. She had only just found the supplies and called out to the others, who'd been searching a nearby bedroom and now came running.

A doorstop prevented the cupboard door from opening fully, so it was with considerable bumping and squeezing that Reynie and Constance crowded in beside Kate to take a look. Milligan simply stood behind them and looked over their heads, while Sticky hung back, too embarrassed to jockey for position. (He'd made himself look quite foolish with that footprint business, he thought, and though no one had teased him – not even Constance – he felt the embarrassment keenly.)

'They must have made several trips hauling all this stuff here,' Kate said as she looked at all the supplies.

The cupboard was a shallow one, little more than a wall of shelves, but those shelves were admirably stocked with water, tinned food, nuts, dried fruit, powdered milk and – most important – digestive biscuits, chocolate bars and marshmallows for roasting over a fire. (The sight made the children's mouths water; they hadn't eaten anything in hours.) In addition to these provisions were two battery-powered lanterns and enough sleeping bags and extra blankets for everyone.

It seemed possible that the next clue would be hidden among the supplies, so after they had all drunk their fill of water and eaten a few hurried mouthfuls of food, they switched on the lanterns and started going through what remained in the cupboard. It was an irritating task, for the door didn't open wide enough even to let Kate hand things out to them without bumping her elbows. When she'd done this for the third time, she suggested they take the door off its hinges to make things easier.

'Forget the hinges,' said Reynie.

'He's got it!' cried Constance, who'd been watching his face.

'Got what?' said Milligan. He hadn't seen Reynie stir except to glance around at the other doorways.

Reynie paused, blinking – he was still unused to

Constance's keen perception – then shook his head and knelt by the doorstop. 'This is the most awkwardly placed doorstop in history, don't you think? Not to mention the only one in the house. It reminds me of that table in the hotel room – and I think it was meant to. Here, Kate, help me pry it up.'

Kate opened her Swiss Army knife and prised the doorstop loose. It turned out to be a hollow piece of wood, and tucked inside it was a note that read:

If you seek to reach us soon,
Peek beneath the town's twin moon.

'Another riddle,' Sticky said with a grimace. 'I was hoping for a map.'

'Maybe the next one's a map,' Kate said. She read the clue again. 'Or maybe there's a secret passageway beneath this twin moon thing.'

'Or a trail that starts at that spot,' Reynie suggested.

'Whatever,' said Constance, 'let's just hurry up and find it. What *is* this twin moon?'

They all looked to Sticky, who shrugged regretfully. 'I've never heard of a such a thing.'

'Mr Benedict's a twin,' Reynie said. 'Maybe he's referring to himself as 'the town's twin'. But then what would the moon be?'

No one knew.

'It may be more straightforward than that,' Milligan said. 'Maybe one of the buildings used to be a tavern or an inn. The Twin Moon sounds like a name for that kind of place. We should look around for an old sign, or an engraving on a door or some other kind of symbol.' He was already heading downstairs, but halfway down he stopped and cocked his head.

The children had moved to follow him, but Milligan shot them a warning glance and laid a finger to his lips. Had his expression not frozen them in their tracks, the scuffling sound they heard now would have. Footsteps. The sound grew louder, then stopped. There was someone at the front door. Milligan took out his tranquilizer gun.

Suddenly Constance gasped. 'Milligan, don't! It's—'

Even as she cried out the door flew open, a figure burst into the front room, and only Constance's warning and Milligan's quick reflexes spared the intruder a dart in the shoulder.

'— Number Two!' Constance finished.

Kate shone her torch down the stairs, and sure enough, there was Number Two, looking up at them from where she'd fallen onto her hands and knees. She squinted into the torch beam with wild, disorientated eyes.

'Constance?' she said, for it was Constance who had called out her name. 'Have I – have I come *home* then? And here I . . .' Number Two chuckled weakly. 'Here I thought . . . oh, Constance, thank goodness! I was dreaming I was still on that terrible island!'

SENTRIES·ON·THE·SILO

Number Two was delirious from hunger and exhaustion. Mr Curtain hadn't realized how much food she required, and she had deliberately not told him she needed more, for in order to convince him she would have had to explain *why*. And there was no way Number Two would reveal that she needed an enormous amount of fuel to compensate for how little she slept, because it was her near-constant wakefulness that allowed her to work away at the fastening pin in her handcuffs, hour after hour and night after night, while everyone else slept.

'Mr Benedict kept trying to give me some of *his* food,'

Number Two said as Reynie spooned cold soup into her mouth. She coughed, and most of it dribbled down her chin. 'I wouldn't take it. He had little enough. I'm afraid he was angry with me for refusing him. I hope he isn't still angry. Is he?' She looked at Reynie with worried eyes.

'Of course not,' Reynie soothed. 'He never was.'

Milligan had carried Number Two to a first-floor bedroom, easing her onto a rope bed that Kate had covered with a blanket. Her skin had lost its pale yellow hue (it looked positively waxen in the lantern light); her clothes were wrinkled and soiled; and her short-cropped red hair looked frazzled, like an old shag carpet. Even after she had eaten a bit, the poor woman was quite out of her head. The only thing Milligan felt certain about was that she had escaped while her captors were sleeping. When asked where she'd been held prisoner, Number Two had waved her hand as if shooing a fly and said, 'Oh, you know, in that cave on the island.' They asked her several times, and in several different ways, but she would be no more specific than that, and after a few minutes she slipped into a fitful doze.

'Keep an eye on her,' Milligan said solemnly. 'I'll be right back.' He patted Number Two on the knee and went out.

Constance watched him go. 'He certainly seems grim. But isn't it good news that she's escaped? And didn't he say she was going to be all right? And now we know that Mr Benedict really is okay, so . . .' She turned to the others, who averted their eyes. 'Hey, *you* all look grim, too. What's going on?'

After a pause, Reynie said, 'Whoever was guarding Number Two will wake up and find her gone. If it hasn't already happened, it certainly will by morning.'

'Which means they'll come looking for her,' Kate said.

'And find *us*,' said Sticky, who had begun to polish his spectacles.

'I see,' Constance said, rather wishing she didn't. She made a dry, gulping sound. 'Do you . . . do you think they'll know to look here first?'

'Maybe not,' said Reynie. 'The only footprints we've seen belong to Mr Benedict and Number Two, so the Ten Men and Mr Curtain must have caught up with them somewhere else. My guess is Number Two came back to the village because she knew there was food here – but Mr Curtain probably doesn't know that. If he knew they'd been here, I think we'd see signs of a search.'

Constance felt somewhat reassured. 'So the Ten Men won't necessarily know where to look.'

'They're excellent trackers, though,' Kate said helpfully.

Constance gave a small moan and put her face into her hands.

Reynie felt like doing the same thing. The irony of their situation was pretty bitter, after all. Number Two's escape might well have ruined her chances of being rescued – and it had put the rest of them in jeopardy, too. Whatever Milligan's plan had been, he would have to alter it now to protect the children. Or *try* to protect them, at any rate. Reynie shivered and glanced at Sticky, who was just tucking away his polishing cloth.

'Sometimes I wish I wore spectacles,' he said.

'You can always use mine if you like,' said Sticky, and they exchanged feeble smiles.

Milligan soon returned with a report that he'd made a

quick pass through the village to look for the 'twin moon' but had met with no luck. 'So here is what we're going to do,' he said, and his tone and expression made it clear there would be no arguments this time. 'I am going to search for that cave. You are going to stay here. One of you must attend Number Two at all times. If she gets her wits about her again, find out where the cave is – or where the twin moon is, for that matter. Just learn whatever you can. If I don't locate the cave myself in a few hours, I'll be back to check on you.'

'What if you do find it?' Kate asked.

'Then I probably won't return before morning. If that happens, I want you to head back to the forest by the bay. Make sure you're hidden in the trees before it gets light out. If Number Two is strong enough, bring her along; otherwise leave her here and I'll see to her. I know you don't like that idea,' Milligan said, seeing their disturbed expressions, 'but it's what you must do. Number Two prizes your safety every bit as much as I do. And at any rate, it's an order.'

Still more orders followed: they could use the lanterns, but they were to keep the shutters and doors closed so the light wouldn't be visible from outside. They must also keep a lookout – he would show them the best place – and send up a signal flare if there was any sign of danger. And if that should happen, they must all run to the storm shelter – taking time for nothing else – and bar the door until Milligan returned for them.

'The shelter can't keep Ten Men out for long, but it should hold them off until I get back,' Milligan said. 'Don't worry, if you're keeping a good lookout, I'll see your signal flare in plenty of time.'

306

'Won't the flare draw *their* attention, too?' Sticky asked.

'If you see Ten Men,' Milligan said, 'it will mean they're coming to check the village regardless. This way I'll know you're in trouble.'

The children had been frightened for some time now, but with every word Milligan spoke – even the ones he meant to be comforting – their apprehension increased. When he unexpectedly turned off the lantern, their hearts quickened, and they reached for one another in the darkness. The window shutters opened, revealing Milligan's silhouette in the moonlit frame.

'I want to show you the lookout spot,' Milligan said, beckoning them over to the window. He pointed down the path to the west. The last building in the village was also the tallest, a sort of wooden tower with a ladder attached to its outside wall. 'Two of you will take a post on top of that old grain silo. The structure is sound and the roof's in good shape. If you're careful, you'll be perfectly safe.'

Kate immediately volunteered to go. Reynie said he would join her.

'We'll take turns,' Constance said. 'Sticky and I can take a shift in a couple of hours.'

Sticky stared at her, then said slowly and mechanically, like a robot, 'Um, yes, that is a great idea, Constance.' It was a difficult thing for him to say. The rooftop of that silo seemed awfully far from the ground, and awfully exposed.

'It is a good idea, actually. You'll want fresh eyes.' Milligan closed the shutters and turned on the lantern, then knelt down and gathered the children close to him. 'Listen, all of you, this is going to work out fine. Just be brave and steady, and we'll get through it. One way or another I'm going to find Mr Benedict. By tomorrow morning you'll be far away from danger, and by tomorrow night we'll all be together – including Mr Benedict and Number Two – safe and sound. All right?'

The children nodded, and they all wished one another luck. Then Kate and Reynie followed Milligan out of the house and down the village path. Behind them the full moon was just peeking over the mountain; when they had climbed the tall ladder to the silo roof, they could see almost half of it.

'I'll check these woods to make sure they're clear,' Milligan said, indicating the swathe of trees that ran alongside the village and away to the west. 'You won't need to watch them. Keep your eyes on that empty stretch of ground just to the north, between the woods and the thickets. Anyone coming from that direction will have to cross in plain view.' He turned and pointed. 'Same thing to the south. The meadow is wide open, see? If anyone comes, you'll be able to see them from far off. That leaves only this mountain,' Milligan said, indicating the middle mountain looming over them, 'but there's no good cover on its lower slopes. No one will surprise you coming down that way.'

'What about the tunnel?' Kate asked. 'If they come through there they'll be on us before we know it.'

'They won't,' Milligan assured her. 'Number Two is in no condition to have travelled very far or very fast. She has to have come from this side of the mountains – otherwise we'd have spotted her on our way here. So this side is where they'll begin their search.'

What Milligan said made sense. Still, Reynie stared nervously at the dark hole in the rock. He couldn't help but imagine something emerging from that blackness, and he shuddered at the vision. Now was not the best time to have a good imagination.

Milligan put a hand on Reynie's shoulder. 'I would booby-trap it just to be sure,' he said, 'but it's your escape route. The tunnel's the fastest way to the other side. All right? Now let me show you how to send a signal.' Milligan took a flare gun from inside his jacket. It was about the size of a water pistol and just as simple to operate. 'Flip the safety switch here, aim at the sky, pull the trigger. Got it? I'll see the flare and come at once.'

Milligan kissed Kate on the forehead and tousled Reynie's hair. Then he grabbed the rails of the ladder and slid all the way to the ground – just as Kate had done from the barn rooftop a few days ago. *Was it really only a few days ago?* Reynie thought. It seemed like something from a previous life.

Milligan disappeared into the trees, and Reynie and Kate turned solemnly to their duties. They stood back to back in the middle of the silo roof. Reynie looked south over the meadow; Kate looked north to the open stretch of ground beyond the woods. The moon had fully risen over the mountain top now, bathing everything in ghostly light.

'There he goes,' Kate whispered after a while. Reynie turned to see a figure darting across the open ground at the far edge of the woods. Suddenly the figure stopped and waved in their direction with a wide, slow sweep of his arm. Kate returned the gesture. From this distance Milligan appeared as tiny as an insect, and as he turned and ran farther north he grew smaller still. Soon he had vanished into the thickets.

They glanced at each other but said nothing. Both felt the weight of their duty upon them. Reynie watched south. Kate watched north. The island seemed preternaturally still. The trees did not stir, nor was there the faintest breeze. It was as if the wind exhausted itself by day and so must rest at night. Thirty minutes passed, then an hour. In tense silence the two young sentries stared out upon the moonlit landscape, hoping against hope that what they were looking for would not appear.

Two hours later Constance came down the village path toward the silo. Kate had been worrying about this, and in a whisper she told Reynie she thought Constance was too little and clumsy to climb up to the roof, to say nothing of how easily distracted she was. What if she stopped paying attention? But Reynie had given this some thought as well, and his opinion was that if Constance committed herself, they could rely on her. Besides, what was there to distract her on top of the silo?

'If you say so,' said Kate, who generally deferred to Reynie's opinions, 'but I'll feel better if I help her up and give her a safety line. Can you cover for me?'

Reynie spent the next couple of minutes looking anxiously south, then north, then south again. He was afraid to look away from either direction for more than a second at a time, and as a result he appeared to be doing vigorous neck exercises when Constance appeared at the top of the ladder.

'What in the world are you doing?' Constance said. 'You look ridiculous!'

As Reynie explained, Kate took out her rope and tied it

around the little girl's waist, tethering it to the top of the ladder so that she couldn't possibly fall more than a metre or so.

They must have discussed this precaution down on the ground, for Constance raised no arguments, though she did complain that the rope was pinching her. Reynie continued looking back and forth, back and forth. He was much relieved when Constance took over Kate's post and let him concentrate on the meadow. Kate went to fetch Sticky, who had stayed behind with Number Two.

'No change?' Reynie asked Constance. They were standing back to back.

'She opened her eyes once and begged me to do my own laundry,' Constance said. 'I told her I prefer that she do it, which is what I always say. I didn't want to make her more confused than she already is. She sighed and went right back to sleep.'

Before long Sticky came up the ladder. Without taking his eyes from the meadow, Reynie handed him the flare gun (he'd decided the flare gun was a responsibility he would *not* trust Constance with) and passed along Milligan's instructions. Sticky nodded and took up Reynie's post, crossing his arms to keep himself from reaching for his spectacles. Now was not the time to be polishing them, no matter how strong the urge.

Reynie wished them luck and went down the ladder. He took his time heading back along the path, glancing around to see if anything clue-related caught his attention. Nothing did, but that might have been because Reynie had a hard time concentrating. Spending two hours at rigid attention was exhausting, especially at the end of a long and tiring day – and Reynie was pretty sure this had been the longest, most tiring day of his life. Between dawn and dusk they had visited the museum library, run from the police, faced a Ten Man, outsmarted Risker, and flown to this island, where the difficulties and danger had only increased. Reynie knew full well that at this very moment, Ten Men might be prowling the island, searching for Number Two, but he was suddenly so weary and bleary that he didn't even have it in him to be anxious. He supposed that was one benefit of exhaustion.

Kate took one look at him and sent him upstairs with one of the lanterns. 'Go get a blanket and lie down. I'll wake you if anything happens. Honestly, Reynie, you're dead on your feet!'

Reynie couldn't argue. He could hardly even mount the stairs. In a sort of dream state he took a blanket from the cupboard and staggered into a bedroom. Some part of his brain was just alert enough to consider saving the lantern batteries, and he turned off the lantern and opened the shutters to let in the moonlight. Then he threw his blanket onto the old-fashioned rope bed and fell in after it. The ropes and fastenings were loose, so the bed sagged pitifully – he would not 'sleep tight', as the old saying went – but Reynie couldn't have cared less. Tight or loose, he could sleep through a train wreck. He could sleep through a tornado.

He could even sleep through the sound of Constance's screams, which is exactly what he did.

Pleasant Dreams and Other False Comforts

At the moment Reynie was crashing into sleep, Sticky was on the silo roof trying not to do the same thing. The impossibly long day had caught up with him, too. It hadn't occurred to Sticky that he would be in danger of falling asleep – not when he was on lookout duty, not when he was so afraid of what might happen. And yet, staring at the same spot minute after minute in the quiet night, he found his eyelids growing heavier and heavier, and Sticky became aware of how truly sleepy he was. Was this what Mr Benedict felt like all the time? He began to pinch himself every so often. Then, after a while, Sticky would realize he had forgotten to pinch himself and his eyelids were drooping dangerously, and with a jolt of fear he would stiffen and blink and stare hard over the meadow. With his pulse pounding in his ears – an unnerving sound that reminded him of footsteps – Sticky would try to determine how long he'd been unfocused. A second or two? A few minutes? Longer? He would glance at the full moon, but unlike Kate he was no judge of distances or proportion. The moon seemed to be more or less overhead, just as it had been ever since Sticky came outside.

Please don't let me have missed anything, Sticky would think, taking deep breaths to calm himself. And soon, as he began to see that everything was all right, his fear would fade, his breathing would steady – and Sticky would fall right back into the same predicament. Pinching, drowsily forgetting to pinch, then starting awake with wide eyes and a flash of panic.

Eventually Sticky realized he was posing a danger not just to himself but to his friends as well, and though his pride withered at the thought of giving up, he began to consider how to manage it without looking like a coward. He was afraid the others would think he was fibbing about his sleepiness – Constance, after all, seemed to be having no trouble staying awake – but even if he came up with a decent excuse, to fetch Reynie or Kate he would have to abandon his post. This seemed entirely too dangerous, for he didn't feel he could trust Constance to cover both directions. He had already tried talking to Constance to keep himself awake, but she had shushed him at once. 'I can't concentrate if you talk,' she hissed, and he could tell she meant it. Conversation might help *him*, but it would distract *her*, which would leave them vulnerable to the north.

Sticky racked his brain. Pinching himself wasn't working. Hopping on the spot was too noisy and might distract Constance. What could he do? Sticky's weary mind, searching for an answer in the best way it knew how, presently settled upon an image from a book. A man had tied burning twigs to his fingers; when the twigs burned down to his skin the pain would wake him. That wasn't a bad idea, Sticky thought, his eyelids sagging. What book had that been? It was unusual for him not to remember. He certainly remembered where he'd been when he read it, though – safe at home with his parents. It was winter; he was wearing extra socks. Sticky closed his eyes and watched himself turning page after page, engrossed in the story. It was pleasant reading there by the window. Then his father came into the room and asked what he was reading.

'I can't remember,' Sticky said aloud. His eyes flew open. He'd been dreaming.

'Remember what?' Constance asked. 'Never mind. Don't tell me. Just keep quiet, for crying out loud. You startled the snot out of me.'

Sticky's breath was coming hard and heavy. He stared out into the night. The meadow seemed oddly bleary, more like an abstract painting of a meadow than an actual one. His spectacles had slipped too low on his nose. Sticky quickly settled them higher and stared out again. Was anything there? No, thank goodness. The meadow was empty. The nearby mountain slope was empty. There was nothing to see, and Sticky felt the overwhelming relief of someone who has made a terrible blunder and got away with it.

That can't happen again, he scolded himself. *You're just lucky they didn't come. In fact, you're lucky you didn't fall off the roof.* It would have been a very nasty fall, too. What was it – five metres down? Ten? Kate would know. Sticky took a careful step forward and peered down over the edge of the roof.

A Ten Man stood looking up at him.

Sticky gave a strangled cry and leapt back in terror. His leap carried him straight into Constance, who had been turning to see what was the matter, and in horrified disbelief Sticky saw her tumble backwards and fall off the roof. She screamed as she went over, then screamed again – though only for a split second, for Kate's rope, catching her about the middle, cut her off with a jerk.

At first Sticky didn't realize what had happened. He thought Constance had hit the ground. Then he heard her feet banging against the side of the silo, and he scrambled forward to haul her up. Sticky snatched at the rope, forgetting the flare gun in his hand until he had already let it go. *No, no, no!* he thought as he watched it fall. It landed near the Ten Man, who had come around the silo to look up at them with a bemused expression, as if contemplating two bickering sparrows in the eaves.

The Ten Man picked up the flare gun and slipped it inside his suit jacket. He took out a radio and said, 'I have activity in the village.' He said something else Sticky couldn't hear, for Constance (who had just recovered her breath) kept yelling at him to pull her up. The Ten Man put away the radio and began to climb the ladder. He moved elegantly – the briefcase seemed not to impede him in the least – and the scent of his cologne rose up before him.

316

Constance, smelling the cologne, fell abruptly still. She stared helplessly at Sticky, afraid to look down. Below her, the Ten Man's shoes made soft tapping sounds on the ladder rungs.

'There, there, chickie,' said the Ten Man. 'Let me help you with that.'

Reynie was coming slowly awake. At first he was extremely disorientated. He had been having unpleasant dreams until something had awakened him. Everything was dark and quiet. He didn't think he was in his own bed, and in the moonlight from the window he could just make out the unfamiliar ceiling above him. No overhead light. He blinked and swivelled his eyes, too sleepy even to move his head. He didn't see any furniture. Was he still dreaming? Where *was* he? The bed sagged in the middle and had no footboard, and in the gloom he could make out twin humps at the end of it. His feet. Still in their shoes, for some reason. And behind them, just beyond the end of his bed, Reynie thought he could see . . .

A figure. Crouched in the darkness.

He could see the eyes.

Reynie's skin prickled – it felt as if ants were swarming over him – and he stopped breathing. He couldn't move. For a moment his mind was blank with fear, and then it seized desperately upon an explanation. He was dreaming. Not just a dream – a nightmare. The most terrifying, most realistic nightmare of his life. Reynie forced himself to breathe, though all he could manage were shallow gasps. It was Mr Benedict's nightmare, he realized suddenly. The figure crouched at the end of the bed – the Old

317

Hag. Reynie had been thinking about Mr Benedict, and so naturally . . . yes, that had to be it.

Still too scared to move, Reynie tried to wake himself up. *A nightmare*, he thought. *Just a nightmare. Wake up now.*

Reynie saw the eyes blink. He shivered. It looked as if the silent creature was trying to make him out in the darkness. Oh, it was no wonder these visions haunted Mr Benedict so terribly! *Wake up*, he commanded himself. *Wake up*! With great effort, Reynie finally managed to sit up.

And when he did, the figure's eyes widened and it sprang forward with a hiss.

Reality came roaring back. He was in the abandoned village on the island. And now someone, a stranger, was trying to yank him out of the bed. Reynie fought back, but the stranger was far stronger than he was, and after a few grunts and cries and stinging slaps he felt himself heaved out onto the wooden floor, striking it first, and very painfully, with his chin. For a moment he saw pinpoints of lights in the darkness, like fairy dust. He was seeing stars. And he was still trying to clear his head when a brighter light shone into the room and fell on his attacker's face.

It was Martina Crowe. Her long black hair, mussed from the struggle, fell all about her face, but there was no mistaking that vindictive expression.

There was also no mistaking the bearer of the torch.

One moment Kate stood in the doorway, taking in the sight of her friend being held down by Martina Crowe. The next moment the torch rose high into the air, almost to the ceiling, and Kate disappeared in darkness. Reynie's and Martina's eyes instinctively followed the light (which was exactly why Kate had thrown it) and so neither of them

318

understood what was happening when, in the same moment, Kate crashed into Martina and sent her sprawling. Martina thought Reynie had somehow managed to strike her a blow. To Reynie it appeared as if Martina had magically transformed into Kate, for his friend now occupied the exact space from which Martina had been so roughly expelled.

Kate caught the torch before it hit the floor. 'Come on,' she said, pulling him to his feet and out of the door, which she banged closed as Martina came hurtling across the room toward them. Wedging her foot against the crack at the bottom, Kate calmly handed her torch to Reynie and opened her bucket.

Martina slammed herself furiously against the other side. 'There's no point running, you idiots!' she screeched through the door. 'You have nowhere to run!'

'Grab a blanket from the cupboard,' Kate told Reynie, and as he did so she took out her marble pouch. 'Roll it up tight and stuff it into the crack,' she said, pointing with the toe of her shoe. 'That'll slow her a bit. Then give me the torch and head for the stairs.'

Reynie stuffed the blanket as best he could into the crack between the door and the floor, jerking back once when Martina kicked the door close to his head. Kate pulled her foot away so he could wedge the last bit of blanket, then quickly put it back. When Reynie had finished and retreated to the stairs, Kate switched off the torch. Reynie heard a clattering sound. She was backing toward him, emptying her pouch of marbles onto the hallway floor. The door rattled again, and this time they could hear Martina's cursing more plainly – the door was inching open. The

319

wedged blanket would delay her only briefly.

'Go,' Kate whispered.

They hurried down the steps and into the bedroom where Number Two had been sleeping. The lantern still burned. The shutters were wide open. The bed was empty.

'Oh boy,' Kate said. 'Not good.'

'What's happened? Where is she, Kate?'

'She woke up when Constance screamed. She was still out of her head, and she insisted on going to see what was wrong. I thought I convinced her to stay put, but—' Upstairs there was a shocking thump, followed by the sound of marbles skittering down the stairs. They heard Martina groan.

'Quick,' Kate whispered. 'Follow me.'

They went out of the window. Kate led him behind the house, to the side opposite the path, and together they scurried behind the buildings in the direction of the storm shelter. Suddenly a bright flash came from the direction of the mountain, accompanied by a great crashing sound like a thunderclap. Reynie and Kate flung themselves down behind a heap of wood – a blown-off roof – and then, recovering, looked for storm clouds overhead. They saw only the full moon in a clear night sky.

'That was an explosion,' Reynie whispered. 'What's going on, Kate?'

'I don't really know. After I left Number Two I ran straight to the silo, but no one was there, so I ran to check the storm shelter. It was empty. When I came out again I saw that Number Two had opened the shutters and light was just pouring out for anyone to see. I ran back to shut them and check on her, but then I heard you and Martina fighting upstairs. That's all I – wait, do you hear that?'

Reynie heard it all right. A rumbling sound, again like thunder, only softer this time and steadier. It travelled from the direction of the meadow, growing louder and louder until the rumbling seemed to come from the ground all around them. Then the Salamander rolled into view. It was coming down the village path. Reynie and Kate crouched behind the fallen roof and peeked out.

A great armoured beast ten metres long and three metres wide, the Salamander surged forward on heavy revolving treads. Its sides were the dark blue-black of gunmetal and shone dully in the moonlight. A Ten Man stood in front with his hands on top of a large wheel, like a captain at the helm of a ship. Behind him Reynie could just see the top of Sticky's bald head and his wide, frightened eyes. Whether Constance was with him or not was impossible to tell.

The Salamander rumbled on, moving in the direction of the house they had just fled. They heard Martina calling out to the Ten Man in an angry, urgent tone, and the rumbling stopped. Only then could they hear the hum of the Salamander's powerful engine.

Reynie looked at Kate. 'If I distract them, can you—?'

'You know I can,' she said, her eyes flashing. 'Go. We'll meet you in the shelter.'

Reynie took off running back the way they'd come, keeping behind the buildings. When he saw the Salamander he yelled 'Over here!' and kept running. He dashed all the way to the back of the last building in the village, the one facing the mountainside. There he drew up short. Another Ten Man was strolling down the slope toward the village, briefcase in hand and a contented expression on his face, as if he'd just completed a most satisfactory transaction. Behind him lay a pile of rubble that used to be the tunnel entrance. That explained the explosion they'd heard.

Reynie pulled back into the shadows, flattening himself against the building's rear wall. He listened. He heard no voices, which probably meant he was being stalked. Peeking around the corner, Reynie watched the Ten Man walking down from the collapsed tunnel. Perhaps he would unwittingly reveal something. A frown, a wave, a look of acknowledgment – anything that might help Reynie know which way to run. He wanted to draw attention once more, then make his way back to the shelter, running for all he was worth. If Kate could snatch Sticky and Constance away, she was fast enough to drag them into the shelter in a matter of seconds. The question was whether Reynie could make it himself.

The Ten Man was about fifty metres away, and in the strong moonlight Reynie could see his face fairly well. He seemed perfectly unconcerned about anything. Just another ordinary well-dressed businessman carrying a briefcase down a hill, in the middle of the night, into an abandoned village on a forgotten island. The sort of thing one saw in bad dreams. Reynie stared and stared. The Ten Man was wearing glasses, and when he glanced up the lenses glinted, reflecting the moonlight.

Like twin moons, Reynie thought with a start, and he suddenly understood where to find Mr Benedict's clue.

But even as the answer came to him, it also occurred to Reynie that the Ten Man had looked up for a reason. And was still looking up, in fact. What was he looking at? Something high up at the other end of the village. The grain silo.

It had to be. Someone had probably climbed onto the roof for a better view – trying to discover Reynie's hiding place. And sure enough, just then Reynie heard the Ten Man in the Salamander calling, 'See anything?'

'Not yet,' Martina called back. She was up on the silo, temporarily out of the chase. There would be no better moment.

Reynie burst from behind the building and dashed over to the path. Startled, the Ten Man in glasses cried out – then laughed and shook his head as if some cute, wayward bunny had bolted its cage. He seemed in no particular hurry to give chase, but he did start moving in Reynie's direction. Reynie didn't look back at him again. He ran straight toward the Salamander, which was parked far down the path on the other side of the village well. Its driver, the Ten Man at the wheel, saw him coming and moved to get out. With one leg over the side, however, he hesitated, evidently debating whether to bother jumping down when it was easier to stay put and let the others handle Reynie.

Jump down, Reynie thought. *Jump down and give Kate a chance.*

The Ten Man frowned appraisingly at Reynie, unable to make up his mind.

Kate made it up for him. Streaking out of the shadows beyond the Salamander, she was moving so fast when she vaulted up over the side that there was barely time for its occupants – Sticky, Constance, and the Ten Man – to look astonished before she'd slammed into the Ten Man and sent him toppling into the path below. He hit the ground hard, his arms and legs sprawling quite inelegantly, and as he climbed to his feet his face was cold and furious.

Kate had already leapt from the Salamander with Constance over her shoulder and raced away up the path. She thought Sticky was right behind her. But Sticky was much slower getting over the side, and Reynie started yelling, hoping to divert the Ten Man's attention away from him.

The Ten Man ignored Reynie, however, and went for the quarry at hand, plucking Sticky from the side of the Salamander as easily as he might have taken a shirt from a department store rack. And much as he might have done in a store, the Ten Man held the skinny boy in front of him by the shoulders, as if gauging the fit. Sticky wriggled and kicked, his feet dangling. The Ten Man looked disappointed. He pulled Sticky close, pinning him with one hand while with the other he took the handkerchief from the breast pocket of his suit.

'Hold still now, ducky,' the Ten Man said. 'Let's have a little nap.'

Reynie had some vague, doomed notion of charging full tilt into the Ten Man if only he could get there in time. But he was still several metres away. Sticky, meanwhile, was jerking his face this way and that to avoid the treacherous handkerchief, and with a look of annoyance the Ten Man pressed his cheek against Sticky's head to hold him still. Sticky jerked his head forward as hard as he could – and the Ten Man yelped.

'He scraped me!' the Ten Man snarled, his eyes wide with angry disbelief. 'The little duck scraped me with his *head*!' Surprised though he was, the man still had hold of Sticky, and no doubt he would have returned to his handkerchief attack with renewed vigor had not Reynie, at that exact moment, charged into him with outstretched arms, lowered head, and eyes squeezed tightly shut.

There was an instant's confusion, during which the Ten Man swiped at Reynie's nose with the handkerchief and missed, Sticky threw a wild punch at the Ten Man and succeeded in boxing Reynie's left ear, and Reynie, recoiling from that painful blow, accidentally struck the Ten Man's chin with the crown of his head. Then the Ten Man was tottering backwards, stunned, and Sticky was free and running after the girls toward the shelter.

Reynie, unfortunately, had staggered backwards himself, and it took him a moment to catch his balance. By then the Ten Man had recovered and was moving to block his path. Reynie wheeled about and darted off between two buildings. Out of the corner of his eye he saw the other Ten Man, the bespectacled one, coming up the path and looking amused. He was reaching into his briefcase.

Reynie ran behind one of the buildings and stopped to listen. No footsteps. No voices. He peeked around the corner. The Ten Man from the Salamander had regained his composure now and was nonchalantly tucking away his handkerchief, whereas the bespectacled Ten Man was sitting on the low stone wall of the well, his briefcase open on his lap, as if it had just occurred to him that he needed to go over some important papers. He glanced up at Reynie, smiled, and flicked his wrist. Something whistled past Reynie's ear and into the darkness. For a moment he was so surprised he didn't move.

'You missed,' said the other Ten Man with a snort. 'You owe me a pencil.'

'Double or nothing,' said the bespectacled one, reaching

into his briefcase again.

Reynie turned and ran as fast as he could.

The storm shelter's door was on the path. He would have to go back out in the open. He passed one building, then another, then veered and raced out to the path again. He was now well away from the Salamander and directly across from the shelter. He didn't see the Ten Men any more – they must be circling behind him – and the shelter door was still open. This was his chance. But just as he started for the door, Martina emerged from between two buildings nearby, and Reynie knew the chase was over. Martina was faster and had a better angle. She was going to cut him off for sure.

'You're mine, Muldoon,' said Martina, her face twisting in vengeful delight.

Reynie skidded to a stop in the middle of the path. 'Close the door!' he yelled. 'Close the door, Kate!'

Kate appeared in the dark doorway, but she didn't close the door. She was holding her catapult, drawing a marble. Reynie felt a burst of hope – he still had a chance! With an excited, incoherent cry, he lowered his shoulders and rushed for the door. Martina lunged to cut him off . . . Kate let fly with the catapult . . . and Martina fell to her knees, howling and clutching her head.

'I saved one marble for you!' Kate called as Reynie ran inside. Then she saw something that made her jerk her head back. An object streaked past her nose and stuck in one of the wooden beams behind her with a loud *thwack*! Even in the darkness she could see it was a pencil – it must have been a very sharp pencil – and it quivered in the wood like an arrow. Kate slammed the door and threw the iron bolt.

'We made it!' Reynie gasped, scarcely believing it. The windowless storm shelter was pitch black inside. 'Sticky, Constance, are you there? Are you all right?'

'Kate nearly broke my ribs,' Constance complained, which Reynie took as a good sign.

'I thought I was gone for sure,' said Sticky. 'I thought we all were.' In the darkness Reynie felt Constance grab hold of his hand.

Kate shone her torch on the wooden beam where the Ten Man's pencil had stuck. She tried to yank it out, but it might as well have been set in cement. She couldn't even break it off.

'I wonder what they're doing,' Sticky said, putting his ear to the door to listen.

'Why, they're waiting for us to let them in,' said a deep voice, and Reynie thought he might throw up. The voice had come from directly overhead.

Kate's torch found the Ten Men in the rafters. There were two of them, squatting on their haunches and peering down at the children with malevolent smiles, like gargoyles in business suits. They seemed gigantic and spidery, all elbows and knees, and their shadows took up the whole of the ceiling.

'But . . . but how . . . ?' Sticky stammered.

'It isn't such a mystery, dearies,' said one of the Ten Men. 'You've just been outsmarted.'

Pandora's Box,

or Things Best Left Closed

'**K**eep still if you value your ears,' said one Ten Man with a grin. He showed them a small cylindrical device in his hand. 'I don't want to have to use this pointer on you – it takes all night to recharge the battery.'

The children, who did rather like their ears, were soon placed in handcuffs and made to stand against the back wall of the shelter. Meanwhile the other Ten Man opened the door to admit the rest of his crew. There were four of them in all, not counting Martina (who was holding her head and, for the moment at least, appeared too furious for words), and each was as well-dressed, calm, and cheerful-looking as his comrades. The shelter was suffused with the smell of expensive cologne.

'Garrotte,' said the largest Ten Man, speaking to the one with the laser pointer, 'be a friend and fetch us a lantern, won't you? Now that you mention batteries, we might as well spare our torches, too.'

'That's a lovely idea, McCracken,' said Garrotte, who was a bearded man with pointy ears and a flattish nose. In his dark suit he looked unnervingly like a giant bat. 'Would you care for any victuals as long as I'm going? Will we have a midnight picnic?'

McCracken chuckled. 'Just the lantern, thank you, Garrotte. I'm still full from supper.'

Given the nature of their work, the Ten Men's pleasant demeanour was more disconcerting than anger or harshness would have been, and indeed it would be hard to find anyone more disconcerted than the children. Even Kate was in a heightened state of alarm, not only because they were captured (though that did contribute somewhat) but also because she recognized the largest Ten Man's name – McCracken – and knew him by reputation.

Milligan had mentioned him before. The leader of all the Ten Men, McCracken was also the most elusive (Milligan had never laid eyes on him), and Kate now had the dubious honour of meeting him before her father did. He was an imposing figure – a huge man with shoulders like bed-side tables, perfectly coiffured brown hair, and piercing blue eyes – but his reputation was more imposing still. According to Milligan, McCracken was the most dangerous Ten Man of all, and now here he stood, smiling at them in the darkness.

'You might as well open your little peepers, cookie,' he said to Constance, who had squeezed her eyes closed, trying to imagine herself elsewhere. 'We can see *you* even if you can't see *us*, you know.'

'Leave her alone,' Sticky squeaked, his words inaudible although he had intended to shout. McCracken didn't even notice he'd spoken. Sticky swallowed, trying to find his voice. He was experiencing something close to a breakdown, not from fear (although he was certainly afraid) but from an overwhelming feeling of shame. All thought of pride or personal safety had long since flown from him now. The only thing Sticky wanted was to save his friends from whatever lay in store as a result of his terrible blunders. Yet he had no means of saving them – his talents were of no use here – and his mind was spinning in a tumult of frustration and despair.

Reynie was in quite a jangled state himself. What had struck him at once – and most unpleasantly – was how quickly McCracken had appraised the situation and taken control of it. In a matter of minutes he'd learned of the children in the village, deduced where they would hide, and gone into the shelter's rafters to await them. It was McCracken who had spoken to them from the rafters, and he had spoken correctly: the children had been outsmarted, which meant McCracken was very smart indeed.

Reynie took a few deep breaths. If they were to have any chance of getting out of this, he had better calm down and think.

Martina Crowe, meanwhile, had mastered her anger well enough to speak and had begun barking orders at the Ten

330

Men. To the children's surprise, the Ten Men seemed to answer to her. None of them appeared to like it very much (though McCracken seemed amused), but whenever Martina spoke they answered, 'Yes, ma'am' and did what she said. She couldn't have gained this authority through any action of her own – Mr Curtain must have granted it to her – but it was hers, regardless, and Martina clearly relished it.

The first order she gave was for McCracken to chain up the children so they couldn't run again. McCracken had obviously planned on doing that – he'd just taken a length of slender chain from his briefcase – but he only smiled and said, 'Yes, ma'am,' and finished what he'd begun. Each child's wrist had already been handcuffed to the next child's, with Kate at one end, followed by Constance, Sticky, and Reynie. Now McCracken cuffed Reynie's free hand to the length of chain, which appeared to be nothing more than a lot of paper clips linked together – the sort of thing a bored businessman might create while sitting through a long telephone conference. In fact (as McCracken cheerfully explained) the chain was made of high-tensile metal, perfectly unbreakable by human hand.

'Not even I can break it,' said McCracken, wrapping the other end of the chain around one of the shelter's wooden beams and securing it with a padlock. He winked. 'And I'm good at breaking things.'

'Stop socializing with them, McCracken,' Martina snapped. 'Give me the key to the handcuffs.' She thrust her hand out peremptorily, and McCracken, with an unconcealed smirk, put the key very daintily into her palm. The children stared at the key, which seemed the perfect symbol

331

of their predicament. They were now in the hands of Martina Crowe.

And Martina Crowe hated them with a passion.

Martina Crowe hated most things, actually. She hated the children in particular, but the children only represented the top of a long list. She also hated weakness and foolishness, and because she regarded most behaviours as weak or foolish, these two categories contained many subcategories, which in turn contained still *more* subcategories, and so on until very few things were left outside the range of Martina's hatred. One of these few things, however, was barking orders. Martina was fond of barking orders, and especially fond of barking them at Ten Men. She also enjoyed distributing them evenly, so that no one was left out. For instance, after she'd demanded the key from McCracken, Martina looked imperiously at the bespectacled Ten Man and barked, 'Find me something to sit on, Sharpe!' Then she ordered Garrotte, who had just returned with a lantern, to place it on the floor in the centre of the room. And finally she snapped her fingers at the fourth Ten Man (a bald man with only a single eyebrow – the one over his left eye – which gave him a perpetually wry expression), and barked, 'Close the door, Crawlings!'

Reynie watched Crawlings bar the door with a feeling of great desolation, as if it were his own tomb being sealed. He hoped Milligan had only been delayed, but when Milligan came back – *if* he came back – how could he rescue them if he was locked outside? He'd chosen this building for its sturdiness, after all. And even if he did manage to get inside, Milligan would still be greatly outnumbered, and the children would be chained up and couldn't even make a run for it.

Crawlings joined the other Ten Men by the lantern, where Martina had ordered them to gather. Sharpe, the bespectacled Ten Man, had failed to find her a seat, and Martina gave his briefcase a covetous glance but said nothing. Evidently the briefcases were off limits to her. No doubt she hated that.

'Well, McCracken,' Martina said, 'do you want to explain how she got away?'

'She hasn't got away,' McCracken responded. He was casually picking his teeth with the sharp end of the pencil that had been stuck in the beam. Reynie had watched him pull it from the wood as easily as one might draw a thumbtack from a bulletin board. Kate had seen it, too, and her jaw had dropped.

'She hasn't got away?' Martina said with a sneer. She glanced around the shelter and threw up her hands. 'I don't see her. Where is she? Is she hiding behind one of these beams?'

'She's in the woods. Sharpe saw her heading into the trees, and I had him blow the tunnel entrance so she can't cut through to the other side of the island. We can track her down that much faster now.'

'Then why aren't we tracking her?'

'I thought perhaps we should deal with the little darlings first,' McCracken said. 'They didn't materialize out of thin air, you know. Someone must have brought them. Better to find out right away who it was, don't you think?'

Martina acknowledged this with a grunt. The truth – which was clear enough to everyone in the room – was that she wanted nothing more than to focus on the children, but thought it best to establish that failing to catch Number Two would be the Ten Men's fault and not her own. Spinning on her heel, she marched over to stand before Kate. Of all the children, Martina bore a particular enmity toward Kate, who had done the most to embarrass her at the Institute (to say nothing of the past few minutes).

'How do you explain your presence here, Wetherall?' she demanded.

'Magic,' Kate said, coolly returning the older girl's stare. 'How's your forehead, by the way? You might want to put some ice on that.'

Reynie noticed that Kate had slipped her free hand inside her bucket. *Don't do anything stupid*, he thought. *Don't get yourself hurt, Kate.*

Martina touched the swelling bruise on her forehead. Her eyes flashed. 'And *you* might want to consider your *position*.' She held up the handcuffs key that McCracken had given her. 'Do you see this? I am in control here, Wetherall, and *you* are the one in chains, so if you don't want to find yourself—'

Kate stamped on Martina's foot, snatched the key from her hand, and butted her in the chest with her head.

Martina staggered backwards, her cry of pain cut short by the head butt, which had knocked the wind out of her. She turned toward McCracken, her eyes wide with outrage, and jabbed a finger toward Kate, who was scrabbling at her handcuffs with the key.

'Yes, ma'am,' McCracken replied to the unspoken order. He made no attempt to conceal his amused smile, but neither did he waste time striding across the room and grabbing Kate's wrist. 'I did enjoy that, plucky,' McCracken said to Kate, 'but that doesn't mean I won't also enjoy this.' He squeezed. Kate gave a gasp of pain and opened her hand. The key fell to the floor.

McCracken checked the handcuffs. They were still locked tight. Martina, meanwhile, had snatched up the key and backed out of Kate's reach. Recovering her breath she said, 'I want you . . . to make . . . that girl . . . pay!'

'Yes, ma'am,' said McCracken, opening his briefcase.

'I thought you wanted to know how we got here, Martina,' said Reynie quickly.

Martina looked at him suspiciously. 'Don't try to put this off, Muldoon. Your snotty friend's going to get hurt no matter what you say or when you say it.'

Reynie shrugged. 'Okay, well, if it doesn't matter to you – or Mr Curtain – then I can certainly wait to tell you what's going to happen.'

'What's going to . . . happen?' Martina repeated. She glared at him. 'What do you mean?'

'If we don't return to the boat by morning, Risker will contact the authorities,' Reynie said. 'So I suggest you think long and hard about whatever actions you're planning to take now.'

The room was quiet. Then all the Ten Men looked at one another and burst into laughter. Martina laughed, too, and she shook her head a long time before saying, 'Risker? You mean that greedy coward in Thernbaakagen? Thank you for the warning, Muldoon – it will be very useful – but we're not really worried about someone like *Risker*. I'm surprised he agreed to bring you here in the first place.'

Reynie was doing his best to look crestfallen – crestfallen

but defiant. 'Well, he did! We paid him half the money Mr Benedict left us and agreed to give him the rest when we got back to the boat! But if we *don't* get back, he's going to—'

'Where is this money?' McCracken interrupted.

'Nowhere you can get to it,' Reynie said.

'And where would that be?' said McCracken. From his briefcase he took out an elegant, leather-clad cigar box, gave it a shake, and set it on the ground between Reynie's feet. A strange, sharp clicking sound came from inside the box, followed by a barely audible squeal. McCracken nudged it with the toe of his well-polished shoe. 'Shall I open that? Or do you want to tell me where the money is?'

Reynie stared at the cigar box. He began to perspire. 'It's . . . it's on the boat. Hidden in my bag.'

McCracken clucked sympathetically. 'Then Risker's gone, my dear. He took your money and left. That's the sort of fellow he is, you see. Oh, we'll check to be sure, but I think you can be confident he's forgotten you. How did you even know about Risker, hmm? How did you know about this island? Tell me quick, and I might put away my box without opening it.'

With the other children listening in bafflement – they had no idea what Reynie was up to – Reynie told McCracken the truth. He said they had sneaked away from their families to find Mr Benedict and Number Two. He explained about the clues Mr Benedict had left for them as part of a surprise trip, about how they'd hoped to follow the clues until they found their friends, at which point they'd intended to contact Rhonda Kazembe. He told McCracken about everything – everything except Milligan and the final

336

clue – and because what Reynie said was true, it was a perfectly convincing account.

McCracken seemed impressed. 'You made that trip all by your little selves? My, what big boys and girls you are!' He picked up the cigar box and held it very close to Reynie's perspiring face. 'Sure you don't want just a peek?'

He chuckled and gave the box a shake; the clicking sound inside grew louder. 'No? Don't want to meet Pandora?' He shrugged and put the box back into his briefcase.

Garrotte spoke up. 'What do you think, fellows? Will Risker make things inconvenient for us?'

'I rather doubt it,' said Crawlings. 'If he's stolen the chickadees' money, he isn't likely to contact the authorities.'

'Don't be a fool,' snapped Martina, irritated to have been left out of the discussion. 'We still need to report this to Mr Curtain. Give me your radio, Crawlings.'

Crawlings raised his single eyebrow. 'Oh dear, I never said we shouldn't report it, did I? But I'm afraid my radio's of no use.' He pretended to look apologetic. 'There's no reception in the cave, remember?'

Martina cursed under her breath. With a haughty toss of her hair she said, 'I'll need to take the Salamander, then. Garrotte, you drive me. The rest of you wait here. We won't be gone long.'

'Why not bring the children?' asked McCracken.

'Because I say so,' Martina growled.

She offered no explanation beyond this, but Reynie felt pretty sure he knew what she was thinking. Here in the shelter they were under Martina's direct control. That would change once they were brought to Mr Curtain, and Martina was in no hurry for that to happen. No doubt she had some nasty punishment in mind for them – perhaps one inflicted by the Ten Men, who must obey her – and didn't wish to lose her opportunity. She probably hated to wait even a minute, but she wouldn't dare put off her report to Mr Curtain.

'Before I go,' Martina said, jerking her thumb toward Kate, 'we need to take her bucket away and search her pockets. She's a tricky one. Here, McCracken, you hold her while I search her.'

It was shrewd of Martina to have McCracken hold Kate, who might otherwise have relieved her of several teeth. As it was, Kate was left unable to speak or even breathe as Martina searched her – very thoroughly and none too gently – from head to foot. When McCracken released her, Kate fell to her knees, clutching her midsection and gasping for breath.

'That's just for starters,' Martina said with a satisfied smile. 'Wait till I get back – then things will *really* get fun. Let's go, Garrotte. McCracken, you keep a close eye on them, you hear me? I don't want any chance of their getting away.'

'They won't be getting away.'

'Just do as I say,' said Martina. She grinned at Kate, who was struggling to her feet, and held up the bucket so Kate could see her leave with it. Then she went out, followed by Garrotte, and McCracken barred the door behind them.

'Why bar the door?' asked Crawlings. 'We'll just have to open it again when her highness returns.'

McCracken grunted. 'You're a fine fellow, Crawlings, but you have yet to learn proper caution.'

'I'm cautious enough, aren't I?' Crawlings said. 'Oh sure,

I've had a bad scrape or two, but I'm cautious, McCracken. I'll wager I'm as cautious as you!'

'And yet I'm in possession of both my eyebrows, and you're not.'

Sharpe snickered. 'He has you there, Crawlings!'

'At any rate,' said McCracken, 'there's something about all this that doesn't quite fit, and when I work out what it is, I want to be ready.'

'Shall we do an inventory?' asked Crawlings.

'Wouldn't hurt,' said McCracken. 'At the very least it will pass the time until her ladyship returns.'

As if in response to some unseen signal, the Ten Men knelt in unison and set their briefcases before them. They were in the middle of the room, where the light from the lantern was strongest, and the children – also in unison – flinched at the sound of the dreadful briefcases being unbuckled.

Outside, the Salamander rumbled out of the village. Then all was quiet except for the Ten Men going through their briefcases. It was clearly a serious business, yet the men surveyed the contents of their briefcases with expressions of happy expectation, even jollity, as if they were selecting chocolates from a holiday tray. The children watched in horror as they laid out tidy rows of sharpened pencils; an assortment of ink pens in various colours; staple removers (which resembled nothing so much as metallic piranhas); sleek-looking calculators; stacks of brilliant white business cards; elegant letter openers tucked into monogrammed leather sheaths – and, of course, the dreaded laser pointers.

Crawlings held up his pointer. 'What do you think?' he

said, wriggling his eyebrow and jerking his chin toward the children. 'Shall I take just the very tip of one of their noses? I'm thinking of a collection.'

McCracken frowned. 'You'd waste your only shot on the tip of a nose? This is what I mean about proper caution, Crawlings.'

'Oh, don't be so serious,' said Crawlings. 'I was only sporting for the kittens' sake.' He grinned at the children. Evidently he very much enjoyed frightening them. 'At any rate, you know I prefer to use this.' He lifted up what appeared to be an ordinary clipboard.

McCracken nodded approvingly. 'That's because you're so good with it.'

'It's true,' Sharpe said, patting Crawlings on the back. 'I've never seen anyone so smart with a clip—'

'You're nothing but a bunch of monsters!' Sticky blurted, finding his voice at last, and the other children stared at him in shock. 'Why aren't you disgusted with yourselves? I mean, look at you! You like *hurting* people! You like frightening *children*!'

He fell abruptly silent, every bit as shocked by his outburst as the others had been and regretting it extremely. What kind of fool wanted to make a Ten Man angry? He hadn't even realized he was going to speak. With his breath coming in ragged gulps and his emotions still awhirl, Sticky braced himself for the response.

But the Ten Men only looked over at him with expressions of mild interest, and McCracken chuckled and said, 'We don't like frightening children in *particular*, sweetie. It isn't our fault you're still a child, is it? Now, why don't you leave the grown-ups to their discussion? You wouldn't want to distract us, would you? We might grow annoyed.'

Sharpe fanned himself with his clipboard. 'You know, McCracken, I get so *warm* when I'm annoyed. It makes me want to loosen my tie.'

'Very warm indeed,' Crawlings murmured, pretending to mop his bald head with his handkerchief. 'I may have to take *my* tie off, too.'

McCracken eyed the handkerchief. 'Again, Crawlings. Proper caution.'

'Oh, for heaven's sake, don't be such a mother duck, McCracken. I'm not going to blow my *nose* with it.'

McCracken and Sharpe laughed at this, and Crawlings carefully folded the handkerchief and returned it to his pocket. The Ten Men resumed their dark discussion.

Sticky was shaking so violently his handcuffs jingled. He longed to polish his spectacles, but with his wrists cuffed to Constance and Reynie it was too difficult to manage.

'It's okay,' Reynie whispered. 'It's going to be okay.'

Sticky looked at him. 'H-how?'

Reynie had no idea. He looked down the line at Constance and Kate. Constance, evidently impressed by Sticky's outburst, was staring at him as if she'd never seen him before. She seemed to be holding up fairly well. Kate, on the other hand, was still clutching her midsection, and it occurred to Reynie that McCracken might really have injured her. He was about to ask if she was all right when Kate suddenly cocked her head to the side, and Constance stiffened. They had heard something. Kate squeezed the smaller girl's hand – as if to warn her not to speak – and turned to face the wall.

McCracken glanced up. 'What's the matter, honey? You

don't like watching us get our things together?'

'I think I'm going to throw up,' Kate said.

'Ah! Mixed up your insides a bit, did I? Happens sometimes. Well, that's a good girl, then. You do your business against the wall where we won't have to step in it.' He went back to his briefcase materials.

There was enough slack in the chain for Reynie and the others to huddle close to Kate and pretend to comfort her. In fact they were looking at what Kate had just detected and pointed out. A tiny drill bit was boring through the masonry between two stones in the wall. The bit made only the faintest scratching sound as it poked through the masonry, no more than an insect might have made, and this scratching was what the girls had heard. After a moment the bit withdrew, leaving a worm-sized hole, and in its place appeared a tightly rolled scrap of paper. Kate removed the paper. It was a note from Milligan:

Stay where you are until I appear. Then run straight for the door. Do not hesitate even for a moment.

Kate passed the note to Constance, who read it and passed it to the boys.

'Everything all right?' Crawlings called over to them. 'Lost your cookies yet, dear heart?'

'Not yet,' Kate called back in a strangled voice.

'Leave her alone!' Sticky shouted, forgetting himself again. He clapped his hands over his mouth, accidentally yanking Reynie and Constance's hands up as well.

'Easy, Sticky,' Reynie cautioned, though he couldn't help noticing that Constance seemed to benefit from Sticky's

342

impudence. Each time he lashed out at the Ten Men, she looked less frightened and more like her usual defiant self.

Sharpe snickered and muttered something to the other Ten Men about 'that bald one spoiling for a handkerchief'. The others murmured their assent.

The Ten Men had begun putting their things back into the briefcases and were talking in low voices now, which to Reynie seemed far more sinister than when they'd been speaking up for the children's benefit. He felt his own stomach turning as badly as Kate's appeared to be. Milligan was coming for them, but how were they supposed to run for the door? They were chained up!

Constance looked at him and whispered, 'But how are we going to . . . you know, how do we *do* it?'

'Hold on,' Kate muttered. She began to cough, then to gag, and then to spit. Over by the lantern the Ten Men smirked and snorted. Kate thrust her head forward a few times like a pecking chicken, made one last, repulsive retching sound, and fell silent. For a moment she stood with her hands on her knees, breathing heavily through her nose. Then she looked over at her friends, winked, and gave them a huge grin.

Clenched between her teeth was a key.

Kate had switched one of her old farm keys for the handcuffs key. That was why Reynie had seen her slip her hand down inside her bucket – she'd been seeking, by touch, a key that might pass for the one McCracken had given Martina. Anticipating a search, Kate had swallowed the handcuffs key and dropped the farm key when McCracken grabbed her. Reynie understood all this at once, but

Constance and Sticky only stared, confused. Hadn't they seen McCracken take that key away?

'We'll explain later,' Reynie whispered. He was afraid the sound of the handcuffs opening would catch the Ten Men's attention, so he told Kate to go back to retching, which she did promptly and with great gusto. As she made one horrible noise after another, with her friends gathered around as if to comfort her, Kate unlocked all their handcuffs and adjusted them to fit much larger wrists. The children would appear to be cuffed but could easily slip loose when the time came.

But when would it come? That was the most pressing question now, for they needed to be ready when it did.

The Ten Men were standing up, their briefcases repacked and buckled closed, and were shaking hands all around as if they'd just concluded an agreeable meeting. Milligan still had not appeared. McCracken stuck a pencil behind his ear and walked over to the children. 'Guess what?' he said in a tone of cheerful excitement. He knelt in front of Constance, who shrank away, avoiding his gaze. 'You're a lucky ducky, little one! You get to help McCracken!'

'Help you?' Constance asked.

'Oh, yes! You see, I've been going over things in my mind, and I'm still not satisfied with the way your story all fits together. I think you're hiding something from old McCracken, you naughty things, and I'm going to find out what it is!'

'If you don't like my story,' Reynie said, 'then why aren't you talking to me?'

McCracken didn't take his eyes from Constance. 'Because in my experience the smallest child is the one most likely to tell you what she isn't supposed to.' He put a finger under Constance's chin and lifted it so that she was compelled to look up. 'Am I right, little one? Do you think I might be able to convince you to give me your secrets?'

Constance stared at the sharp pencil behind the Ten Man's ear, and her lip began to quiver. Rather than cry, however, she screwed up her face and screamed furiously at McCracken – screamed loud enough to make him wince and step back. She screamed until her breath ran out, and then she glared at him, panting hard, her face purple as a plum.

McCracken looked at Constance as if he were disappointed in her. 'Now why would you do that, muffin? Why would you want to make old McCracken angry? Don't you realize your little adventure is over? Don't you see there's no one to help you now?'

'That's what *you* think!' Constance snapped.

McCracken wrinkled his brow. Narrowing his blue eyes, he fixed the tiny girl with a cold and penetrating gaze. Constance looked as if she'd swallowed a scorpion and was praying it wouldn't sting her on the way down.

'Why, I don't believe that's the way you'd speak about someone like Risker,' McCracken observed. 'Oh no. Not that sorry fellow far away in his boat. You're expecting someone else, aren't you?'

'Yes, we are!' Reynie said, hoping McCracken would think he was lying out of desperation. 'We're expecting—'

'You be quiet,' McCracken said, pointing a warning finger at Reynie. 'None of your trickery.' He turned to the other Ten Men. 'Any ideas about this?'

Crawlings's eyebrow shot up. He snapped his fingers,

reached inside his suit coat, and took out Milligan's flare gun. 'The skinny bald one dropped this! I thought the children were using it to signal to one another.'

'Is that right?' McCracken said, scratching his head. 'A flare gun? Well, that was silly of you, Crawlings! They wouldn't need a flare gun to signal to one another – they were all right here in the village. So who was our friend *really* signalling, do you think?'

'Nobody. He dropped it before he could fire the flare.'

'Perhaps, Crawlings, but don't you think our blowing up the tunnel entrance will have acted as a substitute?' McCracken pursed his lips. 'You'd better climb on up into the rafters. Sharpe, you unbar the door. We'll want to make it easy to get inside.'

Crawlings winked at the children with his right eye – –the one without an eyebrow – which made his face look bizarrely lopsided. It was an unsettling sight, but far more unsettling was the way he skittered up one of the beams like a spider and disappeared into the shadowed rafters.

The Ten Men were setting a trap.

Reynie looked anxiously at his friends. Kate was clenching and unclenching her fists, not meeting anyone's eye, too upset for words. Constance had begun to cry, and with a pained expression Sticky was telling her not to feel bad, that they were in this mess because of him, not her.

'That's true,' Constance sniffed. Then she straightened into an attitude of attention, as if she'd sensed something, and a moment later they all heard the rumbling of the Salamander outside.

'There's Garrotte and Martina,' said Sharpe, backing away from the door and loosening his tie.

'Maybe it is and maybe it isn't,' said McCracken. He turned off the lantern, throwing the room into blackness. 'We'll just wait and see who walks through that door.'

McCracken soon had his answer: No one would walk through the door at all. In fact, to the surprise of everyone in the shelter, the door itself ceased to exist.

THE·STANDOFF·IN THE·SHELTER

With a tremendous cracking and squealing, the thick wood of the shelter door splintered into a hundred pieces; the iron bolts tore free of their fastenings; stones toppled down all around, sending a fine powder into the air – and the nose of the armoured Salamander filled the space where the door had been. Someone inside the Salamander threw a switch, and the room was suddenly flooded with light. Masonry dust hung in the light like an amber-coloured fog. 'Move!' Kate yelled, slipping free of her handcuffs and grabbing Constance. With the boys at her heels, she ran straight for the Salamander, coughing against the dust and squinting in the floodlight. She passed directly over the spot where McCracken and Sharpe had stood an instant before. Like roaches at the flip of a light switch, the Ten Men had scattered and were nowhere to be seen.

Milligan seemed to drop from the sky. He landed a metre or so in front of the Salamander, silhouetted by the floodlight, with masonry dust roiling about him like billowing smoke. He knelt and aimed his tranquilizer gun into the shelter's strange grove of wooden beams. First to the left, then to the right. He'd seen which beams the Ten Men had disappeared behind and was covering them both. 'Help the others get in, Kate! Quick now! Into the Salamander!'

Kate was already dragging Constance past him. 'Look out, Milligan! There's one in the rafters!'

At the words 'look out' Milligan sprang forward, and in the same instant a yellow pencil appeared, as if by magic, quivering in the floorboards where he'd just been kneeling. He aimed his tranquilizer gun into the rafters but saw only shadows and wood. Behind him Kate was boosting the others over the side of the Salamander.

'Put down your weapon!' a voice called from above.

'In a minute,' Milligan growled.

'You'll do it now,' said the voice, 'or the girl with the ponytail gets a nasty haircut.'

Kate had just heaved Reynie into the Salamander when she heard this. She looked into the rafters. At first she saw nothing. Then, to her horror, she saw something that resembled a twitching caterpillar. It was Crawlings's eyebrow, wriggling excitedly. Most of the Ten Man's body was hidden in shadow, but he was making sure Kate could see his face and, more important, the laser pointer he was aiming at her.

'Kate?' Milligan called. From his position he couldn't see what she could. When she didn't answer, he glanced back and saw her staring helplessly into the rafters. Milligan didn't hesitate. He set his tranquilizer gun on the floor.

'Milligan, don't!' Kate cried, finding her voice again. But it was too late.

'Kick it away from you,' Crawlings called.

Milligan sent the tranquilizer gun sliding across the floor with his boot.

'Go to the back of the room, pick up a pair of handcuffs, and lock yourself to that chain. Close the handcuffs so tightly they pinch.'

Milligan went and cuffed himself to the chain, which was still padlocked to a beam. He yanked on the chain to demonstrate he was firmly secured, and as soon as he did so Crawlings dropped to the floor a few yards away, aiming his pointer directly at Milligan's chest. He was smiling with pure delight. 'Did I hear her right? Are you really Milligan?'

Milligan said nothing, only leant forward as if he wanted nothing more than to lunge at Crawlings. But the chain was stretched taut behind him – he was at its outer limit – and Crawlings called out, 'Did you hear that, boys? It's Milligan! We've got the famous Milligan handcuffed to a pole!'

McCracken and Sharpe emerged and moved to the middle of the room. The corner of McCracken's lip jerked upwards, as if he were trying not to laugh. 'Milligan, eh? What a pleasant surprise!'

Crawlings stepped closer to get a better look, keeping an eye on the chain to make sure he didn't step within Milligan's reach. He kept his laser pointer aimed at Milligan's chest. 'You of all people! The Ten Man's worst enemy! My, oh my! Wouldn't it be lovely if I were the one to get rid of you once and for all?'

Milligan mumbled something.

Crawlings leant slightly forward. 'What's that?'

Nobody saw what Milligan did. Or at least not what he really did. What it *looked* like he did was step forward and return an embrace that Crawlings had apparently decided to give him. And then Crawlings was unconscious on the floor, and Milligan was holding the laser pointer.

'I said this chain was longer than you realized,' Milligan muttered.

McCracken and Sharpe stood a few metres apart from each other in the middle of the room, staring with great attention at the laser pointer in Milligan's hand. Their smiles had disappeared, and they were holding very still.

'That was clever of you,' said McCracken, recovering. 'What did you do, gather some of the chain behind you to make it look shorter? That's impressive sleight of hand, my friend. You fooled him completely. Well, go on, finish him off. Don't beat about the bush.'

Milligan ignored him. 'Kate, get in the Salamander and go straight to the place we agreed upon. You can handle it. It's more or less like a tractor.'

'Milligan, we can't leave you here!'

'Of course you can!' McCracken called, without turning his head. 'He has a pointer. He'll be fine.'

'Milligan!' Reynie called from the Salamander. 'McCracken said those things only fire one shot and then have to be recharged!'

'You heard that, did you?' McCracken said, looking coy and sheepish, as if he'd been caught stealing biscuits. He shrugged. 'They've got me there, Milligan. I did say that. Now here's the deal. I know you must be tempted to have young Kate fetch that weapon of yours. But if you do, I promise you one of us will do her great harm. Sorry, but that's just the way of it. We can't let you take us both out. One maybe, but not both. Isn't that right, Sharpe?'

'Just as you say, McCracken. That's the code.'

'So let those little dears go, then,' said McCracken. 'That's a fair deal. Let them go, and the three of us will stay here and have a nice chat.'

Milligan never took his eyes from the Ten Men. 'Kate, leave right now. That's an order. Don't be afraid. Our friends will meet you there.'

'But—'

'*Now*, Kate!'

Kate climbed into the Salamander. She didn't speak to the others – who at any rate were speechless themselves – but only blinked tears from her eyes to study the levers and knobs. None of them could believe what they were about to do. They were going to leave Milligan alone, chained to a beam, with two Ten Men. And he had only one shot.

Kate backed the Salamander from the wrecked doorway and out into the village path. She shifted a lever and the Salamander stopped, its engine humming. Kate looked longingly back toward the shelter.

'We should go,' Constance said in an apologetic tone.

'We need to do what he said, Kate – we need to go back to the bay forest.'

'We aren't going to the bay forest,' Reynie said, and the others looked at him in surprise. His expression was very grim but determined.

'Where are we going, then?' Constance asked.

'To save Mr Benedict. We're his only chance now.'

'But we don't even know where—'

'Oh yes, we do,' Reynie said.

It was long past midnight, and the full moon's reflection no longer shone at the bottom of the village well – no twin moon down there now – but as Reynie pointed out, Mr Benedict would have counted on their solving the clue regardless of the hour, just as he would have counted on Kate's ability to retrieve whatever he'd left for them. And indeed, it took Kate mere seconds to fetch her rope from the top of the silo (where Crawlings had untied Constance in order to capture her) and secure it to one of the posts that used to hold up the well's missing roof. Flinging off her shoes, she climbed down into inky darkness.

'I have it!' Kate called after splashing around only a moment. She soon climbed back up with a sealed glass jar. It had been anchored beneath the water, she said, with a short length of cord and a heavy rock. And inside it was a map.

After all the confusion and mystery, the final leg of the children's journey seemed strangely straightforward. The map was simple and easily read, and on it, near the top of the southernmost mountain, was a boldly marked X. There wasn't even a need to decide on a route; they could just follow the Salamander's tracks across the meadow.

'Find a seat,' Kate said after she'd helped everyone into the Salamander. She took her position at the wheel. The Salamander's interior was rather like that of a normal touring boat, with storage compartments lined beneath the gunwales and two short rows of uncomfortable benches. Reynie, taking a seat on the front bench, kicked something over on the floor beneath. Kate's bucket.

Kate took it from him without a word. The bucket's recovery was small consolation, but she did seem to stand a little taller with it belted to her side. She took a last look at the ruined shelter door, beyond which, in the moonlit gloom, Milligan remained trapped with the Ten Men. She grimaced and turned away. She grabbed the wheel, shifted a lever, and the Salamander started forward with a powerful lurch.

Reynie, Sticky, and Constance flew backwards off their benches.

'Hang on!' Kate called, her ponytail streaming out behind her.

The Salamander roared out of the village and into the meadow, where its floodlight plainly revealed the twin tracks of crushed grass. Kate steered into the tracks and followed them. She swerved only once – to avoid the prone bodies of Martina Crowe and Garrotte the Ten Man, both of whom lay unconscious but otherwise unharmed in the middle of the meadow, where Milligan had ambushed them on their way back from reporting to Mr Curtain. The other children never saw what Kate saw. Nor did Kate ever tell them how tempted she had been not to swerve. But she did, and the Salamander rumbled on.

Soon they were rising up the lower slope of the mountain. The slope grew steeper and steeper, and before long the other children were covering their eyes, afraid to look, for the view from the Salamander floor (they hadn't managed to recover their seats) was of nothing but moon and sky. There seemed to be no ground beneath them at all.

Kate stood at the helm, her teeth gritted and every muscle tense. She had a better view than the others and was straining to make out the Salamander tracks, which had grown much harder to find as the meadow gave way to rock. (It would make for a bad end if she unwittingly veered off the route and into some hidden ravine.) Kate was also paying close attention to the feel of the machine beneath her. The Salamander's engine was working at full capacity, yet their speed had slowed considerably and the treads had begun to slip. When the slope grew even steeper and the Salamander's progress slowed to a crawl, Kate shut off the engine. They were very near the mountaintop. From this point it would be faster to hike.

The others opened their eyes and felt their stomachs drop. They appeared to be suspended in the sky. Kate was studying the map by torch. 'The cave's not far. Let's go.'

Outside the Salamander they discovered a goat path, which made their climb easier. The air here was sharp and cool, and vegetation was scarce. A few mountain flowers and weeds poked out between the cracks of boulders, and a few stunted, twisted trees stood in patches of sandy soil, but mostly there was only rock. Reynie was wondering how a plant as fragile as duskwort had ever existed in such a place when Kate broke in on his thoughts.

'We're here,' she murmured, pointing.

355

There was no mistaking the cave. Bright light poured from its entrance as well as from smaller openings in the rock above it, giving the appearance of an enormous stone jack-o'-lantern with a candle inside. The light even appeared to flicker as a candle would. It took Reynie a moment to realize that the flickering effect was created by someone passing back and forth across the light source, somewhere down inside the cave.

Reynie gave an involuntary shudder. He had hoped never again to see Mr Curtain. Yet now, twelve months and thousands of miles later, the time had come.

Elsewhere on the island, in the storm shelter of the abandoned village, a most unpleasant negotiation was coming to an end.

When the children had fled in the Salamander, they had thought they were leaving Milligan chained to a beam, alone in the darkness with two Ten Men. They weren't entirely correct, however, for even as Kate was descending into the well to retrieve the map, the Ten Man known as Crawlings was regaining consciousness. He lay on the ground near Milligan's feet, blinking groggily and drooling, trying to get his wits about him. The shelter was dark, illuminated but faintly by the moonlight shining through the ruined doorway. Crawlings became aware of McCracken talking. Then he heard the rumble of the Salamander on its way out of the village. With a groan he hauled himself to his knees, rubbed his eyes – and saw Milligan holding a laser pointer. *His* laser pointer. Crawlings leapt to his feet, looking wildly about.

'Hold still,' Milligan said, and Crawlings froze.

'Welcome back, Crawlings,' said McCracken's voice from behind him.

'What – what's going on?' said Crawlings, not taking his eyes from Milligan.

'Let's see,' said McCracken. 'You allowed yourself to be knocked out, yielding your weapon to the enemy in the process, and Sharpe and I were compelled to stand here while the children escaped in the Salamander. I hate to say it, Crawlings, but Mr Curtain will not be pleased.'

'I should say he won't,' said Sharpe.

Crawlings spat onto the floor. He was fully awake now and furious at having been humiliated. 'Well, why are we just standing here? There are three of us, aren't there? That pointer only has one shot.'

'We were just discussing this,' said McCracken. 'I was explaining to Milligan that the pointer is extremely sophisticated, a chemical-based laser weapon Mr Curtain designed for us, and that perhaps he should think twice about attempting to use it. For instance, does he even know he's pointing it the right way? He wouldn't want to accidentally shoot *himself*, would he?'

'You forget I've collected a few of these,' said Milligan.

'Oh, that's right,' said McCracken with an easy smile. 'I'd forgotten. Still, when the time comes to shoot, you'll want to be careful. You don't want to miss and set one of the beams afire – or the roof, for that matter. Seeing as how you're chained up, a fire would be inconvenient for you.'

'I'll keep that in mind,' said Milligan.

'What's the point of any of this?' Crawlings said irritably. 'He can't stop all of us and he knows it.'

'He wants to give the children a head start,' said

McCracken. 'But Crawlings's point is well made, don't you think, Milligan? Really, now. You're wasting everyone's time. What's the use of prolonging the inevitable?'

'Maybe I enjoy it,' Milligan said. He aimed the laser pointer directly at McCracken. 'But if you're in such a hurry to resolve the situation, go ahead and make a move.' McCracken frowned. 'Oh, but Milligan, remember what will happen! You'll fire your one shot, and perhaps – *perhaps* – you'll be lucky enough to disable one of us. But there will still be two of us left to deal with you, and . . . well, we *will* deal with you, Milligan. Won't we deal with him, boys?'

'With pleasure,' said Crawlings, whose head ached terribly from whatever Milligan had done to him.

Sharpe snickered. 'Oh yes, indeed. We're great dealers!'

'But I have an idea you'll like, Milligan,' said McCracken. 'If you toss over that pointer, we'll forgo any unpleasantness and simply deliver you to Mr Curtain. Who knows? Maybe you'll get lucky – maybe he'll have some use for you. That's your best chance of survival, at any rate. Believe me, it won't be easy for us. We'll be making quite a sacrifice not to punish you for treating us so impolitely.'

'A *big* sacrifice,' muttered Crawlings.

'A giant one,' agreed Sharpe.

'But if you don't toss over the pointer . . .' McCracken shrugged. 'Well, it's not going to be pretty.'

'No, it'll be ugly, all right,' said Sharpe.

'*Really* ugly,' said Crawlings.

'How ugly, exactly?' said Milligan, as if he thought it a fascinating question. 'As ugly as you?'

Crawlings scowled, his eyebrow slanting inward. He tightened his fists and glanced longingly at his briefcase.

McCracken was chortling. 'Even uglier than Crawlings, I assure you, Milligan! And I'm afraid it's time to make your decision. I'm going to count to three, and then we're all going to move. You can toss over the pointer or use it as you see fit. The choice is yours. Are you ready? Here we go. One . . . two . . .'

'I've made my decision,' Milligan said.

'Thought you might,' said McCracken with a condescending wink. He held out his big hand. 'Toss it carefully, please. Those things are expensive.'

But Milligan didn't toss the pointer at all. Returning McCracken's wink, he spun around and fired at the chain – cutting it clean through.

'Crafty!' exclaimed McCracken, already reaching into his briefcase. The other Ten Men, recovering from their surprise, began to shake their arms, exposing their silver wristwatches. 'Crafty but pointless. We're standing between you and the door.'

Milligan had no intention of trying to escape, however. He feinted one direction, then leapt across the shelter and snatched up his tranquilizer gun.

'Another bold move!' came McCracken's voice as Milligan ducked behind a beam. There was an electrical hum in the air from the Ten Men's watches. 'But you'd still have done better to surrender. It *is* three against one, you know!'

'Not for long,' Milligan growled, and he jumped out from behind the beam.

So began one of the fiercest and strangest battles ever fought, a battle that involved all manner of business supplies, elegant clothing and accessories, and no shortage of trickery and taunts. It was a battle that would rage for hours, and which, when at last it came to an end, would leave the abandoned village entirely in ruins and only one man standing to survey the wreckage. It was also a battle that would leave the young members of the Mysterious Benedict Society in even greater danger than before – for alas, the one man left standing wasn't Milligan.

The Cave at the Top of the Mountain

At the exact moment the terrible battle with the Ten Men was beginning in the abandoned village, Reynie and the other children stood outside the entrance of the mountaintop cave. The air emanating from within was damp and strangely warm, and had a faintly sulphurous odour. Inside, at the end of a narrow, tunnel-like passage, the cave opened into a much larger space, a cavern in which stalactites and stalagmites bristled from above and below. The children could see everything quite well, for the cavern was illuminated by a series of floodlights erected on metal stands. Nothing moved. No voices sounded. But the children had seen the flickering shadows; they knew someone was down in there. Reynie recalled how the island, when seen from a height, had resembled a monstrous beast. Now they were walking right into its mouth.

At the end of the passage, where the cavern opened up, the children stopped to study their eerie surroundings. The stalagmites here rose out of the ground every dozen or so steps; the stalactites, even more numerous, crowded the cavern ceiling and hung so low that an adult could have reached up and touched their pointed tips. Everything, from floor to ceiling, appeared slimy and grey; everything glistened in the bright floodlights. And the soft buzzing of those lights was the only sound the children could hear – until they heard a man cough.

They swivelled their eyes toward one another, hearts hammering. The cough had been simple and short, a normal-sounding cough, and had come from close by. Signalling the others to stay put, Kate crept several steps further. She paused. Reynie saw her eyes widen. Holding a finger to her lips, Kate beckoned them to join her. The children moved forward on tiptoe.

There, in a sort of clearing among the stalagmites, was Mr Benedict.

He sat several paces away from them, with his back against the only stalagmite in the clearing. His head was down, his eyes were closed, and his hands were behind him in what looked to be a very uncomfortable position. A metal loop had been driven into the stalagmite beside him; Reynie guessed that it was to this loop that Number Two had been handcuffed, and that Mr Benedict was probably cuffed to one just like it. That would explain why his hands were behind him at such an awkward angle. Seeing Mr Benedict made Reynie's heart swell – there was that familiar head of white hair and that familiar green plaid suit, both rumpled as ever! – but his burst of happiness instantly gave way to concern, for who knew what sort of condition Mr Benedict was in?

Despite the surge of emotions they felt at the sight of Mr Benedict, the children kept their composure. Silently, with all their senses on alert, they glanced around for sign of Mr Curtain. Not far from Mr Benedict stood a narrow work table covered with equipment – a microscope, several phials and stoppered bottles, and various oddments and tools – and beneath it was a stack of perhaps fifty black metal containers that resembled shoe boxes. Whether all this belonged to Mr Benedict or Mr Curtain was impossible to tell, just as it was impossible to tell if there was a key on the table, a key that might release Mr Benedict. Reynie strained his eyes looking for one, but he was too far away, and it seemed too risky to go over there right now. Someone had been moving around in this cavern, almost certainly Mr Curtain, and the children had yet to spot him. They mustn't let themselves get sneaked up on.

Reynie cast a nervous glance toward the passage behind them, then began to study the cavern floor, searching for human-shaped shadows. Was Mr Curtain hiding behind a stalagmite, ready to burst out at the right moment? Kate tugged his arm and pointed. Far off to their left was an opening in the cavern wall, beyond which there appeared to be a separate chamber, equally well lit. It, too, was thick with stalagmites and stalactites, and at first glance had seemed part of the cavern in which they stood. Reynie felt a rush of hope. If Mr Curtain was in that other chamber, they might be able to free Mr Benedict without ever encountering his wicked brother.

'What do you think?' Kate whispered to Reynie.

It was a soft whisper, but even so, Mr Benedict's eyes sprang open. The effect was disconcerting – no matter that he was their friend and they were here to rescue him – and the children, startled, almost cried out.

'You're here?' Mr Benedict whispered, his expression incredulous. 'But how—?' He cut himself off and whispered urgently, 'Never mind! Listen to me, children. There's little time. You must destroy the duskwort! We can't let Ledroptha discover its whereabouts!'

'But we have no idea where it is!' Kate whispered. 'You'll have to show us!'

Mr Benedict frowned. 'You don't know? But I thought . . . never mind. It's all right. Just – wait. Hold still a moment. Be quiet now. There he goes.'

The children, frozen in their spots, swivelled their eyes all around. A movement beyond the opening in the cavern wall caught their attention – and then they glimpsed what appeared to be a human head and torso floating past in the other chamber. A prickling sensation travelled up everyone's spine. Constance gave a muffled whimper. The ghostly sight would have been frightening even if they hadn't known what it actually was. But they did know. There had been no mistaking Mr Curtain in his wheelchair. They'd seen that long, lumpy nose and shock of white hair, and the gliding motion was undeniably that of something rolling across the ground. Yes, they had all seen it, and yet, strangely, none of them had *heard* it. Reynie thought this must be a trick of acoustics, some bizarre effect peculiar to the cavern.

Regardless, Mr Benedict had somehow sensed the wheelchair passing by; and he seemed to sense, too, when it was safe to speak again. He nodded at the children. 'It's all right,' he whispered. 'But he'll come back any moment. You must hurry!'

Reynie's arms were covered in goose bumps. 'What should we do?'

'Untie my hands,' Mr Benedict said. 'Hurry now, and we'll escape together!'

Reynie hesitated. Something seemed amiss, but in the urgency of the moment he couldn't immediately identify it. Kate, though, had already taken out her Army knife – cutting through a rope was obviously faster than untying it – and she began hurrying toward Mr Benedict just as Constance yanked on Reynie's arm. Reynie, looking down, realized that she'd been trying to speak but had been too terrified to make a sound. Her eyes were huge. She was frantically shaking her head.

With a flash of horror, Reynie understood the reason for his misgivings: Mr Benedict would never have asked them to untie him – not when lingering here so clearly jeopardized their safety. No, Mr Benedict would have told them to run.

Reynie dashed after Kate, waving his arms. Not daring to cry out (for fear of a Ten Man lurking in the other chamber) he whispered, 'Kate, stop! *Stop!*'

Kate heard him and looked back, which was exactly the worst thing she could have done. She had already drawn too close to Mr Curtain – for it could be none other than Mr

Curtain leaping to his feet with such a look of malevolent triumph – and before she understood what was happening, the wicked man had seized her.

Reynie charged in at full tilt. But no sooner had Mr Curtain grabbed Kate than he let her go, and as Kate slumped to the floor with a stunned expression, Reynie noticed the shiny silver gloves on Mr Curtain's hands – one of which shot forward and took him by the arm. Instantly he felt as if a fireworks display had been launched inside him; his body seemed composed of a million white-hot sparks. It was astonishingly painful, and Reynie's relief was intense when the fireworks faded, leaving what appeared to be a clear black sky. Or no, not sky . . .

Reynie opened his eyes and saw Mr Curtain's blurry, smiling face floating above him. He heard Sticky's voice as if from a great distance, telling Constance to run. Then he felt something cold, hard, and metallic tightening around his wrist.

'Not again,' Reynie mumbled, still dazed.

'Oh yes,' said Mr Curtain. 'Again.'

The children were handcuffed to one another in order of their capture. Kate was cuffed to one of the metal loops in the stalagmite – Mr Curtain had been sure to deal with her first – and Reynie was cuffed to Kate. Next came Sticky, who despite having seen what those silver gloves had done to his friends had charged at Mr Curtain in an attempt to save Constance.

'Run, Constance!' he'd yelled. 'Run and don't look back!'

Moments later Sticky was on the ground, shocked senseless, and when he came around again he was handcuffed to

Rcynie. Together they watched bleakly as Constance was brought back from the cavern entrance, where SQ Pedalian had been waiting. She was sniffling and crying and had gone perfectly limp, and SQ was compelled to carry her.

'There, there, Constance,' SQ was saying in a genuinely concerned tone. 'Don't be upset. This is all just a misunderstanding. I mean you've just misunderstood. I mean you've been naughty. Do you understand?'

'That's enough, SQ,' said Mr Curtain, removing his silver gloves and slipping them inside his suit coat. 'Just cuff her to Mr Washington there and say no more.'

It was odd for the children to see the former Executive in ordinary clothes – gone were the smart tunic and sash – but in all other respects he seemed the same. He was tall and gangly, his feet were enormous, and he appeared to be acting against his kind-hearted instincts out of some dim-witted loyalty to Mr Curtain. With the mechanical, efficient movements of one who has performed the same task countless times, SQ cuffed Constance's wrist tightly to Sticky's. Constance winced as the metal pinched her skin, and SQ winced in sympathetic response. But he remembered Mr Curtain's order and said no more.

Mr Curtain regarded the captive children as if contemplating a magnificent piece of art. His cheerful expression had an unsettling effect, for it made him seem more like Mr Benedict than himself. 'Thank you all so much for coming,' he said. 'I really could not have asked for a better gift.'

'It was the least we could do,' said Kate. She was quite scared, but she'd rather die than show her fear to the loathsome man who had just shocked the daylights out of her. He had also taken away her Army knife, and with it her

367

hopes of prying out the metal loop.

Mr Curtain clapped his hands. 'Such bravado! Of course, I expected no less from you children. And, as I hope you now realize, I *did* expect you. Many of my former Executives hold government posts, you see, some of them quite close to Benedict. When you children went off on your own, I was informed at once. My informants were baffled by your disappearance, but your intentions were no great mystery to *me*. The only question was whether you would succeed in finding your beloved Benedict. Oh, how I hoped you would!'

'Where *is* Mr Benedict?' Reynie demanded. 'Or are you such a coward that—?'

'Reynard! For shame!' Mr Curtain waggled his finger disapprovingly. 'Do you really think I'm unprepared for your tactics this time? Last time, you'll recall, you *betrayed* me, which is the only reason you caught me off guard. This time I know you for the conniving and deceitful little wretch that you are. You won't fool me into getting angry, Reynard. I won't be disturbed into falling asleep. *Au contraire*!'

'What?' said Constance, who with some effort had stopped crying. She glared at Mr Curtain. 'What do you want?'

'What do you mean, what do I want?' asked Mr Curtain, who seemed confused by her question.

Constance scowled. 'You said, 'Oh, Contraire!' So what? What is it?'

Mr Curtain burst into his too-familiar laughter, which sounded like nothing so much as a wounded screech owl. 'It's just as SQ said, Miss Contraire! You *misunderstand*!' He shook his head in mock sympathy. 'Never mind, my dear. The point is, I am perfectly undisturbed, and I shall remain so. Oh yes, I shall remain in control of my faculties, which means that *you* shall remain in my power.' He tapped his fingertips together. 'However, I do grow fatigued. I believe I shall fetch a chair.'

With a mysterious, expectant smile, Mr Curtain put his hands behind him and stood at attention, as if waiting for something. Before the children had time to wonder what it was, they witnessed one of the most disturbing things they had ever seen.

Mr Curtain's wheelchair appeared without sound. It shot out of the other chamber like a rocket, speeding around the stalagmites toward its owner, but its wheels made absolutely no sound on the cave floor, and its motor and gears were quiet – even, somehow, *more* than quiet. The effect was like watching a silent film, except that this was real life. The only noise the children heard was the jingle of their handcuffs (for they were all shuddering). The wheelchair was some kind of rolling nightmare, and strapped into its seat was the real Mr Benedict. His hands were cuffed to the armrests, his head lolled forward on his neck, and his spectacles were in danger of falling from his nose. He appeared to be fast asleep.

'As you see, I've designed an excellent remote control,' said Mr Curtain, showing them a tiny control box he'd been hiding behind his back. 'SQ, put him with the others. Be careful, now – I'm convinced he sometimes only pretends to be asleep.'

SQ removed Mr Benedict from the wheelchair, propped him gently against the stalagmite, and handcuffed one of his wrists to the other metal loop. As SQ worked, Mr Curtain was taking his accustomed place in the wheelchair, which appeared to be his old one – a complicated machine with multiple knobs, buttons, and pedals – but which obviously had undergone certain alarming modifications.

'I imagine he worked himself into a sleeping fit trying to warn you,' Mr Curtain said in an amused tone. 'He's been in a sorry state of distress ever since Martina reported you were on the island, and his distress only increased when SQ spotted you coming up the mountain and I arranged to take advantage of your foolishness. Oh, he protested at the top of his lungs! Or I should say he appeared to. I had activated my new device by then, so his annoying cries went unheard.'

'Noise cancellation?' murmured Sticky in surprise. 'But no one's ever achieved it on such a scale . . .' He fell silent, not having meant to speak in the first place.

Mr Curtain had overheard him, though, and he raised his eyebrows. 'I see you've kept up with your reading, George! Yes, I've installed a brand new device – one of my own invention and thus vastly superior to anything else of its kind – that nullifies all sound in its immediate vicinity. I'm well-versed in the manipulation of invisible waveforms, as you know. Indeed, compared to my Whisperer, this project was no more challenging than . . .' Mr Curtain trailed off with a chuckle. 'But I digress. The point is, you couldn't hear Benedict shouting, and I've no doubt he upset himself to sleep.'

'How come we can hear *you* talking?' Constance said. 'It would be nice if we couldn't.'

Mr Curtain twitched, which was the first sign of

annoyance he had shown. 'I deactivated the device, Constance, with the push of a button. If you were more attentive, you would know that.'

'I'm attentive enough to see you're as nasty as ever,' Constance retorted. Her long-anticipated reunion with Mr Benedict, occurring under such upsetting circumstances, had produced in her a very agitating mix of relief, concern and fear – emotions she naturally expressed with angry defiance. In fact she was about to deliver an insulting rhyme when Mr Curtain silenced her with a threatening look.

'SQ,' Mr Curtain said, 'be a good fellow – by which I mean not quite such a blundering fool – and take a few steps away from Miss Wetherall. I dislike the way she's eyeing the key in your hand.'

Having locked Mr Benedict near the children, SQ had lingered unthinkingly close by. At Mr Curtain's warning, he shoved the key deep into his pocket and backed away from Kate with a look of disbelief. At the Institute he'd been fond of the children, and despite all that had happened, SQ found that he was comfortable with them – and far too trusting. He shook his head angrily. 'You should be ashamed!'

'I was only admiring how well you handled that key,' Kate said. 'I think you've got less clumsy, SQ!'

SQ brightened. 'Do you think so?'

'SQ!' Mr Curtain snapped. 'Be silent, and bring the smelling salts from the table.'

'Should I bring the serum, too?' SQ asked, hurrying to the table.

'Absolutely not. As I've told you repeatedly, you are never to touch it. The serum's too precious to trust in your awkward paws, SQ. You should know that.'

'I was just thinking about what Kate said, about how I seem to be—'

Mr Curtain rubbed his forehead. 'She was *lying* to you, SQ. It was the key she was admiring, not your skill with it. Now wake up Benedict, move away, and for the last time, be silent.'

SQ obediently passed the smelling salts beneath Mr Benedict's nose. Mr Benedict sniffed, started, and suddenly looked up. His green eyes, normally so clear and bright, were terribly bloodshot and rimmed with red – he seemed exhausted beyond measure – but they flashed with joy when they fell upon the children, only to grow troubled when he perceived their predicament.

'Ah,' Mr Benedict said ruefully, pushing up his spectacles with his free hand. 'How good it is to see you, my friends, and how I wish you hadn't come.'

'They've come to save you, Benedict!' cried Mr Curtain. 'They sneaked into my Salamander and raced to your rescue! Aren't they doing a fine job?'

'I think they've done admirably,' Mr Benedict said, then turning to SQ he added, 'SQ, you know *I* don't mind having you close by, but I imagine my brother would prefer you to stand a bit farther away from his prisoners.'

'I've told you never to call me that!' Mr Curtain snarled as SQ hastily retreated. 'You are not my brother! A brother would not have ruined years of my work! A brother would not have taken away that which I prized most! My brother? No, Benedict, you are decidedly *not* my *brother*!'

'And yet we do look rather alike,' Mr Benedict pointed out.

Mr Curtain pressed his lips so tightly together the colour left them; and his knuckles, too, went white from clenching the arms of his wheelchair. Spinning around so that his back was to Mr Benedict – the chair moved noiselessly; he must have triggered its silencing device – Mr Curtain took several deep breaths. (No one could hear him, but his shoulders rose and fell dramatically with each breath.) The fact of his kinship to Mr Benedict was clearly upsetting to him, just as it once had been – and perhaps still was – to Mr Benedict. A year had passed since each had discovered a long-lost brother and a formidable enemy at the exact same time, and Mr Curtain had evidently spent every moment of it cultivating his bitterness.

Regaining his composure, he turned back to face Mr Benedict. His mouth began to move, but no sound came out. With an irritated grimace, he pressed a button on the controller in his hand and started again. 'Very well,' he said. 'I will acknowledge that you are my brother – a brother who ruined my ambitions and is thus the very worst kind of traitor. Are you satisfied?'

Mr Benedict opened his mouth to speak, but Mr Curtain cut him off.

'That was a rhetorical question, Benedict. I do not care in the least if you are satisfied or not.' He rolled his eyes and moved a little closer in his wheelchair. 'And now to business. Since you have slept through recent developments, Benedict, allow me to apprise you of the situation. I had hoped these children would know about the duskwort, but by their own account they do not. Therefore—'

Mr Benedict interrupted him. 'I've told you repeatedly, Ledroptha, that if you'd only release Number Two and me,

I would make sure you were informed about the duskwort. That offer still stands. Once my friends and I are safely out of reach, I promise to have the information sent to you.'

'I know what you offered,' Mr Curtain said irritably. 'And yet even if I trusted you, Benedict, the offer wouldn't exactly suit my plans. I am not going to let you go. I am not *ever* going to let you go.'

'Won't I grow awfully cumbersome?' Mr Benedict said. 'I hate to be a burden.' Mr Curtain sneered. 'You joke, but the jokes will soon end. No, you will not be cumbersome. I don't intend to let you go, but I don't intend to keep you around, either. I intend to replace you.'

It was with obvious delight that Mr Curtain explained his carefully laid plans. The months he'd spent watching, waiting, preparing. How he'd ordered the theft of the truth serum – the better, he explained, to extract key passwords and information that would help him pass for Mr Benedict. Under his new identity, Mr Curtain would regain access to his Whisperer – and with it the ability to manipulate the memories and opinions of others. In short order, those officials who opposed the 'new' Mr Benedict's ambitions would find themselves unceremoniously yanked from their posts, with no memory of having opposed him at all. And with the help of his former Executives, so well placed in government, Mr Curtain – known to everyone else as Mr Benedict – would rise swiftly to a position of unequalled power.

In a way, Mr Curtain explained in a mocking tone, Mr Benedict had done much of the work for him. He had but to take advantage when the opportunity arose. 'My associates were ready to pounce the moment you strayed beyond your protection. But then I learned that you'd made plans for travel without disclosing the reasons to anyone. This, I thought, was suspicious behaviour, and I determined not to apprehend you until I had learned more. And oh! What I learned was well worth the wait, don't you think? Duskwort! The most precious plant imaginable! And you – of all people – unwittingly prepared to lead me right to it!' Mr Curtain uttered a clipped screech of laughter that sounded like a hiccup.

'Ledroptha,' said Mr Benedict, 'why are you telling me this now?'

Mr Curtain ignored him. Speaking directly to the children, he continued, 'When I caught up with him here, I knew the duskwort was close by. Benedict and his assistant – I refuse to call her by her ridiculous code name – clearly intended to use this cave as a temporary laboratory. They had everything they needed: a comfortable location sheltered from the wind, a microscope, good lighting. To my great annoyance, however, I discovered that I'd arrived before they had gathered any of the plants for study. I could never have guessed their pace would be so tortoise-like! Here they were, ludicrously unaware of the duskwort's precise location or even of its appearance – just sitting on their hands and waiting for some mysterious associate to contact them with the necessary information.'

Mr Curtain gave Mr Benedict a contemptuous glance. 'Luckily,' he went on, 'after wasting only a few drops of my truth serum, I realized the most efficient way to find this person would be to appeal to the protective instincts of Benedict's friends. It was a perfect plan – no, a plan beyond perfection! I would receive the information I sought, then return to Stonetown in triumph! I would have the duskwort *and* my Whisperer! Can you imagine?'

The children shuddered. They could imagine only too well. Mr Curtain's dream was everyone else's nightmare.

'Of course,' Mr Curtain said, 'I would have to revel in private. In public I would be compelled to grieve for my assistant, that poor nervous woman who would have failed to 'escape' with me. I'm sure you can understand why your friend couldn't return with me – not knowing who I really was. No, I'm afraid she would have met her untimely demise at the hands of that cruel Mr Curtain. Or else – I haven't decided yet – she would remain his prisoner, hidden away somewhere in a far corner of the world, where all the government's top agents would be dispatched to search in vain. This, of course, is why my men are tracking her down even as we speak. I may be undecided about her fate, but I certainly can't have her running loose.'

'Ledroptha,' said Mr Benedict gravely. 'It doesn't have to be this way.'

Mr Curtain looked at him askance. 'Oh, but I *choose* for it to be this way. And the arrival of the children has simplified matters. You asked a minute ago why I'm telling you all this now. The answer is that I needed to be cautious. I did not care to give you information you might use against me. You had already proven yourself too untrustworthy for my truth serum to be effective – you always managed to say something technically true but completely unhelpful. But that was when the serum was administered without – how shall I put it? – without additional *ingredients*. And now those ingredients are in my possession.'

Mr Curtain took out his shiny silver gloves. The children

instinctively recoiled. Grinning at their reaction, he patted the gloves against his knees. 'I suspect that with the children here you'll be more inclined to tell me what I wish to know. What say you, Benedict? Shall I put on my 'kid gloves'?'

Mr Benedict looked at his brother with an expression of profound concern. 'Ledroptha, you can't possibly—'

'Do not tell me what I cannot do!' Mr Curtain shouted. He quickly closed his eyes and took a deep breath. After a long moment he opened his eyes again. 'You can say what you please,' he said in a calmer voice, 'but if your answers are not helpful to me, the children will pay the price.'

Mr Curtain shot forward in his wheelchair – narrowly missing the children and Mr Benedict – and retrieved a small phial and dropper from the nearby table. He spun the chair around and rolled over to Mr Benedict. 'Let's get started, shall we?'

Mr Benedict gazed steadily into his brother's eyes. 'How can I know that you won't hurt the children anyway?'

'A fair question,' said Mr Curtain, drawing a single drop of liquid from the phial. 'Allow me to put your mind at ease.'

Mr Curtain lifted the dropper, threw back his head, and let the drop fall into his open mouth. Instantly his eyes bulged and he wagged his head, as if he'd swallowed turpentine. 'I promise,' he said, speaking quickly in a strained voice, 'that if you tell me all I wish to know, I will not hurt these children. I'll use the Whisperer to remove their memories of this event, and so they will be no threat to my plans and can live the remainder of their lives in safety. I will not offer you anything better, but that much, at least, I promise.'

The two men stared at each other, Mr Curtain with a

look of defiance, Mr Benedict with an assessing, contemplative expression. At length Mr Benedict started to speak, only to be interrupted by Constance, who shouted, 'He's lying, Mr Benedict! That wasn't the truth serum at all! He switched the phials while you were asleep!'

Mr Benedict started, then looked visibly upset, as if he'd just received terrible news. In a voice so low only the children heard it he said, 'I knew he was lying, dear girl.' Mr Curtain was staring at Constance in amazement. 'Well, well, *well*,' he said in an appraising tone. 'Now how could you possibly know I switched the phials?'

Constance stared back in dismay. She didn't know how she'd known about the phials. She only knew that she hadn't wanted Mr Benedict to be fooled, and that her revelation seemed to please Mr Curtain very much.

'I did switch them, but it was long before you arrived,' Mr Curtain was saying, mostly to himself. His fingers drummed excitedly on the armrests of his wheelchair. 'And yet you knew . . . you *knew*. Oh, my, what a useful little girl you are, Constance. I had no idea!'

'Ledroptha,' Mr Benedict said quickly, 'promise to leave her alone – no need for the serum – just make the promise, and I will tell you everything you want to know.'

Mr Curtain smiled an oily smile. 'I'll make no such promise, Benedict. I will, however, promise not to harm any of the children for the time being – but only if you answer at once. That is my offer. Shall I put on my gloves, or . . . ?'

'That won't be necessary,' Mr Benedict said. 'Just make the promise.'

'I promise,' said Mr Curtain. He gave Constance a sly look. 'Am I telling the truth, my dear?'

Constance gazed fearfully at him, then nodded.

Mr Curtain made a pleased murmur. He turned back to Mr Benedict. 'Now tell me quick, and no more games! Who is this person you spoke of? And don't you dare ask which person! You know who I mean: the one 'extremely close' to you – the only one who can secure the information for me! That's exactly what you said! Now who is this person?'

Mr Benedict looked frankly at his brother. 'You.'

'Me?' said Mr Curtain, taken aback. His eyes narrowed, and he put his hands over his mouth, breathing into them as if they were cold. It was evident he was attempting to stay calm. 'What do you mean, me? How could I possibly secure this information for *myself*?'

'You could have done so at any time simply by letting us go, which was the offer I made you repeatedly,' said Mr Benedict. 'Had you released us, I would have revealed the information.'

Mr Curtain threw his hands into the air. 'But you said you didn't know!'

'I said no such thing.'

Mr Curtain's wheelchair bucked forward, and with surprising agility he leapt from his seat and landed inches away from Mr Benedict. He shook his finger in Mr Benedict's face. 'And what if I had threatened to hurt your companion? You wouldn't have revealed it then?'

'I most certainly would have,' said Mr Benedict. 'But it would still have been you who secured the information with your threats.'

'So you phrased it that way to prevent further questioning!' roared Mr Curtain, finally understanding. 'You

379

knew I didn't want to waste any more serum! You knew I wanted to save it!'

'That was my understanding, yes.' Mr Benedict returned his brother's furious look with a calm, inscrutable gaze.

The children watched hopefully. If Mr Curtain was angry enough, he might fall asleep, and they could try to make an escape. Maybe . . . But after only a moment of outraged quivering, Mr Curtain relaxed. He smiled, nodded, and put his hands behind his back. His wheelchair came up behind him like a well-trained pet. 'Good enough,' he said, taking his seat. 'In the end, your treachery has worked in my favour. You must be terribly disappointed in yourself, Benedict. Now I shall have my duskwort *and* my Whisperer, and these children are proving useful as well . . .' He turned his wheelchair and cast a probing glance at Constance.

'Ledroptha,' said Mr Benedict. 'Shall I show you what I discovered now, or would you prefer to wait?'

'Yes,' said Mr Curtain, turning eagerly back to him. 'Show me at once.'

'I'll need you to turn off the lights, then.'

'What?'

'The floodlights. Turn them off. There's a control box on the table.'

'*I know* where the control box is,' said Mr Curtain. 'And I have left the lights on for good reason – so that nothing you did would go unobserved.'

Mr Benedict gave him a patient smile. 'I was aware of this, of course. But if you wish to see what I've been hiding from you, then off they must go.'

Mr Curtain regarded him coldly. 'Before I turn them off,

do I need to make clear what punishments the children will suffer if this is an attempt to trick me?'

'I don't believe such an explanation is necessary, no. I assure you I intend to do nothing at all while the lights are out.'

Mr Curtain backed his wheelchair to the table and picked up the control box. He examined it carefully, then – just to be safe – rolled over and handed the box to SQ, who'd been watching the proceedings in dutiful silence and at a dutifully safe distance. 'Very well, Benedict. Let us hope you haven't needlessly endangered your young friends. SQ, flip the switch!'

SQ did as he was told, and the cave was thrown into perfect darkness. But the darkness lasted only a moment, for the walls, stalagmites, and stalactites soon began to glow with luminescent streaks of green.

'What you're seeing is a form of translucent moss,' said Mr Benedict. 'It is what makes the rock appear slimy and wet in the light. In the darkness, as you can see, it is iridescent.'

For a long time Mr Curtain sat in startled silence. Then he laughed. Softly at first, then louder and louder – and screechier and screechier – until the walls of the cavern reverberated with the great screeching peals of Mr Curtain's triumph.

OLD FRIENDS

and NEW ENEMIES

The hours that followed were wretched ones indeed. Mr Benedict and the children were compelled to watch as Mr Curtain and SQ diligently scraped duskwort from every surface within reach. It was Mr Curtain who had brought the black metal boxes stacked beneath the table, the children discovered. Although he'd had no idea of the plant's appearance or location, he'd long been a scholar of the duskwort legends, and some years ago had secured – in a dark corner of the world – a scrap from an ancient book offering instructions for the transport and preservation of the fragile plant.

Evidently nothing more elaborate was required than darkness, moisture, and a certain degree of heat, and Mr Curtain had devised special containers to meet these conditions. Whenever he or SQ opened a metal box to slide in another layer of the precious moss, steam wafted out as if from a modern-day witch's cauldron.

'To think,' said Mr Benedict, watching his brother stretch to reach a high patch of duskwort on a stalagmite, 'if we had worked together, Ledroptha, we might have accomplished a great deal. We each knew things the other did not.'

'And still do,' said Mr Curtain, standing on the seat of his wheelchair to reach the duskwort more easily. (The wheelchair, in response to an unseen signal, eerily circled the stalagmite as if it had a mind of its own.) 'But as you've now witnessed, I'm perfectly capable of making you reveal the things I desire to know. I see no advantage in 'working together,' as you put it.'

'The advantage,' Mr Benedict began, 'would lie in—'

'I do not care to hear any more of your opinions,' interrupted Mr Curtain, peeling away a strip of slimy moss. 'Foolish opinions distract me, and I have no time for distraction.'

'You do seem rather in a hurry,' Mr Benedict observed.

'What did I just tell you about your opinions?' Mr Curtain snapped. 'Once again you betray your simplicity, Benedict. How do you think I have avoided capture if not from choosing never to tarry, never to linger? Take the present case: even if I did not receive word from your Miss Kazembe, I fully intended to leave this island today.'

'And abandon the duskwort?' Mr Benedict asked, sounding mildly surprised.

'Again, Benedict. Simplicity of thinking. I intended to leave SQ, of course, to continue searching for it while I investigated the matter elsewhere. One way or another I would have found the duskwort, I assure you.'

At this, SQ paused in his work. From his stunned expression it was clear he'd had no inkling of this plan to leave him alone on a deserted island.

'As usual, however,' Mr Curtain went on, 'I have achieved my goals in the most efficient manner possible. Still, it never serves to stay in one place for long. Therefore I proceed, as always, with due haste.'

'If you're in such a hurry,' Kate put in, 'why don't you force us to help you gather the duskwort?'

Mr Curtain uttered his screechy laugh. 'I have quite enough help, thank you, Miss Wetherall! And I should have quite enough duskwort even if I were compelled to leave most of it behind. No, I believe it's better if you remain locked up.'

'I can't see why you don't just dump us off the mountain,' Kate said. 'Now that you have your stupid plant, we're not much use to you.' (Her friends squirmed uncomfortably at these words, even though they knew Kate was trying to create an opportunity for escape.)

But Mr Curtain, who also knew what she was up to – subtlety had never been Kate's strong suit – only screeched again and said, 'On the contrary, you may be useful indeed! I've been giving the matter some thought, you see, and the fact is that once I have a proper distillation of the duskwort, it should be simple enough to keep you asleep – helplessly, quietly asleep – except on such occasions as I deem appropriate. Say, whenever I require more information. Benedict has already proven himself quite weak where you children are concerned.'

'Well, I suppose that isn't the dumbest idea you've had,' said Kate, just to show pluck, for Mr Curtain's suggestion had made her feel sick with dread. 'There are rather a lot of us to keep hidden, though. Do you have some kind of shrinking machine, too?'

'Properly stacked, Miss Wetherall, I should think you would all fit nicely in a single locked cupboard.' Mr Curtain pursed his lips, pretending to consider. 'But you're right, it may prove too much of an inconvenience. I'll need to reflect upon it. What do you say, Benedict? Would you prefer to be got rid of entirely, or to sleep your life away in a cupboard?'

'I *am* partial to long naps,' Mr Benedict said. 'But I've never been got rid of before, so it's difficult for me to say.'

Mr Benedict's implacable calm seemed to ruffle Mr Curtain, whose smirk faded, replaced by an icy stare. 'Then it's lucky you will not be the one who chooses. Now do be quiet, all of you. I've had enough of your distractions. I hate to interrupt my work again, but I assure you – and this is a promise – the next person who utters a word will receive my full attention.'

There was no doubting Mr Curtain's sincerity on this point – or what he meant by 'full attention' – and the remaining hours of the night were spent in awful silence, under threat of those shiny silver gloves, with no sounds at all save for those of Mr Curtain and SQ working away.

Reynie's mind was also working away – and furiously, at that – but to no good effect. He had tried countless times to think of a means of escape. Tried and failed. And meanwhile he was imagining all sorts of things he would prefer not to imagine, such as the terrible reunion of Mr Curtain and his Whisperer, and what would happen to Rhonda, Miss Perumal, and all the others whose nosy questions Mr Curtain would never tolerate. Nor, unfortunately, did Reynie's imagination stop there. Instead it wandered bleakly on, out of Mr Benedict's house and into Stonetown, where Reynie saw a crew of Ten Men stalking the slumbering streets, every last resident having been sent to sleep by a 'proper distillation' of Mr Curtain's duskwort. Try as he might, Reynie could not avert his mind's eye, and so he saw with frightful clarity the ease with which Mr Curtain's men carried away all those who dared oppose their master. There would be no struggles, not even a cry of complaint. Just a city waking up in the morning with one less opponent of Mr Curtain.

Mr Curtain would have what he'd always wanted. He would be in absolute control. All that was required was that he change his name to Nicholas Benedict. Most people would never guess what was happening.

The children would be out of the way by then, of course. That much was certain. The question was what Mr Curtain was going to do with them. Try as he might, Reynie couldn't think of any possibilities that didn't make him sweat.

His only hope – however slim – was that Milligan might save them, and as night drew nearer to morning, Reynie clung to it with increasing desperation. When Mr Curtain mused aloud that it was taking his Ten Men much too long to track down the escaped Number Two ('the woman', he called her), and sent SQ out of the cave with a radio to contact them, Reynie tensed in expectation. Perhaps Milligan was waiting outside and would ambush him! But SQ returned with the report that the radio waves were silent. This news caused Mr Curtain to furrow his brow suspiciously, and it gave Reynie some reason to nurse his fragile hope a bit longer . . .

But that hope fell apart completely just before dawn, when McCracken came limping into the cave.

Kate let out a gasp, then burst into tears, for the Ten Man's appearance could mean only one thing. The other children looked at one another in despair, and Mr Benedict, his own eyes brimming as he heard Kate's devastated sobs, reached out to comfort her – then slumped sideways against the stalagmite, asleep.

McCracken observed all this with amusement as he limped over to await Mr Curtain, who at the sound of his approach had retreated – in perfect, creepy silence – to the other chamber. SQ had likewise disappeared, but the Ten Man stared shrewdly at a nearby stalagmite as he called out, 'Code Seven, Mr Curtain! No need for an ambush!' In a patronizing tone he added, 'SQ, I'll remind you that Code Seven means 'all clear'. Your boot tips are plainly visible, at any rate.'

As SQ emerged from his hiding place looking sheepish, Mr Curtain rocketed into view at such a speed that his wheelchair seemed certain to slam into McCracken. He skidded to a stop at the last instant, however, and McCracken acknowledged his entrance with an admiring bow. If Mr Curtain had actually struck him with the chair, McCracken would have been sent flying, and as a Ten Man he had great esteem for impressive displays of force.

It was lucky for McCracken he *hadn't* been sent flying, for he was already in a terrible state. He was using his necktie as a sling for an injured arm, his face was bloody and streaked with soot, his elegant suit was tattered and scorched, and his briefcase positively bristled with tranquilizer darts. His expression, however, revealed an obvious satisfaction, and when he spoke it was in his usual calm, deceptively pleasant way, as if he'd simply come to report on the weather.

'We ran into a spot of trouble,' McCracken said, in response to Mr Curtain's look of disapproval. He nodded toward the children. 'Where'd you find the chickies?'

'They found *me*,' Mr Curtain said coldly, 'having stolen *my* Salamander, which was in *your* care. And I've captured and held them, which was more, apparently, than your imbecile crew could manage. Do remind me why I pay you.'

McCracken grinned, revealing a number of missing teeth. 'We're good for your morale. Anyway, you didn't have to deal with Milligan.'

'Benedict's agent? He's on the island?'

'Ohhh . . . so they didn't tell you,' said McCracken, lifting an eyebrow.

Mr Curtain shot the children a venomous glance. 'They did not. Milligan, eh? I suppose his involvement explains why I haven't heard from Jackson or Jillson.'

'No doubt,' McCracken agreed. 'But you needn't worry about further interference. Milligan's been dealt with.'

'I take it you dealt with him yourself,' said Mr Curtain, looking the Ten Man up and down. 'You're in a pathetic condition.'

'Not just me. It took the lot of us. I must say Milligan was like no one I'd ever fought. Fast as a tiger and clever as a fox. But he never had a chance, really. The man had an absurd reluctance to do anyone real harm. You should have seen the lengths he went to just to avoid killing Crawlings, who was doing everything he could to dash him to pieces. Once I discovered that weakness, it was only a matter of time until I finished him.'

'So you did finish him?' Mr Curtain asked. 'Skip to the end, McCracken. And you, SQ, stop standing there like a lamp post and get back to work.'

'The end was rather a disappointment,' said McCracken as SQ hurriedly resumed scraping and packing. 'Our fight had taken us high up on the middlemost mountain, where I had backed him onto a cliff at the edge of a ravine – the other men were out of commission by this point – and he was enduring a shocking number of hornet stings rather than come out from behind a boulder he was using to shield himself. But I was gradually moving into position to finish him off, and when he realized this, he chose a less painful end. He jumped.'

Reynie put an arm around Kate's shoulders, but she scarcely noticed. She had stifled her tears now, mastering herself in order to listen to McCracken's account. She stared at the Ten Man, radiating fury.

'Now, I didn't see his body,' McCracken admitted. 'My torch was shattered by then. But in the moonlight I could see a good twenty metres down, so he fell at least that far, and he was in a sorry condition to begin with. I doubt he lived, but if he did, he's surely wishing he hadn't. A fall like that will have broken every bone in his body.'

'You're going to wish *you* hadn't lived!' Kate snarled,

lunging forward. She spoke and moved with such ferocity that everyone in the cave flinched – everyone but McCracken, who chuckled as Kate's handcuffs, still locked to the metal loop, jerked her off her feet. Reynie and Sticky grabbed onto her, holding her back for fear she'd break her arm trying to get at McCracken.

'I've come to see what you prefer to do now,' said McCracken, turning back to Mr Curtain. 'I still need to track down Number Two, but first I should gather the men. Martina, too, I suppose – I saw her and Garrotte in the meadow. Milligan waylaid them on their way back to the village.'

Mr Curtain frowned. 'I thought you said he avoided doing real harm.'

'And so he did, but he left everyone unconscious, and Crawlings has some broken bones that will heal better if I have help to lift him properly. If you don't care about that, I can just toss him into the Salamander with my good arm. Or, if you prefer, I can wait for the others to regain consciousness and give me a hand. Sharpe and Garrotte appeared to be coming around – they fluttered their eyes a bit when I kicked them – and I predict they'll be awake soon. But I thought I should let you decide. I knew you hoped to leave before noon today.'

Mr Curtain received this news with considerable annoy-ance, but he appeared determined not to grow vexed. 'Take SQ,' he said brusquely. 'And hurry up. We're almost ready to load.'

SQ started to set down the metal box he'd been carrying.

'No offence,' McCracken said, smiling at SQ in a way that showed he did, in fact, mean offence, 'but I think it ought to be *you* who helps me, Mr Curtain. As I said, Crawlings has broken bones. It wouldn't do to have him dropped.'

SQ, greatly offended, dropped the metal box on his foot.

'Fine,' Mr Curtain said as SQ hopped around moaning and clutching at his foot. 'I'll come. SQ, stop prancing and get back to work.'

McCracken had set down his briefcase and was probing at a loose tooth with his fingertips. He pulled it out, examined it with mild curiosity, and slipped it into his pocket. 'There's something else. Milligan told the children that some friends were coming for them.'

'Snakes and dogs,' muttered Mr Curtain. 'Did he say who? It can't be an official rescue party or I'd have been notified. I assume no one radioed while you were outside.'

'I did hear from Bludgins. Evidently Rhonda Kazembe has sent the pigeon back with a note. She claims to have identified the person you seek and begs for a few more days to locate him.'

'A desperate ploy,' said Mr Curtain, with a gesture of dismissal. 'I've already located what I seek. But you have no word on these people who are coming?'

'No, and Milligan didn't mention any names. But we know where their boat will land, if it hasn't already. The only decent place is in that southeastern bay. If you like, once my men are up we can drive over—'

Mr Curtain waved him silent. 'Any confrontations can wait, McCracken, and it would be best to avoid them altogether. What I want from you is an assurance that our escaped prisoner cannot contact these people and tell them where Benedict is.'

'Well,' said McCracken, 'if she hasn't already met up with them – that is, if they haven't already sent a rescue party across the island . . .'

'Most unlikely,' said Mr Curtain. 'The bay will have had an exceptionally tricky tide last night, McCracken – I know a thing or two about tides, you see – and I doubt any craft can have navigated to shore before now.'

'Very good,' McCracken said. 'Then I can assure you we'll capture Number Two before she causes any trouble. I suspect she's still hiding in the woods by the village. With the wind's help we should have no trouble burning the woods and smoking her out.'

'You had better be right,' Mr Curtain said tersely.

The conversation then shifted to the wheelchair, which Mr Curtain was loath to leave behind. Because of his injured arm, McCracken couldn't carry both the chair and his briefcase down the steep goat path to the Salamander, yet the chair was too heavy for Mr Curtain – or indeed for any but the strongest of men – to carry that far. McCracken pointed out that Mr Curtain wouldn't actually be using the wheelchair much, to which Mr Curtain replied that McCracken didn't use his brain much, either, but still preferred to keep it with him. And so the discussion continued.

Kate, meanwhile, was rifling surreptitiously through her bucket, trying to find anything that might help. At length she muttered, 'I can't work out how we're going to manage this.'

'You mean how we'll escape?' said Reynie in an undertone. 'I can't either.'

'I didn't mean *that*,' Kate replied, as if surprised at the very notion. 'Of course we'll escape!'

'We will?' Sticky asked hopefully. 'How?'

'Oh, we'll think of something,' Kate whispered, which was not quite as specific a plan as Sticky had hoped for. 'What I'm wondering is how we'll meet up with Milligan and find Number Two before those creeps do. How will we rescue her?'

'Wait – you think Milligan is alive?' Constance whispered.

'Obviously! I mean, I didn't think so at first, but then I realized Milligan would never jump to his death – not when we were still in danger. He must have had something else in mind. Probably he just hasn't been able to find us. He told us to go to that bay forest, after all. That's where he'd have gone to look for us.'

Reynie was less optimistic than Kate, but she did have a point. 'Let me get this straight. We're chained up in a cave with no idea what Mr Curtain's going to do to us, and your biggest concern is how we're going to rescue Number Two?'

'Exactly!' Kate whispered.

'I just wanted to be clear on that,' said Reynie, and though he had only a small impulse to smile, this was nonetheless the best he'd felt in some time. 'I think the place to start would be to rescue ourselves, Kate.'

'I know, but we need more time! If they're going to burn those woods—'

'We have more time than they think,' Constance put in. 'They'll have trouble burning anything. It's getting damp outside. Misting or drizzling. Don't look at me like that, you know I can sense these—'

'SQ!' barked Mr Curtain. The children flinched and looked up to see him glaring at them. 'If any one of our prisoners speaks again – any single one of them, SQ – you will report it to me on my return, and they will suffer the consequences. That's an order, understood? No one is to speak. I will have none of this murmuring among themselves.'

'Yes, sir,' said SQ. He cleared his throat. 'And, er, sir? Might I suggest that McCracken carry your wheelchair while you carry his briefcase? Just down to the Salamander, I mean.'

The two men stared at SQ, then looked at each other in surprise.

'Out of the mouths of babes,' grunted McCracken.

'I'll steer my chair as far as the path,' said Mr Curtain, already moving. 'Then we can exchange burdens.'

He glided swiftly away up the passage, with McCracken limping along behind him and with never a word of thanks to SQ – nor even a glance of acknowledgment – for having made the amazingly practical suggestion that the two of them work *together*.

Still smarting from McCracken's insult and Mr Curtain's cold treatment, SQ Pedalian had only just returned to his work when Mr Benedict spoke to him. No one had seen Mr Benedict wake up, and in fact he spoke now in a careful, measured tone, with a very sleepy quality, as if perhaps he hadn't woken at all.

'SQ,' Mr Benedict said in this strange, somniferous tone, 'I know you have much to do, but if you can spare just a moment, these handcuffs are chafing me again.'

SQ turned to Mr Benedict with a look of distress. 'Oh, no, Mr Benedict, you shouldn't have spoken! Don't you realize I have to report you to Mr Curtain now? It was a direct order, you know! You'll be punished!'

Mr Benedict fixed SQ with a steady gaze. 'I realize that, SQ,' he said, still in that slow, sleepy tone, 'and it's quite all right. You must do what you must do, my friend. I bear you no ill will.'

Plainly relieved, SQ smiled, then stifled a yawn. 'Still,' said Mr Benedict, 'the handcuffs, as I said, are chafing my wrist most terribly. Just as they always do.'

SQ stared at him, not in hesitation or even with suspicion, but as if it were taking a long time for Mr Benedict's words to register in his brain. The children, bewildered, said nothing. They dared not even breathe. They could see Mr Benedict was up to something even if SQ couldn't. SQ yawned again but didn't take his eyes from Mr Benedict's.

'You are very tired, aren't you, SQ?' said Mr Benedict.

SQ continued to stare. After a moment, he nodded dumbly. 'I really am,' he whispered.

'I know you are, my friend,' said Mr Benedict. 'And so am I. You should sit with me a moment and rest. But first, please unlock my handcuffs, just as you've kindly done before. I would like to rub some feeling back into my wrist.'

And then, to the children's profound amazement, SQ Pedalian walked over to Mr Benedict and unlocked his handcuffs. At first Mr Benedict did not stir; he only thanked SQ and rubbed his wrist gratefully. Then he patted the ground beside him.

'Sit for a moment,' Mr Benedict said.

'For a moment,' intoned SQ, his eyes heavy-lidded, his

shoulders slumped. He sat beside Mr Benedict and leant back against the stalagmite.

'You should feel how these pinch,' said Mr Benedict, and very casually, as if adjusting a cufflink on SQ's sleeve, he slipped the open handcuff onto SQ's wrist (the other was still attached to the metal loop) and tightened it. 'There, isn't that uncomfortable?'

'It *is* a bit constraintive,' SQ murmured, frowning. 'I mean constrictual. I mean . . .' He trailed off, his expression troubled.

'We should take them off,' said Mr Benedict. 'Here, give me the key.'

SQ gave Mr Benedict the key. Leaning forward to obscure SQ's view, Mr Benedict slipped the key to Kate, who lost no time in freeing herself and the others. Then Mr Benedict drew the children away from the stalagmite, where SQ still sat cuffed to the metal loop. SQ blinked rapidly, as if coming awake. He stared at the children, and then at Mr Benedict, in perfect bafflement.

'I am sorry, SQ,' said Mr Benedict. 'Some part of you must understand that I mean that.'

SQ shook his head violently as if to clear it. His expression darkened; his lip began to quiver. 'But . . . but you can't be serious! You can't have *lied* to me!'

'I never did,' said Mr Benedict.

SQ was stunned. 'But all those other times – you never tried anything! You promised you wouldn't! I even gave you a drop of the truth serum to be sure!'

'Yes, but I made no such promise this time, SQ. Nor did I promise to release you – I said only that we should take your handcuffs off. Which we should. In a better world and time, I would gladly release you. And I hope to see you again in just such a world, and at such a time. You have a bright soul, SQ I'm extremely sorry to leave you in this predicament, but leave you I must.' Mr Benedict turned away with a sorrowful expression. 'Come, children, we should hurry.'

Kate hoisted Constance onto her back, and together the escaped prisoners made quickly for the passage. Behind them, SQ sat with his face growing darker and darker, his eyes darting back and forth as he worked through what Mr Benedict had said. He was plainly trying not to believe what had just happened.

'You hypnotized him?' Constance asked as they hurried up the passage.

'Something like that,' said Mr Benedict gravely, 'although much coarser. Persuading him was possible only because he trusted me not to betray his kindness. I've just dealt a terrible blow to the best part of SQ Pedalian, children. We must all hope he recovers.' Mr Benedict touched Reynie's shoulder. 'I hope *you* haven't given up on the SQs of the world, Reynie. As you see, there are a great many sheep in wolves' clothing. If not for SQ's good nature, we'd never have escaped.'

They were now approaching the cave entrance, from which they could hear an unearthly moaning – it was dawn, and the island's daily wind had risen – and Reynie was just reflecting that they hadn't escaped *yet* when the wind's moaning was drowned out by a howl of anguish echoing through the cave behind them. SQ had finally accepted the reality of his situation. In furious outrage he screamed after them, 'You're just like Mr Curtain said! I believed you, Mr

Benedict! I trusted you! I should have known! I should have *known*!'

At the cave entrance Mr Benedict stopped to look back. Perhaps it was a result of his exhaustion, or perhaps it was because he was the direct cause of SQ's suffering, but his expression was as mournful as any of the children had ever seen it.

'If only—' he began, but he never finished his thought, for at that moment he fell asleep.

Sticky spared Mr Benedict a vicious knock on the head by being in his way when he fell. Thus it was Sticky who suffered the knock, bruising his forehead on the hard ground as he fell with Mr Benedict on top of him. Tugging free, he gently rolled Mr Benedict onto his back and resettled the sleeping man's spectacles before resettling his own. He shook Mr Benedict's arm. 'Wake up, Mr Benedict! Wake *up*!'

SQ's howls had stopped as abruptly as they'd started, and the only sound now was the moaning of the wind and Sticky's entreaties as the others looked anxiously on. Mr Curtain and McCracken had been gone no time at all. If they'd forgotten something and came back . . . Reynie cast a nervous glance out beyond the cave. Dawn may have broken, but there was no sunshine. Grey clouds scudded low over the mountain, and – just as Constance had predicted – a fine grey mist hung over everything, swirling in the wind like smoke.

'He isn't waking up,' Sticky said, patting Mr Benedict's cheek.

'Uh oh,' said Constance. 'This can happen when he's

really worn out. Sometimes wc can't wake him for hours.'

'Well, he's surely as exhausted right now as he's ever been,' Sticky said. He looked up at Reynie. 'This isn't good.'

'Let's see if we can fashion a stretcher,' said Reynie. 'We can't afford to wait. We need to get to that bay forest.'

'What about Number Two?' Kate protested.

'Our best chance of helping her now is to get to the forest. Like you said, that's where Milligan expected us to go, so that's where we should look for him. If he isn't there, maybe his friends will be, and we can get them to help us. But there's no chance of any of that if we're caught. We need to move!'

Move, of course, was a word with great natural appeal to Kate, and she was instantly swayed to Reynie's perspective. Still, she doubted the boys could handle the other end of a stretcher all the way to the bay, even taking turns, and there was also Constance to consider. 'What we need is a sledge. We can drag Mr Benedict and Constance together. I'll be right back!' She dashed down the passage into the cavern.

The others were still trying to rouse Mr Benedict when Kate returned. She was dragging the table that had been covered with tools and equipment. With the help of the tools, her bucket, and her Army knife (which Mr Curtain had left on the table), she'd removed the table legs and re-attached them lengthways to act as crude runners. She'd also stripped the wiring from several floodlights and fash-ioned lead lines and grips with which to pull the sledge. It was quite a makeshift contraption, but no less remarkable for the speed with which Kate had assembled it.

'I wanted to bring those smelling salts,' Kate said, seeing

Mr Benedict was still asleep, 'but SQ had them in his pocket and I thought it best not to go near him. He was glaring at me like he wanted to wring my neck.'

They hoisted Mr Benedict onto the sledge; then Constance climbed on and held him steady while the others grabbed the lines and yanked to test them. The metal runners made an awful scratching, grinding sound on the rocks, but with Kate and the boys pulling, the sledge moved fairly quickly.

Satisfied, Kate said, 'I'll need to find the easiest route down,' and she hurried off to scale the peak above the cave, leaping from boulder to boulder as if she were one of the island's resident mountain goats. In no time she stood high above her friends, scanning the eastern side of the island with her spyglass. She quickly determined the best route: first a short northwesterly descent to a prominent goat path that led almost all the way down the mountain; then slant-wise across a long gravel slope (giving as wide a berth as possible to some treacherous bluffs); and finally across the black rock plain to the bay forest, which from here appeared as a dark shadow in the general greyness. Kate looked for any sign of Milligan but found none. The forest, the bay, and the ocean beyond were lost in the shroud of mist.

Far below, Reynie was looking up at Kate, anxious to hear her verdict, when a curious feeling came over him. He wasn't sure what it was. He stared and stared, trying to place it. Kate stood silhouetted against the grey, cloud-scattered sky, wind flapping her ponytail behind her. Cliff swallows, heedless of the damp, darted in and out of holes in the rocks about her, and high above them circled a bird of prey, no doubt contemplating which swallow would constitute its breakfast. Meanwhile, dark clouds raced overhead as if on a film strip run on fast-forward, and these combined with the fluttering of the swallows and the circling of the larger bird made Reynie's stomach twist with vertigo . . . yes, vertigo, that must be the curious feeling. Or . . . no, Reynie wasn't satisfied with that answer. What *was* this feeling, then? It almost seemed like déjà vu – as if he'd experienced something very much like this before.

Kate scrambled back down to report. 'It's going to be awfully hard,' she concluded, after describing the route. 'I think it will take at least two hours to get to the forest, maybe three, depending on how much you boys can pull. That's if we don't have an accident going down the mountain.' She reached back to re-tie her ponytail, which had come loose during her climb. 'And there's something else.'

'What's that?' asked Reynie, sensing bad news.'

'I don't see how we're going to avoid being spotted. If they find Number Two, they'll come back here and discover we're gone – in which case McCracken and Curtain are sure to climb up and take a look around like I just did. If they *don't* find her, they'll keep circling the island on their Salamander looking for her. Either way, as best I can figure it, they're almost certain to see us crossing that rocky plain. We're going to be completely exposed for a long time. We'll have a big head start, so we might outrun them ...'

'But then what?' Constance said. 'They'll know where we are, and we can't even be sure there's help waiting for us!'

Reynie rubbed his temples. Constance was right, of course. And if McCracken's prediction was accurate, then two of the other Ten Men would be awake by then, and

401

possibly Martina as well. There would be an awful lot of sharp pencils flying around that forest, and plenty of legs to chase down fleeing children.

'Maybe we should find a place to hide and wait for Mr Benedict to wake up,' Sticky said. 'He'll know what to do.'

Kate shook her head. 'He might sleep for hours. We need to work this out ourselves.'

By 'ourselves' Kate mostly meant Reynie, and she and the others instinctively turned to him now. Reynie frowned. He was trying hard to figure something out, but his mind kept nagging him with that strange feeling of déjà vu. What *was* it he had been reminded of ? He'd been looking at Kate, and the sky, and the circling hawk . . . wait. Had it been a hawk? He started, then looked up into the sky. No, not a hawk. A peregrine falcon.

'Kate! Look there! Is that falcon—'

'Why, it's Madge!' Kate exclaimed. She took out her whistle and blew it. The falcon streaked down out of the sky, alighting on Kate's wrist just as she finished tugging on her protective leather glove. 'Good girl, Madge!' Kate said, stroking the bird's feathers. 'I'm so sorry I don't have any treat to give you. I'll have to owe you one.'

A small leather pouch was tied to Madge's leg. Kate hastily undid the clasp and took out a letter. 'It's from Cannonball!' The children all gathered close to read:

Dear Kate,

How we hope this finds you! We know you're in danger, and I'm writing as quick as I can to tell you of our situation and to see how we may help. In case any of the details are important, I'll give you all I have.

402

Last night we were hiding in the forest, anxiously awaiting your appearance, when we heard an explosion. Soon after that Number Two stumbled out of a mountain tunnel into our view. She'll be all right, but at the time she was in such a condition we felt obliged to carry her to the skiff (our landing boat) and then to the Shortcut for bandages.

She protested loudly – much too loudly, in fact, as her hearing had been affected by the explosion. She's a bit out of her head, too, but it was clear enough that she believed you to be in danger, and that she'd gone looking for you in the tunnel only to find herself cut off (and quite battered by rocks) when the entrance blew. She insisted we leave her and go to find you children. But this would have contradicted Milligan's instructions, and we dared not risk upsetting his plans even if Number Two's injuries hadn't required immediate attention. She's safely bandaged up now, though, and has fully recovered her senses. It was her idea to send Madge with a note, and – now she tells me I'm taking too long, so let me hurry on.

We're aboard the Shortcut, a few miles out to sea. Our plan was to return immediately to the forest, but we've run into difficulty. The skiff's motor was damaged on shoals as we left the bay – there was a horribly tricky tide – and the skiff is now quite noisy and painfully slow. We worry that using it might endanger you by calling attention to the bay. Milligan advised that we must be stealthy above all else. Is this still the case? Send word, Kate, and let us know what we should do!

Things to consider: Captain Noland, per Milligan's directions, contacted the Royal Navy at dawn (mere minutes ago as I write) but their patrol boats may not arrive for some time. The captain can't bring the Shortcut too close to the island for fear of grounding her, but in the skiff we can reach the bay shore in two *hours at most. We'll await you there or come for you as you think best – just tell us where to look!*

We're counting on Madge to find you with her sharp eyes. When you send her back, just say 'frog food' and she'll fly straight to me – I've been feeding her those steak bits ever since we took her aboard. Do hurry, Kate, and send your reply!
Cannonball (Joe Shooter)

The moment he finished reading, Reynie began to pace. What he really felt like doing was curling into a ball. The letter should have encouraged him, but under the circumstances it was heartbreaking. If they sent Madge right away with a reply, and if everything went exactly as hoped, the slow and noisy skiff would reach the bay just as the children arrived. But Kate was right – they would almost certainly be spotted crossing that rocky plain; the Salamander, then, would be hot on their trail, and Milligan had said the Salamander was very fast on land and water both. Even if they made it to the skiff . . . well, a damaged skiff would be easy pickings. They would be snatched up by Mr Curtain's crew long before they reached the *Shortcut*.

The others were all groaning now, having slowly come to understand what had distressed Reynie right away: There was no way out of this.

'At least Number Two is safe,' said Sticky gloomily. 'That's something, anyway.'

The others nodded but said nothing. They were all relieved Number Two was safe. Her good news was their bad news, though, for Mr Curtain and his Ten Men, not finding her in the western woodland, would continue to circle the island. That made it even *more* likely the children would be intercepted before they reached the bay.

Reynie glanced down at Mr Benedict's sleeping face, frowned, and went back to pacing.

'Maybe we should try to hide,' said Constance. 'Those patrol boats will come eventually, right? Maybe they'll get here in time to save us.'

'We'd have to be awfully lucky,' said Kate. 'I say we run for it and hope for the best. Milligan's probably in the forest, remember. If we can just get to him, he can help us.'

Sticky was feverishly polishing his spectacles. 'What do you think, Reynie? Should we run for it or hide?'

Reynie gritted his teeth. What *did* he think? It would be hard to hide everyone from the Ten Men for long. And even if the patrol boats arrived soon and sent their crews ashore, Reynie doubted their chances against Mr Curtain's group of nasties, especially since the Ten Men had the Salamander. But running? Reynie's mind returned to the skiff. *Noisy*, Cannonball had said – so they couldn't even hope to avoid detection in the heavy grey mist. And unlike Kate, Reynie didn't count on Milligan's being able to help them. No, hiding seemed the better option, although it was a nearly hopeless one, and although . . .

Reynie paused in his pacing. He did see one other option. He had seen it from the very beginning, in fact, but had kept shoving it aside. If it worked, it was their best chance of escape. But if it didn't, all would be lost – and for it to work Reynie must depend upon something he felt could not be depended upon.

'Reynie?' Kate prompted. 'What do you say?'

Reynie stared at the sleeping figure of Mr Benedict. They had risked life and limb for him, had come to the ends

405

of the earth to save him. If Mr Benedict were awake right now, what would he have Reynie do?

He felt a tugging at his sleeve. Constance was gazing up into his face. 'You should trust him,' she said.

'Trust him?' Kate repeated. 'Trust who? Reynie, what's she talking about?'

Reynie returned Constance's gaze. He knew she was right. He knew what Mr Benedict would have him do. The question was whether he had the courage to do it.

'Reynie?'

'Give me a pen and paper,' said Reynie, making up his mind. 'I know what we need to do!'

What Shines in Darkness

Descending the mountain with the sledge was the most arduous physical challenge either of the boys had ever attempted, and if not for Kate they would never have succeeded. Her excellent eyes, her sense of balance, her gauge of distance and slope – to say nothing of her unusual strength – saved the boys from deadly tumbles more than once. And all the while the sledge had to be kept aright to spare Mr Benedict and Constance, who struggled mightily to keep him on the sledge without falling off herself. Halfway down the mountain Reynie and Sticky were already trembling and aching from their exertions – and they were pulling *downhill*.

By the time they reached level ground even Kate was exhausted. Despite the cooling mist and the unfailing wind, her face radiated heat, and her leg muscles and lungs burned from their unusual strain. Gazing out through the mist across that wide rocky plain, remembering how hard crossing it had been just the night before, Kate's shoulders drooped. She doubted the boys could make it without a long rest – probably several long rests – and there was no way she could pull the sledge alone. Still, the crossing must be attempted. She looked at Reynie and Sticky, both of them gasping and doubled over.

'We can't rest long,' she said apologetically. 'A minute or two, and then . . .'

Sticky straightened abruptly. His face, dripping with perspiration and taut with fatigue, bore a look of resolution so intense it startled Kate. 'No, let's go now. We can't afford to rest.'

Sticky's tone struck Reynie just as his expression had struck Kate, and when Reynie looked up wonderingly he noticed something missing. 'Sticky, what happened to your spectacles?'

'They fell off and slid down an embankment. I didn't want to waste time going after them. Never mind, I can see well enough to see we have a long way to go.' He took one of the sledge grips in a hand already raw from pulling. 'I'm ready when you are.'

Reynie, who didn't feel ready in the least, wiped his brow and made an effort to stand up straight, while Kate drew her shoulders back, suddenly encouraged by Sticky's display of fortitude. 'Where did all this toughness come from?' she asked.

Sticky gave her a weak smile. 'I've been saving it up.'

'Well, now is the perfect time to spend it,' said Kate, impressed.

Indeed, over the long, gruelling trek across the plain, Sticky gave all of them hope. It was Reynie who'd had the idea and Kate who'd plotted their course, but it was Sticky who sacrificed the most – and in the process inspired the others to greater effort. His skinny frame quaked with exhaustion, sweat streamed from his head, and more than once his legs wobbled and went out from under him, but each time he rose, collected himself, and set to the task again with a fierceness they'd never seen. The fact was that Sticky had finally been given a chance to make up for his errors – a chance to get his friends out of danger – and he was passionately determined to succeed, no matter the cost to himself.

When Reynie slipped, Sticky helped him up. When Kate uncharacteristically despaired aloud at their progress, Sticky assured her they would make it, and somehow managed to double his efforts. Time and again his body faltered; time and again Sticky hauled himself up and pressed on. It was a noble thing to behold, and as the group at long last drew near the forest, Reynie found himself thinking that even if they were caught, he was grateful to have seen Sticky at his finest.

'We're actually going to make it,' said Constance incredulously, and it was true – their pace had slowed to a crawl, and the boys' hands were blistered and bleeding, but they lacked just a few yards until they could leave the exposed plain for the shelter of the forest.

'Of course we'll make it,' Kate wheezed as she strained

forward. 'We just need to . . . hey, what's that?'

The others saw it, too, a lumpy black object on the ground ahead. The object blended in almost perfectly with the rocky ground, and because of the mists they hadn't seen it until they were almost upon it. It wasn't a large rock, or even a group of rocks, but appeared to be a long, shallow pile of mud – though where such a lot of mud would have come from was impossible to guess. And then, as the children came closer, they saw that the object was Milligan.

Kate cried out and stumbled forwards, landing on her knees beside her father, who had opened his eyes at the sound of her voice. As she wiped mud from his face and begged him to tell her he was all right, Milligan gave her a relieved smile.

'Now that I see *you're* all right, I can't compl—' He was cut off when Kate threw herself upon him, mindless of the mud.

Milligan groaned, then whispered hoarsely, 'Better stop hugging me, Katie-Cat. Afraid I'll black out again. From the pain, you know. It's considerable.'

Kate had drawn back with a horrified expression. 'Oh! I'm so sorry! How badly are you hurt? Did you really fall off a cliff?'

'Jumped, actually,' said Milligan.

'But how did you get here, then? McCracken said you must have broken every bone in your body!'

'Not all of them,' Milligan muttered. (He seemed to be trying not to move his mouth very much.) 'And I got here by dragging myself, mostly. I was on my way to save you.' He swivelled his eyes toward the other children and Mr

Benedict on the sledge. 'Is everyone all right, then? How is Mr Benedict?'

For a moment Kate couldn't answer. She simply shook her head and stared. Now that she'd got over the shock of discovering Milligan here, she was coming to realize just how bad he looked. She'd seen him in a frightful condition before – in fact it was only a year ago that she'd seen him covered in mud just like this, and injured as well – but this was much worse. He looked as though he'd been trampled by a stampede. His face was so bruised and swollen with hornet stings he was scarcely recognizable; his shirt and trousers were in tatters; his hat and jacket were gone . . . and yet he'd been coming to save her. Kate took his hand and held it, noticing as she did so the handcuff and short length of chain dangling from it. She felt anger swelling up inside her.

Milligan winced, and Reynie, standing behind Kate, gently reminded her not to squeeze.

'Mr Benedict's all right,' Kate said, easing Milligan's hand back to the ground. 'We're all fine. But how did you survive if you fell – I mean jumped – into a ravine?'

Milligan swallowed with some difficulty and said, 'The bottom was all mud. I'd been there earlier looking for the cave, so I knew.'

'But McCracken said it was more than twenty metres down!'

'Well . . . I was able to slow myself a bit by dragging along the face of the cliff, and of course I had to land just so . . .' Milligan winced again, though no one had touched him, and his breath came in ragged bursts. 'Still, I'm afraid in the darkness I . . . slightly misjudged the distance.'

'Kate,' Reynie murmured. 'We need to get him into the trees.'

'Right! Okay, Milligan, we're going to lift you onto the sledge and—'

Milligan made a noise of dissent. 'Listen, Kate, I think I'm going to . . .' he swallowed '. . . black out again, so listen carefully. Leave me . . . cover me with pebbles or something if you must . . . and make for the bay. You can't escape if you're dragging me, and I am ordering you to escape, do you hear? Go now . . . leave me behind . . . that's an order, so don't even think—' Milligan abruptly closed his eyes and fell silent.

'Can't *anyone* stay awake around here?' Constance moaned.

'Let's get him onto the sledge,' Sticky said, coming around to help lift Milligan. 'I assume we're disobeying his order.'

'Of course we are,' said Reynie. 'We have to save him.'

'I was hoping *he* would save *us*,' said Constance.

Kate said nothing. Her grief had rapidly transformed into something else, and she was clenching and unclenching her fists, boiling with anger at the Ten Men for what they'd done to Milligan. She despised McCracken in particular, but all of the Ten Men had played a part. In her fury, Kate wanted revenge more than anything, and for a moment it blinded her to all else.

'Kate!' said Reynie, shaking her shoulder. He'd been calling her name again and again. 'What's the matter? We have to move him! If we can get into the trees, they might not even see us! We're almost *there*, Kate!'

Kate looked up and saw the boys staring at her wonderingly. She leapt to her feet – but it was already too late. She

412

saw it on Constance's face. The tiny girl was staring out into the mist with a look of deepest dread. And the next moment they all heard what she had sensed.

The rumbling.

In horror the children saw the Salamander appear at the far northern edge of the plain, a black shadow moving through the mist like a shark through water. Whipping out her spyglass, Kate found McCracken at the helm – with his own spyglass fixed on her. Beside him stood Mr Curtain, gesturing angrily, and behind stood Martina, Garrotte, and Sharpe, all awake now and surely seething with vengeful wrath. In the spyglass they seemed close enough for Kate to reach out and hit, and she wanted badly to do just that – they weren't the only ones seething with vengeful wrath. But even in her anger Kate was sensible enough to realize this encounter was ill-timed. She and the others were doomed. She only hoped she could get a lick at McCracken before he overpowered her.

'How long do we have?' Reynie asked her. 'We can't beat them to the bay, can we?'

'At that speed? With us dragging the sledge? We'll be lucky to make it ten metres into the trees. At least they'll have to go to the trouble of getting out. That's some comfort.'

The others found this no comfort at all, however, and Reynie glanced despondently at the sledge – the prized burden that ensured they'd never make it to the bay. He found himself staring into the eyes of Mr Benedict, who was sitting up straight and yawning.

'I must have . . . ah, I see,' said Mr Benedict, running a hand through his hair. He looked at Reynie in chagrin. 'I chose a terrible time to sleep, I'm afraid.'

He appeared to grasp their predicament at once, for before Reynie could even think of what to say, Mr Benedict had lifted Milligan from the ground and, with a rallying cry to the children, set off into the forest with the injured man in his arms. The others exclaimed and hurried after him, Kate slinging Constance up onto her back almost as an afterthought.

'Be careful!' she cried. 'He's badly hurt, Mr Benedict!'

'So I can see, my dear, but I have no doubt he'll recover,' Mr Benedict puffed as they ran through the trees. 'Your father is the most resilient man I've ever known. He'll be fine.'

Reynie wished he shared Mr Benedict's confidence. At the moment it seemed unlikely that any of them would be fine. Already the Salamander had reached the forest edge and veered off to go around – it was too big to pass through the trees – but not before Reynie heard a telltale pause in its rumbling that indicated a Ten Man or two had been dropped off to follow them. The Salamander would skirt the forest and meet them at the shore, and any retreat through the woods was now out of the question. Their escape had become, just as Reynie had predicted, an all-or-nothing situation.

A few desperate moments more and the haggard, gasping group emerged from the trees and stumbled onto the rocky shore of the bay. There was the beached seaplane, still covered in Milligan's tarpaulin. There, in the far distance, was the Salamander, rumbling around the edge of the forest and turning toward them. And there, in the choppy waters of the bay itself, was . . . nothing.

Sticky took one look at the empty water and fell to his knees.

Mr Benedict stared out at the mist-shrouded bay with a perplexed look. 'I take it something is amiss.'

Reynie, stricken, covered his face with his hands. 'I did what I thought . . . I mean, I hoped . . . oh, I can't believe I hoped—'

Mr Benedict made a gentle shushing sound. 'Whatever you chose, Reynie, I'm sure it was the right thing. Now you must brace yourselves, my friends, for—'

'Hold that thought,' said Kate, pointing at the bay.

They looked, and so awesome was the sight that for a moment all thought of danger fled their minds. Seen through the mist, the dark hills at the mouth of the bay appeared to be moving, as if they were the legs of the ancient Colossus. But this was a trick of the eye. In fact a gargantuan shape had loomed up behind them, was even now rushing between them, and now – to the thrill of the stranded, desperate watchers on the shore – the enormous, magnificent body of the *Shortcut* hove fully into view, splitting the waters of the bay.

As the ship appeared, its horn blasted with such shocking volume that most of the onlookers covered their ears. The onlookers included those in the Salamander, who had hardly needed the horn to call their attention to the *Shortcut*'s arrival. Every single one of them was gaping in awe, and even the unflappable McCracken had swerved wildly away from the water before looking back in disbelief. And well he might have disbelieved. So disproportionate was the great ship to the bay, so vastly out of place, it might have been a whale in a bathtub.

'This way!' Mr Benedict shouted.

Though less than a second had passed since its appearance, the *Shortcut* was already bearing down upon the shore. The children ran after Mr Benedict, toward the side of the bay opposite the Salamander. Never once did they tear their eyes from the ship, which was churning up gigantic waves – not only of water but also of mud, for the *Shortcut's* keel was furrowing the bottom of the bay like a farmer's plough.

Captain Noland, just as Reynie had asked him to, was grounding his precious ship to save his friends. Moments later the *Shortcut* had come to rest, and the island bay and its shore resembled the scene of some unimaginable disaster. Pieces of the destroyed seaplane were strewn everywhere on either side of the ship, whose bow jutted well into the forest, having crushed any number of trees in its path. On one side of the ship, the Ten Man called Garrotte was digging himself out from a mountain of mud – it was he who had pursued Mr Benedict and the children through the forest, and he'd been just about to catch up with them when the ship crashed ashore, nearly drowning him in water and muck. Behind Garrotte the Salamander was moving toward the ship at the behest of a furious Mr Curtain. On the other side of the *Shortcut*, the group of castaways it had come to rescue were likewise hurrying toward the ship, from whose deck Cannonball and a handful of other sailors were tossing down lines.

Footholds and handholds had been cleverly knotted into the lines, two of which supported a stretcher, and almost before they knew it the children, Mr Benedict, and Milligan had been whisked up and away onto the deck high above.

'There's no time!' Reynie declared the moment he set foot on deck. 'We have to get everyone into the security hold!'

'Don't worry, Reynie,' said Cannonball, who in his excitement was grabbing all the children and hugging them in turn. 'Captain Noland's already given the order. He's coming from the bridge to lead you down. My friends and I intend to stay and fight them off, but—'

'That's out of the question, Joe,' said Mr Benedict, with unusual severity. 'I admire your bravery, but you'd stand no chance. You won't even slow them down. You must come with us.'

By this time Captain Noland had joined them, his expression a curious mixture of joy and shock at what he'd just done.

'I commend you on a perfect landing, Phil,' said Mr Benedict, and the captain laughed and embraced him.

With Cannonball and another stout sailor carrying Milligan on the stretcher, they all hurried from the deck. Even as they were starting down the ladder, grappling hooks began to sail over the deck railing, finding purchase with ominous clangs. Mr Curtain and his Ten Men were coming aboard.

'The Royal Navy has two patrol boats on the way,' Captain Noland said as he led them down into the belly of the ship. 'They'll be here in half an hour.'

At the door of the security hold he ushered everyone else inside before coming in himself. Then, with a spin of the handle and the throwing of a bolt, the heavy metal door was secured.

'Children!' cried a familiar voice, and Number Two emerged from the crowd of sailors and security guards crammed into the hold. Her hair was concealed by a winding bandage, and she was scarcely strong enough to hug them all – Reynie and Sticky each took her by an arm – but her face glowed at the sight of them.

Mr Benedict was eyeing the locked door. 'Half an hour, did you say, Phil? Are you certain of that?'

'Yes, they just radioed to tell me. They aren't far.'

Mr Benedict pursed his lips. He turned to face the small crowd. Everyone's face betrayed great apprehension and not a little confusion. Captain Noland hadn't had time to explain anything to his crew, who knew only that some menace was approaching from above. The extra security guards hired by Mr Pressius, thinking themselves under attack by pirates, were arguing in urgent, agitated tones about whether or not to hand over the decoy diamonds.

Mr Benedict raised his hands to gain their attention, then very quietly said, 'I advise complete silence, everyone. Our pursuers must find this hold before they can attempt to enter it. Let's not give them any help.'

Instantly a hush fell over the room, and a period of tense, silent waiting began. They could all hear the distant thumps and bangs from overhead as Mr Curtain and his crew made their way methodically through the ship. The security hold was several levels below deck, and there were many passageways and cabins to search. Mr Curtain was taking no chances of letting his quarry slip by him. Ten minutes passed. The noises grew louder. Twenty minutes passed. Still louder. Twenty-five.

And then the frightened assembly in the hold heard voices outside the door, followed by a burst of screechy laughter.

'There's no longer any need for silence,' Mr Benedict announced. 'Move away from the door, everyone. Press into those far corners as well as you can. Joe, will you lend a hand with Milligan?'

Everyone squeezed as far away from the door as they could; they were pressed so tightly together it was difficult to draw breath. Milligan lay in his stretcher near the front of the crowd, with Kate kneeling beside him, her arm thrown protectively over his chest. Behind them Reynie, Sticky and Constance were holding tightly to Number Two's arms (or in Constance's case, to her legs), while Mr Benedict stood with his arms folded, regarding the door as if it were a puzzle.

'What do they want, anyway?' one of the security guards whispered. His face was white with fear.

'Our friends,' said Cannonball.

'You mean . . . ?' said the guard, his eyes widening. 'You mean if we let them have this bunch,' he waved his hand to indicate Mr Benedict, Number Two and the children, 'they'll leave the rest of us alone?'

The children caught their breath. Mr Benedict raised an eyebrow.

Captain Noland spun on the guard, fixing him with a steely gaze. 'On this ship,' he said through clenched teeth, 'we do not sacrifice the innocent to save our own skins.'

'Hear, hear!' growled Cannonball, and a chorus of approving voices rang out from among the rest of the crew, as well as from some of the other security guards.

Reynie and the other children (except Constance, who was staring at the door with a frown of concentration) looked gratefully about at all these frightened people

419

willing to risk themselves for strangers. Mr Benedict raised his hand and offered a friendly wave of appreciation. If he was disturbed by the fact that someone had just suggested throwing him and the children to the wolves, he didn't show it. Nor did he seem surprised by the courage and decency of the others. He simply made his wave, then knelt beside Constance, who was still staring at the door.

'What are they doing, my dear?'

'Something bad,' Constance whispered. 'They have a plan to get in, and they know we'll be hurt, but they don't care. Oh!' Her eyes grew very wide. 'They intend to—'

But what Constance said next was overwhelmed by the sound of a loudspeaker outside the ship.

'Attention! You in the ship! Come onto the deck with your hands up!' boomed a voice over the loudspeaker. The Royal Navy had arrived.

Everyone cheered, and from beyond the door came the sound of loud cursing and arguing, followed by thumping noises as Mr Curtain and his crew rushed away from the door and up the several levels to the deck. At this the cheering grew still louder and more boisterous – so much so that it was some moments before Constance, who'd been frantically repeating herself over and over, could make herself heard.

'— to blow the door open!' she was shouting. 'They've planted a bomb!'

There was a sudden collective intake of breath, followed by a moment of shocked silence, and then pandemonium broke out as several people nearest the door tried to move farther away from it, while those at the back tried hard to not to be crushed against the wall. The only ones to move

420

toward the door were Captain Noland, who unlocked it as quickly as he could, and Kate Wetherall, who sprang forward the moment he did.

Stuck to the outside of the door what appeared to be an ordinary business calculator was emitting a faint, electronic beep. Kate's sharp eyes immediately made out the display: 31.

The 31 changed to 30. Then to 29.

Snatching the device from the door, Kate turned and bolted up the passage. Captain Noland shouted after her, 'No, Kate! Let me!' But Kate was already scurrying up a ladder, quick as a monkey. She raced along the passages as fast as her weary legs would carry her. As long as she didn't slip, she thought, she had a fair chance of reaching the deck in time. And once on deck . . .

A strange thing began to happen then. As Kate ran down passage after passage and climbed ladder after ladder – and as the calculator continued its menacing countdown – her mind began to sort through a great jumble of images and thoughts. She saw the Ten Man in Thernbaakagen, the one who had intended to lash them with his whip. She saw Mr Curtain standing over her with those wicked, shiny gloves, and she heard him speaking gleefully of what he planned to do to Mr Benedict. But more than anything she thought of Milligan, of what McCracken and the others had done to him. Was this her life flashing before her eyes? If so, why did she have the odd feeling that she was making her mind up about something?

She was almost to the deck now. She glanced at the calculator display: 15. 14. 13.

Kate flew up the final ladder and over to the railing,

where her eyes were met with a scene of utter chaos. Two Royal Navy patrol boats were coming around the ship's stern, loudspeakers booming and floodlights crisscrossing every which way through the mist. The Salamander was directly below, its occupants – Mr Curtain and the Ten Men – looking up at Martina Crowe, who had become tangled in a line on her way down and was hanging by her foot some ten feet above them, screaming for Mr Curtain to help her. All of this Kate observed in a split second.

In the same split second, Mr Curtain saw Kate at the railing with the calculator in her hand. He gave a visible start. 'Move!' he ordered McCracken. 'Leave Martina! Leave her, I say!'

McCracken sent the Salamander roaring backwards, its treads spewing mud and water, but Kate was in perfect position. It would be so easy to stop them. A well-placed throw – and Kate was nothing if not a good shot – and the calculator would land directly in the Salamander's path. The explosion would wreck it. Sure, it might kill the wicked men inside, but those men had had no qualms about such matters when they'd stuck the bomb on the security hold door, had they? If anyone deserved to be sent sky-high with their own evil contraption, it was these men, and no doubt about it.

Kate saw Garrotte flick his wrist. She leapt to the left – a razor-sharp pencil whistled past her shoulder. *You've just made it even easier,* she thought, cocking her arm to throw. The men in the Salamander, powerless to do anything else, bent down and shielded their heads with their arms. They were sitting ducks. This would be the easiest thing in the world . . .

Except that Milligan was right.

Kate was not like Mr Curtain and his nasty associates. Not at all. Back on that rooftop in Thernbaakagen Milligan had told her as much, and she saw now what he meant. Seeing those men there, helpless to stop her from doing what they themselves would never hesitate to do, Kate realized – with a certain degree of disappointment but also a degree of pride – that she could never do it, could never do something that would make her more like her enemy and less like her father. And so, instead of throwing the calculator into the Salamander's path, she flung it out over the bay, where it splashed into the water. An instant later the *Shortcut* trembled with the concussion of an underwater explosion, and from the spot where the calculator had splashed a geyser of water shot twenty feet into the air. The patrol boats, though a safe distance away, rocked back and forth in the waves caused by the blast.

From the Salamander a cheer erupted, followed by laughter, and Kate watched as the machine moved rapidly away on the bay shore, where the patrol boats were helpless to stop it. The Ten Men were clapping – applauding her decision with scornful delight. As the Salamander rumbled away, Mr Curtain smiled and blew Kate a kiss.

Kate made sure he saw her wipe it off.

Apologies, Explanations, and Most Agreeable Notions

'I don't like it,' Constance said. 'How am I supposed to find anything?'

'You mean you *used* to be able to find things in here?' Reynie asked.

'That's not the point,' said Constance.

The young members of the Mysterious Benedict Society were sitting in a circle on the floor of Constance's bedroom, which during their absence had been thoroughly cleaned and tidied. Indeed the whole house had been scoured, and many of its draughts sealed up and leaky taps fixed, for the Washingtons and Perumals, having no other outlet for their anxious worry, had been keeping themselves busy. Constance had been back only a week, which was hardly enough time to return things to their proper state of disorder, and she'd complained about her room every chance she got.

'It's a little better, isn't it?' Kate said, pointing to the pile of laundry on Constance's unmade bed. 'You haven't washed anything since we got back, and your top drawer is completely empty except for a mouldy hot dog. I don't even want to know why *that's* in there.'

'Why were you going through my drawers?' Constance demanded.

'Looking for this,' said Kate, waving the travel journal Mr Benedict had given them. 'And I see you cheated – you took another turn.'

Constance stuck up her nose. 'When inspiration calls,' she said, 'I have no choice but to answer.'

The children had begun making entries in the journal – just as Reynie had promised Constance they would – and the first entry had been made by Constance herself, who had composed a rather disgusting haiku about the trials of seasickness. Kate had followed that entry with a page of lemon-juice scribblings she insisted mustn't be revealed for ten years, and Reynie had written a lively, two-page summary of their adventure – an account that ended with the revelation that Mr Curtain had *not* escaped with fifty boxes of duskwort, as the children had at first believed.

It was thwart-wort, Reynie had written, every last bit of it, and Mr Benedict knew it. He and Number Two had scoured that cave before Mr Curtain ever showed up. Half

425

a century was more than enough time for the few specimens Han de Reizeger had seen to overcome the duskwort. Mr Benedict kept this information to himself, correctly guessing that should Mr Curtain ever be forced to choose between confronting his enemies or making a quick escape with his precious moss, he would choose the latter. And so it was thwart-wort, not duskwort, that Mr Curtain salvaged from that mountain cave, and even though he and his men would manage to slip away in the mists, he had yet to discover his final disappointment.

Reynie had not written about the other, more personal disappointment that they all felt. The duskwort had promised a possible end to Mr Benedict's sufferings; now it was simply the stuff of history and legend. And though Mr Benedict refused to mourn its loss, which had prevented certain catastrophe at the hands of his brother, everyone who loved him wished things could have turned out otherwise. All of this Reynie found too difficult to express with suitable eloquence, and so he'd concluded his entry with a simple but cryptic line that could apply just as easily to Mr Benedict or Mr Curtain: *One more dream destroyed.*

Now it was Sticky's turn to make an entry – they had agreed he should go last, so that he didn't accidentally use up all the pages before the others had written anything – but Constance had skipped his turn and made another entry herself.

'It's fine,' Sticky said, lifting up his bandaged hands. 'I can't hold a pen very well with these on, anyway.'

'Your mum won't let you take them off?' asked Reynie, whose own hands were mostly healed from the cuts and blisters inflicted in dragging the sledge. Sticky was the only one still wearing bandages.

'Not yet,' Sticky said with a shrug. He leant back on his elbows and jauntily crossed his legs. These private meetings in Constance's room gave him some much-needed relief from his parents' attentions – they spent half their time babying him and the other half berating him for his reckless behaviour – and his gratitude put him in an expansive mood. 'Let's hear what you wrote, Constance. I can't wait.'

'Oh, you're really going to like it,' Kate said, handing the journal to Constance with a mysterious smile.

Constance cleared her throat. 'This poem is entitled 'The Terrible Fall'. 'She waited a moment for her title to sink in – she obviously thought it a very good one – and then, in a dramatic voice, she began to recite.

The night was black, the owl did call.
I stood upon the silo tall,
Never suspecting I would fall . . .
Thanks to the boy who bumped me.

Though frightened, I had stayed alert.
No thoughtless slumberings did divert
Me from my task, till I got hurt . . .
Thanks to the boy who bumped me.

'For the twentieth time, Constance,' Sticky said, his expansive mood greatly diminished, 'I'm *sorry*. Did you have to write a poem about it?'

'I know you're sorry,' Constance said, speaking up to be heard over Reynie and Kate's tittering. 'Now please hold your comments until I'm finished. There are three more verses.'

The remaining verses would have to wait, however, for just then Number Two knocked on the door. 'Sorry to interrupt whatever you're plotting,' she said when they let her in, 'but Moocho wanted me to tell you the pies are almost ready. Mr Benedict has cleared the officials out of the house, and Captain Noland and Joe Shooter are expected to join us. It should be a cosy gathering.' She reached into the pocket of her yellow pants suit and took out a measuring tape. 'Also, I've been wanting to measure you. Stand up, please.'

With resigned expressions, the children stood. They were all happy to see how Number Two had recovered – she was almost her old self again – but they also knew she was determined to 'make them something special' as a token of her gratitude for risking their lives on her behalf. Kate had seen her drawing up patterns that morning, and the four of them had been avoiding Number Two ever since. They were trapped now, though, and one by one they submitted to being measured, with only Constance raising any complaint.

'You've all grown so much!' said Number Two, jotting the figures down on a scrap of paper. 'I suppose that's to be expected. At some point your bodies have to catch up with your hearts.'

The children rolled their eyes. Number Two had been given to such mushy pronouncements ever since she'd returned to her senses. (At first Kate had argued that these were actually a sign she was still delirious, but Number Two had scolded her into submission, then hugged her and

428

kissed her until Kate had fled.) Reynie, for his part, was secretly counting on Constance to annoy Number Two back into being her old, no-nonsense self.

'There!' Number Two declared. 'Now if you'll finish up whatever mischief you're engaged in—' Here she interrupted herself, setting down the scrap of paper to dig anxiously in her pockets. She took out a packet of raisins and emptied it into her mouth. 'Just a quick snack before pie,' she said, chewing hungrily. 'Now do come along soon. Moocho will be disappointed if you don't get it hot.'

When Number Two had gone, Constance noticed the scrap of paper with their measurements written on it. 'She forgot this.'

'Lose it,' Reynie whispered.

The entire house was now suffused with the wonderful sweet smell of cherry pie, and with eager faces and watering mouths the children hurried down to the dining room. There they found Mr Benedict, Rhonda Kazembe, Number Two, and the Washingtons and Perumals all gathered around the long table, with seats left open for the children and the expected guests (extra chairs had been brought from all over the house). Moocho Brazos was busily setting out plates, pots of coffee and tea, and pitchers of milk. 'Five minutes,' he said when the children came in. 'Also, Mr Washington, if you get a chance . . .' He handed Sticky's father a doorknob. 'I'm sorry, these old things with their weak screws—'

'Never mind,' said Mr Washington. 'I'll have it back on in a jiffy.'

Moocho thanked him and went back into the kitchen.

'Isn't that the second doorknob of the day?' asked Mrs Washington.

'I believe he's as excited as the rest of us,' said Rhonda, rising to greet the children with warm hugs, just as she'd done a hundred times since their return. 'After all those days of worry, every day without it feels like a celebration!'

Constance waved her arms madly about as if being attacked by bees, but Rhonda managed to hug her regardless.

'If you think you're excited *now*,' said Kate, 'wait till you try Moocho's pie. I'd better go ask Milligan if he wants ice cream with his.'

Rhonda cleared her throat. 'I, um, just checked on him, Kate. He's still asleep.'

'Still? Is it real sleep or is he pretending again, do you think?'

Rhonda exchanged glances with Mr Benedict, who remained inscrutably silent. A few days before, Milligan had returned from the hospital to rest and heal in Mr Benedict's house. He was in a fairly mummified state, all bandages and casts, and was unable to leave his bed, but he could not have had more attentive nurses – or more nurses, full stop – than his friends and family in the house. What was more, the children were attempting to keep Milligan entertained by talking to him, singing to him, reading to him (Constance recited several poems, including one called 'A Slight Misjudgment in the Darkness'), and even performing skits. They'd been doing this ever since his return, more or less without interruption, and Milligan had taken to pretending he was asleep in order to get some peace.

'I suppose I might have seen him peeking at me a little,'

Rhonda admitted. 'But you know it's for—'

'Oh, good grief,' interrupted Kate, already at the door. 'He won't want to miss Moocho's *pie*, will he?'

Reynie took a chair between Miss Perumal and her mother, both of whom patted him affectionately. They couldn't have him close enough these days – Miss Perumal looked anxious every time he left the room – and Reynie had been patted so often he worried he might be ground to dust. ('Consider yourself lucky,' Miss Perumal had said the day before, when he'd jokingly complained about it, 'that the pats aren't significantly *harder*.' And she'd fixed him with such a stern look that Reynie reminded himself not to make such jokes in the future. His return had been greeted with enormous relief and happiness, but like Sticky he'd also found himself in considerable trouble.)

Across the table, Constance had taken a chair next to Mr Benedict, and making a sly grab for the sugar bowl (which Rhonda quickly slid out of reach), she announced that Captain Noland and Cannonball had just arrived. The Washingtons and Perumals looked at her curiously, for it seemed impossible that she could know this, and Miss Perumal's mother said in a too-loud voice that she must have misheard what Constance said – was it something about lowlands and cannonballs? – but Sticky went straight to the window. He saw an annoyed-looking Mr Bane scraping falcon droppings from the gate, and Madge perched in the elm tree looking satisfied, but no captain or Cannonball. Drawing a chair to the window (because of his bandaged hands, he had to hug it awkwardly between his arms), Sticky climbed up for a better view.

'I don't see them,' he said finally.

'Oh, they're already inside,' Constance said. 'Mr Bane let them in. He wasn't happy about it, either, but I suppose Mr Benedict told him he must.'

'I did indeed,' said Mr Benedict.

Sticky scowled. 'You let me drag this chair over and stare all around even though you knew they weren't outside? Why didn't you tell me?'

'Because it was funny to see you do it,' Constance said.

The Perumals and Mr Washington were looking more and more confused by all this, but Mrs Washington was distracted by Sticky's risk-taking behaviour. 'Do get down from there before you fall,' she said, pressing a hand to her forehead. 'You make me so nervous.'

Sticky started to argue, thought better of it, and finally sighed and stepped down from the chair just as Captain Noland and Cannonball appeared in the dining room doorway. They were welcomed with a great deal of enthusiasm, which the men gladly returned. Indeed, Cannonball's natural enthusiasm overpowered everyone else's, and by the time they were all seated again, Sticky was wearing Cannonball's cap and Reynie's hair was frightfully mussed from tousling. Miss Perumal, having heard of the captain's love of coffee, had already set him a cup of Moocho Brazos's gourmet brew. Captain Noland expressed his thanks and lost no time in taking a sip. He smiled – it was a very strained smile, Reynie thought – and set the cup carefully back onto its saucer. Still smiling, the captain twitched, swallowed, and politely commented upon the coffee's excellence. He did not touch his cup again.

After some moments of friendly, boisterous conversation, Mr Benedict tapped his teacup with a spoon. 'Will you all please turn your attention to Phil? I understand he's pressed for time, and he has a few things he wants to say before he goes.'

Captain Noland looked up and down the table. For a man who had just wrecked his ship – and, as a result, his cherished career – he seemed perfectly happy, even exuberant. At the same time, there was a hint of sheepishness in his manner, which was quickly explained when he said, 'If you will indulge me, everyone, I have some apologies to make – apologies and explanations. Especially to you, Reynie. I'm afraid once we were aboard the patrol boats there was too much confusion for us to talk. I'm very glad to have the chance now. Ah, and here's Kate, just in time!'

Kate had entered the room frowning – she'd failed to wake Milligan up from his 'sleep' – but she brightened when she saw Captain Noland and Cannonball. After a hearty exchange of greetings, she took her seat, and the captain resumed his speech.

He looked at each of the children in turn. 'I realize how distressed you all must have been when you reached the bay shore and the *Shortcut* wasn't there yet. I want you to know that my delay wasn't a result of indecision. I simply thought it best to time our arrival exactly. Reynie's note said to meet you in two hours. I feared that if your pursuers hadn't found you yet, the *Shortcut*'s early arrival might tip them off. As you saw for yourselves, there's no discreet way to ground an ocean vessel. So though I hated to wait, it seemed wise to follow Reynie's directions precisely. Of course, if we arrived too late, we intended to come ashore and fight for you.'

'Luckily it didn't come to that,' said Mr Benedict.

'Indeed,' agreed the captain, and here his expression grew quite serious. 'I must say, Reynie, how honoured I am that you trusted me to come. Deeply honoured, and not a little surprised. I imagine you've told the others about our exchange in my cabin, the one involving the decoy diamond?'

'Sorry, I know you told me to keep it between us,' Reynie began, 'but under the circumstances—'

'Never apologize to *me*,' Captain Noland hastily interrupted. 'I'm the one who must apologize. In retrospect, you see, I've realized what a lubber's move it was to give you that decoy and ask you to keep it secret. I must have seemed quite the scoundrel, especially with all that creeping about and closing doors and whatnot.'

'I did wonder about that,' Reynie admitted.

'I was nervous to have you in my cabin,' Captain Noland said. 'If Mr Pressius had seen you he would have disapproved of your wasting my time – that is how *he* would have viewed it, you understand. As for my asking you to keep the decoy secret, well . . . I have an explanation, though hardly an excuse. The truth is I had asked Mr Pressius for decoys to give to all four of you. I wanted to give you keepsakes as an expression of my admiration and thanks. But Mr Pressius refused, offering instead to sell them to me for a price – a price so exorbitant I felt I could only afford one. I'm extremely embarrassed to tell you all of this. I was far from my best during that voyage.'

'It was just a misunderstanding,' said Reynie, not wanting to point out how serious that misunderstanding had been. The captain, he realized now, had never dreamed Reynie might suspect the decoy was an actual diamond. No doubt he'd feel even worse to learn Reynie had thought him capable of swiping a precious gem.

'Thank you for saying so,' said Captain Noland, 'but it's a misunderstanding for which I take responsibility, and I can only hope you'll all forgive me.'

With the exception of Constance – who declared that she *would* forgive him, since he'd asked so nicely – the children hastened to assure the captain that apologies and forgiveness were hardly necessary. After all, he had sacrificed everything dear to him on their behalf, and what more could be asked of anyone than that?

'Speaking of which,' said Constance, 'shouldn't you be miserable? There can't be a company in the world that'll hire you now that you've run a ship aground. How can you seem so cheery?'

Almost everyone had wondered about this, but it was such a sad and unfortunate situation that no one would have mentioned it. All around the table there was a general wincing at Constance's comment, as if several people had bitten their tongues at once. Captain Noland only grinned, however, and Cannonball reached down to tousle Constance's hair.

'Because he's got another ship, Constance!' Cannonball boomed. 'That's why he's so cheery! And he's got me a post on it, too! In fact we're to be at the harbour in an hour's time, and by this very evening we'll be at sea!'

Everyone cheered and exclaimed with surprise, and when Captain Noland had been offered congratulations by all, he scratched his beard and said, 'It is wondrous news, isn't it? I still can scarcely believe it. For some reason, Mr Pressius made a public announcement saying he'd authorized me to ground the *Shortcut*, that I'd acted with remarkable heroism and expert seamanship in the service of humanity, and that he knew of no greater captain in the world!' Captain Noland laughed and shook his head in amazement. 'As you might expect, the offers came pouring in after that. Cannonball and I had our pick of the lot.'

'But Mr Pressius *didn't* authorize you to ground the ship,' Kate said. 'So why on earth did he say all that?'

'He gave me no explanation,' said Captain Noland, turning to look probingly at Mr Benedict. 'But he did let slip that he'd been in contact with *you*, Nicholas, and I have a sneaking suspicion I owe you my life once again. You seem determined to keep me in your debt.'

Mr Benedict smiled. 'Not at all, Phil. I actually did very little, and I risked nothing. There's been a curious incident, you see, one of which you're probably unaware, as it's been kept quiet for several reasons: Mr Pressius's diamonds were stolen.'

'Stolen!' Cannonball cried, exchanging glances with Captain Noland, who seemed equally stunned. 'You mean after all that hoop-de-doo with decoys and extra security, someone actually did steal them?'

Mr Benedict raised an eyebrow. 'It is my opinion that Mr Pressius made such a grand show of protecting his diamonds precisely to make their theft seem legitimate. Having taken such pains to protect them, he could hardly be suspected of arranging their theft. I have reason to believe, however, that he did just that. Mr Pressius stands to receive a fortune in insurance money for those stolen diamonds – much more money, in fact, than they were worth.'

436

'You mean he arranged the theft to get the insurance money?' Sticky said.

'So my source has suggested, and when I communicated this to Mr Pressius, he was quickly swayed to my perspective that Phil should receive his enthusiastic recommendation. His only condition was that I keep my suspicions to myself. He seemed to be under the impression that I could actually *prove* them.'

'But you can't?' said Kate.

'I have no proof whatsoever,' said Mr Benedict. 'But I neglected to mention this to Mr Pressius.'

Cannonball guffawed. 'You snookered him! Bravo, Mr Benedict! Nobody deserves it more than *that* bullfrog, I can tell you!'

Everyone laughed at this but Miss Perumal's mother, who seemed startled and put a hand to her ear. 'What's this about a bullfrog?'

Reynie leant close to her. 'I'll explain later, Pati.'

'But what about Mr Pressius?' Constance cried indignantly. 'Are you really letting him get away with that scam?'

'It may be he misunderstood my position on the matter,' said Mr Benedict with a sly smile. 'Still, I'll need to proceed with caution. There—'

'Ta-da!' shouted a deep voice just then, and Moocho Brazos, his massive arms bearing a gigantic platter of steaming hot pies, swooped into the room. There was a burst of applause at his appearance, and all discussion of more serious matters fell away as the group set eagerly upon the marvellous desserts. Captain Noland and Cannonball were compelled to eat their slices in a hurry – they were due at the harbour – and with wistful glances at the several remaining pies, they pushed back their chairs and bid everyone a fond adieu.

After the two men had gone and everyone had eaten at least one slice of pie, the conversation returned to Mr Pressius's diamond deception. Reynie wanted Mr Benedict to explain how he knew about it. 'You mentioned a source,' he said. 'Is this person's identity a secret?'

'Actually, you know her well,' Mr Benedict said. 'Her name is Martina Crowe.'

The children's jaws dropped. How, they asked, could Martina possibly have known about Mr Pressius?

'You'll recall,' said Mr Benedict, 'that Martina fell into our custody after my brother abandoned her to save himself. Well, I've had a few talks with her since then. Martina's been most eager to repay my brother's disloyalty – she's an impressively vindictive person, I must say – and has told me everything she knew about his plans. Unfortunately, though she may have been his most trusted Executive, he actually trusted her very little and told her even less. She *was* vaguely aware, however, of an arrangement with a jewel merchant that would result in my brother's being substantially enriched.'

'Don't tell me,' said Kate. 'Those diamonds were stolen by a couple of well-dressed jerks with briefcases.'

Mr Benedict tapped his nose. 'Indeed they were, Kate. And so it appears my brother maintains considerable funding for his operations. Still, we have reasons to be encouraged.'

'Encouraged?' said Constance, screwing up her face, and the other children made similar expressions of doubt. 'What could possibly be encouraging about all this?'

Mr Benedict's eyes twinkled; he seemed pleased to be asked. 'Take these developments with Martina, for instance. Aren't they a fine example of how even scurrilous behaviour may lead to some good, if only we're clever enough to take advantage?'

After some hesitation, the children said they supposed this was true.

'And I realize there's no shortage of wickedness in the world,' said Mr Benedict, with a significant look at Reynie, 'but is it not heartening to know that so many are willing to fight for the good? Think of that young librarian, Sophie, who made certain you escaped. Think of SQ, who risked my brother's wrath to make me more comfortable. Think of Captain Noland, and Joe Shooter, and all the others – even strangers – who were prepared to sacrifice their safety, perhaps even their lives, on our behalf. That's something, is it not?'

None of the children could argue with this, not even Constance, who could argue with anything. It *was* something, after all.

Mr Benedict swept his arm out to indicate the grown-ups around the table. 'And though we'd never have wanted you to attempt such a thing, you *did* save my life, did you not, in the face of incredible odds? Have you not proven yourselves once again to be the bravest, most resourceful children in the world?'

The children had to admit they found this notion the most agreeable of all.

Acknowledgments

I would like to thank the many friends and family members who have supported my work (I'm blessed with excellent unofficial publicists and agents) as well as the booksellers, librarians, teachers and especially readers who have given the Society such a warm welcome. I also wish to call attention to a few whose contributions to the present book have been particularly invaluable: my thanks to Paul Galvin for *The Iberian Adventure*, Tracie Stewart for *Secrets of the Dutch*, Ken and Marianne Estes for *Love and a Box Turtle* and everyone on the 15th floor – for everything else, and more.